A
COLDWATER
WARM HEARTS
CHRISTMAS

Also by Lexi Eddings

The Coldwater Warm Hearts Club
A Coldwater Warm Hearts Wedding

Published by Kensington Publishing Corporation

A COLDWATER WARM HEARTS CHRISTMAS

LEXI EDDINGS

KENSINGTON BOOKS
www.kensingtonbooks.com

KENSINGTON BOOKS are published by

Kensington Publishing Corp.
119 West 40th Street
New York, NY 10018

Copyright © 2018 by Diana Groe

All Kensington titles, imprints, and distributed lines are available at special quantity discounts for bulk purchases for sales promotion, premiums, fundraising, educational, or institutional use.

Special book excerpts or customized printings can also be created to fit specific needs. For details, write or phone the office of the Kensington Sales Manager: Kensington Publishing Corp., 119 West 40th Street, New York, NY 10018. Attn. Sales Department. Phone: 1-800-221-2647.

Kensington and the K logo Reg. U.S. Pat. & TM Off.
BOUQUET Reg. U.S. Pat. & TM Off.

eISBN-13: 978-1-4967-1969-0
eISBN-10: 1-4967-1969-7
First Kensington Electronic Edition: October 2018

ISBN-13: 978-1-4967-1968-3
ISBN-10: 1-4967-1968-9
First Kensington Trade Paperback Printing: October 2018

10 9 8 7 6 5 4 3 2 1

Printed in the United States of America

To my dear husband, the man who can fix anything . . .
even if it means he has to hire someone else to do it!

Acknowledgments

A writer may spend countless hours alone crafting a story, but bringing a book to market requires the hard work and talent of dozens of people. I'd like to thank a few of them here.

First, my tireless agent, Natasha Kern. She has been my cheerleader, trusted advisor, and best supporter throughout my writing career. I'm also blessed to name her my friend.

Next, my dear editor, Alicia Condon. Her grace, wit, and style never fail. I'm so thankful for her sharp eyes and deft touch on my work.

All the Kensington team has contributed to the success of my books, from Paula Reedy in production, to Jane Nutter in publicity, to Kristine Noble who designed my gorgeous cover. Closer to home, I need to thank Marcy Weinbeck, my beta reader and friend. Even though we are on opposite sides of the political spectrum, she and I regularly solve the world's problems when she's not letting me bounce story ideas off her.

Lastly, to my readers, family, and friends. Some of you may see yourselves on the pages of my books. If so, know that you're there with much love. Thank you to Kathy Bunn, for allowing me to use Charlie Bunn, her father's name, for one of my characters. And thanks to Zafer Gonncu, my #1 Daughter's brother-in-law, for allowing me to use his name for the new Bates College math professor.

Have a blessed holiday season!

Lexi

Chapter 1

It hurts to see a younger version of yourself making the same mistake you did.

—Angela Holloway, a high school English teacher who longs to keep the drama in her life safely hidden between the covers of her books

Marianne Dashwood, you little idiot. Angie shook her head and closed the dog-eared copy of *Sense and Sensibility. Why are you mooning around over a jerk like Willoughby when Colonel Brandon would walk through fire for you?*

Tucked into the big corner booth at the Green Apple Grill, Angie set the book aside and took a sip of her coffee. The rest of the Coldwater Warm Hearts Club would be wandering in pretty soon for their weekly breakfast meeting, but ever since Angie had joined the group, she'd always been the first to arrive.

Punctuality was next to godliness in her last foster parents' home. Probably because that foster dad had been a railroader. He'd been such a stickler for being on time, she'd occasionally thought she'd rather be caught pregnant out of wedlock than turn up late someplace.

As if my getting pregnant wouldn't require a miracle of biblical proportions anyway. Kind of need a guy for that.

Lester Scott ambled by and topped off her coffee without asking if she wanted more.

"Say, Teach," the old Vietnam vet said. "You oughta try the new breakfast special."

Lester was one of the Warm Hearts Club's success stories. Before the club members got hold of him, he'd been a homeless alcoholic. Now he was employed, sleeping indoors, mending fences with his estranged family, and had been sober for nearly a year and a half.

Of course, that had all happened before Angie joined the group. During her time in the Warm Hearts Club, she hadn't helped anyone yet.

But I'm working on it, she told herself. She just hadn't found the right project.

"What's the new breakfast special?" Angie asked.

"Well, it's sorta my idea, you see." A proud smile turned up the corners of Lester's mouth. "You know how it's kinda popular nowadays for folks to say they're vegetarians?"

"Yeah."

"So anyways, I figured the Green Apple menu needed a Vegetarian Omelet."

Angie glanced at the plastic-covered menu. "I don't see it listed here."

"Oh, that's 'cuz it's new. You get a three-egg omelet made with onions, peppers, cheese, and your choice of ham or pork sausage."

"Ham or sausage?" Angie arched a brow at him. "Vegetarians don't eat meat. You know that's the definition of the word, right?"

"That's what I thought, but I also don't think folks around here would like a meatless omelet so much," Lester said with a frown. "How's about this? We could call it the *Hypocrite's* Vegetarian Omelet."

Angie laughed. "I love it when words mean things, Lester. That's exactly what you should call it."

The old fellow beamed down at her. "So, you want one or not?"

Usually, Angie made do with cream cheese and a bagel, but today was an in-service day for the teachers at Coldwater Cove High. Since there was no cafeteria when classes weren't in session, she'd probably be noshing on vending machine cuisine for lunch at her desk.

"Sure," Angie said. "Bring me a Hypocrite's Vegetarian Omelet."

Lester whipped out his order pad. "Ham or sausage?"

"Both! If I'm going to be a hypocrite, I may as well go all in."

"Sure thing, Teach. Why go hog when you can go whole hog?" Lester headed back to the kitchen, whistling tunelessly through his teeth.

Angie opened her book again, but glanced up when the trio of bells jingled over the door to the Green Apple. She recognized the pair of high school kids who hurried in, the brisk wind sending a dry leaf or two swirling after them.

Shivering in the sudden draft, Angie pulled her old cardigan tighter around herself. The sweater was so worn it would have looked at home in the *Matrix* movie, but it was too comfortable for her to trash. Plus, it was warm. Early November mornings in Coldwater Cove always started with a breath of winter.

The newcomers were students of hers, Emma Wilson and Tad Van Hook. She was a JV cheerleader and he was a power forward on the Fighting Marmots varsity basketball team.

The jock and the cheerleader. Clichés exist because there's truth in them.

Emma was pretty in a windswept prairie sort of way, with long sandy-brown hair and a dusting of freckles over her pert nose. Despite the blustery weather, she wore a flirty short skirt and a gauzy tank topped by a pink denim jacket. Her small feet were snugged into turquoise cowboy boots. Rawboned and handsome, Tad was head and shoulders taller than Emma and had three years on her to boot.

Angie's lips drew into a tight line. She'd seen this play before.

A senior and a freshman. It hardly ever works out.

But things seemed to be going well for young love at the moment. They were both laughing and holding hands as they settled into the booth behind Angie without noticing her.

She picked up her book again and tried to concentrate on the foibles of Miss Austen's heroines. She didn't mean to eavesdrop. Even though nosiness was akin to an Olympic sport in Coldwater Cove, Angie wasn't the gossipy sort. It wasn't her fault she could hear the conversation going on behind her.

"This is so sweet of you, Tad," Emma said, a smile making the pitch of her voice drift upward. "You've never actually taken me out on a date, you know."

There was a longer pause than there should have been.

"It's just breakfast, Em."

"Well, it's sweet, is all. Sort of takes our thing up a notch."

Tad cleared his throat. "Um . . . what do you mean . . . our thing?"

She giggled, sounding even younger than she was. "You know, silly. Us. You're my guy. I'm your girl. We're a thing."

The silence was deafening. Angie caught herself reading the same sentence over and over. *Sense and Sensibility* just couldn't compete with the real-life drama unfolding in the next booth.

"We're a couple, right?" Emma insisted.

"Um, I mean . . . well, sort of, I guess. I mean, we have fun. What we got . . . it's like casual, you know. We hang together . . ."

"Hang together?" A tiny bead of fear shimmered in Emma's tone.

"Yeah," Tad said with disgusting cheerfulness, willfully ignorant of her distress. "Hang."

"But . . ." Emma's voice dropped to a shaky whisper. "Don't you think of me as your girl?"

Angie cringed for her. This conversation was sounding all too familiar. But instead of being a JV cheerleader, Angie had been several years older, an English major finishing her freshman year at Baylor. And the guy hadn't been a jock. He'd been about to graduate summa cum laude, bound for law school.

Several states away.

"Look, Em . . . It's . . . well . . . no," Tad admitted. "I don't think of you like that."

This time the silence blared from Emma's side of the booth. Finally she found her voice. "How *do* you think of me?"

"Um . . . as a friend. Someone I hang with?"

Emma sucked in a sharp breath and made a soft sound. Not quite a sob, but more than a snuffle.

Oh, precious lamb. Angie's chest ached for the girl. At the same time, she wanted to leap up and give her a shake.

Give it up, sweetie, Angie wanted to tell her. *He's not the guy you think he is. He's not your white knight. He doesn't know who you really are, and he doesn't care. You're a notch on his belt. Don't look now, but he's about to bigger, better deal you. In fact, he's already moved on. If you'd ever read Jane Austen, you'd know he's a Willoughby, through and through.*

If Angie didn't quit biting her lower lip, she'd make it bleed, but she couldn't say anything. It wasn't her place.

Emma kept trying. This time, though, her voice was frosty.

"Well, if I'm not your girl, if we're not a couple, I'd like to know what you think a relationship is. Because to me, I mean, after all we've done . . . well, it seems like we're the real thing, whether you want to admit it or not."

"Look, Em. Why are you making this so hard? I like you, okay? I mean, I like hanging with you."

"And when you say hanging, you mean . . ." Her voice had slipped back into whine mode.

"You know, how we do. We hang. Now and then."

Lester swooped by to take their breakfast order. "So, kids, what'll it be?"

"We're not ready," Tad said curtly.

No joke. Neither of them was ready for a real relationship. Tad should be considering which basketball scholarship to accept and Emma ought to be working on bringing up her GPA.

Silence reigned again, but Angie would've bet her unused vacation days that neither of them was studying the menu.

"So," Emma finally said. "Are we going to *hang* at the Winter Dance?"

"Um . . . I dunno. Maybe. Sure. Why not?"

"Great!" The perky cheerleader was back. "I've already picked out my dress!" She launched into a steady patter, a running one-sided conversation about the terrible importance of finding the just right shoes to go with the "totally bangin'" dress she was going to wear.

Oh, Emma, can't you tell he doesn't care? Not about your dress. Not about your shoes. Not about you.

Angie was suddenly glad Tad wasn't in her Advanced Placement English class. She would have been tempted to flunk him on principle. She wished he'd just go ahead and dump Emma instead of stringing her along with hopes of the Winter Dance.

Or maybe Emma might somehow find the backbone to walk away from him.

Stand up, Emma. Angie willed the girl to move, but she didn't hear the slightest creak from the green vinyl seats. *Come on. Tell him he's history. Tell him you're worth so much more than a halfhearted "why not?" And tell him if he ever grows up enough to figure that out, he's going to be sorry he let you go.*

But Angie knew she wouldn't.

Emma was probably going through some mental gymnastics. She was trying to convince herself that Tad loved her, really. He just didn't know how to show it. He'd come around, though. Maybe at the Winter Dance . . .

Angie knew these things because she'd *been* Emma.

Once. About ten years ago.

She hadn't wanted to believe that Peter was slipping away, even though he gave her the same signals Tad was sending Emma. Angie made excuses for him. She refused to believe it when her friends warned her. Even after he left for good, she couldn't accept it. She fantasized about how he'd eventually come to his senses and realize he needed her as much as she did him. He'd come crawling back, a gorgeous ring in hand. Even in her fantasies, she had zero pride. She always fell back into his arms.

Angie was halfway through her first semester of student teaching before she finally admitted to herself that Peter would never come back, never come looking for her. Only one of them had been in love and it wasn't Peter.

She still wanted to curl up into the fetal position when she thought about it.

Which fortunately wasn't often.

Because Angie Holloway was off men for the foreseeable future. They turned women into soppy little doormats, and she was done letting anyone wipe their feet on her.

"Hey, you the teacher?"

The rough baritone made her look up from her unread Austen. The rumbly voice belonged to a guy whose dark hair was thoroughly tousled, as if he'd just risen from bed.

Okay. That's a totally inappropriate thought. No good comes from imagining a guy in a bed. Or freshly out of one either.

"You her?" he asked again.

She wondered how he could've made it in the door, set off

the bells, and stomped up to her table without her noticing before now. She must have really zoned out.

It's Peter's fault. Even remembering him for a little bit turns me into a mess.

Angie couldn't decide what color this new guy's eyes were. A cross between dark gray and deep blue. Despite the brisk day, he was wearing no jacket. His jeans looked like they'd been worn by hard work instead of coming from the factory pre-ripped and faded. She could barely make out the words "Parker Construction" sewn in red thread over the pocket of his washed-out black T-shirt.

"Lookin' for an English teacher," he said, more forcefully. "Angie Something-or-other. You her?"

"It's Holloway, not Something-or-other. And yes, I am she." His poor grammar was like an itch she couldn't scratch. "Do you ever speak in complete sentences?"

He shrugged. The man's shoulders were massive. "If I have to." A smile curved his mouth. His teeth were so white he belonged in a toothpaste commercial. "I'm Seth Parker. Heather sent me for you."

As what? A present?

Her friend, Heather Walker Evans, was always trying to set her up with someone. Heather and her husband, Michael, had trotted out computer nerds and local shop owners, a few ranchers and one emergency medicine resident at Coldwater General who couldn't keep from talking about the gory details of his day over dinner. Angie had lost count of how many awkward double dates she'd squirmed through.

Through which I squirmed, she corrected her own ungrammatical thought. Grammar was order amid chaos. It was her touchstone, her safety net. She fell back on it with gratitude.

But Seth Parker was still there, standing by the booth. This was the first time Heather had ambushed her with a Neanderthal—albeit a smoking hot Neanderthal—who probably wouldn't recognize a dangling participle if it smacked him in the face.

Still, something about the logo on his shirt niggled at her memory.

Parker Construction.

The company had just won the bid to build an addition to the high school. They were known for tackling big projects all over southeast Oklahoma with a reputation for delivering high quality and on time completion.

Could this guy be *that* Parker? She doubted it. The strong, silent type had a lot to commend it, but this man spoke in monosyllables. How could he run a successful company?

"Come on now." He turned and headed for the door. When she didn't follow, he stopped, and cocked his head at her. "You coming?"

"I am not in the habit of going off with strange men."

"Nothing strange about me, miss. I'm common as an old shoe." He opened the door and held it wide for her. "Meeting's been moved to the courthouse. Like I said, Heather sent me for you."

So it wasn't a setup. The Warm Hearts Club meeting had just been moved. Feeling foolish, Angie rose, and headed for the door. "Oh. You might have said so."

"Thought I did."

"Wait up, Teach!" Lester called after her. "Don't you want your omelet?"

"Sorry, Lester. I have to go."

"I'll take it," Tad Van Hook spoke up. "I need to eat and get out of here. Emma's waffles are going to take forever."

Emma slumped a little in the booth, but Tad didn't seem to notice.

"I can put it in a to-go box for you, Teach," Lester said.

"No, that's okay. Give it to Tad," Angie said as she swept past Seth, who was still holding the door for her. At least, he was a well-trained Neanderthal.

And no one deserves a Hypocrite's Vegetarian Omelet more than Tad Van Hook.

Chapter 2

I'm a sucker for lost causes and damsels in distress.
Someday, I'm gonna have to learn to say no.

—Seth Parker, who wishes there was a blueprint that
would help him figure out what's going on in
someone else's head

Heather Walker Evans, founding member of the Coldwater
Warm Hearts Club, waved to them as Angie and Seth joined
the group gathered on the courthouse steps. "I think we're all
here now."

Angie did a quick head count. Valentina Gomez, Marjorie
Chubb, Ian Van Hook, Virgil Cooper, Charlie Bunn, and Junior
Bugtussle stood in a semicircle around Heather. Now that she
and Seth Parker were there, everyone was present and ac-
counted for.

"Let's get started," Heather said, opening the little notebook she always carried. Her husband Michael might be a
techno-wizard, but Heather was old school. If she didn't write
it down, it wasn't real.

Angie sidestepped to position herself a little behind Mr.
Bunn. She'd always hated the cold and she was sure the gregar-
ious old man wouldn't mind being used as a windbreak, even
on such a blustery day.

Plus, it moved her a bit farther from Seth Parker. The guy
made something inside her quiver in a tingly, it's-good-to-be-

female sort of way, which was ridiculous. She liked polished, well-read, sophisticated men.

Scratch Seth Parker on all counts.

"Any reason we're meeting on the courthouse steps instead of inside the Grill?" she asked, hoping her teeth wouldn't chatter from the chill.

"We're gathered here because this is the site of our next group project," Heather explained. Each Warm Heart had personal causes they supported. Ian Van Hook ran an anti-bullying campaign at the high school, for example. Heather regularly stepped in to spell a beleaguered caregiver. And Mr. Bunn organized the Royal Order of Chicken Pluckers to raise money for the Lutheran Ladies' charity fund. Whatever their chosen cause, club members had discovered the great secret of pouring themselves into other people's lives. Helping others wasn't just about getting a warm glow in return for do-gooding. Putting someone else's needs first for a bit brought their own lives into perspective and made them grateful.

"Cheaper than therapy," Heather had often said, "and someone else benefits, too. Win-win!"

But along with individual acts of kindness perpetrated by the club, they sometimes joined hands to take on larger projects.

"What's the plan, Heather?" Ian asked. A freshman at Bates College, he was the youngest member of the group and, coincidently, first cousin to the Hypocrite's-Omelet-eating Tad.

"We are going to organize and present the annual community Christmas pageant," Heather announced.

Marjorie Chubb, captain of the Methodist prayer chain, scowled at this news. "But Shirley Evans has been running that show for years."

She didn't add "with an iron fist," but they were all thinking it. Mrs. Evans was a stickler for detail, and everything about the pageant had to be just so.

"Well, if we're doing the pageant ourselves, that suits me better than possum pie for supper. She nagged me half to death last year because I didn't spread the straw to suit her," Junior Bugtussle said. "Not that I didn't lay down enough, mind you, but that I didn't make the straw look *the way* she wanted it to. Don't that beat all?"

"Say what you will, Shirley Evans could herd cats if she had to," Seth Parker finally put in. "We'll miss her ability to organize."

Surprise, surprise. The man can speak in complete sentences.

Angie knew she was being snippy, even if it was only in her own head, but just being near this Parker guy irritated her. It wasn't that he looked like Peter. Her first love had been a golden Adonis, blond with vibrant green eyes, and Peter was well aware of his striking looks. Seth didn't seem the sort to trouble with combing his hair if he could cover it with a ball cap instead, let alone primp for hours the way Peter had. But Seth was still attractive in a rough sort of way.

And after Peter, attractive men activated Angie's self-protective radar.

That must be why my insides are pegging out the "heartache-on-the-horizon-o-meter."

"Seth is Shirley Evans's nephew, on his mother's side." Mr. Bunn leaned toward Angie and stage-whispered this bit of intelligence as if it were a state secret. "His father married Delcie Higginbottom—that's Shirley Evans's maiden name, you know. Delcie was Shirley's sister. Of course, if you go back far enough, everybody's related to everyone around here."

Since Coldwater Cove was her first teaching job straight out of grad school, Angie had only lived there for a few years. She was still trying to untangle the "who's related to whom" web, so she appreciated the heads-up from Mr. Bunn.

"You can't sling a dead cat 'round these parts without it hittin' kin to somebody or other," Junior pronounced loudly enough for everyone to hear. To those who missed Mr. Bunn's whisper, Junior's comment must have seemed totally unrelated to the general discussion and unexpectedly gross. To cat lovers, like Angie, it was just plain offensive. When Angie glared at him, Junior added, "Not that I'd be slingin' no cats anyhow."

"Why can't Shirley do the pageant?" Valentina, the dispatcher for the sheriff's department, asked. She helped find work for recently released cons in her spare time. Usually at Mr. Cooper's Hardware. "I hope it's not because of a health problem."

Everyone knew that last year, Shirley Evans had been diagnosed and treated for breast cancer. She'd tackled the disease as she did everything.

"Like she was killing snakes," her husband George had said.

After a lumpectomy, Shirley opted to take radiation and chemo treatments at the same time, all while still managing to organize her daughter Lacy's wedding to Jake Tyler.

Of course, when Lacy and Jake eloped at the last minute, the ceremony had turned into a surprise wedding for her son Michael and Heather Walker, Angie's friend. But from the over-the-top decorations to the bridesmaids' dresses that were such a violent pink they'd make a flamingo blush, the event bore Shirley Evans's stamp of approval. The fact that the bride and groom could be changed ten minutes before the ceremony began, without another single alteration to the proceedings, bore witness to Shirley's masterful command of details.

One might question her taste or her methods, but no one could argue with the results. Shirley Evans flat out got things done. Every time.

No wonder it'll take the whole Warm Hearts Club to replace her running the Christmas pageant.

"Shirley's health is all right," Seth said to put Valentina's mind at ease. "She got a good handle on that cancer scare. All her follow-up tests come back great, she says."

"Then why would she give up the pageant?" Marjorie asked. If pressed, Marjorie would undoubtedly say she wanted to know because she wondered if there was a problem she ought to pass along to her fellow "prayer warriors."

Angie suspected she was just nosy by nature.

"I don't think we should be gossiping about Mrs. Evans's reasons," Angie said.

"It's not gossip if you intend to pray over it later," Marjorie said with a firm nod. "Besides, the pageant won't be the same without her."

"I don't mind tellin' you, I'm kinda counting on that." Junior Bugtussle beamed. At least someone was happy to hear that Shirley Evans's holiday reign of terror was coming to an end. "She took a whole lot of pleasure outta bossing me around—I mean, runnin' the pageant. Sorta makes a body wonder why she wouldn't want to do it again this year."

"I can't say," Seth said.

"You mean you won't say." Marjorie pursed her lips.

Seth shrugged. "Guess Shirley will fill you in when she's ready."

Angie shoved her hands into the pockets of her cardigan and wished she'd put on a jacket that morning. They could have just as easily had this discussion tucked into the corner booth at the Green Apple. She'd kill for a warm cup of coffee between her palms. "I still don't understand why we changed the club meeting place."

"I thought being here would give us inspiration," Heather said. Normally, the pageant consisted of a live nativity with the Methodist Church choir singing alongside. Of course, Shirley made a few tweaks to it from year to year. Like last Christmas, when she decided they needed snow, and Mother Nature refused to cooperate. She costumed Charlie Bunn in solid black, which according to Shirley rendered him nigh invisible, and had him stand on a ladder behind Ike Warboy, who was playing Joseph. Then Mr. Bunn was instructed to toss handfuls of borax soap into the air so the flakes could drift down onto the Holy Family.

Lucinda Warboy, who regularly took the role of the Blessed Virgin, claimed it took the kink right out of her naturally curly hair for weeks.

On the plus side, the courthouse steps had never been so clean.

But whatever other changes were made to the pageant each year, Shirley Evans always staged it on the courthouse steps. And on Christmas Eve, the whole town turned out to see what new twist Shirley would wrap around the old story.

It was a Coldwater tradition Angie wasn't sure they should mess with.

With which we should mess, she mentally corrected.

"I'm hoping we can do things differently this year," Heather said.

"Like how?" Valentina asked cautiously. She evidently remembered the borax snow, too.

"Well, for starters," Heather said, "Seth has agreed to build a manger for us on the courthouse lawn, so the main event will already be moved a bit."

"The mayor will be relieved not to have to tromp through straw all December," Marjorie said with a sidelong glance at Junior.

"That weren't my fault," he said. "I wanted to heap the straw off to the side, but Mrs. Evans said to spread it around. If a little is good, she'd always say, a lot is a whole bunch better."

"The Evans family motto." Heather sighed. "There's no arguing with it."

Since marrying Shirley Evans's son, Heather had evidently tried.

"Another thing we ought to change is the cast. I've been a wise man for the last ten years," said Mr. Cooper, owner of the local hardware store. "It's high time somebody else had to haul around that trunk full of gold."

As with everything else, Shirley Evans believed in excess when it came to pageant props. Why present the Christ Child with a small cask of painted poker chips when you could offer the holy infant a steamer trunk full of them?

"While we're on the subject of the cast," Marjorie said, "don't you all think Lucinda Warboy is getting a little long in the tooth to be the Virgin Mary? I mean, just because she can usually provide a real baby to be the Christ Child, that doesn't mean she ought to keep being Mary every year."

Lucinda and her husband Ike produced infants on an astonishingly regular schedule. In fact, if all their children had been boys, they'd only be a couple of kids shy of fielding their own football team.

"The cast is something for the new director to decide," Heather said. "We'll all be involved in this project as needed, but you know how it is when something is supposed to be done by committee. If it's everybody's job, nobody gets around to doing it. We need a leader, someone to spearhead the pageant." She paused and met Angie's gaze.

No. Don't you dare.

"I nominate Angela Holloway."

Angie swallowed hard. It was one thing to direct the high school kids in bad renditions of *Macbeth*. It was quite another to take on the annual production that had become a town legend. She wished Heather was trying to set her up on another bad date instead.

Valentina jumped in with, "I second."

"All in favor signify by saying—"

"Aye," they all said in chorus with no prompting at all.

This may not be a date, but it's definitely a setup.

"If there are no objections—"

Angie's hand shot up. "I object."

"Duly noted, but ignored. You've been drafted so you might as well make the best of it," Heather went on with a grin. "That's settled then. Now, we don't expect you to do it all alone, so Seth will be your assistant."

"Her what?" he said gruffly.

And the man's back to incomplete sentences.

"Or codirector, if that's how you two decide you want to put it. You've already agreed to build whatever sets we need, Seth, and since you're Shirley's nephew, I thought you could introduce Angie to her. I'm certain Shirley will want to make suggestions."

"That's guaranteed." Seth frowned. "Why can't *you* introduce her to Shirley? She's your mother-in-law."

"True," Heather admitted. "But if there are going to be major changes to the pageant this year, and I hope there will be, in the interest of family harmony, it's best if I take a back seat."

"Coward."

Heather raised both hands. "Guilty, but still not telling Shirley we're changing the pageant."

"I'll pray for you," Marjorie said piously to Seth. "Not that you'll need it. After all, you and Shirley are kin."

"We'll need it. Being a nephew doesn't offer that much protection." Seth grimaced.

"Don't worry," Mr. Bunn whispered. "Blood really is thicker than water. Family first."

Angie didn't know much about that. She had none of her own.

The carillon in the bell tower at tiny Bates College started to chime. The morning was slipping away and most of the club members had jobs or classes to get to.

To which to get. No, that's silly. Even I can't like my syntax that tortured.

The group dissipated, leaving only Angie and Seth standing on the courthouse steps.

"Well, that's it," Heather called over her shoulder. "Call if you need something, Angie."

How about a new life? danced on her tongue but she swallowed it back. It sounded whiny, and she wasn't a whiner.

She liked her job. Mostly. Working with teenagers was a challenge, because they all seemed to be afflicted with the world-revolves-around-me syndrome. But every now and then, she found a student who really caught a spark of what she was trying to convey and they blazed up like a house afire. It was thrilling when literature opened a window to a wider world for a young mind in this insulated place.

Not that Coldwater Cove wasn't a fine place to live. Angie was beyond grateful that she didn't have to deal with the violence or drug problems facing some of her old classmates who taught in big cities.

But sometimes, she felt as if she were living out her last name. Literally.

She was trudging along a "hollow way."

When Heather wasn't trying to fix her up with a date, she was promising that if Angie took being a Warm Heart seriously and gave some of herself away by helping others, it would make her own life easier.

So far, there was no joy in that department.

Of course, it wasn't Heather's fault that Peter had already taught her she couldn't trust her heart to others.

It's pretty hard to give yourself away when you know you need to hold back.

Still, it was zero fun to go home to an empty apartment

each day. Even the Siamese cat she'd inherited from the previous tenant didn't fill the void. Angie loved cats, but Effie was more a calamity waiting to happen than a comfort. It was a little ironic that Angie was taking over the Christmas pageant from Shirley Evans, because she'd sublet her apartment from Shirley's daughter Lacy, who'd moved to Boston. At the time, Angie and Lacy had agreed that the Siamese wouldn't move well. After all, Effie had been in the apartment when Lacy first leased it, too.

An Evans apartment, an Evans cat, an Evans Christmas pageant—it seemed her whole life was filled with leftovers from the Evans family. Including the tall, lean, nearly nonverbal Evans nephew standing beside her.

"May as well get it over with," Seth said.

"Get what over with?" *Oh, my gosh, it's contagious. Incomplete sentence. Preposition dangling at the end. I'm starting to sound like a Neanderthal, too.*

"Meeting my aunt Shirley. Why? You got someplace else you need to be?"

"Sadly, no." Since it was an in-service day, she had no classes to teach. Angie could work at the desk in her classroom, but she could just as easily spend the time at home. Her lesson plans were already fleshed out till the end of the semester and had been turned in for approval. The only other thing she might be doing today was providing a lap for a cat who'd be just as happy with a pillow. Effie merely tolerated her.

Talking to Shirley Evans about the pageant was starting to look like Angie's best choice.

" 'Lay on, MacDuff,' " she quoted, with a palm up gesture to Seth.

"Huh?"

"It's Shakespeare," she explained. "It means 'lead on.' "

"You coulda just said so."

"I just did." The irritation she'd felt toward him from the moment she first clapped eyes on him had been simmering all through the club meeting. Now it boiled over. "What are you? Illiterate?"

He frowned at her. "I read."

"Yeah? Like what?"

"Well, lately, this book that says we should treat other people the way we want to be treated."

A bucket of cold water would have been less of a shock to her system. He was right. She was behaving badly and, worst of all, she wasn't sure why.

"I'm sorry," she said. "That wasn't like me. Or rather, that's usually not like me. I mean, I don't normally say such . . ." Evidently, his lamentable way with words really was catching. Angie's shoulders slumped. "If you have time to introduce me to Mrs. Evans, I'd appreciate it."

Ever a man of few words, Seth nodded. Then he pointed toward a shiny Parker Construction pickup parked in front of the courthouse. "My truck's over there. Let's go, Teach."

Chapter 3

Limeberger's Mortuary. We'll be the last to let you down.

—*The Coldwater Gazette* classifieds

Seth opened the passenger side door of his big dually for her, wishing he'd been driving something sleeker, maybe a mustang convertible, instead of his company truck. The cab was clean enough, but the vehicle was built for hauling construction materials, not passengers. Especially not ones as petite as the little English teacher.

Like a cherry bomb, he decided. *She may be small, but that mouth of hers definitely packs a punch.*

Seth held out a hand in case she needed help, but she scrambled up into the cab unassisted. He went around the vehicle, climbed in, and punched the start button. The engine roared to life.

"So I take it you don't want the job," Seth said, more to fill the uncomfortable silence than anything else.

"What do you mean?" she snapped. "I love my work."

He'd never met anyone so touchy, and he had no idea what had set her off. "I meant the pageant."

"Oh."

Her left knee was bouncing up and down like a little jackhammer.

God save me from high-strung women.

Still, he wondered why he even noticed how uncomfortable

she seemed to be. He usually didn't pick up on such things, and it bugged him that he might be the cause of her jumpiness.

"No, I'm not crazy about doing the pageant," she admitted. "But I guess someone has to if your aunt won't. And since I have experience with directing, I'm the logical choice."

"So the pageant isn't what got your panties in a bunch?"

"Excuse me. Did you just make a comment about *my panties?*" The knee stopped bouncing.

"Sorry. Guess I coulda said that better. I just meant, it's obvious you're not happy about something. If it's not the pageant, what is it?"

He glanced at her long enough to catch her giving him a scowl in return. "Hey, you don't know me well enough for it to be me."

"No, but I know your type." She crossed her arms. Instead of a defiant gesture, it almost seemed as if she were hugging herself.

"What type is that?"

"Male," she said, tight-lipped.

"Really? You're at war with half the human race?" Seth rolled his eyes at her. "That's the snarkiest girl-power type thing I've heard in years."

She held her ground for a heartbeat or two, but then her tight lips relaxed and she heaved a sigh. "I'm sorry. You don't deserve that." She let her arms drop to her sides. "I guess what I'm really upset about is a couple of students of mine. There's something going on between them that reminded me of . . . well, an incident this morning sort of set me off."

She cared enough about the kids she taught to be upset over them. That wasn't the worst character trait in the world. "So some problem with your students is what's making you behave badly?"

"I said I was sorry."

"I'm just trying to understand what's eating you." Though why he should bother was a mystery to him. He had enough on his plate with the new high school project. Seth didn't need to add to his growing to-do list by trying to rescue every damsel in distress who stumbled across his path.

Force of habit, he told himself grimly.

"Are you studying to be a shrink in your spare time?" she asked, the snarky tone back in spades.

"No." Seth turned down Oak Street, planning to drop off the teacher at his aunt's house on the next block and make a break for it. He felt as if school was about to be let out. "I generally like putting things together, not trying to take them apart."

"So you're like a psychologist, only backward. A shrink takes their client apart to discover what's wrong before helping them put themselves back together." When she looked at him this time, it was with faint surprise. "That's actually a pretty astute observation coming from someone like you."

"Someone like me, huh? Bet you think I don't know what astute means."

"That depends." She smiled at him with deceptive sweetness. "Are you trying to decide if it's a compliment?"

"It's as much a compliment as you're likely to give." *Dang! She cuts like a chainsaw.* "I don't get you, Teach. Women don't normally dislike me on sight."

"I imagine they don't."

Seth had no idea what that meant, but he was tired of her sniping. He pulled the truck to the side of the street and stopped. Then he turned off the motor and silently counted to ten.

"Look," he said, "if we're going to work together on this pageant thing, let's settle something right now. I won't bring trouble from my business to this partnership and you won't bring whatever brand of crazy is buzzing around in that brain of yours to it either."

She blinked at him. Then she drew a deep breath.

"Okay," she said softly.

He waited.

"I said okay."

There was still something bothering her. He read it in the tightness of her jaw, in the whiteness of her knuckles as she clutched that dog-eared book to her chest like a shield.

Strange that he should be so in tune with the feelings of Angie Holloway, of all people.

He didn't like it one bit.

She really wasn't his type. He liked women with more meat on their bones and less acid on their tongues. Angie would have to stand twice to make a decent shadow. And he certainly wasn't used to being insulted right out of the gate.

But when she turned to look him full in the face, she reminded him of a half-drowned kitten. Beaten down by life, and spitting mad about it. He never could resist a hard case. He'd help her if he could.

Whatever it was she was dealing with, at least she was fighting back. He was just sorry he'd stepped into her crossfire.

"Well, okay, then," he said and started up the truck again. "Let's start fresh. Tell me something I don't know about Angie Holloway."

"I'd rather you go first," she said with surprising meekness. "If you don't mind."

He suspected a trap, but someone had to go first.

"Okay. I got my BS in construction engineering at Texas Tech."

"You can earn a degree in construction?" Her tone said it was an honest question, not another verbal slap.

"Construction *engineering*." Seth might not be so good with words, but he was a whiz with structural analysis and the geometry of a plumb line.

"Mr. Bunn said Shirley Evans is your aunt." She picked at a

loose thread on the hem of her sweater. "Does a lot of your family live around here?"

"Not *a lot* of them. *All* of them," he said. "A few of us have gone away for school or to work in a city someplace for a while, but eventually, we all come home."

The gentle Ozark hills, the sparkling lake, the sleepy little town of Coldwater Cove was as much a part of his DNA as his steely eyes and thick, capable fingers.

"How about you?" Seth asked as he turned into the Evanses' driveway. "You got family hereabouts?"

"No."

Seth turned off the engine, but didn't move to get out of the truck. He was waiting for her to follow up her "no" with an explanation of why she'd come to Coldwater, or where she grew up, or something about her family wherever they were. But Angie just stared down at the book in her lap.

"You know, for an English teacher, you're not too keen on how a conversation works," he said. "You know something about my family. What about yours?"

She raised her head to meet his gaze. Her eyes were the saddest brown he'd ever seen.

"I don't have family. Anywhere."

Then she opened the passenger side door and slid out of the truck cab. She started walking toward the house, but stopped and turned back to face him when she realized he hadn't moved yet.

"Are you coming?"

Dang. He'd intended to drop her with his aunt and then take off. Now he had to stay. There was no way he'd leave an orphan to fend for herself in the Evanses' household.

If George and Shirley discovered she was alone in the world, they'd smother her alive with sympathy and affection. Seth knew without being told that Angela Holloway would hate that.

He hauled himself out of the truck and dogged her through the open garage door. A collapsible ladder that dropped from the attic space had been folded down and was propped on the cement floor. From the scraping sounds coming from above them, Seth figured someone was rummaging around up there.

Along with the thumps and bumps, whoever it was also grumbled a few choice words that wouldn't be appropriate in church.

"Hello," Seth called up the ladder. "That you, Uncle George?"

"Who wants to know?" A grimy suitcase tumbled down the ladder's rungs and Seth had to jump out of the way. It landed on the garage floor with a thud and a billowing cloud of dust.

"It's Seth and—"

"And Miss Holloway," the retired lawyer finished for him. George Evans appeared at the top of the ladder and climbed down with his back to them. "Heather called to let us know you'd be coming. Coffee's on."

Seth shook his head at Angie, trying to warn her. The sheer awfulness of George Evans's coffee was the stuff of family legend.

"I'd love some, Mr. Evans," she said, as if to spite him.

"Don't say I didn't warn you," Seth whispered.

"What was that?" Mr. Evans said as he reached the bottom of the ladder and turned to face them. "You want some too, Seth?"

"Nothing for me, George. Already had my caffeine fix today."

A cup of George Evans's brew had enough caffeine to last for a week.

"Well, come on in then," George said. "Shirley's looking forward to meeting you, Miss Holloway. She's a great supporter of your students' plays."

That meant Shirley had dragged him to all of them.

"I'll be sure to thank her. And call me Angie, please," she said, all smiles.

Sure. She smiles at the old geezer.

"Only if you call me George," said the old geezer in question as he picked up the suitcase and started into the house. Once they tromped through the laundry room and into the kitchen, he called out, "They're here, Shirley."

A Yorkshire terrier appeared in the doorway to the next room, yapping its head off, as if to herald his mistress's approach. Then, in a fragrant cloud of Estée Lauder, Shirley Evans waltzed in.

Somehow, she always manages to make an entrance.

"Angela Holloway, I'm so glad to meet you," she said, holding out a hand for Angie to shake. Shirley was so queenly, Seth always wondered if folks should bow and kiss her ring instead.

His aunt's smile was dazzling, but then her delicate nose twitched and she looked around Angie and Seth to find the source of her displeasure. Her gaze settled on the dusty Samsonite George had plopped down in the middle of the kitchen.

"This will never do, George. That old suitcase is filthy."

"It'll clean up okay."

She sniffed again. "It's moldy on the inside. I can smell it from here."

"That's why God invented Lysol," George countered. "Cleanliness is next to godliness, you know."

"I'm sure you think that's scriptural, but it's not. It's—wait a minute. If you think you can distract me from the issue at hand with a theological debate, you've got another think coming, George Evans." Shirley gave him the stink-eye. Seth backed up a pace or two, lest her evil expression spill over onto him. "You just don't want to spend the money to buy a decent set of luggage."

"Why should I when we already have some?"

"Luggage that hasn't been used since Nixon was president," Shirley said. "We'll discuss this later, George. Get that out of my kitchen, and I mean now."

George picked up the luggage and headed for the garage, grumbling a few more of those choice words under his breath. Shirley turned her attention back to Angie and Seth, motioning them toward the doorway from which she'd just emerged. "Why don't we move to the living room? Oh, say, would you kids like some iced tea?"

"Mr. Evans already offered me coffee—"

"But she'd rather have iced tea. Thanks, Aunt Shirley." He grabbed Angie's elbow and half led, half dragged her to the living room. "Trust me. You do not want Uncle George's coffee."

"I like to make my own choices, if you don't mind," the teacher hissed, then called to Shirley, who was still in the kitchen filling glasses with ice. "I'll wait on the coffee, Mrs. Evans."

"Are you sure, dear? My George makes it pretty stout."

"By that she means the coffee's strong enough to grab the spoon and beat you with it if you try to add cream or sugar," Seth warned.

"I'm sure the coffee will be fine," Angie called back to his aunt, giving Seth a "See? I'll do whatever I dang well please" grin. "Are you planning a trip someplace, Mrs. Evans?"

"Oh, yes!" She reappeared with a tray of assorted cookies, a pitcher of iced tea and three glasses. Evidently, she had ignored Angie's coffee request and was determined to serve her tea anyway.

For once, Seth could only be grateful for his aunt's stubbornness.

"Didn't Seth tell you?" Shirley offered them the cookies. "George and I won the grand prize in the Limeberger Funeral Home Bucket List Contest."

"No, he didn't tell me about it," she said. To Seth's surprise,

Angie took three ginger snaps and bit into one with gusto. He'd figured her for a salad grazer, not a sugar fiend. "What's the Bucket List Contest?"

"It was all over the *Coldwater Gazette*. Oh, you must not read the paper. So many young people don't these days. Anyway, you've heard of a bucket list, haven't you?"

Angie nodded, her mouth still full of cookie.

"It's all the things you want to see and do before you die," Seth supplied, before tucking into his own sugary treat.

"That's right, but hardly anybody gets their bucket list done. So Limeberger's decided to offer a chance to tick off the things on your list if you prepay for your funeral," Shirley explained. "I had to talk a blue streak to get George to agree to it, but I finally convinced him. After all, the odds are good we'll need a funeral someday, so we may as well arrange the one we want ahead of time."

"That makes sense," Angie said.

"It does, doesn't it? And even that old lawyer of mine couldn't make a case against it." Shirley turned toward Seth and said, almost as if Angie weren't in the room, "I like her, Seth. I think she'll do."

He sent the teacher an apologetic look. His aunt was always trying to set him up with someone. He'd never been able to convince her that he didn't have time for a relationship. And even if he did, he was sure his aunt's pick wouldn't be his. "I suspect Angie's afraid to ask what she'd do for."

"For what I'd do," she corrected.

"What?"

"Never mind. It's grammar."

Her dismissive look said he wouldn't understand. Seth ground his molars together. He might not be the smoothest guy in the county, but none of his exes had ever made him feel like such a total doofus. All it took with Angie Holloway was a word or two and a roll of her big brown eyes.

"Go on, Mrs. Evans," she urged, all sweetness to his aunt.

"Where was I? Oh, yes. So George and I both picked out our caskets and vaults and bought a joint plot. We went ahead and preordered a headstone—they have such pretty ones nowadays—and then we decided on music and favorite scripture verses and who we wanted to give the eulogy. I'll swear, it's almost as much work to plan a funeral as it is to run the Christmas pageant." Shirley gave a self-deprecating chuckle. "But you'll find that out for yourself soon enough, my dear. Anyway, as much trouble as it was to enter the Bucket List Contest, it was worth it in the end because we won the grand prize."

George joined them, bearing a cup of his vile devil's brew for Angie. She accepted it from him and wrapped both her hands around the steaming mug.

But she didn't take a drink.

Maybe she believed his warning. Seth hoped so. He wouldn't wish a mouthful of his uncle's coffee on his worst enemy.

"Tell her what the grand prize is, Shirley," George said.

Shirley's eyes danced with excitement. "Next January, we're going around the world!"

"We won a world cruise, 'a' being the operative word in that sentence," George said emphatically in his best lawyerly tone. "As in referring to one. Singular. The prize was for *one* of us to circumnavigate the globe."

"So, of course, we had to buy a second passage," Shirley said as she offered her husband a snickerdoodle. "I'd have so hated to leave George at home alone."

"You could always send me postcards," he said morosely, but he didn't turn down the cookie.

"Stop it, silly." She gave George's knee a playful swat. "You're just as excited about this as I am."

"My bank account is, that's for sure."

"Well, anyway," Shirley went on, "the prize was for an inside cabin. And I don't know how you'd feel about it, but if you're trying to see the world, you won't see much of it from inside a tin can."

"We could always go find a couple of deck chairs," George said. Seth had the feeling his uncle had already tried this reasoning and lost with it, but old lawyers never like to give up an argument.

"I've heard the wind can be horrible on a top deck." Shirley patted her elaborately styled hair. "So we upgraded to a balcony cabin. That way we can enjoy the view any time we like and be a bit sheltered while we're at it. You'll love it, George, you'll see."

"With my luck, the ship will sink." Seth's uncle sighed. "And we won't even be able to use those prepaid funerals."

Chapter 4

Cremation Deal to Die For. Call Limeberger's Mortuary for more info on this pre-need special.

—*The Coldwater Gazette* classifieds

"But you kids don't want to hear about the pair of us and our cruise," Shirley said. "You're here for the pageant book."

Angie set her mug of coffee on the table. Her hands were finally warm, but she hadn't taken so much as a sip. Even without Seth's warning, she would have steered clear of drinking the pitch-black liquid. It smelled all right, but it looked like tar that hadn't set yet. "There's a book?"

"Oh, yes, the pageant book." Shirley Evans dragged an oversized binder off the coffee table and plopped it into Angie's lap. Filled with newspaper clippings, fabric swatches, and Polaroid pictures from pageants past, it must have weighed ten pounds. "This is the collected wisdom of twenty years of running the Christmas pageant. You'll find sections on lighting and costumes and—oh! While I'm thinking about it, you really should replace Mary's blue cloak. Lucinda used a cheap grade of wool for the last one she made, and it pilled something terrible when it came out of the wash."

"The Virgin Mary looked like she was covered in tiny blue meatballs," George said.

"I thought that was because of the borax snow," Seth put in.

George nodded. "Might have been a combination of the two."

"In any case," Shirley said, wrestling the issue back from

the men, "the one we have in storage is completely unusable. We need to make sure we present just the right picture for the live nativity. So we can't have Mary looking like a bag lady."

"Well, she did give birth in a stable." Angie figured it wouldn't hurt to show she knew a little about the Christmas story, even though she hadn't been in Sunday School for years. "It's not like she was a fashion queen."

A quick breath hissed over Shirley's teeth. "You are talking about the Virgin Mary."

Angie nodded. "Who was probably a pregnant teenager and—"

"Oh, we don't say pregnant, dear. Not about the Virgin Mary," Shirley corrected. "We say 'with child.'"

"Okay, she was 'with child' out of wedlock, and had just ridden ninety miles on a donkey, so I doubt she'd have made the cover of *Vogue*."

Shirley Evans's cheeks flushed a deep scarlet. Angie wasn't sure, but she thought there might be wisps of steam coming from her ears.

Time to change the subject.

"What else is in the notebook besides lighting and costume notes?" she asked.

"Well, there's the script."

"A script?"

"Yes, of course," Shirley said. "You can't expect the live nativity players to be mimes, after all. Besides the conversation between Mary and Joseph, each person who delivers a gift to the Christ Child has a piece to say, too. Of course, if it's cold, sometimes the microphone doesn't work too well. When that happens the actors just have to shout their lines."

Angie tried to imagine Mary and Joseph shouting at each other and drew a total blank. Any semblance of family in her past had been a hodgepodge of uncertainty. She'd bounced from home to home, sometimes placed with families who were looking at dysfunctional in the rearview mirror. But she expected more from something called "the Holy Family."

"Don't worry, dear. The cast knows what to do." Shirley patted her forearm. "There's a list of names and phone numbers after the script. Unless they're dead, they'll agree to do the pageant again this year."

Angie wasn't so sure. After all, Mr. Cooper had already tried to beg off being a wise guy.

Wise man, she corrected herself. After her comments about Mary, if she called the magi "wise guys," she'd probably get an earful about how she wasn't taking the pageant seriously.

"But you're not dead and you're not doing the pageant," Angie said. "You said yourself that the cruise doesn't start till January."

"Yes, but there are ever so many things to do between now and then. We have to get passports and visas and vaccinations—"

"Vaccinations?" George sputtered.

"Yes, dear. Some of the places we'll visit require them. And then there's the packing and planning excursions and—"

"And frankly, I put my foot down and told her flat out she had to either do the pageant or the cruise because she wasn't doing both," George said in a tone that brooked no argument. "Shirley wore herself to a frazzle last year what with the wedding and the cancer and then the pageant to boot."

"And so I chose the cruise this year," Shirley said. "I hope that's not selfish of me."

"Of course not," Seth said. "You won the cruise fair and square. Nobody turns down a grand prize."

"Why couldn't it have just been a leg lamp?" George grumbled under his breath.

"About the cast," Angie said, hoping to steer the conversation back to the pageant. "I was thinking we might have auditions for the parts this year. You know, just to give someone else a chance. You never know who might want to step forward."

Shirley sniffed, as if she smelled something worse than the old suitcase. "I suppose you can if you want to. You're the director. But mark my words. You'll be borrowing trouble."

Angie didn't have to borrow trouble. It had been heaped upon her from the moment Heather staged that totally rigged vote this morning.

"Oh! I almost forgot." Shirley took the book back from her and began thumbing through it frantically.

"What are you looking for, Aunt Shirley?" Seth asked.

"Great-Granny Higginbottom's donut recipe."

"What does a donut recipe have to do with a Christmas pageant?" Angie asked.

"Why, we always have Granny Higginbottom's donuts at the cast party after the pageant is over. Without fail. It's tradition."

Angie's mental dictionary leaped into high gear.

Tradition: (n.) An excuse for doing something the same way over and over far beyond the point where it makes sense.

"What if the new cast wants something else for their party?" Take-out pizza sprang to mind.

"Oh, they won't. Everyone loves Granny's recipe. These donuts are heaven on a paper plate. And they're a perk for being in the pageant. It's the only way to get one," Shirley said. "How else do you think I've been able to keep the same folks working on the pageant year after year?"

Um . . . a combination of guilt and bullying?

"But there's a problem this year," Shirley said.

Angie was certain of that.

"Granny's recipe is a family secret," Shirley explained. "No one but a Higginbottom can make it."

"Well, if that's the case, I don't want to upset your family,"

Angie said with relief. The best thing she made in the kitchen was reservations. "We'll serve something else for the cast party."

"I'm a Higginbottom." Seth leaned back and crossed his arms over his chest. "On my mother's side."

"Oh, that's right." Pleased, Shirley clapped her hands together. "And you're the codirector, aren't you?"

"Manger builder," Angie corrected, narrowing her eyes at him. She could have said "set designer," but it would have been giving him too much credit.

"And codirector," Seth said with a self-satisfied grin. He made her uncomfortable and he knew it.

Drat the man.

"Heather said we should hash that out later. So now it's later," Seth reasoned. "Codirector has a nice ring to it."

"But—"

"If you want a new manger built, I'd say we just settled it."

"Well, that'll do then," Shirley said happily. "As long as Seth guards the recipe from prying eyes and you promise me faithfully that you won't pass it on to anyone, you can make the donuts, dear."

"Me?" Angie couldn't boil water without burning it. "Why can't the codirector do it?"

"To be honest, there's never been a codirector so I'm not sure what Seth is supposed to do, but making the donuts *is* part of the director's duties. They're all listed on page three of the pageant book," Shirley said.

Angie flipped to page three and found a list as long as her arm.

"Now, I always make the donuts the night before the pageant so they'll be good and fresh," Shirley said. "Of course, you might want to make a trial batch ahead of time to be sure you've got it right. Some of Granny's recipes can be tricky."

Angie had no doubt. Messing with a tradition was like tiptoeing through a minefield. She wasn't likely to make it through in one piece. In fact, this whole pageant thing was looking a lot trickier than getting high school kids to spout Shakespeare.

Seth leaned forward and helped himself to another snickerdoodle. His chest rose and fell under the black T-shirt in a way that showed how heavily muscled he was. Angie averted her gaze. The last thing she needed to be doing was noticing little things about Seth Parker.

"According to family legend," Seth said, "Granny used to leave out a few ingredients or fudge on baking times so no one else could make the dish quite like she could."

"And she had a few tricks you had to catch her at or you'd never learn them," Shirley said. "For instance, when she moved to town and finally had an electric range to cook on instead of a wood stove, she'd get up and do the donuts at two in the morning so she could be certain she'd be able to heat the oil good and hot."

Angie's brows shot up. "And it needs to be two in the morning for that?"

"Not now," Seth said. "Electrical service wasn't as reliable back then. If too many people were on the line at the same time . . . pfft!"

Angie's shoulders slumped. "Any donuts I make are likely to pfft, no matter when I fry them."

"Don't worry," George said. "Seth here will help you."

"Hey, I only volunteered to build a manger."

"Sounds to me like you insisted on being codirector a minute ago, son," George said. "The job is yours with all the risks, responsibilities, and appurtenances thereto. Here, Angela, let me warm up that coffee. I think you've let it go cold."

She didn't want to offend him. He'd been so nice, but that coffee of his had a sheen to it, like used motor oil. "There's no need, Mr. Evans—"

"George, please."

"George," she repeated. "I really must be going. It's an in-service day for teachers but there's still work for me to do."

Shirley Evans smiled brightly at her. "Well, I expect you're a bit overwhelmed anyway."

That was an understatement. Angie would have to climb out from under the pageant book weighing down her lap and claw her way up the drapes to be just overwhelmed. But she thanked the Evanses and handed the big honking book to her "codirector." She and Seth made their way back through the kitchen and out the garage door.

"If you have any questions, give me a ring," Shirley called after them.

"Or just stop by," George suggested. "Coffee's always on."

"He's not kidding," Seth said under his breath as he opened the truck door for her. "Just don't drop by after Wednesday. By that time in the week, the coffee's been reheated so many times, it has a life of its own."

After he closed the truck door, Angie watched him go around to his side. Seth Parker had an easy gait, a confident stride, that made him eminently watchable. And even though the gentlemanly ritual of opening and closing a lady's door had gone the way of the dodo, he did it so naturally, not a single feminist bone in her body rebelled.

It was a small thing, but she couldn't remember the last time a guy had done something like that for her.

Sorry, Gloria Steinem. It still feels nice.

"So where can I drop you?" he asked as the truck's engine rumbled to life.

"The Bates College library is fine." She would have rather gone home, but if she wasn't going to sit at her desk in her classroom, she should at least use the day to research which play she'd tackle with her ninth graders next spring.

"Want me to keep the pageant book for you?" he asked. "It's a step from the college to your place and that notebook is so big, it'd be awkward for you to carry it that far."

"Okay. Thanks." If he'd said it was too heavy, she'd have tried to carry it just to spite him. But the book was unwieldy and filled with so many loose clippings and notecards and swatches, she was sure to lose some of it. "How do you know where I live?"

"Remember where you are, Teach. Everybody in Coldwater is all up in everybody else's business. Besides, Lacy Evans is my cousin. You think I wouldn't hear who she sublet her place to?"

"Oh." Growing up, Angie had drifted from one foster home to another. No one ever seemed to care where she was. Now a whole town was keeping track of her, which was a little disconcerting. Worse, the Neanderthal at the wheel—*all right, the well-trained, polite, quite possibly intelligent in a nonverbal way Neanderthal*—had also made her whereabouts his business.

She felt a little exposed, as if he'd somehow caught her naked.

"So I'll bring the book by this evening." He didn't ask. He simply told her he'd be coming by.

"All right." Angie couldn't think of a reason why he shouldn't, but her insides fluttered uncertainly, like a sparrow caught in a sudden downdraft.

When they reached the charming little jewel that was the Bates College campus, they came to a stop in front of the two-story brick colonial that had been turned into the library.

"When you bring the book over, don't be surprised if I can't come to the door right away," she said. "You'll have to give me a minute to put Effie away."

Seth chuckled. "Oh, yeah. Lacy's attack cat. Heard you got saddled with that hairy bundle of badness."

"Effie's not bad. She's just misunderstood."

"Aren't we all?" A crooked smile lifted one corner of his mouth. "Want me to bring pizza and beer?"

A pizza? Beer? He was coming over, and he was bringing dinner. Angie's "man-on-the-move" defensive system sprang into high gear.

"Is that your ham-handed way of asking me on a date?"

"Heck, no. Get over yourself, Teach. I just don't want to starve while we figure out this pageant thing."

"Oh. Okay, then."

Before he could hop out and open her door, she did it herself, but she didn't make a clean getaway. He stopped her from climbing out of the truck with a hand on her forearm.

"Just for the record," Seth said, "if I did ask you out, it wouldn't be for pizza and beer. See you around seven."

Angie slid out of the cab and watched him pull away, his back tires spinning a little before gaining traction. Only after he turned the corner and was out of sight did she realize that she'd left her copy of *Sense and Sensibility* on top of the pageant book.

The margins were cluttered with her notes about the text. She'd underlined favorite passages. Angie groaned. She couldn't have given this man, this perfect stranger, a clearer glimpse into her heart if she'd ripped it from her chest and presented it to him on a platter.

Chapter 5

*"The more I know of the world, the more I am
convinced that I shall never see a man whom I
can really love. I require so much!"*

—*Sense and Sensibility* by Jane Austen

"**W**ell, that explains a lot," Seth said with a grunt. Once he
reached the high school job site, he noticed that Angie had left
her paperback along with the pageant notebook in the cab of
his truck. He flipped it open, hoping she'd written a phone
number inside so he could let her know he had it and would
bring it back to her when he dropped by this evening.

No joy. She had written her name in it, but not her number. So he thumbed through the book, hoping she maybe had
marked her place with a business card or something. He ran
across a highlighted passage instead.

The English teacher really did seem to require so much,
and Seth Parker evidently didn't come up to the mark. He'd
never felt so weighed in the balance and found wanting.

She was as prickly a girl as he'd ever met. She had yet to
smile at him. Not a real smile anyway. Oh, she'd cast a few sly
grins his way, mostly when she seemed to think he was some
sort of simpleton. That kind of smile he could live without, but
it didn't stop him from wanting to see if he could earn a real
one from her.

He wondered if she ever laughed. If so, he got the feeling
she didn't do it often.

He shoved the book into his glove box and went to join his crew. They were breaking ground at the high school, so he'd be playing in dirt and gravel all day. If he worked hard enough, he ought to be able to put the squirrelly little teacher out of his mind.

After a couple of hours, he decided meeting Angela Holloway was like having a smashed thumb. The more you tried not to think about it, the more it throbbed.

The double doors of Bates Library were sturdy and heavily carved, fashioned of old oak and embellished with polished brass fittings. Dark lines of wood grain pushed through the patina of age and swirled around a lead glass transom overhead. Angie opened one of the doors and entered the circa 1890s house that had been repurposed for the college's use.

There were a number of rooms leading off the wide main hallway, all filled with books and periodicals and maps, but the best part of the space was the center atrium, where the ceiling soared two stories to stained glass skylights. On the upper level, the stacks of books led off from a narrow walkway that could only be reached by the wrought-iron spiral staircase in the far corner.

Angie inhaled deeply. There were few things in the world that smelled better than a library. She used her tablet for convenience sake, but nothing could match the scents of old leather and slight mustiness that accompanied real books. In the pregnant quiet of a library, there were thousands of minds waiting on the shelves for her. Each one called to her, ready to engage her in a private conversation, in an adventure, in a love affair that, even when it ended, left no guilt, no sorrow, and no regrets.

"Angela Holloway, is that you?"

She started at the sound of the voice, but she'd heard it so often in her dreams, she recognized it at once. This time, though, she wasn't dreaming. The guy was really there, leaning one elbow on the circulation desk. He didn't exactly meet her gaze. His always seemed to drift a little lower to her lips.

Oh, the things his mouth could do to hers.

Her lips tingled a little.

Dressed in chinos and a polo shirt, he looked as if he'd just stepped from the pages of GQ. Angie would have said he hadn't changed, but that wasn't true. He was even more devastatingly handsome than she remembered.

She pulled her ratty sweater closer around her. *This is what I get for wandering around town dressed like a bag lady.*

"Peter," she whispered.

When he smiled, the years melted away. The way her heart pounded, they might still have been back at Baylor.

The impulse to turn and run was strong. She wanted to, but it was as if someone had glued her feet to the floor. Then Peter closed the distance between them, and gathered her in a quick, sexless hug before she could straight-arm him.

How does he do that? How can he pretend we don't have a history? That, for one breathless semester, we weren't the sun, moon, and stars to each other?

Oh, that's right. He's a lawyer.

Peter had explained to her once that pursuing the law meant he had to be able to compartmentalize, to put things into mental boxes and not let the edges touch.

She wondered if he'd tucked *her* into one of his little boxes, or if he'd thrown out memories of that time in his life completely. Straightening her spine, she decided that if he could act like this was just a chance meeting between old friends, she could too.

He wasn't entitled to her pain.

Angie found her voice. "What are you doing here?"

"There's a career fair tomorrow," he said. His voice was as resonant as James Earl Jones, but with none of the Darth Vader wheeze. "I've been invited to give a presentation about going into law."

"On the theory that the world needs more lawyers?"

He smiled. "You and your Shakespeare. Still think we should kill all the lawyers?"

"Only some of them," Angie said with poisonous sweetness. *Just the ones who stomp on people's hearts.* She settled for giving him an indignant smirk instead of a clout to the head.

"Anyway, I'm here to extol the benefits of postgraduate study," he said, apparently unfazed by her snarky expression.

Oh, that's right. Lawyers have the hide of a rhinoceros to go along with their neat little mental compartments.

"As I understand it," he went on, "most graduates of Bates College end up seeking advanced degrees."

"That's because they can't get a job based on the goofy liberal arts degrees they earn here." Not that Angie was anti-liberal arts. She was an English major, after all, but Bates didn't offer the usual courses of study. "Judging from the library, the college used to be pretty mainstream, but now they specialize in more . . . *esoteric* offerings."

Esoteric-(adjective) 1. Something designed to be understood by only a few who possess specialized knowledge, or 2. (and this is my personal definition) What you call something when it would be rude to call it weird.

Now that she thought about it, running into Peter Manning in Coldwater Cove was pretty . . . *esoteric,* too.

"Esoteric, huh?" Peter looked around. The library reeked of tradition. "How do you mean?"

"Bates offers degrees in things like Popular Culture and Online Society, Decision Science, Ecogastronomy—"

"What's that?"

"Not sure, but if you have to ask, is it any wonder the grads can't find a job that uses their newfound knowledge?" Angie shrugged. "You can even earn a BA in puppetry here at Bates."

"Puppetry?" Peter shot her a surprised grimace. "You're kidding."

"No joke. Puppetry."

Bates College didn't even offer an education program so its grads could pass on their niche market expertise to others as teachers. Not that trying to get high school kids to warm up to the Bard was a dream job, but teaching paid the bills. And Angie loved teaching.

Except maybe when her students' problems opened up her old wounds. . . .

"Even if they study underwater basket weaving, as long as they have a bachelor's degree, a decent grade point, and score high enough on the LSAT, my alma mater wants to talk to them," Peter said. "It doesn't matter what their undergrad background is. Nothing is ever wasted on a lawyer."

"Yeah," Angie drawled, "I'm trying to imagine using puppetry in a courtroom."

He laughed and the circulation librarian shushed him.

"That's your fault, Angie," he whispered. "You always made me laugh."

And you always made me cry.

But she didn't say it. He didn't deserve to know she still bore, if not the exquisite ache, at least a vivid memory of the wound he gave her heart. So she lifted her chin and faced him squarely.

"So after your talk tomorrow, you'll be heading home," she said, wondering if he'd stayed in DC after he finished law school.

He shook his head. "Not immediately. After the career fair, I'm going to be a guest lecturer in a couple of classes for a few days."

"Your firm doesn't mind?"

"My name's on the letterhead, so if I want to take some time away, I can always ask one of the junior partners to step in."

"Of course," she said. "I should have known you'd make partner in record time. You never did anything by halves, did you?"

"Even when it wasn't the right thing to do." His habitual smile faded, and his gaze turned intense. "I wish I . . . Angie, I just want you to know—I never forgot about you."

She made a small hmph-ing noise. "That must be why you called and wrote so often."

He shook his head and gave her his best self-deprecating sigh. Angie bet members of a jury ate him up with a spoon.

The female ones anyway.

"Law school was a crazy time for me. You have no idea the pressure I was under.

"Still ending sentences with prepositions, I see." *He should know better than that, but he's trying to turn on the Manning charm.* Grammar was the best shield she owned. Angie crossed her arms and leaned against the nearest bookcase.

He smiled. "And you're still a grammar freak. Glad some things haven't changed."

"But some things have." Fluttery feeling in her chest notwithstanding, she was proud of herself for not swooning into his arms at first sight.

"You know, I tried to find you after I landed my first job."

Those flutters grew more insistent but she tamped them down.

"But you'd gone to grad school someplace and moved away from Waco," he said. "I contacted some of our friends, but nobody had a forwarding address for you."

That wasn't surprising. She'd lost touch after they scattered to take up their new post-graduation lives. Her college buddies were off to Dallas, Atlanta, Chicago, and Seattle. They were all totally jazzed about teaching in challenging urban districts.

Angie had stayed in academia to get her Masters, even though it hadn't been necessary to teach, and then accepted a job in little Coldwater Cove because it seemed like a cross between Mayberry and Lake Woebegone. She had no family, no safety net. When she was a kid, she'd fallen through the cracks in the foster system. A child who didn't act out tended to be ignored. Now that she was an adult, she didn't want to end up someplace where no one would notice if she wasn't there.

"You're not even on Facebook," he said accusingly. "Who does that?"

"People who value their privacy."

"Come on, Ange, it's like you're in witness protection or something. How could you expect me to find you?"

"I didn't ask you to." *Oh, shoot. Now I'm dangling prepositions, too.*

"That's just it. I didn't expect to find you here. There I was, talking to the librarian, minding my own business, and suddenly you walked in." He cocked his head. "Think it's a sign?"

"A sign that you still try to get by on charm."

He took a step closer. "Is it working?"

"No," she lied.

Knowing how he operated didn't negate its power. There was something beguiling about Peter. Always had been. It was more than attractiveness. He had a way of making everyone he was with feel as if they were the most important person in the world.

Angie just hadn't been able to keep him with her.

"Look, Ange." He reached a hand up and planted it against the bookshelf, his splayed fingers close enough to her left ear that she could imagine them ruffling through her hair. Her whole body stiffened. "I know just rolling into town can't make up for the past."

She snorted. "You think?"

"But that doesn't mean we can't start over, as friends, I mean. Let me take you to dinner."

She relaxed a bit, but then Emma and Tad's conversation scrolled through her head. Angie could almost hear Emma gushing over how nice it was of Tad to take her to breakfast. The girl had infused a simple meal with far more meaning than Tad intended.

But Angie wasn't doing the same thing. She knew Peter didn't mean anything by the invitation. And wouldn't it prove she was over him, once and for all, if she accepted his dinner invitation? If they shared a cordial meal and then parted ways as soon as they polished off dessert, maybe it would take away the sting of their final days together.

"Peter, you can't take me to dinner." The look of surprise on his face was so worth it. Then she pulled out her phone and went on, "But you can *meet* me for dinner. We'll go Dutch. Give me your number and I'll text you where and when."

This was so much better than her fantasies of him groveling and her swooning. It felt good to be in control. She'd pick the place. She'd dictate the terms of their encounter. She could wear something nicer than her *Matrix* sweater and faded jeans.

And if that something left Peter full of regret, so much the better.

Chapter 6

Now at the Green Apple Grill for a limited time!
Hypocrite's Vegetarian Omelet, chock-full of ham or sausage.
Have our six-ounce steak on the side. We won't tell if you don't.
What happens at the Green Apple, stays at the Green Apple!

—*The Coldwater Gazette* classifieds

Seth wasn't a big reader. Not that he couldn't, of course. It was just that he hardly ever sat still long enough to read a whole book, and when he did, it was more likely to be nonfiction, engineering, or applied science. Why should he dive into someone else's imaginary world when the real one around him kept him busy enough?

And in trouble enough.

Angie Holloway's pixy face seemed to hover before him at odd times throughout the day. It was hard to concentrate on moving earth and laying cement when she kept creeping back into his head.

But despite his usual lack of interest in fiction, after he got home and showered off the day's work, the teacher's paperback began calling to him. When he leafed through it, he didn't read the story. It was the notes in the margins of *Sense and Sensibility* that drew his eye.

The English teacher obviously spent a ton of time in someone else's imagined world.

The characters seemed real to her. They must, or she wouldn't be alternately scolding or consoling them in so many of her scribblings in the white space around the text. There was hardly a page without an underlined passage or two.

For example, the words "She was stronger alone" were underlined three times and, just in case that wasn't enough, Angie had highlighted them with a yellow marker.

"Guess those are her words to live by," he mumbled. Well, it sounded like she had to be stronger alone since she had no family.

Seth tried to imagine what that must be like and failed. He'd grown up with a houseful of brothers and sisters and a gaggle of cousins spread all over the county. It was great. He didn't even mind his mom and his aunt Shirley trying to fix him up with "the right girl."

He wondered if somehow they'd gotten to Heather and that's how he happened to be shackled to Angie Holloway at the moment.

He could just hear his aunt Shirley saying, "You could do worse, Seth."

He didn't see how.

He and the English teacher had nothing in common.

Except this blasted Christmas pageant.

He didn't want to be late getting over to her place. It always irritated him when someone stole his time by making him wait, and he tried not to do it to anyone else. So he left earlier than he needed to. First, he made a run by the pizza place and then ducked into the Piggly Wiggly to pick up a cold six-pack. He grabbed some cokes too, in case she was a teetotaler. The soft drinks wouldn't be cold, but she'd surely have some ice cubes.

Angie lived in one of the apartments above the second-hand store called Gewgaws & Gizzwhickies on the Town Square. Over the last few years, the merchants on the lower level around the Square had renovated their empty top floors to serve as residential space. The apartments' front doors were down on the Square, and opened onto long dark staircases leading up. But most residents and visitors used the back doors. The rear of the building featured a French Quarter–style upper deck and long open-air wrought-iron steps.

It was one of the most charming things about the apartments and had been featured in the Tulsa paper once as a prime example of how to combine retail and residential space in rural areas.

Seth took the iron steps two at a time.

On the deck outside Angie's door, a wicker love seat and chairs had been arranged in a conversational manner. The dry remains of a mandevilla vine still snaked out of its large clay pot and clung around the iron post supporting the deck roof. Seth could picture the little teacher curled up in a corner of the love seat on a summer's evening, poring over her *Sense and Sensibility* and sipping a glass of sweet tea. Maybe there'd be a slight breeze and the hem of her sundress would ruffle up a bit.

Down boy. He gave himself a mental shake. He didn't usually indulge the randy side of his imagination and, in this case, he was pretty sure he was wasting it on a woman who wasn't at all interested in him anyway.

Still, he wasn't one to back down from a challenge, and if nothing else, Angela Holloway was that.

Seth set the pizza and pageant book down on the nearest chair's side table and knocked on her door.

No response.

He rapped again.

This time, the curtains in the kitchen window parted when a large Siamese hopped up on the sill. The cat stared at him with bored superiority.

Even when Effie had belonged to his cousin Lacy, he'd never been able to make any headway with her. Lacy had always claimed that Effie was a one-person cat . . . who was still in search of her person.

Maybe the English teacher was having better luck with the hand-me-down pet, but he doubted it. If someone had dumped the sullen creature on him, he'd have found some other sap to take the cat off his hands pronto.

The animal laid its ears back and hissed at him.

"You can't blame a guy for what he thinks, cat. Only for what he does."

Seth banged on the door again. This time he heard a faint, "Wait a minute, I'm coming," accompanied by the tapping of heels on hardwood. He picked up the pizza and pageant book.

When Angie opened the door, he decided the wait was well worth it. She was wearing a little black dress with strappy heels. This morning her hair had been bunched up in a sloppy ponytail. It was down now, falling to her shoulders like dark rain. She'd applied some makeup, not a lot, but enough to make her big eyes seem even larger. Her pink mouth shaped itself into a surprised little "oh!"

She looked nice. Date nice, he realized. She'd been so insistent that this *wasn't* a date, he'd only tugged on clean jeans and a flannel shirt after his shower.

"Whoa, Teach. You clean up pretty good."

"Well. I clean up pretty well," she corrected, rolling those big eyes at him. "I suppose you think that was a compliment."

"That's how I meant it." He came in and put the pizza and drinks on the kitchen counter. Then he plopped the pageant notebook onto one of the barstools. The cat hopped up into the other one and continued to glare at him with malice. The animal clearly did not like visitors, even ones who brought pizza. Seth took the hint.

"We can put this stuff in your fridge if you'd rather go out to eat," he suggested.

Angie glanced at the big clock over the sink. "Actually, I am going out. Look, I'm sorry about this, but to be honest, I forgot you were coming by tonight."

Way to make a guy feel like he just stepped in cat crap.

"It's not like I planned this." At least she had the grace to look a little embarrassed. When he didn't say anything, she rattled on, "You see, I ran into an old . . . friend at the college. Totally by accident. And so now we're meeting for dinner to catch up. Like I said, I'm really sorry."

When she tented her fingers before her, he noticed she'd painted her nails the same shade as her lipstick.

"I didn't mean to inconvenience you. This dinner just sort of happened," she said, her brows drawing together in distress with such earnestness, he couldn't be upset with her. "Can we reschedule a time to go over the Christmas pageant stuff?"

He shrugged. "Sure."

What else could he say?

Her lips lifted in an approximation of a smile. It still wasn't the one he wanted from her.

"Thank you, Seth. I really appreciate your being so nice about this."

"No problem." Pointedly ignoring the cat, who'd graduated from glaring to a low growl with each exhalation, he moved the pageant book and settled onto the other barstool. If Angie was going to stand him up, he deserved a few details. "So who's the guy?"

"Who said it was a guy?"

"I don't think you'd get this dressed up for a girls' night."

"Um . . . you'd be surprised how often women dress to impress other women, but actually, I don't go out much at all. Look, I was brushing my hair when you knocked." She raised the brush in her hand. "Do you mind if I keep getting ready?"

"Go ahead."

She leaned her head to one side, and ran the bristles through the glistening strands. Her slender neck and one little shell of an ear was exposed, pink and soft-looking. Seth's mouth went dry.

When she finished with her hair, she disappeared into the other room, probably to put away the brush. Seth drew a deep breath. His skin prickled as if static electricity was dancing along each nerve. He felt as if he'd been caught out in an open field, exposed while thunderclouds gathered, lightening crackled, and the sky prepared to drop a torrential rush on his head.

Why this woman should make him so hyperaware of her, he didn't know. She still wasn't his type.

A subtle hint of fragrance followed her back into the kitchen. No cloying flowers or baby powder. She'd spritzed on a surprising mix of vanilla, soft woodsiness, and a spicy hit of pepper. She smelled like . . . well, like everything he wanted a woman to smell like.

That settled it. "You *are* meeting a guy tonight."

"Yes, I am, if you must know," she said as she lifted a small foot to adjust the strap on one of her heels. "Peter Manning is his name, and he's from . . . well, I don't really know where he lives now."

"And you know this guy from where?"

"We met as undergrads," she said. "He and I used to see each other when we were at Baylor."

See each other naked, you mean? almost popped out of Seth's mouth, but he stopped himself. The past was the past. He'd hate to give chapter and verse on his failed relationships and he sure didn't know Angie well enough to poke around in hers.

Still, he couldn't help wishing this Peter Manning clown would suddenly sprout a big red zit on his nose.

He popped the top on one of the beers and took a long pull. "So what happened between the two of you?"

"That is none of your business."

"Hey, I'm the one getting stood up here. You owe me."

"I'm not standing you up. This would have had to be a date for that to happen. I'm just—"

"Rescheduling me, then."

"Yes. We're rescheduling." Her dark eyes snapped. "And I said thank you for being so understanding."

"You're welcome. Don't try to change the subject. Besides, understanding is what I'm after. What happened with this Peter Manson?"

"Manning."

"Right." Seth took another swig from the longneck. "You dump him?"

She shook her head. "He dumped me."

Dang, that's why she's trying so hard. He had to admit what she was doing was working. If he'd dumped a girl who could rock a simple black dress like that, he'd want to kick his own rear up between his shoulder blades. "The guy's an ass."

"You don't even know him."

"Don't need to," Seth said. "Stands to reason he's an ass. He'd have to be to dump someone like you."

"You don't know me either."

He put down his beer. "I'd like to."

Her mouth opened and closed a couple of times. She looked a little like a bluegill trying to decide whether or not to strike the lure jigging in the water in front of it.

"Why?" she finally asked.

He wasn't sure. When he'd first met Angie, he'd pegged her as difficult, but not high maintenance. No woman who'd be caught dead in that ratty old sweater she'd been wearing could be called high maintenance. Still, she was an irritable fussbudget who thought she was better than he. But after he'd read some of the things she'd written in the margins of that book, he was beginning to see a different sort of person altogether.

Angela Holloway was sensitive. Empathetic and caring. She had a dry wit. As fragile as she looked, he'd been surprised to discover a core of determination in her that was solid as steel.

And between the lines of her sometimes meandering commentary on the Austen novel, he'd read a deep hurt.

If something was broken, Seth's go-to response was to fix it. He never could resist a stray, which was why he had two dogs at the moment. If someone was down on their luck, he was first to lend a hand. He figured it was only right since he'd been blessed with a loving family, a decent education, and a business he'd grown into the most successful construction firm in the southeast part of the state. He needed to give back.

It wouldn't hurt to give back to Angela Holloway. But he was beginning to suspect this need to figure her out was about much more than his usual instinct to help.

Something about the English teacher called to him. He didn't understand it, but that didn't make it less true. However, he figured he'd totally creep her out if he admitted that. Obviously, she didn't feel the same pull toward him.

Yet.

"I want to get to know you because I figure it'll make it easier for us to work together on the Christmas thing." That was true, as far as it went. "Besides, you said you don't go out much. Seems to me you could use a friend."

"If I need a friend, I'll take out an ad in the *Gazette*."

She was determined to push him off. It was a classic self-protective move. He didn't remember much from the psych class he had to take to earn his degree, but that particular strategy had stuck in his mind. Angie was trying to drive him away before he could leave her.

She was okay with being solitary when she could convince herself it was by her choice. Not so okay with being alone when the choice was someone else's.

"All right, then," he said. "I'll be back tomorrow night to go through the whole pageant notebook with you."

"You really think that's necessary?"

"Hey, if you want to do it all yourself, it's no skin off my nose." He could play push away, too.

"No, you're right." She put the pizza and the drinks in her fridge. "We can warm up the pizza tomorrow. Thanks for bringing it, by the way."

"No problem." He rose to go. "Have fun with Mr. Manicotti."

"Manning."

"Whatever."

As he headed for the door, someone knocked on the other side. Seth opened it to find another guy standing out on the deck, a bottle of wine in one hand, and flowers in the other.

And there wasn't the slightest hint of a zit on his nose.

Chapter 7

In the immortal words of Suzanne Sugarbaker,
"The man's supposed to kill the bugs."

—Shirley Evans, on the difference between men and women

"You must be Dick Manning," Seth said flatly.

The other guy frowned. "Peter. Peter Manning."

"Right. Angie, he's here."

She had to peer around Seth, who didn't feel like unblocking the doorway immediately.

"I didn't tell you where I lived, Peter." Angie gave the newcomer a frown.

At least someone else is on the receiving end of her scowl this time.

Manning smiled at her.

It reminded Seth of the expression Effie made after she licked her own butt.

"This is a small town," the guy said. "The lady at the desk of the Heart of the Ozarks motel was happy to give me your address, Ange."

"Ange?" Seth repeated.

"Yes, Ange," she said. "Just because you have a name that can't be shortened, don't pick on those of us who do."

Okay, now she's back to frowning at me. I oughta keep my mouth shut.

She turned to Manning. "I thought we agreed that we'd meet at Harper's."

Located on the lower level of the Opera House, Harper's

was the nicest restaurant in town. The menu was a bit pricey for most folks, but the food was as good as you could get in a fine restaurant in any city. The place got a little rowdy on Karaoke Fridays. During the week, it was sure to be quiet and dimly lit by the little candles in the center of the linen-covered tables.

It was as intimate a setting for dinner as you could find in Coldwater Cove.

Seth's gut burned.

"I thought it'd be nice to have a drink here at your place before we walk across the Square to the restaurant," Peter said, handing her the bottle of white wine. "Chardonnay. Your favorite. Have you got a corkscrew?"

She took the wine from him, but set it on the counter instead of rummaging through her drawers for an opener. "I'm not much for wine anymore," she admitted.

"Maybe she's more a beer kind of girl," Seth said.

She shook her head. "I really don't like beer either. I thought you were leaving, Seth."

Seth ignored her not-so-cordial invitation to make himself scarce. He didn't like the looks of this Manning character. "Not until you introduce us."

She sighed in exasperation. "Peter, this is Seth . . ."

"Parker," Seth finished for her in case she'd forgotten his last name. He stuck out his hand. Manning took it and gave him a surprisingly strong shake for someone who was probably a spineless wiener. No calluses, though. Seth would bet any amount of money the guy had never done an honest day's work in his life.

Manning narrowed his eyes at Seth. "And you and Angie know each other . . . how?"

"Actually," Angie cut in, "Seth and I just met today. We're working together on a community project."

"What sort of project?"

"The annual Christmas pageant," Angie said.

"Is that so?" Manning said, turning to Seth. "I didn't take you for a *pageant* sort of guy at first glance, but I think I see it now."

Trust a lawyer to deliver a smack without moving any muscle but the one in his tongue.

Seth wished he could knock the guy into next week just on principle. He deserved it for dumping someone like Angie, but Seth figured she wouldn't appreciate the gesture. Still, it was fun to imagine how much losing his shiny front teeth would mess up her old boyfriend's looks.

But Angie's cat didn't seem to care what her mistress might appreciate. From the corner of his eye, Seth saw Effie sink into a crouching posture and give her bottom a preattack shake. Then, with a hair-raising yowl, the cat launched herself across the room. She did a bank shot off the counter, sending the wine bottle crashing to the floor. Droplets of chardonnay and splintered glass flew and the rest of the wine glugged out of the remains of the bottle. Then Effie leaped onto Peter Manning, giving special attention to the hand that was holding the bouquet.

He yelped like a twelve-year-old girl and dropped the flowers.

The cat continued to shred the blooms until a bulbous-bodied spider climbed from the ruins. The arachnid scuttled across the kitchen floor, trying to get away, but ran into the rapidly spreading puddle of chardonnay and began to flounder instead.

"Oh, my gosh! That's a black widow," Angie cried.

Seth stomped down on it with his heavily booted foot. "*Was* a black widow."

Peter Manning's eyes widened and his Adam's apple bobbed in a gulp. He looked like he was about to wet himself. "Aren't they poisonous?"

"Yeah," Seth said as he pulled a paper towel off the roll hanging from Angie's upper cabinets and cleaned the spider goo from the bottom of his boot. Then he knelt to sop up the wine as well. "Black widows like to hide out in cut flowers and produce from down south. Then they hitch a ride up here. You maybe ought to check for 'em, before you give any more flowers to a lady."

"Peter had no idea the flowers had a spider in them, Seth."

Why is she defending this loser?

"Yeah, well, just to be safe, how about I take the rest of the bouquet out to the dumpster? Just in case Charlotte brought a friend with her."

"Charlotte?" Angie asked.

"Yeah, like in *Charlotte's Web.*"

A quick smile slid over her lips. "That was my favorite book when I was a kid."

"Mine too," he said. It was a small thing, but it felt like the first point they'd agreed on from the moment they'd met. Something inside him hummed. "Of course, Charlotte wasn't a black widow."

"No, she was a good spider, clever and loyal," Angie said. "I cried so hard when she died in the end."

Seth chuckled. "Will you think less of me if I admit I did too? 'Course, I was only eight at the time."

"Eight? You were a pretty early reader if you were already into big chapter books by then."

"Okay, okay," Peter said, obviously trying to interrupt the steady flow of points Seth was making with Angie. "Let the record show we all like spiders as long as they're in a children's book."

"Or outside," Seth said. "I never kill a spider if it's minding its own business."

Angie nodded. "Me, neither. But in the house, if it has more than four legs, it deserves to die."

"Yeah," Seth agreed.

"Ange, I'm surprised at you. That's a rather bloodthirsty attitude you've developed. You used to be much more Zen about this sort of thing." Manning raised a brow at her. "We really ought to have trapped the spider in a jar and taken it outside instead of smashing it."

"Maybe you coulda done that if you hadn't been too busy screaming," Seth suggested.

"I wasn't screaming," Peter protested.

"Yeah, you kind of were," Angie said.

"I . . . I was just surprised by it. Let's go, Ange."

"Okay, let me get my jacket." She headed for the other room, then stopped in her tracks. "No, wait. I haven't fed Effie yet."

Seth immediately saw a way to make a few more points with her. "I'll feed the cat. Then I'll pick up the mess"—he gestured toward the ruined pile of daisies and carnations—"and lock up when I leave."

"Would you?"

"I'm used to cleaning up construction sites. Guess I can manage a little feline mess."

"Thanks, Seth." Her expression clearly grateful, she breezed off into the other room. It still wasn't the smile he was looking for, but it was a big improvement.

"She's way out of your league, you know," Peter said once she was out of earshot. "You'll never catch a girl like Angela."

"Maybe not," Seth agreed. "But if I did, I wouldn't be stupid enough to throw her back."

Peter made a noise in the back of his throat that sounded suspiciously like Effie's little fake growls. Before he could say more, Angie came back into the kitchen, wearing a fitted leather jacket over her dress.

"There's a can of tuna in the pantry, Seth. Thanks, again."

"Okay, you and Manfred have fun."

"Manning," Peter corrected.

"Whatever, dude."

After they left, Seth bagged up the floral debris and opened a can for the cat. When he set the plate of tuna down on the floor, Effie sniffed at it delicately and gave it a lick, but before she tucked in to her dinner, she rubbed against Seth's legs.

She even gave him a throaty purr.

"Well, cat, what do you know? This just may be the beginning of a beautiful friendship."

Chapter 8

In literature or in life, it's hard to get very far if
you keep rereading the same chapter.

—Angie Holloway, who admits to getting stuck sometimes

As Angie had expected, there wasn't a big crowd at Harper's and they were immediately shown to a table in a pleasantly dim corner. The window of wavy old glass next to them opened out onto the Square with its Victorian courthouse framed by the quaint collection of shops. The street lights around the courthouse were electric and had been installed fairly recently, but they were styled after old Victorian gas lamps. Come December, the bulbs would be changed from white to red and green to add a festive flair to the Square.

"What's good here?" Peter asked after he held the chair for Angie to sit.

Two different guys opening doors and holding chairs for me in the same day. She knew the feminist in her ought to be affronted, but it was kind of nice to be pampered once in a while. Sort of made her feel like a Jane Austen heroine.

"The trout is fresh," Angie said. Lake Jewell was good for more than boating in the summer. Anglers of all ages fished its crystal waters year-round. The cold, spring-fed lake was perfect for rainbow trout.

After a quick look at the menu, Peter ordered rib-eye steaks for both of them. Angie had forgotten how much he liked being in control and would have complained that she'd rather have had surf than turf, but he'd already insisted on the way over that he was paying. A lavish supper at Harper's wasn't in her budget. If she'd been on her own dime, she'd have had to go with the chef's salad, no starter and no dessert.

Once their server left the table, an awkward silence stretched between them. A flood of memories from her time with Peter came rushing back to her, leaving her slightly breathless. Peter Manning had been the catch of the campus. She'd been so astonished when this godlike fellow turned his attention to her. Wild Saturday nights together morphed into lazy Sunday mornings. He'd been her first and only love. She didn't think it was possible to be that happy.

Then the relationship that had started with a bang ended with a whimper. He'd crushed her so completely, she hadn't thought she'd ever recover.

Now, her insides didn't seem to remember that part of it.

Her heart didn't have a toggle switch.

What would a Jane Austen heroine do? she wondered. *She'd fill the empty air with polite small talk and no one would ever know what a mass of contradictory emotions seethed in her heart.*

"So, where do you live now, Peter?" she asked. Sometimes, Austen was so right. If not for her favorite author, Angie might have done something stupid like gushing over him as if she were as clueless as her student Emma.

"My firm is in DC, but I live in Bethesda and take the Metro to work each day," he said, resting his forearms on the table as he leaned toward her. "If I want to get out of the city for a while, I get the Beemer out of the garage and run down to my weekend house near Virginia Beach."

"A weekend house. Sounds lovely."

He shrugged. "It is, I guess, but I don't get to use it very often. My accountant says it serves me better as a rental property right now."

"It seems sad that you have a house you can't use." Her

apartment was fine as far as it went, but Angie longed for the permanence of a real home. She always had.

"Who says I'm not using it? The write-off really helps my tax situation."

Oh, to make enough money to have a tax situation! "Well, maybe you'll retire there someday."

Peter had taken a sip of his water and nearly choked on it. "Are you nuts? The place would drive me crazy in half a week. The cell service is spotty at best and the area my house is in rolls up its sidewalks at eleven."

She chuckled. He had Coldwater Cove beat. The Square was usually deserted by nine unless it was Karaoke Friday or the local big band was playing dance music in the little ballroom upstairs in the Opera House.

"A place in the country is okay for a getaway now and then, but not to live in permanently. Give me the city, even on a bad day." He leaned forward a bit. "So are you going to tell me what you're doing in a town like this?"

"I happen to like Coldwater Cove."

Peter shook his head. "I never figured you for life among the hairy unwashed. That Parker fellow is my exhibit A, by the way."

"He's not so bad." Angie wondered what Peter would think if he met Junior Bugtussle. The self-confessed hillbilly wasn't unwashed exactly. His wife Darlene would never stand for that, and made sure his overalls were always clean and well mended. But Junior certainly qualified as hairy. Angie thought he could pass as an escapee from *Duck Dynasty*. "Actually, Seth owns a successful business here."

"Last time I looked, a still in the hills didn't qualify as a business," Peter said dryly.

"I'll have you know Seth owns a major construction company. He employs a lot of people," she said testily. "Probably more than your law firm does."

"I'd be happy to compare bottom lines with him."

"I don't get the feeling that making a buck is the only reason Seth works," she said. If he was volunteering for the Warm Hearts Club, it stood to reason he wasn't just looking out for himself. "He doesn't seem to be all about money."

"That's a shame," he said harshly. "It's the only way to keep score."

"Why does everything have to turn into a contest with guys?" she asked. At least that flutter in her chest had settled down now. She realized that she liked Peter less when his mouth was moving.

Peter must have sensed she was mentally pulling away from him because his tone turned more conciliatory. "Look, Ange, I don't want to argue. Really. I want to hear about you and what you've been doing with yourself. So why don't you tell me how you come to be working on that community project with that guy?"

That guy has a name, she almost said, but decided she'd defended Seth Parker enough for one night. It was becoming a habit she didn't much care for.

For which I don't much care.

Angie launched into the whole tale of how she'd been drafted to run the pageant. She shared about meeting Mrs. Evans, her detailed instructions for the annual event, and the community's high expectations for the pageant.

"Sounds like you've inherited a mess," Peter said sympathetically.

"It's my own fault," she admitted. "I got a reputation around town for being a serious director when I tackled Shakespeare with my ninth graders last year."

"What was that like?"

"Let's just say I was too ambitious by half. But my students finally warmed up to *Macbeth,* and we made a decent amateur production of it." She was proud of her kids. At first, Elizabethan English was like another language to them, but after a few weeks, they started calling each other by their character names as they passed from one class to another in the hall. "Unfortunately, our opening night was not without a wardrobe malfunction or two."

"No kidding?"

"I messed up big time," she said. "I should have told my students that when you wear a kilt, you need to bend from the knees. On opening night, the boys who stooped to lift Duncan's body and bear him away mooned the whole theater."

Peter laughed. "I bet that went over like a lead balloon."

"Fortunately, they had gym shorts on under their kilts." Angie shook her head. "If someone had told them real Scotsmen go commando, I'd have been fired on the spot."

"Maybe that wouldn't have been so bad." He reached across the table and ran his fingertips across the pulse point at her wrist. Stupid little tingles raced up her arm, so she pulled away and reached for her own water glass. She tried to make it seem casual. He didn't need to know how he still made her feel. "If you'd lost your job here, maybe I could persuade you to come to Bethesda with me."

Her breath hitched a time or two. *With me,* he'd said. He couldn't possibly mean it.

"That's silly," she said. "We're not the same people we were at Baylor."

"Maybe not, but some things don't change." He sent her such a smoldering look it was a wonder the tablecloth between them didn't catch fire.

She had to lighten the mood. "Time has a way of changing everything. If we hadn't run into each other at the college today, you still wouldn't know where I am, and you wouldn't care, so don't go all Sexiest Man Alive on me."

That made him smile. Then his expression sobered.

"Seriously. Come back to DC with me. We'll never miss a single Bard in the Park. I mean it, Ange."

Ange. He was the only one who'd ever called her that.

Angie could hear her own heartbeat thudding in her head. She wished her pulse wouldn't shoot up like that, but it was proof that she wasn't immune to Peter's brand of uber good looks and smooth charm.

"Peter, let's lay aside the fact that we really don't know each other anymore"—*and maybe never did*—"it's just not practical." She willed her insides to stop jittering. "I'm certified to teach in this state. I wouldn't be able get a job in Maryland until I met a slew of new requirements. I'd have to take a ton of classes and would probably lose a whole year of work. Maybe more."

"Then don't come with me to find a job. I work hard enough for both of us. Hang out at my place and give yourself some time off." He cocked his head and shot her another intense look designed to turn her insides to Jell-O. "You might find there's something else you want to do besides teach Shakespeare to kids who are never going to get it anyway."

When she used to fantasize about Peter coming back for her, it was always a cross between the end of *An Officer and a Gentleman* and *Cinderella.* Her pretend Peter always begged her to take him back, and he always had a ring in his pocket.

When she considered his real offer for her to "hang out" at his place, she decided it was vaguely insulting. It reminded her of Tad Van Hook and his fondness for "hanging" with Emma. It didn't mean anything to Tad. And this offer didn't mean anything to Peter.

She deserved more than that.

"Peter, you can't waltz into town as if years haven't gone by and expect us to pick up where we left off." Her words were measured and clipped. She fought the urge to stand up, lean across the table, and slap his ridiculously handsome face.

Why, oh why, couldn't his insides live up to his outsides?

"Why not, Ange?" he said, clearly not realizing she was ticked. "Even felons get parole."

"Yeah, but you've done no time."

"Yes, I have. I've been without you all these years."

She snorted. "I doubt you were lonely. In fact, I have trouble believing you don't already have someone back east."

"I don't," he said. "When you bill eighty hours a week, there's not much time left for other things. More important things."

"It sounds like your plate is still pretty full. There's no room for anyone else."

"Yes, there is. I'm better at compartmentalizing now."

She leaned back and crossed her arms. "How could I forget your little mental boxes?"

"It's not just mental. I do it in all areas of my life now. For example, my firm's work doesn't interfere with my pro bono cases," he said. "And my personal life is separate from each of them."

She had to turn the conversation away from either of their personal lives. "*Pro bono,* huh? What kind of cases do you take for the public good?"

"I handle litigation for the UCFF."

"What's that?"

"United Civil Freedoms Front," he explained. "It's a national organization that serves as a sort of watchdog. We make sure government entities don't trample the rights of the people."

"Sounds good," she agreed. "I'm glad you've learned to give back. That's sort of the point to the CWHC here."

"What's that?"

"The Coldwater Warm Hearts Club," she said with a smile. It was fun to elevate their little group to the status of a national organization. "We help people, too, but according to my friend Heather, we have an ulterior motive and we know it."

Peter's brows arched in a question. "What kind of motive? Political? Religious?"

"No. Selfish. Heather claims when we help others, our own lives get better. Or if not better, at least it's easier to deal with our problems if we lighten the load others are carrying."

He made a hmph-ing sound. "Pretty pragmatic for a service organization. How does a community Christmas pageant figure into this picture?"

"It's a way of bringing people together."

"Usually a crèche on a courthouse lawn divides people."

"To paraphrase the natives, 'You aren't from around here, are you?' This pageant is so steeped in the town's history, everyone turns out for it."

"And no one minds the use of public space for a religious purpose?"

"I've never heard anyone complain."

Their salads arrived just then, and Angie was relieved when Peter started telling her about the summer he'd spent at Oxford between his second and third year of law school. She discovered the secret to keeping the conversation light was to ask Peter questions about himself. It was a topic he never tired of.

Strange that she'd never noticed that about him before.

After they polished off their steaks and finished with a delightful crème brûlée, she rose to leave. He started to come with her.

"No, Peter. Thanks for dinner, but I can walk across the Square by myself. That's another reason I love Coldwater. It's safe as houses."

He tried not to take no for an answer, but Angie was insistent. It was the best way she could think of to avoid an awkward scene at her door. She wanted to believe she was strong enough to resist Peter, but there was that troubling fluttery feeling that rose up when he looked at her a certain way, or said something in just the right tone of voice. She felt like a jar filled with honey bees, all drowsy and softly buzzing.

It might have been the wine she'd had with dinner, but there was still something about this guy that set her humming. If she let him kiss her, all bets might be off.

Once he got back to his room in the only motel in town, Peter pulled out his cell phone. Not even one bar. He wandered across the parking lot until a single bar popped up. He punched the third number on speed dial.

Sabine answered on the second ring. A heavy bass boomed in the background. She was clubbing someplace and had to shout to be heard over the din.

"Peter, is that you? So, what's it like in flyover country? Julian bet me you'd drop off the map. Here there be dragons and all that."

He leaned against the streetlight post. "No, no dragons, but I hear there are some catfish in Lake Jewell that are big enough to swallow a MINI Cooper."

She laughed. "That's what I love about you, Peter. You always make me laugh. Can you cut yourself loose a day or two early? I miss you."

"Me too," he said noncommittally. Her use of the word love was casual enough, but just hearing her say it was enough to make him wince. He and Sabine had a friends-with-benefits arrangement that he had no intention of allowing to morph into something deeper. Not only were they business partners, they also did pro bono work for UCFF together. Recreational sex with Sabine was all well and good, but introducing actual feelings into the relationship could cause things to deteriorate post haste.

Sabine would really be ticked if she found out he'd manufactured a reason to come to Coldwater Cove because he'd been trolling the internet looking for Angela Holloway. It wasn't that his life in DC wasn't full and rich, and getting richer all the time if he considered only his brokerage account. But there was something missing, something empty inside him he hadn't been able to fill since he'd left Angie at Baylor. Maybe he needed to win her back. Maybe he just needed to bang her one more time to get her out of his system. One way or another, he needed to close the book on Angela Holloway.

Peter had finally found her when her semidisastrous production of *Macbeth* made the online version of the *Coldwater Gazette*. After combing the insipid little paper for months, he'd called Bates College with an offer to speak to its students about pursuing law. It was dumb luck that he'd bumped into Ange so quickly, but he should have expected it. Coldwater Cove was a very small town.

"It'll be a couple of days before I'm done here," he said to Sabine, "but I have some news."

Sabine must have made her way to the ladies' room because the head-banging music faded into the background. "What's up?"

"You know how you've been looking for a good test case for the UCFF?"

"Yeah?"

"I've found one for you." He imagined her eyes lighting up. "It's got everything—church and state issues, misuse of civic funds and resources. There are even public employees involved. It's perfect."

"Stop it, Peter. You know how hot I get when you talk litigation."

"Well, hold that thought." He wandered back across the parking lot toward his room to sprawl across the slightly saggy bed. "I'll be home Friday."

It was probably a good thing Ange turned down his offer to come home with him. Sabine could make him miserable when she was angry.

Sometimes, the path of least resistance was the right way to go.

Chapter 9

No spiders in the chocolate. I checked.

—Peter Manning's note, tucked into
a big box of chocolate-covered cherries

Of course, Peter hadn't actually checked. He couldn't have. This box of sugary goodness came by way of UPS. But the card still made Angie smile.

She put the berries away in the fridge and decided to pretend they weren't there until Seth had come and gone. She felt a little mean about hiding them since he'd provided the pizza for their working supper, but chocolate-covered strawberries weren't the sort of thing you gave a guy you were just collaborating on a Christmas pageant with.

With whom you are collaborating on a Christmas pageant, she amended. *Tidy grammar, tidy life.*

Even if she ate a strawberry now, it would bring back thoughts of Peter and she didn't want to dwell on his handsome face longer than necessary. She'd done well last night, if she did say so herself. Barring a few odd flutters in her gut, she'd proven to be pretty well inoculated against him. She must have developed some "Anti-Peter" antibodies in the wake of their stormy break up. She was protected against him now.

His out-of-the-blue suggestion that she pull up stakes and move across the country to live with him—*correction! "Hang out" at his place*—had made her wish she still carried a pound of pennies in a sock in her purse. When she was an undergrad, she never went anywhere without that makeshift weapon. Though she'd never had to use it, she felt safer walking home from a late night at the library, knowing she had means to protect herself.

Granted, a smack alongside Peter's head with that sock would be an extreme reaction to his ham-handed offer. But a girl had to protect her heart as much as her physical safety, didn't she?

"Hang out" at his place. Honestly, he's as big a jerk as Tad Van Hook.

The only difference was that Tad was a self-involved teenage boy whose brain, according to scientific research, hadn't fully developed yet. Peter's gray matter was supposedly firing on all cylinders.

She sighed and put Seth's pizza into the oven to warm. Loaded with pepperoni, sausage, peppers, olives, and smothered with cheese, it promised to be filling. The savory smell began to fill her little kitchen. With a glance at the clock, she realized he wasn't supposed to arrive for another fifteen minutes.

Those stupid strawberries were calling to her. Trust Peter to remember they were her weakness. She'd have just enough time to enjoy one before Seth arrived, but she'd have to be sure it was gone or she'd have to offer him one.

And that would never do. It would be weird to serve him something another guy had given her. He'd know she hadn't run out and bought them for herself. Or for him.

Chocolate-covered strawberries were so decadent. Sensual, almost. The kind of thing lovers gave each other.

If she trotted out the strawberries while Seth was there, she'd have to deal with his questions and general surliness on the subject of Peter and she didn't want that.

It was too much drama for her. She preferred to keep all the angst in her life between the pages of her books, where it belonged. Which reminded her that with all the excitement of bumping into Peter, she'd forgotten where she'd left her copy of *Sense and Sensibility*.

With a sigh, she gave in, took a strawberry from the fridge, and bit into it.

Ah! Nirvana . . .

It was a good thing they were wrapped in milk chocolate. If the berries had been drizzled with dark chocolate instead, they'd have to be labeled a controlled substance.

Despite the milk chocolate, all the tension drained from her as she sank into sugar bliss. Everything would work out okay.

Even the book would turn up. Sooner or later.

Seth pulled his truck to a stop behind Angie's building, turned off the engine, and listened to it sigh and click as it cooled.

He wished he could cool off as easily.

Last evening he'd narrowly resisted the urge to circle the Square to check when Angie made it home. Because that seemed more than a little stalker-ish, he forced himself to go back to his place instead.

It didn't stop him from stewing.

He'd tried watching a pay-per-view fight on TV, but it didn't hold his attention. He put on some loud music and lifted weights for an hour. All it got him was sweaty and sore. Finally, he showered, collapsed into his La-Z-Boy, and decided to try reading Angie's book.

Not just her notes. The actual story this time.

Seth had read the book for a couple of hours last night. It was sort of a record for him. He didn't stop until the print started blurring and he found himself rereading the same sentence two or three times.

He didn't have to get very far into the story to realize he

seriously disliked that Willoughby character. And he wished Colonel Brandon would get over himself long enough to say what he was really thinking.

Willoughby had no hesitation about speaking his mind. The way he described Brandon, as someone people thought well of but didn't much care about, rubbed Seth raw. According to Willoughby, Brandon was the kind of guy "whom all are delighted to see, and nobody remembers to talk to."

"Jackass," Seth said to the fictional character who lived in the book on his truck's passenger seat. He should probably take it back to her, but he was into the dumb thing now. He kind of wanted to see it through, if for no other reason than to find out if Willoughby got what was coming to him.

The book would end up hurled at his wall if John Willoughby didn't come to a bad end.

Seth left *Sense and Sensibility* in the cab of the truck and headed up to Angie's apartment.

When he knocked, he heard a muffled response almost immediately and the door opened a moment later. Angie's face looked a little pinched, as if she was trying to swallow something quickly and it wasn't going down well.

"You all right?" he asked.

She gulped and nodded.

"You've got a little something on . . ." He reached over and wiped off the dark brown smudge at the corner of her mouth with the pad of his thumb. She jerked back at his touch, but he got it all anyway.

"It's chocolate," she admitted.

"In that case." He licked his thumb and grinned at her. "Never woulda figured you for a chocoholic."

"I'm not. I just like a little once in a while." She waved him in. "Besides, they say the type of candy you like says a lot about you. What's your favorite? Snickers or Almond Joy?"

"Are those my only two choices?"

"For the purposes of the online quiz I took the other day, yes," she said with a grin.

Seth shrugged. "What's the difference? Snickers and Almond Joy both have nuts."

"Yeah, but coconut makes Almond Joy the more exotic choice."

"Snickers, then." The last thing he wanted to be considered was *exotic*. "What's your favorite?"

"Anything with dark chocolate."

That wasn't dark chocolate he'd tasted on his thumb. Seemed strange that she wouldn't buy what she liked.

Her oven made a dinging sound.

"Pizza's ready." She indicated that he should sit at the counter where she'd already set out real plates on place mats, cloth napkins, and most surprisingly, flatware, all perfectly lined up as if she was hosting a dinner party in a Jane Austen novel.

"Paper plates would do," he said. *And who uses a knife and fork for pizza?*

"I'm not really big on paper plates. They always get so soggy and icky," she said. "And besides, this is my way of making up for last night when—"

"When you stood me up," he finished with a grin.

"When I rescheduled you," she corrected.

He sniffed the air appreciatively. "Gotta confess I'm half starved," he said as she sliced the pizza with a serrated knife instead of a round slicer. She obviously didn't eat pizza often. "Didn't get much time for lunch on the job site."

"I noticed that you and your crew were working pretty hard." She filled two glasses with ice and set them next to the side-by-side place settings.

"Where's your classroom located in the high school?"

"East side, second floor. Why?"

"No reason." The high school's addition was going up on

the north side of the building. That meant she must have made an effort to find a window where she could look out and see what he was up to. Seth smiled as he settled onto one of the barstools. Effie occupied the other with a surly expression on her feline face that would put the internet star Grumpy Cat to shame.

"Hello, Effie."

She gave him a staccato-like "meh" of a meow, showed him her tail, and hopped down. Evidently, the good will he'd earned by feeding her tuna yesterday had evaporated.

"Nice to see you again, too."

"Thanks again for taking care of her last night," Angie said.

"No problem. How'd your dinner go?" He hated himself for asking, but the words seemed to flow out his mouth without conscious volition.

"It was okay."

"Just okay?"

She shrugged. "It was dinner. What can I say? The Cobb salad was perfect. I had the rib eye, but I really wanted the trout. The crème brûlée was to die for. Anything else you want to know?"

Yes, but knew he shouldn't ask. He shook his head, then plowed ahead anyway. "How long is he hanging around?"

She didn't pretend to misunderstand whom he meant. "Peter will be in town a few days, lecturing at the college. Not that it's any of your concern."

"Who said I'm concerned?" He so wanted to ask if they were seeing each other again, but he settled for. "Manny just seemed like . . . the careless type."

"Manning," she corrected. "Careless how?"

"Well, the guy did bring a poisonous spider into your home."

"But—"

Before she could start defending Peter Manning, he headed her off with, "I just don't want to see you get hurt."

That made her close her mouth abruptly. Then she tucked a wedge-shaped spatula under the edge of one slice of pizza and set the whole pie on the counter before him.

"What do you want to drink? I've got beer and coke, thanks to you, or sweet tea or water."

"A coke is fine."

She got one for him and one for herself from the fridge and sat down in the other barstool next to him. Without preamble, she served him a slice, put one on her own plate and started eating.

Seth had been raised to pray before his meals, but Angie must not have. So he just shot a silent prayer skyward. God would understand.

"Thanks for bringing this over, Seth," she said between gooey, cheesy bites.

"You're welcome." He noticed that she cut her pizza with her knife and a fork, never touching her food with her fingers. He couldn't bring himself to follow suit. "What's with the silverware? Most folks eat pizza with their hands."

She set her fork down and shrugged. "I don't like touching my food."

"My uncle George always says fingers were made before forks."

"Yeah, well, if we weren't supposed to use forks, Martha Stewart would be out of a job."

"You don't eat anything with your fingers?"

"Not if I can help it."

"How about French fries?"

She wagged her utensil in the air. "Fork."

"How do you eat an apple?"

"I wash it, cut it into wedges, put it on a plate, and . . ." She waved the fork again.

"Bet you're fun to take camping."

"Hey, they make portable mess kits complete with a knife, fork, and spoon," she said, with a bite of the pizza dripping cheese from her fork. "So, I can't be the only one who doesn't want to eat like a Neanderthal."

"You callin' me a caveman?"

"If the loin cloth fits . . ."

He picked up his fork and cut a bite off his slice of pizza. No way he was going to let her think he was a Neanderthal.

"Even warmed up," she went on, "this pizza is pretty good."

Peter Manning might have taken her to the most expensive restaurant in town, but all he got was an "okay."

Pretty good was better than okay.

"So how come you had a steak last night if you really wanted fish?" Seth asked.

"Peter ordered for both of us."

"That's weird."

"No, it's sort of a throwback. There was a time when gentlemen always ordered for the ladies. Peter's old school that way."

"Sounds more like he has to be in control."

She gave a head-bob of a nod. "Yeah, that's one of the things I don't miss about him."

Seth was more curious about whether there were things she *did* miss, but forced himself to take a pepperoni-laden bite instead of asking. He'd chew it until the urge to dwell on her ex passed.

He might have to chew a long time.

Chapter 10

It's pretty hard to fix something if you don't know what's wrong.

—Seth Parker, who knows there
must be more to Angie Holloway
than a walking dictionary

"So have you had a chance to look at the pageant book?" he asked.

"A little. To be honest, I think I'll throw out most of it and start fresh."

He snorted in surprise. "Don't tell my aunt Shirley."

"Oh, I'm pretty sure someone else will beat me to that," she said wryly. "I've been here long enough to realize gossip is an art form in Coldwater Cove."

"Yeah, but folks mean well," Seth protested. "The only reason everybody's all up in everybody else's business is because they care."

She made a hmph-ing noise. "Yeah, well, once I start dismantling their Christmas traditions, they may *care* me right out of town on a rail."

"No chance of that. I got your back."

She smiled at him. It was a shy, thank-you sort of smile. Still not the one he was after, but it would do.

"So what's out for sure?" Seth asked.

"We need new actors to start. If we hold auditions for the parts—and I think we definitely should—we'll probably also need all new costumes. Do you know someone who could take care of that?"

"Not big on sewing circles myself, but I'll ask around." His aunt Shirley would know. It might also be something he could delegate to Marjorie Chubb. She was more than the captain of the prayer chain. She headed a couple of serious quilting circles and a local group that styled themselves the "Fabric Guild."

"Even though the Methodist choir usually provides the music, I was thinking it ought to be a community choir for a community pageant, not just people from one church."

Seth nodded. "That's a good idea, but the Methodists do have the biggest choir in town, so you can't shut them out." He forked up another bite of pizza. Not eating with his fingers wasn't so bad. "Talk to Mr. Mariano about it."

"The high school music teacher?"

"Yeah. He also directs the Methodist choir, so he'd be the logical person to ask about including other singers in the group."

"Okay." Angie hopped up from her place at the counter and padded over to a small desk in the pint-sized living room. She returned with a yellow legal pad and pen. After writing the number one, she wrote *Contact Mariano re: expanded choir* in an easy, flowing script. "When I first started teaching at Coldwater High, there was a rumor swirling around that Mr. Mariano was actually a Mafia don in witness protection."

Seth chuckled. "That rumor's been around since I was in school. The witness protection bit is new though."

"Do you think it's true?"

"Naw, I think Mariano started it himself just to keep his students in line. I mean, think about it. Who's gonna cross the Godfather?"

"Wish I'd thought of something like that. But to be honest, the young people here are pretty easy. They're so polite. My first week of teaching here, I'd never been 'ma'am-ed' so much in my life."

"Being respectful to your elders is kind of drummed into your head early in this part of the world."

"Not being an 'elder,' I didn't take it well at first," she admitted. "No woman wants to be called ma'am. Especially not before she turns thirty."

So she was a year or two younger than he. "Don't worry. I'd never call you ma'am."

"What would you call me?"

"Pretty." The word was out of his mouth almost before it registered in his brain. He probably should have said beautiful, but she wasn't classically lovely. Pretty was more accurate. The way her nose tilted up ever so slightly made her face insanely cute. She parted her hair on the side, but it always seemed to fall forward so she had to keep it tucked behind her ear. He liked it better when she left it alone and the dark cascade swept over the outer corner of one of her brown eyes. It made her seem mysterious.

Sexy.

He'd been so sure she wasn't his type. Boy, was he wrong.

He glanced at her to see if she was looking back at him. She seemed to be totally absorbed by the pizza on her plate. But her lips were curved in a small smile.

Two little smiles in one day. Not bad.

"I want the script rewritten, too," she said as if they hadn't just had a moment. "The characters in the current version sound as if they'd swallowed a King James Bible."

"Isn't that kind of like Shakespeare?"

"Yes, the English is from the same period, and nobody loves Shakespeare more than me," she said. "But we're not living in sixteenth-century England. Don't you think it makes more sense for the Christmas story to be accessible to a wider audience?"

"Guess so."

"I know so." She pointed with her fork for emphasis. "I can't even imagine what Junior Bugtussle would make of 'forsooth' or 'anon.'"

"So who will you get to write the new script?"

"I was thinking there must be someone at the college who writes."

"Yeah, for sock puppet theater," he said with a laugh. The curriculum at Bates was the town joke.

"I'm sure someone in the English department could write a little Christmas play," she said.

"You should ask my cousin Crystal," Seth suggested. When she arched a brow in question, he explained. "Crystal Addleberry. She used to be an Evans. Now she's the dean of admissions at Bates. She'll know who to ask about writing a script."

She added the number two and another note to herself to the list.

"Of course, you could write it yourself." If the pithy little things she'd penciled into the margins of her copy of *Sense and Sensibility* were any indication, Angie was a terrific writer. "Your stuff is fresh and funny. Not that the Christmas story is funny, but I think you'd do great."

She frowned at him in confusion. "How could you know that? You've never read a thing I've written."

Busted. "Well, you're an English teacher and all. Stands to reason you can write. Probably better than those eggheads at the college." He needed to change the subject pronto. "So it sounds like you're tossing the pageant notebook my aunt Shirley gave you out the window. Is there anything in there you are keeping?"

She grimaced. "Just the donuts, I think. She seemed so set on having them for the cast party. That's probably one tradition that needs to stay. But I'm having a problem."

"What's that?"

"I can't make sense of the recipe."

"Well, Aunt Shirley did say you should make a practice batch."

She shook her head and started clearing away the remains of the pizza. "I can't very well make a practice batch if I can't even read the recipe."

She took the recipe card from the side pocket of the pageant notebook and laid it on the counter between them.

"Is it written in another language?" she asked.

Seth chuckled. "No, that's English. It's just my granny Higginbottom's terrible handwriting."

"Oh! I'm sorry." Angie didn't want to offend him, but honestly, it was evidence of one of the worst cases of dysgraphia she'd ever seen. "Well, I can make out a few words. Let's see . . ." She narrowed her eyes at the card and read, "I muscle donuts—"

"Made," he corrected. "I made donuts."

"Oh, I see." She followed the scribbles with her finger, and went on, "with that vice land . . . getaday."

"With that nice lard yesterday."

"Nice lard?" She sat up straight and frowned at him. "What the heck makes lard *nice*?"

Seth's hands lifted in a palm up shrug. "I'm guessing it's . . . lard that hasn't gone rancid."

"Okay." Just calling something *lard* sort of implied rancid to her. "Who cooks with lard anyway?"

"It's a very old recipe."

"Yeah, I get that. So, it says, 'I made donuts with that nice lard yesterday.'" She wrote the translation—the script seemed so foreign, she couldn't think of what they were doing as anything other than translation—on her to-do page, then she started trying to read the recipe again. "I . ... kawe?"

"Have," he offered.

"If you say so." She blinked at him and then turned back to the card. " 'I have a good recrift?' What on earth is a recrift?"

"She means recipe. Granny just added a couple of extra bumps in there and made her *p* a little tall. That's why you thought it was an *f*."

"I'm not trying to be insulting to your grandmother, but how can that be an *e* at the end? It looks like a loopy *t*."

"Yeah, it does, but it's an *e*."

"How do you know?"

"'Cause I write the same way," he admitted. "The guys have a heck of a time reading my work orders sometimes. I usually have Pam write them out when I can."

"Who's Pam?"

"My office manager. She keeps things straight at Parker Construction."

Angie found herself wondering about this Pam. Was she young and pretty or old and motherly? She kind of hoped for the latter.

"Dysgraphia can run in families," she said. "Having trouble writing legibly must have made school hard for you."

"At first. Once I learned to keyboard, things got easier."

"And you didn't have problems with reading, too? Dysgraphia and dyslexia often go hand in hand."

He shook his head. "Reading wasn't my favorite thing. Still isn't, but I do okay."

Angie bet he did better than okay. Obviously, he'd had to work harder for his accomplishments than some, but he didn't seem at all bitter about it. If anything, his early struggles might have contributed to his rock-steady character now.

Everything came easily to Peter. She wondered for the first time if that wasn't as much of a blessing as she'd thought.

"Back to Granny Higginbottom . . . 'I have a good recipe so . . .'" She squinted at the card, trying to infer from context because the writing was as intelligible as hieroglyphics. "Here it is?"

"Yeah, now you're getting the hang of it." His smile made her feel as if she'd just recited a Shakespeare soliloquy word perfect instead of just a few lines from an old recipe card.

"I think I've got the next little bit, too." The words looked more like *1 uek futternilh,* but Angie guessed, "One cup buttermilk."

"That's it."

She was on a roll now. "One cup sugar, two eggs . . . features? What's an egg feature?"

"Beaten. Two eggs beaten."

"Okay. What's this squiggle off to the side?" She pointed to a scribble along the edge of the card. "It looks like 'feet ace loquiker.' You're sure this is in English? Sometimes early settlers around here still spoke a European language and slipped a few words from that into the English they were trying to learn."

Seth frowned at the card. Even he had to study it for a bit before he said, "Beat all together."

"I'll take your word for it." She ran her finger over the next item. "One t salt. I'm guessing *t* stands for tablespoon. One t nanillu?"

"Vanilla," he corrected.

"You sure?"

"Pretty darn. That's how I'd write it."

"Okay, now for the really loosey-goosey part." Angie hated recipes that weren't precise. It was hard enough to make them work when everything was laid out clearly. "It says, 'Three or four cups flour.' So which is it? Three or four."

"Looks like Granny's added a note off to the side about that." He pointed to another set of squiggles.

"Really? That looks like margarine something or other."

He chuckled. "Nope. It's 'Maybe more. Go easy.'"

"Go easy, huh? Words to live by." She needed to go easy with Seth for sure. She was coming to like his laugh far too much. "Two t baking . . . peer."

"Baking powder."

"Okay. One t soda. Does your grandmother mean Coke or Pepsi?"

"Neither. Granny means baking soda. You don't bake much, do you?"

She shook her head. "My cooking gives new meaning to the phrase 'burnt offering.' I can make a mean salad and set a pretty table, but I was absent the day God handed out culinary skills."

If she was being honest, she'd admit there was rarely anything in the kitchens of her foster homes to bake. But she didn't need to launch into that sad song and dance. So she turned her attention back to the recipe card.

"What's a dacle of nutwig?" she asked

"Dash of nutmeg."

Angie wrote it all out on her list so she could refer back to it, but still didn't know if she'd be able to use the recipe. "And your grandmother finally ends with, 'makes three dog.'"

"Dozen. Makes three dozen."

She nodded. "Well, that makes more sense. Those are the ingredients, but after I line them up on the counter, then what? Is there a special order I should mix them in? Do I roll the dough flat and use a donut cutter? Is there even such a thing?"

Seth shook his head. "Don't ask me. I'm just the translator."

"Or maybe I'm supposed to roll the dough into skinny

logs and form little loops with them." She tapped the end of her pen on the counter like a percussionist practicing rum-tum-tiddle-ums.

"You're overthinking this."

"And then once I have some semblance of donut-shaped objects, how do I cook them?" she wondered aloud.

"I'm no expert, but I think that's where the nice lard comes in."

"Even if I could find lard that's 'nice,' to what temperature should I heat it? How long does each donut need to cook?" Her shoulders slumped.

"Don't be so hard on yourself. I bet this recipe would stymie cooks who have a lot more experience in the kitchen than you do."

He patted her forearm and then let his hand rest on her wrist. His rough, callused palm was warm. Angie was sure he meant it to be consoling, but the contact had a jolting effect, sending flares of alarm up to her shoulder. She fought the urge to jerk her hand away. It was hard for her to let people touch her.

That was part of the reason Peter had been her one and only. It had taken a lot for her to let him close.

And another reason it cut so deeply when he left.

She wasn't ready to be touched again. Not that Seth was so terrible. He wasn't at all, but she always felt uncomfortable in her own skin when someone invaded her space. When he pulled his hand back, she released the breath she'd been holding.

"Why not just delegate the donuts to someone else?" he suggested. If he was aware of her inner turmoil a few seconds ago, he gave no sign.

"I don't think Shirley Evans would appreciate that. Your aunt was pretty particular about the recipe staying in your family." Of course, the unintelligible handwriting pretty much guaranteed it wouldn't be passed on without an insider to translate.

"Add the recipe to your list of things to talk with Crystal about. She used to be an Evans."

"Perfect." Angie wrote a note on her list. "I'll bet your aunt has already taught her how to make the donuts."

"I wouldn't count on it. Aunt Shirley is as secretive about her recipes as Granny was."

"Well, I'll ask your cousin Crystal about making the donuts anyway." She underlined the idea, planning to fob off the baking to this Evans cousin. "Even if she says no, I'll be no worse off than I am now."

"That's the . . . spirit."

"I'm sorry. You're right. I need a better attitude."

"Are you always this negative?"

"I try not to be, but I guess I am looking on the pageant as a burden," she admitted.

"If it is a burden, at least you only have to shoulder half of it. I'm here for you, Angie."

The way he said it made her think he meant he was there for her in other ways, too. It was tempting to lean on his strength, but she'd learned early that she could only count on herself.

And when she forgot that lesson, Peter had been there to remind her.

"Heather would say that I need to look on the pageant as an opportunity. And frankly, the Warm Hearts credo applies to me in spades. I need something to get me out of myself and thinking about other people for a change."

"You work with high school kids all day. I suspect you do plenty of thinking about others."

"You know what I mean." She took a long drink of her tea to empty the glass and started loading her dishwasher with their plates and flatware. "I was taught not to be the grabby child. Other peoples' needs are supposed to come first."

"Sometimes, it's okay for you to be the one who needs

something," Seth said, his dark eyes warm as he gazed at her. "There's a grace to giving and a grace to receiving. And sometimes, receiving is the harder part."

"Why are you telling me this?"

He stood. "Because I want you to know whatever you need, I'm ready to give."

Chapter 11

They say if you jostle a person, whatever they're full of spills out. Pain always seems to slosh out of me.

—Angela Holloway, who wishes she could pull a thick blanket over her past and put it to sleep forever

"Whatever I need," she repeated.

He had no idea. She needed quite a lot. So much she didn't dare let herself feel it most of the time. If she did, she feared she'd start weeping and never stop.

One night, she woke screaming from a vivid dream of being locked in a closet. She was filthy and hungry and her throat was so dry, as if she hadn't had anything to drink for hours and hours. Once she was fully awake, she realized it wasn't so much a dream as a metaphor for a memory. She'd never been shut in a closet for real, but she remembered the feeling of being closeted. Isolated. Left out. Overlooked. Nobody saw a shy, silent girl who bounced from one foster home to the next because she couldn't seem to connect with anyone. When she was punted to the next home, she doubted she was missed.

She'd slept with the light on for a week after that dream, just so she could remind herself quickly where she was when she woke.

Seth was still looking at her with that searching expression of his. It was as if he could read her secrets. She forced herself to smile at him.

"I don't know what you mean. I don't need anything. Oh, I could probably stand more sleep than I'm getting, but I'm fine." She closed the dishwasher, grateful for something to do with her hands. He might catch them trembling otherwise. She knew better than to let thoughts of her past intrude on her present when someone else was around. "Look, is there anything else you think we need to talk about tonight? About the pageant, I mean."

He shook his head.

"What about the budget?" She smacked her forehead à la the old "I coulda had a V8" commercial. Nothing came free in this world. Something as involved as the pageant would cost a good bit to produce. "I didn't see anything in the notebook about money."

"I'll take care of the building supplies and labor for the manger," Seth said. "We may have to take up a collection for fabric for new costumes, but whoever we get to do the sewing will probably donate their time. The merchants around town are pretty good about sponsorships for anything else we need. The Christmas pageant is about community. People are used to giving back around here. I'll handle it."

"Okay, well . . . then, I think we're done for now." The sooner she got Seth Parker out of her apartment, the more like herself she'd start feeling. She was strong. Independent. She didn't need anybody or anything and she intended to keep it that way. "Meeting adjourned."

He didn't take the hint. "It's still early. Want to catch a movie?"

That was a quality bad idea. She didn't need the temptation to lean on him any more than she already was.

"Oh, I don't think so, Seth. I've got school tomorrow and anyway, the films at the Regal aren't exactly first-run caliber." That was a good refusal if she did say so herself. It wasn't personal. It was about the sorry old movies the Regal Theater offered.

"First runs aren't necessarily all that good," he said, clearly not hearing "no" in her gentle reply. "Sometimes, an old classic is better."

"You have me there." Maybe it wouldn't hurt to go over to the Regal with him. After all, she'd gone to Harper's with Peter and she'd emerged no worse for the wear. "What's playing?"

"*The African Queen.*"

"I've heard about it, but I've never seen it."

"You should."

"I suppose since I haven't, for me, it is a first run," she rationalized. *If we just went as friends . . . If there aren't any expectations on either side . . . Expectations are what get you into trouble.* "Okay."

"Okay?"

"Yeah, I'll go with you. But since this is not a date, I'll pay for my own ticket. Let me get my coat." She scurried into the other room before he could object.

Not a date, she says. Seth stewed about it for as long as it took Angie to return with her coat—not the fancy, fitted leather jacket she'd worn to Harper's. This one was padded and puffy, more for warmth than fashion. Clearly, she felt no need to impress him.

Seth pasted on his game face. She might not think this was a date, but he was going to count it as one.

True to her word, she wouldn't let him pay for her ticket, but she couldn't stop him from buying buttered popcorn and soft drinks for them both. He stifled a laugh when she didn't even eat her popcorn with her fingers. Once the lights went down in the Regal, she tipped up the paper cup filled with buttery kernels and snagged a couple with her clever little tongue.

She laughed at the movie in all the right places, and he noticed she swiped her eyes a time or two toward the end, when
Bogart and Hepburn were about to be hanged together.

He didn't try to hold her hand or put his arm across the
back of her seat. Somehow, he knew, without knowing why,
that she wouldn't like it.

But she did like him.

A little. He was almost sure of it. Sure enough to keep trying anyway.

They stayed until the last credit rolled. The kid who had to
clean up the theater started sweeping the aisles behind them as
they left. When they hit the sidewalk, a wintry wind hit them
in the face. The temperature had dropped considerably while
they were inside.

"Brrr!" Angie said as she turned up the collar of her coat
and shoved her hands into her pockets. "And me without a hat
or gloves."

"Take mine." Seth didn't have a hat, but he handed her his
wool gloves. He wore leather ones for work, but hardly ever
wore these. Usually only when Pam at work caught him heading home without them and insisted he put them on. He
hardly ever felt cold, no matter how brisk the weather.

Angie put her tiny hands into his gloves and jammed her
now oversized fists back into her pockets. "I'm glad you suggested that movie, Seth."

"Me too."

"It's really strange, isn't it?" Her breath puffed in the cold
air as if she were a little she-dragon. "The way Charlie and
Rose ended up together. They're sort of an unlikely couple."

"Well, shared enemies can make folks fast friends," Seth
reasoned. "Charlie and Rose had to fight a river and Nazis—"

"And mosquitoes." Her shiver had little to do with the
brisk wind. "Ugh! And those awful leeches."

"And each other," Seth said. "They didn't think much of each other either in the beginning, remember."

"No, not at first, anyway. I suppose that's to be expected because they were such different people. She was so buttoned up and proper and he . . . well, I guess Charles Allnut could best be described as a slacker."

"Hey, the guy leaped into a leech-infested river and pulled the boat for miles." Seth felt honor bound to defend the movie's hero. Allnut was sort of Everyman. "Doesn't sound like a slacker to me. I'd hire him."

They turned off the Square to walk around to the rear of Angie's building. She picked up her pace. Seth had to lengthen his stride to keep up with her.

"You don't have to walk me up," she said as he started up the iron staircase beside her.

"Sure I do. It's how I was raised. Every female in my family would have my hide if I didn't see you safe to your door," he said honestly. Even more than respect for his elders, his mother and aunts had seen to it that gentlemanly traits were pounded into Seth and his brothers.

"Well, that would be bad. I'd hate to see you lose your hide." She took off his gloves and handed them back to him. Then she started rummaging in her purse as they continued to climb the stairs.

Well, that puts the kibosh on a good night kiss. If a woman wanted one, she'd wait until she reached her doorway to start looking for her keys.

But once Angie stopped in front of her door, she didn't immediately stick the key in the lock. Instead, it dangled from her hand as she turned back to face him.

Talk about mixed signals.

"Do you think they'll be happy?"

"Who?" Just in case he wasn't confused enough about

whether or not she wanted him to kiss her, she had to come up with a completely unrelated question.

"Rose and Charlie, of course," she said in an exasperated tone, as if he hadn't been paying attention.

Yeah, sure. I ought to be able to follow her train of thought even though we stopped talking about the movie about a block and a half ago.

"Why do you ask?" It was his way of stalling until he could come up with a mildly intelligent-sounding response.

"Well, they lived through some harrowing adventures together. Exciting, even," she said. "But once the war is over and their lives go back to normal, do you think they'll be happy with each other?"

She didn't talk about Charlie and Rose as if they were fictional characters. It was more like they were her friends. He should have guessed she'd watch movies with the same emotional investment she made in her books.

"Well, for one thing, I don't think Rose will be a missionary anymore."

Angie chuckled. "She might figure she has enough of a mission with her husband. Charlie is certainly in need of reform."

"I've heard all women think that about their husbands," Seth said wryly. "But the thing is, neither Charlie or Rose will ever be who they were before they met."

Her keys jingled a bit. Was she impatient that he hadn't tried to kiss her yet or anxious for him to leave so she could go into her apartment?

He reached a hand up and leaned it against her door. That should let her know he wasn't ready for her to go in. Two could play this signals game.

"When you let someone into your life, you're gonna change whether you plan on it or not," he said softly. "It sort of comes with the territory."

"How so?"

"My old man described it like this. He said if you put a rock in a bag by itself, no matter how much you swing the bag around, the rock will be exactly the same when you take it out," Seth explained. "But if you put two rocks in a bag, they knock the sharp edges off each other. Leave 'em in there together long enough and they both come out all smooth."

"People aren't rocks."

"No, but we do change each other."

"So you expect to change some girl you meet into your perfect woman?" She crossed her arms over her chest.

Whoa. Message received. If that doesn't shout "Not even a peck on the cheek, fella," I'm a yellow-bellied sap-sucker.

"There are no perfect women, Angie. Or men either," he added quickly. "There's just folks doing the best they can."

"Sometimes their best is pretty awful." Her arms dropped to her sides again.

Okay, her shields are down. I'm goin' in. He leaned toward her, thinking only to brush his lips on her cheek. It wasn't the kiss he'd like to give her, but it was better than nothing.

Suddenly she thrust her hand out in the "shake-me" position. "Good night, Seth."

So no kiss. Oh! Wait a minute.

His time spent in the company of Jane Austen was about to bear fruit. He took Angie's hand and slowly lifted it to his lips. Her hand trembled slightly, but she didn't pull it away when he pressed a soft kiss on her knuckles. He'd closed his eyes, but he still heard the sharp intake of breath hissing over her teeth.

When he let her hand drop and opened his eyes, she was staring up at him, her lips parted in what looked like astonishment.

Astonished is good. Beat that, Peter Manning.

Then, because he could only mess things up from there, he turned and headed down the iron staircase. He kept one ear cocked, listening for her door, but he never heard her open and close it. He stopped at the base of the stairs and looked back up.

She was peering over the railing, watching him go.

Better and better.

"Good night, Angela."

Caught looking, she quickly zipped away from the rail and back to her door. She made short work of the lock, but he didn't move until he heard the door bang shut behind her.

More pleased with himself than he'd been in a long time, Seth hopped in his truck and started it up. Before he put it into gear, he glanced over at the dog-eared copy of *Sense and Sensibility.*

"Thanks, Miss Austen," he said as he pulled out of the small parking area. "Don't tell anybody, but I think you're my new best friend."

Chapter 12

Much is made about the terror of auditioning for a part.
Let me tell you, watching an audition is no picnic either.

—Angela Holloway, currently starring
in *The Reluctant Codirectors*

"Thank you, Zorabeth, that'll do." Angie was about ready to get out a shepherd's crook and yank the current auditionee off the small stage at the far end of the gym. Anything to make it stop. How on earth could Angie be expected to work someone who played the accordion while tap dancing into a Christmas pageant? "Really, that's all we need for now. We'll let you know as soon as we've settled on a cast list."

"Thank you, ma'am." Zorabeth's accordion wheezed a bit as she dropped in a quick curtsey. Her taps clicked on the gym floor as she headed for the door.

"You know sometimes she sings while she tap dances, too," Seth said once Zorabeth was out of earshot.

"You're kidding. While still playing the accordion?"

He nodded and held up three fingers. "Scout's honor. Remember where you are."

Seth was right. Things that might be considered bizarre elsewhere were perfectly ordinary in Coldwater Cove. Zorabeth Klinkensmith was a much sought-after entertainer for the retirement party crowd.

But her act didn't much fit in with angels and shepherds and wise men. Angie was frustrated that they hadn't been able to cast a number of important parts yet. Seth was evidently frustrated, too. His left knee was bouncing up and down.

"Stop fidgeting, Seth," Angie whispered. "You'll make the actors nervous."

His knee stopped and he leaned forward, resting his elbows on them. Granted, the bleachers weren't the most comfortable of seats, but it *was* his idea to use the high school gym for the pageant auditions. He reasoned if an actor could be heard in the gym, they stood a better chance of being heard delivering lines in an open-air pageant, so Angie went along with the plan. If he was uncomfortable listening to the wannabes try to fill the space, it was his own fault.

It had been several days since she'd gone to the movies with him. She'd expected to feel awkward around him after that unexpectedly romantic kiss he'd planted on her hand, but Seth didn't behave any differently toward her. Angie decided to follow suit.

If it didn't mean anything to him, why should it mean anything to me?

"Why should they be nervous?" Seth shifted again, leaning back on the bleachers and stretching his arms. "It seems like we've been at this for hours. Oh wait, we have." He sat up straight and then leaned toward her. "Do we have to make such a production out of each audition? Look, Second Shepherd isn't exactly Oscar material."

"Shh!" Even though she shushed him, she had to agree. So far the parade of pageant hopefuls had yielded no budding stars. "We have to give everyone who's come out to audition a fair hearing."

Angie had been surprised by the long line of potential actors that snaked down the corridor leading to the gym. From grade school kids dragged in by their stage moms to old Mrs. Chisholm, who was wheelchair bound and had to be pushed in by her long-suffering niece and caregiver Peggy, there was a steady stream of folks who wanted to be part of the pageant.

Next up was Junior Bugtussle. His overalls were obviously new, the denim so dark Angie would bet they'd not been washed even once. He bore a striking resemblance to an onion with his hair slicked down tight against his skull. She suspected Junior's wife Darlene was responsible for that unfortunate fashion choice. Hill folk had their own ideas about what constituted looking nice.

"What part are you auditioning for today, Junior?" Angie asked.

"I thought I could maybe be one of them wise fellers," he answered. "It'd make a nice change from just spreading hay around on the courthouse steps."

Angela cringed at the thought of Junior as one of the magi. In her mind's eye, she imagined them as well educated and spiritual, with a regal and dignified demeanor. Junior's mannerisms were more regrettable than regal, and he was more likely to dig a hole than act dignified. But Angie was determined to give him a chance.

"We don't have the final script yet," Angie told him. Actually, they didn't have any script at all. Crystal Addleberry at the college couldn't see her until later that afternoon, and she refused to use the stilted, hackneyed script that came in the pageant book.

Seth hauled himself off the bleachers and handed Junior the page of material they were having the men read.

"Just the passage highlighted in yellow," Angie said. "And speak up, please. We want to find out how well your voice carries."

"Okey-dokey." Junior screwed his face into a furious frown as he stared at the page. Finally, he began shouting the lines as if he were in a pig-calling contest. " 'And it came to pass in those days, that there went out a decree from Caesar Augustus, that all the world should be taxed.'" His voice dropped to a normal tone. "Well, don't that beat all. Even Bible folk had to put up with them durn revenuers."

Seth chuckled and whispered to Angie, "Junior would know about that. His daddy's still doing a stretch at the state pen for trying to avoid taxes on the proceeds of his still."

"No commentary please." She skewered Seth with a glare. "From either of you. Go on, Junior."

"And you might want to dial it back a bit, buddy," Seth suggested. "We don't need you to be heard in the next county."

"All righty, then. 'And this taxing was first made when Cyrenius was governor of Syria.'" Junior pronounced the governor's name as if it rhymed with Miley Cyrus.

Angie decided not to correct him. It wouldn't help a bit.

"'And all went to be taxed, every one into his own city. And Joseph also went up from Galilee, out of the city of Nazareth, into Judaea, unto the city of David, which is called Bethlehem; because he was of the house and lineage of David'—mercy! That there's a powerful long sentence. I plumb ran out of breath and it ain't even over yet." He took another deep breath and continued. "'To be taxed with Mary his exposed wife, bein' great with child.'"

"Espoused," Angie corrected. She couldn't let that slide. "Exposed makes it sound like . . ."

"Like the Virgin Mary forgot her clothes," Seth finished for her.

Junior went so red he resembled a tomato instead of an onion. "Oh! I'm sure she'd never do that." He scratched his head, messing up his carefully gelled do. "Then what's it mean, that 'espoused' thing?"

Angie may not have been in Sunday School for years, but she had been doing her homework on the Christmas story. "There's some confusion about that, but basically it means when couples in biblical times got engaged, it was considered as binding as marriage."

"So Mary and Joseph weren't actually hitched when they fetched up in Bethlehem?"

"Not married as we consider it now," Angie said, "but as far as their culture was concerned, they were. That's why in another passage, it says Joseph intended to divorce her when he discovered she was expecting and knew the child wasn't his."

"Look at you, going all Bible scholar," Seth said.

She rolled her eyes at him. "We want the pageant to be historically accurate, don't we?"

"Well, yeah, but you may have to gloss over a bit. If you don't, you'll have to wait a couple of years for the wise men to show up at Bethlehem. That'd make for a pretty long pageant," Seth said. "You can let a few details slide as long as you get the meat of the story out there."

"But details are what make a story," Angie argued. There was a way to show the passage of time without actually waiting two years. "What do you think, Junior?"

"Me?" He put a hand to his chest. "I don't know nothing about that stuff. I'm still trying to get my head around the idea of Jesus's folks gettin' a divorce. We Bugtussles don't hold to that. Once we ties the knot, it stays tied. Even if it strangulates us."

"Well, Mary and Joseph didn't divorce, so you don't have to fret over it. That's all, Junior. Thanks for auditioning. We'll post the cast list in the *Coldwater Gazette* soon," she said. "Can you please send in the next person?"

Junior ambled out of the gym.

"Actually, Seth, I've been meaning to talk to you about how we should do the magi part." She consulted her notebook and then glanced at him. He hadn't shaved that morning and a fine stubble of dark beard peppered his strong jaw. It suited him. She looked quickly back at her notes. "Of course, we can't put a huge time lag into the pageant, but if we want to be accurate, we have to move the Holy Family out of the stable. By the time the wise men arrived in Bethlehem, Mary and Joseph were living in a house."

"So you want me to build a house on the courthouse lawn, too?"

"Not a whole house," she said. "A façade of one will do."

"I think you're going overboard here."

"Like you did the other night." The words were out of her mouth before she thought about the consequences of saying them. They'd been ignoring the fact that they'd shared an un-expectedly romantic moment. Now it was on the table.

One of his brows arched in question. He was going to make her say it.

"You kissed me. Remember?" Sometimes her knuckles still tingled.

"If I'd kissed you, I'd remember it," he said, his drawl as thick as dark molasses. "Seems to me I only kissed your hand."

She covered the hand in question with her other one. Could he tell it still made her quiver to think about it? "Well, it wasn't appropriate. We're just codirectors. Maybe friends. That's all."

"You didn't object at the time."

"That's because you . . . you surprised me." Why did his eyes have to be so . . . so looking at her as if he could see her secret thoughts?

"As I recall, it all pretty much happened in slow motion," Seth said. "It's hard to surprise someone when you're moving as fast as a three-toed sloth."

Well, that image sucked the romance right out of the memory. "Still, I wasn't expecting it."

"Expectations are overrated."

That smile of his, that crooked, easy smile. It was a small change in his expression, but it was ridiculously attractive. She wanted to slap it right off him.

"You need to learn to take life as it comes, Angela."

"Or goes," she said tartly. Peter would have called her "Ange." He was the only one who ever had. Yet somehow, when Seth said her whole name, it felt more intimate than Peter's shortened pet name for her.

"Speaking of going, I'm guessing Peter Mandrake is gone by now."

"Manning. The guy's name is Manning. You know that's his name. Why don't you use it?"

His grin stretched wide this time. "Maybe because I like seeing those little wisps of steam that come out your ears when I don't. You're ducking my question. Is he gone?"

"I don't know." She shrugged. It did seem a little strange that Peter hadn't contacted her again, other than sending those strawberries. He usually wasn't the sort to give up, even after he got shot down. Not that *that* happened very often. Still, it was a puzzlement. She could have sworn he wanted to see her again before he left town. "I haven't heard from him since we had dinner together."

"He doesn't mean you any good, you know."

She did know, but how could Seth? "You don't know that."

"Sure I do."

"How?"

"The spider was a dead giveaway." Seth stretched his long legs out in front of him and hooked one ankle over the other. Instead of his steel-toed work shoes, he was wearing snakeskin cowboy boots today.

Angie was enough a daughter of Texas to find a guy in cowboy boots incredibly hot. She looked away.

"That spider wasn't Peter's fault," she argued.

"I bet nothing ever was."

Peter did have a knack for wiggling out of responsibility

for things, whether it was a frat prank that went wrong or the way he broke her heart. It was never his fault.

"Trust me, Angie. A guy knows these things," Seth said. "Your Mr. Mango is up to no good."

She decided to stop correcting him and hope he'd get tired of this game. "Peter would probably say the same about you."

Seth nodded. "Yeah, but he'd be wrong. I mean you only the best." He rested the tips of his fingers on her forearm. Surprisingly enough, she didn't feel the need to shrink from his touch. "You deserve it."

Before she could tell him she didn't, the next person trying out for the pageant came into the gym.

It was Emma Wilson. The flirty skirt was gone. Today, she was wearing faded jeans and a T-shirt that had probably started life as red, but now was tending toward dusty pink. She was wearing less makeup than usual, too.

Angie thought she looked better for it. More her own age, which was closer to fifteen than the twenty-five she usually aimed for.

"Hi, Emma. I've missed you in class the last couple of days," Angie said.

"Yeah, well, I've been a little under the weather, but I'm feeling better today." Emma leaned all her weight on one foot and hooked the other behind her calf, standing turkey legged. "I'll make up the work next week, Ms. Holloway."

"I'm sure you will. Now, what part are you interested in playing?"

The girl's shoulders lifted in a shrug. "I dunno. Whatever part you think I can play."

"Good answer," Angie said as Seth handed Emma the page with the verses they'd decided all the female auditionees would read. There was really only one coveted part for women—the Virgin herself.

Unlike Lucinda Warboy, at least Emma was the right age to play Mary.

Emma shifted and put her weight on both feet as she studied the page.

"Whenever you're ready," Seth said.

Emma cleared her throat and started softly. " 'My soul doth magnify the Lord.' "

"A little louder," he suggested.

"No, it's okay," Angie said. Chances were good the young virgin didn't feel like shouting when she first realized she was pregnant out of wedlock. It made sense to start the Magnificat softly. "Go on, Emma."

" 'And my spirit hath rejoiced in God my Savior.' " Her voice was a little shaky, but grew stronger as she continued. " 'For He hath regarded the low estate of his handmaiden: for, behold, from henceforth all generations shall call me blessed.' "

Angie's imagination kicked into overdrive. Emma as Mary would run away from her home in Nazareth to take refuge in her cousin Elisabeth's home. But as she approached with news of the impending birth, she'd discover that Elisabeth already knew. It would give her the courage to praise God in the face of what must surely have been some sidelong looks from her friends and neighbors in Nazareth.

" 'For He that is mighty hath done to me great things; and holy is His name,' " Emma said in a strong clear voice.

Angie leaned toward Seth and whispered, "I think we've found our Mary."

He nodded.

"And I've got an idea." The pageant began to take shape in her mind. It didn't have to be a static scene in one place, the Holy Family frozen in statue-like stillness while shepherds and wise men wandered in and out, like moveable pieces of a large cuckoo clock orbiting the main figures.

In Angie's version, the Christmas story would be presented from its beginning, with the angel announcing the Christ Child's coming. Then the pageant would flow with the characters until they reached the City of David.

So it would have to be structured more like a procession, parading from the far end of Main Street to the manger on the Square. The town's people would have to line up along the street to watch the drama unfold and then fall in behind Mary and Joseph as they traveled along. The audience would be sort of like golf fans, trooping behind their PGA favorites from one hole to the next. In this way, the whole community would make the journey to Bethlehem.

"What have you got rolling around in your head, Angie?" Seth said with a worried frown. "I can see the wheels turning and I don't think I'm gonna like it."

She smiled sweetly at him. This ask required a little sweetness. "How would you feel about building quite a few more pageant sets?"

Chapter 13

*Maybe I can get through Thanksgiving without
everyone finding out. It's only a week or so away.
But Christmas? There's no way I can fake being jolly.*

—Crystal Addleberry, mother of two, respected dean
of admissions at Bates College, and scared to death
her family will discover her husband has left her

"Riley, put that down this instant."

"But Mommy—"

"Don't 'but Mommy' me. You'll drop it and break it. No,
not there. Back where you got it. *No!* Do as I say or you're
going to be sorry. Do you hear me, young lady?"

The woman's voice sounded equal parts resigned and frantic as it echoed down the empty corridor of the Bates College
administration building. The place smelled of lemon oil polish
and mustiness from the myriad books that Angie imagined
were hidden in the offices behind the closed oak doors that led
off the corridor. Stacks of untidy texts and papers ringing the
room were the hallmarks of an academician, after all. Angie
and Seth's footfalls seemed unnaturally loud as they walked toward Crystal Addleberry's office at the end of the hall. Since it
was Saturday, hardly anyone was around, and the effect was
slightly creepy.

Like an empty amusement park or a museum after hours, Angie
thought.

"But it can't sit in the window. The sun will make it melt."

A high little voice wafted down the hall. "The snow globe wants to be someplace else, Mommy."

"Don't we all," came the muttered reply.

Seth leaned into the office and rapped on the open door. "Crystal?"

"Oh!" The knock seemed to startle her even though Seth had assured Angie that his cousin knew they were coming. Unlike the unruly professors' offices Angie had imagined, Crystal's was immaculate. No self-respecting speck of dust would dare show itself. The books on her shelves marched in neat rows. The shades at every window of her corner office were drawn to the exact midpoint and the flourishing philodendron in the corner had probably never let a single leaf turn yellow. "Come in, Seth."

"Thanks for seeing us," he said.

Angie was grateful that he was still willing to introduce her to his cousin after she sprang her new idea for the pageant on him. It was going to mean a lot more work for him and his construction crew, but he'd grudgingly agreed.

"This is Angela Holloway, high school English teacher and drama coach," he told Crystal. "She's directing the Christmas pageant this year."

"Oh, yes. I saw your *Macbeth*." Crystal cleared her throat loudly. "It was . . . a unique presentation."

Well, that's a noncomplimentary compliment if ever I heard one. Angie gave her a nod and a flat smile.

"Nice to finally meet you." Angie had seen Crystal Addleberry around town a few times. She and her husband Noah were Coldwater Cove's power couple. Noah was heir to the Addleberry family's extensive collection of local businesses and real estate. Always dressed to the nines, Crystal set the standard for fashion about town, and, in addition to her prestigious position at the college, she was the mover and shaker behind several charity events.

Dressed in jeans and a shirt so wrinkled it appeared she'd slept in it, Crystal looked far less polished than her office at the moment.

"Please have a seat. Riley, stop climbing on those shelves." Crystal bolted across the office to pluck her daughter from a precarious perch on a shelf that held a number of awards and trophies. The child, who appeared to be about six, was all knees and elbows and limber as a lemur.

"But the snow globe wants to be up there."

"But it belongs here." Crystal deposited the globe back on the windowsill and handed her daughter a cell phone. "Sit down and play Angry Birds. Mommy's busy."

"I don't like Angry Birds," the little girl said. "I wanna play Happy Birds."

"There's no such thing as Happy Birds."

"Is, too. I see them all the time out my window."

Crystal sighed. "Just be still for a bit, and when Mommy is done working, we'll go by the Green Apple for ice cream."

"Will Daddy be there?" Riley's little heart-shaped face looked hopeful.

"Just play your game, honey." Crystal returned to her chair behind the massive desk, swept her longish bangs to the side, and met Angie's gaze with a penetrating stare. Frazzled mom or not, the business woman had arrived. "So, you're directing the Christmas pageant this year."

"That's right."

Strange that Seth didn't mention he claimed the role of codirector to his cousin.

"Well, to be honest, I'm relieved," Crystal said as she leaned back in her chair. "When Mother decided she couldn't do the pageant this year, I was afraid it would fall to me. I'm glad she punted it to the Warm Hearts Club. This really isn't a good time for me to take on anything else."

Is there ever a good time to have a major holiday tradition dumped in your lap?

"As you can see, I'm a bit overwhelmed at the moment with . . ." Crystal's eyes seemed to unfocus for a blink, but then she hurried on. "Well, it's a busy time of year for the college, so before you ask, I can't be involved in the pageant in any way."

Her jaw was tight and her eyes had a puffiness about them no amount of makeup could disguise. Angie thought Seth's cousin was either suffering from acute hay fever, though it was the wrong time of year for it, or Crystal Addleberry had been crying her eyes out.

"Actually, we aren't here to ask you to do anything for the pageant," Seth said. Crystal's shoulders visibly relaxed. "Angie was hoping you could recommend someone on the college staff who could write a new script for it."

"A new script?" Crystal said as if Angie had asked for a new constitution. "Does Mother know you intend to change the old one?"

"We figure it'll be a nice surprise for her," Angela said.

Crystal snorted. "You don't know Shirley Evans, do you? Her credo is 'This is how we did it the first time. So it is now and ever shall be. Yea, verily. Amen.' "

"I thought it was 'If a little is good, a lot's a whole bunch better,' " Seth said.

Crystal rolled her eyes. "That's the Evans family motto."

Angie sighed. Between credos and mottos, sublets and wickedly handsome cousins, every time she turned around, she found herself in the middle of something to do with the Evans family. She resolved to give her friend Heather a good shake the next time she saw her for roping her into this. No matter what she did with the pageant, someone was going to be upset.

What kind of friend puts you in such a no-win situation?

"Does Bates have an English professor who might write something for us?" Angie asked.

"You could ask Dr. Barclay, I suppose," Crystal said, "but fair warning. She's into experimental theater."

"By that, Crystal means the Holy Family might just be portrayed by sock puppets," Seth drawled.

"I like puppets." The little girl left her mother's cell phone on the floor and popped up beside Angie's chair. "Are you doing a play? I could be in it. I know how to dance."

She did a clumsy pirouette and then dipped in an exaggerated diva bow.

Angie smiled at her. "Maybe you can be in the pageant." Angie envisioned her in a lamb costume for a second, but decided she would be so cute, she'd steal all the attention from the Christ Child. "Riley, is it?"

The girl nodded vigorously. "Riley Addleberry."

"Riley is a pretty name," Angie said. "What's your middle name?"

The child's forehead scrunched in a frown.

"Come on, Riley," Crystal urged. "Tell the lady your middle name."

"I don't memember what it is." She shrugged.

"*Remember,* not memember. And yes, you do," her mother insisted. "What does Mommy call you when she is upset with you?"

Riley's lips lifted in a mischievous smile. "Little twink."

"Riley Lynn Addleberry!" Crystal's cheeks flushed a deep scarlet. "What a thing to say."

"Hey!" Seth laughed. "Give the kid a break. And be grateful you never called her anything worse than little twink."

Just then, a tall man with caramel-colored skin, dark hair, and a neatly trimmed beard appeared at Crystal's door. "Mrs. Addleberry, I—oh! I will come back later. I did not realize you were otherwise occupied."

"That's all right, Dr. Gonncu. Please come in." Crystal stood to welcome the newcomer. "This is my cousin, Seth Parker. He owns Parker Construction here in town. And this is Angela

Holloway, who teaches English at the high school." She gestured toward the professor. "Dr. Zafer Gonncu. He's our new professor of mathematics here at Bates."

Seth shook the man's hand. Angie however had slipped into director mode. She was so busy imagining what a splendid magi the middle-eastern professor would make, she offered her hand to him without thinking. Dr. Gonncu didn't move to take it.

"I ask your pardon, Ms. Holloway. My faith prohibits me from touching a woman to whom I am not related," the professor said with a lovely accent. "But I am pleased to meet you and hope you will forgive me this breach of your western etiquette."

His grammar was so flawless, Angie would forgive him anything. "There is nothing to forgive. The fault is mine." Embarrassed, she shoved her hand into her pocket. "I didn't realize."

"Few do. I thank you for your understanding."

"Are we done, Seth?" Crystal asked. "Dr. Gonncu and I have some business to discuss. He's in the process of expanding our math department."

"That sounds exciting," Angie said, though math had never been her strong suit.

"It sounds necessary," Dr. Gonncu corrected. "If our graduates hope to find meaningful employment upon matriculation, the college must offer more advanced math and hard science degrees."

"We call them STEM classes at Coldwater High," Angela said. "Science, technology, engineering and mathematics."

"In my country, we call them basic education," the professor said, with the slightest hint of condescension.

It wasn't the first time Angie had bumped into techno-geeks who thought a subject that didn't involve numbers wasn't worth studying. She also knew a number of computer science majors who could code to beat the band, but couldn't put a coherent sentence together to save their souls.

Balance in all things.

"From what country do you come, if I may ask?" she said.

"Turkey. I taught at university there."

"I understand your emphasis on math, but there must be room in the Turkish soul for the liberal arts as well. After all, your people gave the world Yunus Emre."

His mouth formed a quick "oh" of astonishment. "You know Emre?"

"A little. Enough to know he's one of your country's most beloved poets." Angie cast about for her favorite quote from the thirteenth-century writer. " 'There's no use hiding it— What's inside always leaks outside.' "

Dr. Gonncu smiled. "It loses a bit in translation, but I believe that is from *One who is Real is Humble.* I am honored."

"Well, as much as I'd like to stay and swap poetry, we need to get going," Seth said. "Thanks for the recommendation about the script, Crystal." Then he looked down at his cousin's daughter. "How about if we take Riley to the Green Apple for you?"

Crystal's grateful expression was almost pathetic. "Would you?"

"Sure." Seth offered Riley his hand, but she didn't take it right away.

"I can't touch nobody I'm not related to either," she said with a quick look at the math professor.

"Then you're in luck because we are related. I just missed a few of the family reunions lately, that's all," Seth told the child. "We'll have her back in an hour or so."

"Or longer would be fine," Crystal said. *Hopefully,* Angie thought. "If I'm not here when you get back, please drop her by my folks' house. Go with your cousin, Riley."

"He's not a cousin," she said in a stage whisper to her mom. "He's a man. Cousins are s'posed to be kids."

Seth bent down so they were face-to-face. "I may be all grown up, but I *am* your cousin, Riley. Your mom and I are first cousins, so that makes me your first cousin once removed."

"Removed? What did you do wrong?" Riley asked.

Seth straightened to his full height. "Nothing."

"You musta done something. I get removed when I do something wrong," Riley admitted. "Mommy removes me right up to my room."

"Riley Lynn Addleberry!"

The child put a hand to her mouth and said confidentially, "She called me by my big long name, but I bet she's thinking 'little twink.'"

Chapter 14

Your life gets messy when you let someone else into it.

—Angela Holloway, who prefers characters in books
to real people. You can always close a book. It's
harder to shut out real people once you've let them in

Once the Parker Construction truck stopped in front of the Green Apple, Angie and Seth and his little cousin all clambered out of the tall rig. The brisk wind that had been lashing the town for the last couple of weeks seemed to blow them right through the Grill's door. The bells above it announced their presence with a merry jingle.

"Brr! It's so cold today, I'm surprised you want ice cream, Riley," Angie said.

"Everybody likes ice cream," Riley told her as she climbed into the big corner booth and slid around to the middle of its green faux leather seat. "Don't you like ice cream, Angie?"

"Better call her Miss Holloway," Seth suggested. "She might be your teacher someday."

Riley rolled her big blue eyes. "Don't you like ice cream, Miss Holloway?" she repeated.

"I don't like ice cream when it's this cold outside."

"That's why we eat it inside," Riley said with a grin.

"And that's also why they invented hot fudge sundaes," Seth said. "Have one, Angie. My treat."

"How come you get to call her Angie?" Riley wanted to know.

"Because she's not ever going to be my teacher," Seth said, then shot Angie that crooked smile. It made something inside her hum, and she didn't feel the urge to smack him this time. "At least, not in school. Seriously, have a hot fudge sundae."

Humming or not, Angie decided she really shouldn't be accepting things from this man. He was making her feel all jumbled up and messy. If she let him into her life for more than just the pageant, he'd make a fool of her in the end. She shook her head. "I couldn't."

"Yes, you could," Riley said, her little palms upturned in a full body shrug. "All you need is a spoon."

Angie snorted. Seth didn't have to make a fool of her as long as Riley was around to do it for him. "There's no arguing with logic like that."

Seth signaled to Lester, who was ambling toward their booth, order pad in hand. "We'll have three hot fudge sundaes. You want coffee, too?" he asked Angie.

She shook her head.

"Water all around, then, I reckon," Lester said as he wrote down their order.

"Lester Scott, you don't need a notepad to remember three sundaes," came a voice from a barstool near the kitchen. The quavering tones belonged to Ethel Ringwald, the geriatric wonder who'd been the sole waitress at the Green Apple Grill for years until Lester joined the staff. Now that she had an underling to boss around and the leisure to sit and rest her feet while she did it, Ethel was feeling fine as frog's hair.

"I just want to make sure I get the order right, Miss Ethel," Lester said.

"If you want to get it right, you don't ask them do they want coffee. Everybody wants coffee, so just bring it to 'em. And tell that handsome Seth Parker I think he wants a piece of blueberry cobbler, too," Ethel said loudly. "Winter's comin'. That tall drink of water needs to weatherboard up a bit."

Seth might not be as sophisticated as Peter, but he was defi-
nitely the sort of man women noticed. No matter what their age.
Ethel was right. Seth was handsome. And tall. And . . .
Not for me. So not for me.

Lester turned back to Seth and said in a whisper, "Have the
cobbler, man, or she'll be all over my a—" He noticed Riley
watching him intently and quickly amended, "my back. She'll
be all over my back."

"Sure, Lester. Don't want you to get in trouble," Seth said.
"Bring me some cobbler, too."

"Thanks, man." Lester slapped a hand on Seth's shoulder
and then headed back to the kitchen to relay the order to the
cook. Jake Tyler, the owner of the Green Apple, was still in
culinary school in Boston, so his sister Laura was working the
grill and baking the cobbler these days.

"You didn't come here for cobbler. Are you always so easily led?" Angie asked.

"I've learned not to sweat the small stuff. If it'll help Lester
out, a bite or two of cobbler won't hurt me."

"That must be how Heather roped you into doing the
pageant. She told you a little civic duty wouldn't hurt you."

"Naw. She didn't have to twist my arm very far because I
don't mind doing my bit where I can," Seth said. "Are you still
grousing about being drafted for it? If you're so bent up about
directing the pageant, call Heather and tell her you don't want
to do it. Otherwise, give it a rest, would you?"

Angie flinched. Had she really been complaining that
much? She didn't think so, but at least his curt words meant
she didn't have to worry that Seth was interested in her. Because if he was, he'd just proved he was the worst boyfriend
material in the world.

Besides, it wasn't the pageant she minded so much. It was
spending all this time with him. Couldn't he see how uncom-

fortable he made her? Since she didn't much like his tone, she turned to the six-year-old between them.

"So, Riley," Angie said, "how do you like school?"

"I dunno. I wonder how I can like it my own self sometimes," came the quick reply. "My teacher makes me sit still a lot. Did you like school, cousin?"

"It was okay," Seth said.

"But you didn't like it much," the six-year-old observed shrewdly.

"He did his best and got an education. He graduated." Angie had to promote the value of school no matter what Seth might have felt about it. "That's the important thing."

"Well, I almost didn't graduate," Seth admitted. "Not officially anyway."

"What happened?" Riley asked.

"Well, there I was at my graduation ceremony and my name was called so I was supposed to go up on the stage and get my diploma. But when I got there, Mr. Whittle—he was the principal back then, too. He's been at Coldwater High since the Flood," he added as a quick aside to Angie. "Anyway, he couldn't find a diploma with my name on it. So he tried to hand me a blank one."

"That is not good," Riley said with a solemn shake of her head. "Almost as bad as getting a frowny face on your paper. Or a note sent home to your mom when you weren't doing nothing. Much."

"A blank diploma is pretty worthless," Angie agreed.

"That's what I thought." Seth's easy smile almost made her forget the setdown he'd just given her. "Anyway, Mr. Whittle whispered to me that I should go on back to my seat. They'd find my diploma and mail it to me later. In the meantime, everyone in the auditorium was getting all antsy, waiting for me to take the blank paper he was trying to hand me."

"What did you do?" Angie asked.

"I said, loud enough for folks in the last row to hear me, 'No, sir, Mr. Whittle. I earned a diploma with my name on it and I'm not leaving this stage till you give me one.' "

Angie chuckled, imagining her boss with his cheeks like flame and his eyes all bugged out. "Bet that went over."

"Like a lead balloon," he said. "But since Mr. Whittle could see that I meant it, everyone on stage started combing through the stack of diplomas on the table. I finally found the one with my name on it and waved it in the air."

Riley giggled and waved her own hands in imitation of Seth's triumph.

"Well, everybody in the auditorium started clapping and hooting and before you know it, I got myself a standing ovation," Seth said with a self-satisfied nod. "I may not have been the valedictorian, but I'm the one who made the front page of the *Coldwater Gazette*."

"Don't break your arm trying to pat your own back," Angie said. "It's pretty easy to make the *Gazette*. All you have to do is be the first person to see a robin in the spring, you know."

"Hey, it was my fifteen seconds of fame," Seth said. "You can't take it away from me."

"It's not nice to take stuff." Riley's grin suddenly flattened and her face crumpled in a worried frown. "Somebody taked my dad away from me."

Seth sobered in an instant. "What's that about your dad?"

The child shot him a quick look and then pulled her knees up to her chest. "I don't know where him is. Him and Ethan been gone a couple of days. Ethan, that's my brother and he's ten," she explained to Angie. "He's kind of a poopy-head most of the time, but he's my poopy-head. I wanna know where he is."

Angie's gut felt suddenly hollow. She knew something of

what Riley was going through. This was eerily like the time when one couple in her long string of foster parents split up. One day, she had an older foster brother who alternately played with her or tormented her, and the next, the boy and the man who served as their foster father were simply gone. She never learned what became of either of them. Thirty days later, her overwhelmed foster mom had shuffled her back into the system, where she waited in the county group home to be farmed out to a new family.

Again.

She was suddenly expected to call another set of strangers "Mom" and "Dad."

Again.

Angie looked back at Riley, who was studying her knees with absorption. The girl's bottom lip trembled. Riley's family was disintegrating, just as Angie's foster family had, and she didn't understand what was happening.

Children can't be expected to take this kind of punch to the heart. And a dissolving relationship is no picnic for the adults involved either.

No wonder the normally pulled-together Crystal Addleberry had seemed rattled.

Angie met Seth's gaze. *Change the subject,* she mouthed to him. She couldn't bear to see Riley upset. The child had no control over what the adults in her life did, but she probably secretly blamed herself for the family's crumbling.

Angie always did.

Seth dutifully changed the subject, talking to his little cousin about what she wanted for Christmas. He soon had Riley giggling and trying to figure out how he did a little finger play.

"This is the church," he said as he clasped his big hands together with his fingers laced so they were tucked inside. Riley followed suit. Almost. Her fingers lay across the backs of her small hands.

"This is the steeple." He made a point with his index fingers. Riley did, too. "Open the doors and see all the people."

Seth turned his hands over to show his palms and there were all his other fingers lined up like folks in their pews.

Riley tried to do the same, but because she had clasped her hands wrong and her fingers were on the outside, there were no "people" in her little church. She stared at her hands in puzzlement for a moment. Then her mouth formed a perfect "oh!"

"I know what's wrong," she said. "It must be Saturday."

"Must be," Seth said with a laugh. Then he hugged Riley and the little girl snuggled into his embrace.

He's really good with children.

This could be a very attractive quality in a man. But it wasn't for her. Angie never planned to have any kids. Why bring a child into the world if there was a chance you might leave it?

Then Lester came back with their treats and for a blessed little while, all hurts and disappointments were forgotten, or at least submerged for a bit in a swirl of gooey hot fudge and homemade vanilla.

Angie was glad Seth had insisted she have some ice cream, too. It was always tough when memories from her childhood bubbled to the surface. She needed the treat as much as Riley did.

They passed a pleasant hour eating their ice cream and doodling on the paper place mats Lester delivered too late to be used under their ice cream bowls. Riley drew a picture of a lopsided star and gave it to Angie.

"If you hang my picture on the foot of your bed," Riley told her, "you can look at it while you're sleeping."

When Lester brought out the blueberry cobbler, he included three spoons and they all dived in. When the last of the cobbler was just a memory and a blue stain on Riley's collar, Seth declared it was time to take his little cousin back to her mom.

There were no lights on in the administration building and when Seth tried the door, it was locked.

"Well, little one," Seth said when he climbed back into the

cab of the pickup. "Looks like somebody gets to go see their grandma."

Riley swiveled on the seat between them. "Is it you, Miss Holloway? Do you get to go see your nana?"

"No," she said softly. "I don't have a nana."

"That's okay," Riley said, patting her on the forearm. "You can use mine."

Chapter 15

It's hard to say what tears a couple apart. It's not always something big. Sometimes it's the constant drip of little things that wears out a relationship. A single leak can crack the strongest foundation if you ignore it long enough.

—Seth Parker, who wasn't all that surprised about Crystal and Noah's breakup

Seth tried to keep the conversation light as they bumped around town in his truck, but it wasn't easy. Riley was understandably upset that her mother wasn't where she was supposed to be, and Angela was alternately cheerful toward his little cousin and grumpy toward him. He probably shouldn't have come down so hard on her at the Green Apple, but honestly, he couldn't take the way she sometimes turned negative all of a sudden.

And he never knew when she'd take a turn either. Angela Holloway was the most unpredictable person he'd ever met.

When they reached the Evanses' home, they discovered his uncle George puttering around in the front yard. The old gentleman dropped to one knee to welcome his granddaughter, who scrambled out of the truck and zipped into his arms like a dart into a bull's-eye.

Seth felt a little less sorry for the child. Riley might be about to lose her father, or at least not have him in the same house, but she wasn't short of adults who cared about her. She had her mom, or would have once Crystal found her footing again. Seth had never seen his cousin so shaken.

Now he knew why.

But George and Shirley Evans were the best of grandparents, so Riley would be okay. Seth promised himself he'd start looking in on her and her brother Ethan. He figured wherever Noah had taken the boy, he'd be bringing him back soon. Noah had never been all that present in his kids' lives, according to Crystal, but Seth wasn't sure her take on things was unbiased.

Unless Crystal and Noah could find a way to mend their fences, things were likely to get worse for them and their kids before they got better. Taking Ethan smacked of a preliminary move in a custody battle that would shatter the kids.

Seth hated the whole idea of divorce. Like the Bugtussles, his parents "didn't hold to it." His dad had often claimed folks got divorced over things he and Seth's mom wrangled about with regularity. Commitment to the relationship trumped everything else and they found ways to work out their disagreements.

It was respect for the institution of marriage that had kept Seth from getting too serious with any of the women he'd dated. There was a reason they called it wedlock. And a life sentence in an unhappy one was a long, long time.

But it seemed to work for his folks, and for his uncle George and aunt Shirley, so maybe there was hope.

"What are you up to today, Uncle George?" Seth asked, as much to get a fresh set of thoughts as anything.

"I'm setting a few squirrel traps." He picked up a cage-like contraption and positioned it under one of the hundred-year-old oaks that dotted his front lawn.

"My uncle has been fighting the War of Squirrel Insurgency since I was a kid," Seth said to Angie, softly enough so that his uncle couldn't hear.

With a puzzled expression, Angie mouthed, *War of Squirrel Insurgency?* back to him.

"That's what he calls it."

"The darn things rip off twigs from my oak trees and throw them everywhere just for the heck of it," George complained as he bent to scoop up a handful of twigs.

"Is that legal? To set traps in town, I mean?" Angie asked. "Not to mention cruel," she muttered softly to Seth.

"There's nothing cruel about these traps." Evidently, George's hearing was sharper than Seth figured. "These are the catch and release kind. I figure I'll take the varmints I catch up into the Ouachitas and release them into the hills."

Coldwater Cove was almost encircled by an ancient mountain range that had eroded over the years into softly rolling green peaks.

"Besides," Seth said, "I'll bet Aunt Shirley would never let you tan the hides anyway."

"True, though I tried to convince her that a few hides tacked up on the side of the garage might be a deterrent to the wily little bas—devils," he quickly amended, remembering Riley, who was circling his legs.

"You know, I've always sort of admired squirrels," Angie said, peering up at a couple of sleek brown fellows who stared down at them from the safety of an oak limb.

George sucked in a surprised breath. "Bite your tongue!"

"No, I mean, think about it," Angie went on. "Squirrels are really pretty smart, the way they store up food for the winter months. There aren't a lot of mammals who plan ahead."

"I never thought about them like that," Seth admitted. Several of the guys who worked for him never planned for tomorrow and they usually came to grief. He'd lost track of how often they'd come to him with one sad story or other, asking for an advance on their pay. Unless it was an unforeseeable emergency, Seth always said no. Then he counseled them to start living by his "10/10/80" rule. Give ten percent. Save ten percent. Spend the rest with thanksgiving. Over time, it worked. "Squirrels may be a nuisance, but they actually are kind of enterprising."

"Not you too!" George said as he raised the lever to set his trap. "They're a crafty bunch, I'll give them that, but that doesn't mean we have to form an admiration society for them."

"Uncle George has tried plenty of different tactics to get rid of his squirrels over the years," Seth told Angie.

"So far, the furry rats are ahead, but this method is a game changer. It's sure to work," George said. "I baited the traps with peanut butter. They won't be able to resist."

Just then, the metallic snap of a trap being sprung came from around the side of the house.

"Got one!" George took off at a surprisingly quick trot and rounded the corner ahead of the rest of them, but Angie, Seth, and Riley were at his heels. "Oh, no!"

Angie stopped short, and Seth nearly plowed into her. She covered her eyes with her hands, afraid of what she might see. Perhaps the catch and release trap was not as humane as advertised.

"It's okay, Angie. You can look," he bent to whisper in her ear.

"That's not a squirrel, Grandpa," Riley said with a giggle. "That's Fergus!"

The Evanses' little Yorkie was caught fast in the cage-like trap, a glob of peanut butter on his whiskers and a sheepish expression on his furry face.

"Come on out of there, you silly old thing," George said as he knelt to remove his dog from the trap. Fergus was unharmed, but he trembled like an aspen in autumn until he was freed. Then he bolted around to the front door and scratched at it to be let in.

"Brr!" Angie said, hugging herself against a sudden gust of wind. "The dog's got the right idea."

"This'll help." Seth slipped out of his quilted jacket and draped it over her shoulders.

She pulled it close around her and inhaled deeply. It occurred to Seth that the jacket probably smelled like him, which meant a combination of sawdust, leather-based aftershave, and warm man. Judging from the way she snuggled into it, she didn't seem to mind.

It was a dangerous thing for a guy to let a girl wear his jacket. Especially since the girl in question was trying mightily not to let the guy into her life.

But maybe it would work. He'd heard about things called pheromones and such. Seth wondered if smell was really that important in developing an attraction for someone. He already knew he liked the way she smelled, all soap-clean and fresh without the need for fussy florals.

Though she did totally rock that spicy, earthy perfume she wore the night she went out with Peter Manning.

Angie tucked her arms into the long sleeves of his jacket and zipped it closed.

Maybe the jacket's scent was working and she was warming up to him. Maybe she was just cold and wanted anything that would warm her up. He really couldn't tell.

"Let's follow Fergus's example and head into the house," George suggested. "A little coffee's what we need to warm up."

"Me too, Grandpa."

"Not for you, Riley," George said. "It'll stunt your growth."

"What's that mean?"

George took her by the hand. "It means you'll never grow up."

"Daddy musta drinked a lot of coffee when he was a kid. Mommy says he never growed up." As they walked around the corner of the house to the front door, Riley suddenly noticed her grandmother's lawn art. It was a small windmill, whirling like a dervish in the brisk breeze. "Oh! Miss Holloway, look.

That's where all the wind is coming from. Grandpa should put it up in the attic and you won't be cold no more."

Shirley Evans plied them with ginger snaps and fended off George's attempts to pour coffee to go with them. She gave Riley a coloring book and a can full of dull crayons and let her color up a storm on the coffee table. To Seth's surprise, his aunt didn't ask a single question about how the pageant was going.

High marks for Aunt Shirley.

When they finished their refreshments, Seth carried the tray back into the kitchen for his aunt and managed to pull her aside for a moment.

"What's the deal with Crystal and Noah?" he asked. "Are they splitting the sheets?"

"Hush! George doesn't know anything about it and I'm hoping he won't have to," Shirley said in a furious whisper. "In fact, Crystal doesn't even know *I* know they're having trouble, but someone put an unspoken request on the prayer chain for them, so I figured something was up. That's when I did a little digging on my own."

Chalk one up for the Methodist prayer chain. It distributed information faster than the speed of Twitter and involved a lot more than one hundred and forty characters.

"Do you know where Noah and Ethan are?" Seth asked.

"He's taken the boy to the Addleberrys' ranch." The wealthy family owned a spread about a mile out of town that would put *Dallas*'s Southfork to shame.

"But he left Riley?" Seth asked.

"Ethan's the easy one. Put an iPad in his hand and you'd never know the boy was around. Riley is . . . oh, dear, I just love her to pieces, but she's a caution and no mistake," Shirley said. "I'm so in hopes this whole thing will blow over. It'll be hard on Crystal if it doesn't. She's never failed at anything, you know."

Maybe that was Crystal's trouble. She was always the perfect one, and she expected everyone around her to be perfect, too. It was a tough standard to live up to. Seth didn't want to assume the break up was his cousin's fault, but more than once, he'd felt sorry for Noah Addleberry when Crystal was on a tear about something he'd done or failed to do to her exacting standards.

"Seth, what's Angie's story?" Shirley asked. "Her background, I mean."

The abrupt change of topic caught him off guard. "Danged if I know."

"Well, don't get me wrong. She's a perfectly lovely person, but . . . there's a sadness about her."

Seth snorted. "And here I thought it was just pure cussedness."

"No, it's sadness," Shirley said with certainty. "You have to find out about her."

"Why me?"

"Because someone needs to, and I've seen how you look at her." Shirley scraped the crumbs from the cookie plate and loaded it into the dishwasher. "You're sweet on the girl, Seth. That's plain as mud."

"Plain as mud, huh? Ah, Aunt Shirley you always were a romantic."

"Of course I am," she said, putting a smile into her tone as Uncle George lumbered back into the kitchen with a full carafe of coffee and three cups that had seen no use at all. "After all, I'm going 'round the world on the Love Boat, aren't I?"

Seth frowned in puzzlement at her.

"Oh, you're too young to remember that old TV series, but your uncle and I are going to have the time of our lives, you mark my words."

"Duly marked," Uncle George said grumpily. "But let the

record show, if we founder on the shore of some Godforsaken Gilligan's Island, I was against this thing from the beginning."

Aunt Shirley clasped her hands around George's waist from behind him and laid her head between his shoulder blades. "But you went along with it because you love me, didn't you?"

"Guilty as charged." He patted her hands and then headed back to living room. "Gotta make sure Riley's confining her coloring to the book and not the couch."

"See?" Aunt Shirley said once he was out of earshot. "Grumps aren't that bad to live with once you get used to them. You just need to find out what's ailing your little grump."

My little grump. Seth had to admit the nickname suited Angie to a T.

"It's like I always say," his aunt went on to say. "Every single one of us has a secret that would break your heart if you knew it. If you want to know Angie Holloway, find out what happened to make her so sad."

"I doubt she'll let me."

Shirley swatted his chest. "Seth Parker, you were not raised to shy away from a fight. It's like I said the first time you brought her over here. I like her. She'll do."

"What's that supposed to mean?"

His aunt's smile was as enigmatic as the Mona Lisa's. "If you don't know, you don't deserve her."

Chapter 16

If you ask Riley Addleberry what she wants to be when she grows up, she'll tell you. "A star," she says. Riley doesn't mean a celebrity. She means one of those twinkly dancing lights in the night sky. She says it with such conviction, I half believe she could do it.

—Angela Holloway, who despite being all grown up still isn't sure what *she* wants to be sometimes

"You wanna grab a bite to eat?" Seth asked once Angie climbed back into the cab of his big truck.

Angie put a hand to her belly. "Between the ice cream and cobbler and your aunt's cookies, I probably shouldn't eat again for a week."

"Something simple, then," Seth said. The sun had set over an hour ago, but the sky was still faintly gray instead of inky black. "Maybe a burger?"

"Too heavy. How about a grilled cheese sandwich and tomato soup?" she countered.

"Great. Where do we go for that?"

She snuggled deeper into Seth's jacket. He'd insisted she put it on again when they left his aunt's house. Of course, she was swimming in it, but it was so warm. And for some strange reason, she really loved the way it smelled.

"Well," Angie said, stretching out the word so that it sounded like it had two syllables. Part of her wanted to spend more time with Seth, to listen to him talk in that gravelly drawl of his, to sneak glances at his profile. The man's strong jaw really was a work of art. Another part of her wanted to shove those thoughts to the furthest reaches of her mind. No good could come of needing to be with someone.

But she couldn't stop herself from saying, "We could go to my place."

"I didn't mean to invite myself to supper," he said.

"I know that." The hidden part of her that leaned toward him decided it wasn't that big a deal, just supper together and not even a very fancy one at that. There was no danger of a cheese sandwich being mistaken for a romantic dinner. "You've been such a good sport all day, what with the auditions and going to the college with me and all. I bet your guys miss you at the construction site."

"I try to give them Saturdays off as long as the project we're working is on schedule, which we are. Hey—" He shot her a sidelong glance. "Is this your way of talking me into building a bunch of extra sets for you?"

She hadn't laid out everything for him yet. In fact, her new plan for the pageant was still taking shape in her mind. Until it did, she'd keep exactly how many more sets she needed to herself.

"This has nothing to do with the pageant. In fact, if you come over, I think we should make pageant talk completely out of bounds." Why didn't he just say yes? Couldn't he see this was her way of trying to apologize for being so negative earlier? "Besides, a grilled cheese sandwich is the best thing I make."

"Well, all right then." He turned off Oak Street and headed toward the Square. "Never let it be said I turned down a lady's best."

Best might be overstating things. "Maybe I shouldn't have set the bar so high. It's hard to think of grilled cheese as a best of anything. They're just sandwiches after all. It's difficult to mess them up. And anyone can open a can of soup."

"Angie, I'm sure it'll be great," he said as the truck pulled into the Square and they rounded the courthouse. "Besides, I'm coming for the company, not the food. And I don't mean your dang cat."

She laughed. "Poor Effie. No one wants her company."

Seth turned on the radio and caught the end of the evening news. According to the local weather man, the mercury was heading south in a big way and the cold snap was likely to continue.

"That's the good thing about grilled cheese and tomato soup," Seth said as he pulled into the small parking lot behind her building. "They warm you up on the inside."

Chased by the wind, they double-timed it up the iron stairs and into Angie's snug little apartment.

Another good thing about grilled cheese and tomato soup was that it was quick. By the time Seth set out their plates and flatware and filled a couple of glasses with ice, Angie had the soup heating and the first sandwich ready to come off the griddle.

She hadn't burned it a bit.

Seth tried not to slurp his soup and wondered how best to follow his aunt's advice. Knowing he needed to discover Angie's secret and actually doing it were two different things.

Sometimes, when he got stuck on a construction problem, he needed to change his frame of reference and look at it with fresh eyes. It usually worked. Maybe that strategy would transfer to people too. He decided to approach the Angie problem sideways.

"Guess my cousin and her husband are separated."

"I got that impression," she said between sips of sweet tea. "I'm sorry, but more for Riley than Crystal and her husband. Is that bad?"

"No, I agree with you. Kids suffer most when adults don't act like adults. I wonder what happened."

"I don't think it's any of our business," Angie said primly; then she slanted her big brown eyes at him. Instead of feeling chastised, Seth just thought she was outrageously cute. "Besides, I never figured you for a gossip, Seth Parker."

"Hey, to quote Marjorie Chubb, it's not gossip if you pray over it afterward."

"That's a mighty fine knife you use to slice your conscience." She slid off her barstool. "Want another sandwich?"

He shook his head and she climbed back onto her seat.

"Do you pray?" she asked softly.

"Sure. I used to pray for a pony every night when I was a kid. Now I pray about other stuff." He didn't tell her he'd been praying about her lately. "Don't you?"

"Yeah. Some. Not as much as I probably should," she admitted. "I used to pray when I was a kid, too."

This seemed like a pretty good opening into her past. "What did you pray for?"

"Well, it wasn't for a pony, that's for sure."

"What then?"

She drew a deep breath. "For a mom and dad. Real ones."

Seth was thankful once again for the intact family he'd grown up in, and realized afresh just how much of a rarity that had become. "I know it's none of my business, but I'm only asking because I can see it's left a hurt on you that hasn't gone away. You have no family, you said. What happened to them?"

She stared into her soup bowl for a heartbeat or two. "I

don't really remember. I was nine months old when it happened, but my caseworker told me about it when I was old enough to ask."

Seth held his breath when she stopped. He only released it when she started talking again.

"There was an accident. A bad one. I was in the back seat, but my car seat lived up to its safety rating." Her voice was flat, as if she'd been through this information countless times in her head. Seth would bet she hadn't told many people though. "All I had was a concussion and a few cuts and bruises."

Seth waited, afraid if he interrupted with a question, she'd stop for good.

"My dad was pronounced dead at the scene, but my mother lived."

"Well, that's good."

"You'd think so, but no." Angie shook her head. "She was in a coma for the next six years. They were both only children and none of my grandparents were living. The state of Texas tried to find a relative to take me, but there wasn't anybody. So I was parked in foster care."

"You must have been adopted," Seth said, thinking he'd figured out her secret. She was pining for the parents she never knew. "They always say babies get adopted right away."

"Not me," she said. "Because my mother was still alive, I couldn't be adopted. She might have woken up and recovered, so her parental rights had to be preserved. By the time she died, I wasn't a baby anymore. I was a scrawny seven-year-old with attachment issues."

"Attachment issues?"

"That's what the state psychologist called it," she said. "I was shuffled around to a number of different homes when I was growing up. Sometimes, I was moved because my foster parents got divorced, sometimes there were problems with other kids in the home. Because I've always been small, I was an easy target."

Seth's fingers balled into fists. He wished with all his heart he could go back in time and be there to protect her.

"Each time a kid gets moved, she has to make new connections. It's not just with the new family. Lots of times, I changed day care, too. Later, it meant changing schools. It was hard," she said. "After a while, I couldn't make connections at all."

"Did you get help?"

She nodded. "Some. Not early on. My last foster mom was also a psychologist. She helped me see what was happening inside me. I knew I was different. After talking with her about it, I knew why."

He met her gaze. "Well, I think you're someone special."

She blushed.

Who does that anymore?

"I mean it, Angie. You're smart. You're sensitive and you're really pretty." He wanted to go on, but she cut him off.

"Okay, that's enough. A girl can only take so much." She scooped up both their empty plates and carried them to the sink. When she turned back to face him, she frowned. "What? You look so serious, it's like you're trying to cure cancer or something."

No, but he'd give a lot to be able to help her. "I was just wondering if that attachment thing is what makes it hard for you to form relationships now."

She bristled, but then conceded his point. "It's still not easy for me, but I manage. Once I got to college, I had a circle of friends. And then here in Coldwater, I got to know Heather and she introduced me to a ton of people. I know more folks now than I ever have."

"But how many know you?" he asked.

"What's that supposed to mean?"

"How many of them know you were a foster kid?"

"Everybody deserves a little privacy." She dumped the plates in the sink and came back to sit down before her still cooling soup. "Do you tell everyone you meet about your childhood?"

"Don't have to. Most folks around here watched me grow up." More than a few of them had had a hand in seeing that he learned his manners, too.

"You are a lucky guy, Seth Parker."

"I'd be the first to agree." He laid a hand lightly on her forearm. She flinched a little, but didn't move away. "I'm really lucky Heather talked me into doing the pageant with you."

"I thought we said no pageant talk."

"We're not talking about it. We're doing it. And the important thing about doing it is that I'm doing it with you." He slid his hand down to her wrist and covered her hand with his palm. "We haven't known each other very long, but I really do want to know you better, Angie."

She slipped her hand away from his and let it drop into her lap.

Too fast. Slow down, Parker.

She toyed with her spoon, making little figure eights in her soup. "I don't know if getting to know each other better is such a good idea."

He got it. Manning had taught her men couldn't be trusted to stick around. "I'm not going to let you down."

"You might not mean to," she said. "I'm sure my real parents didn't intend to die and leave me alone either."

Seth drummed his fingers on the counter. "Okay, this isn't a perfect metaphor, but I want you to know I understand a little bit about attachment issues."

"You? Mr. Lived–Here–All–His–Life?"

"Except for college." Seth raised his soup bowl to his lips and drained the contents. "Don't forget I wandered the wide world for a few years."

"Yeah, I'm sure that qualifies you to understand about attachment issues."

"No, actually, I learned about it from my dog."

Chapter 17

Limeberger's Mortuary . . . a better funeral experience . . .
You'll be satisfied with our service or your second one is free!

—*The Coldwater Gazette* classifieds

"Your. Dog?" Angie was ready to spit tacks. He thought he
understood how she felt because he'd had a dog? She'd opened
up to him, shared things she hadn't talked about with anyone
for years. And he wasn't taking it seriously at all.

"Yeah," Seth said with a dopey half smile on his handsome
face. He clearly had no idea how steamed she was. "We got
Lucky at the pound. He was a big hairy mutt, kind of old to
start with, all white around his eyes and muzzle. But he needed
a home and my mom wanted a dog that was already house
trained. Anyway, Lucky was a great dog. He followed me
around all day and slept on the foot of my bed every night."

Her cheeks cooled a bit. Against her better judgment, she
was beginning to be sucked in by his dog story. "Sounds like
you were never lonely."

"Nope, not with Lucky around. But like I said, he was an
old dog when we got him. After only two years, he died." His
voice cracked with emotion. He wasn't being flippant. The dog
really had meant something to him. "It broke me up something terrible."

She nodded. "How old were you?"

"Nine. Lucky was my best friend and he left me," Seth said.
"My dad offered to get me a puppy that summer, but I didn't

want one. I knew it was just a heartache with feet waiting to happen."

"Then you *do* understand." This time, she put her hand on his arm and it felt right. "If you don't let anyone or anything in, they can't hurt you."

Effie meowed.

"Maybe that's what happened to Effie, too," Seth suggested. "I heard she was abandoned by the people who had this apartment before my cousin Lacy."

"I never thought of that."

"Of course, she's only a cat. They don't get attached to much except their supper bowls."

"That's not true. Cats can be very affectionate."

"Ever catch Effie being that way?"

"No, but if she's been abandoned so often, maybe she does suffer from attachment disorder. I wonder if I can help her get over it."

"Yeah, Effie needs help. That's for dang sure, but you haven't let me finish my dog story yet." He took her hand in his. This time, she didn't feel the need to pull away. "After a while, I started thinking that I was being selfish by not wanting another dog."

"Selfish? How do you figure?"

"There are lots of dogs out there that need homes. My folks were okay with me having one. And as it turned out, I needed one," Seth said.

"I get that you like dogs, but they aren't exactly a need."

"They are for a kid. Even if you've got family and friends, who doesn't need a little more unconditional love?"

Unconditional love sounded good. Something soft and sure that you could love and that something would return the feeling no matter what. Angie had no idea what that must be like.

But her childhood wouldn't have been helped by having a dog. It would have been one more thing to lose each time she was yanked to a different home. She'd have worried about a dog if she'd had to leave one. Cats tended to land on their feet.

Just like she always did.

More or less . . .

"So we got a puppy and this one was with me till I graduated from high school," Seth went on. If he noticed she'd been silent for a while, he gave no sign of it. "And yeah, I buried that one too, and I was just as sad about losing him as I was about Lucky. But being sad when a relationship is over is the price you pay for the joy that you had together."

"So, are you trying to tell me that relationships with people are like the ones you had with your dogs?"

"When you put it like that, it sounds stupid. I'm not explaining this very well." He sighed and shook his head. "I guess I'm trying to say you can't judge the future by the past."

"But every single time you take in a dog, eventually, it ends the same. The dog dies and leaves you."

"Yeah, but that's not what I was getting at."

"What are you trying to say, then?"

"You. And that Manning guy. It ended badly, but it doesn't always have to," he said. Angie knew he was seriously trying to explain something since he hadn't purposely mangled Peter's name. "You took a risk with him, but he hurt you and it sucks. I'd be happy to deck him for you if I ever see him again."

"You won't." *Trust a guy to think everything can be settled with his fists.*

"Here's hoping. Not that I'd mind laying him out good and proper," he added quickly, "but you don't deserve to have to be reminded of the past."

Angie sighed. "I still don't get your metaphor. How is my relationship with Peter like your dog story?"

"I guess it's not." His broad shoulders slumped a bit.

"Then what do you mean, Seth?"

He met her gaze with his clear-eyed one. He looked so intent, so earnest, she'd believe anything that came out of his mouth. "Just that I'm not like Peter. If you take a chance on me, I won't hurt you."

Her breath caught in her throat. She reached up a tentative hand and pressed her palm on his cheek for a second or two. Then she jerked it away.

"I believe you wouldn't mean to, but you can't be sure you wouldn't."

"I can be sure I'd do my best not to," Seth said. "Do you wish you'd never known Peter?"

Now he wasn't even calling him Manning. This was obviously a serious discussion.

"Sometimes."

"You know why you don't regret it all the time?"

She shook her head.

"Because, it wasn't all bad with the guy," he said, gritting his teeth as if it half killed him to force the words out. "You must have had some good times."

"We did," Angie admitted.

"And you were able to 'attach' with him, right?"

She nodded. "He was the first. The only, really. I trusted him. I took a risk with him, and . . . he threw me away."

A muscle twitched along Seth's jaw. He looked like he wanted to pound Peter Manning into next week.

"If you took a chance once, that tells me you could do it again," he said.

"It tells me I may not want to," Angie said. "You only have to smash your thumb once to become leery of hammers."

"As someone who's had his share of smashed thumbs, I can tell you, Angie, you can't protect yourself out of life. Even folks who don't have your . . . issues, get hurt sometimes."

"Have you ever been hurt?"

★　★　★

The girls he thought he'd loved and lost traipsed through his mind. It was a short parade. "I was hurt a time or two," he admitted. "You know how teenage boys are."

"Not so much." She shook her head, but she hadn't taken her hand from his. It gave him hope. "I never understood how guys think. It's like you're from another planet."

"They've pretty much debunked that men are from Mars, women are from Venus thing. Everybody comes into this world with the same wants and needs."

She pulled her hand away from his and folded it with the other in her lap. "And sometimes we just need to be left alone."

Dang! We're going backward. "Okay, answer me this. What did Peter Manning do to convince you to take a chance on him?"

She put a hand to her forehead and sighed. "He noticed me."

"That's it?"

"That was a lot at the time," she admitted. "I'd been pretty much invisible for years, but then suddenly this guy started bumping into me on campus every day. First, it was just a nod and a smile. Then one day, he saw me coming off the track—I ran cross-country back then—and he called out, 'How you doing, Legs?' "

"Legs?"

There was that blush again. "Yeah, I wore pretty short shorts when I ran."

"That's it? A guy compliments your legs and you fall for him?" Heck, he'd call her "Legs" all day long if that was all it took.

"No, that was just the beginning. He hung around and when I came out of the locker room, he had a cold Gatorade waiting for me. It was . . . unexpectedly kind."

But not unplanned. Seth could see the pattern in Manning's siege on Angie's heart. He'd bet any amount of money the guy had researched her and knew a lot more about her than the fact that she had great legs. It smacked of covert activities almost, an Operation Angie Holloway. Manning must have discovered her vulnerabilities and taken advantage of them.

All it took for her to think Peter unexpectedly kind was a Gatorade. She must not have experienced much kindness in her life. Something inside Seth ached for the lost child she'd been. "Nobody ever brought you a cold drink before?"

"Nobody ever thought about the fact that I needed one. Peter anticipated everything."

"Of course, he did," Seth said flatly. As rare as attention had been for Angie, she must have been an easy mark.

"Anyway, we became a couple the first semester of my freshman year. I won't lie to you. I fell hard."

Manning had undoubtedly counted on that.

"When did it fall apart?" he asked.

"A week before Peter graduated. He told me he was headed east for law school."

"Did he ask you to go with him?"

She shook her head. "He said he needed to make a clean break so he could concentrate on his studies. But it was more than that," she admitted. "He knew me well enough to know I'd be lost in DC. Big cities freak me out."

"Which is why you're here in Coldwater."

"It's one of the reasons."

"What are the others?" Seth asked.

"Fewer people, fewer risks, I guess. That's the main one," Angie said.

"People are a risk. Every single time. But they're worth it, mostly." Seth leaned toward her a little and she didn't lean away. "At least the ones that promise they mean you well. I do, you know."

She nodded. "I'm beginning to believe you."

Then, to his great surprise, she closed the distance between them and gave him a peck on the cheek.

"What was that for?"

"Because I've been kind of terrible to you since we first met. No, don't deny it." She waved away his objections. "I know I have. It's like I can't help myself. There's this ball of something inside me that lashes out once in a while and you've been catching the brunt of it lately."

"And you thought a quick kiss would make up for it?"

"Well, no . . . maybe?"

"Look, Angie, a kiss shouldn't be a consolation prize."

"What should it be?"

"You want me to show you?"

She swallowed hard. "Yes."

Chapter 18

A kiss is the gateway to the soul. When your lips
touch someone else's, you discover who they are. Once
you kiss them, you can't ever un-know them.
That's the glory and the terror of a kiss.

—Angela Holloway, who's only kissed
one other man in her whole life

What would Colonel Brandon do? Seth wondered for half a heartbeat before telling himself, *He'd kiss the lady, you fool.*

But he was still wary about scaring her off. If he kissed Angie the way he wanted to, he probably would. So he bridled himself and moved in to just brush his lips across hers.

At the last second, she tipped her head in the same direction as his and their foreheads came together with a resounding smack.

"Well, that wasn't very good," he said, rubbing his noggin.

"No, it wasn't," she said with a giggle. "In fact, it was amazingly awful."

"Give me another shot. I can do better than amazingly awful."

"All right," she said with a laugh that sounded suspiciously like a snort. "Just so you don't have to worry about a moving target, I'll hold still this time."

Not if I have anything to say about it. He wanted to feel her move, pressing her lips against his, snugging her body up to his, but this wasn't the time for that kind of kiss.

True to her word, she didn't move. He decided he could risk touching her cheek. It was soft and smooth and surprisingly warm. Probably on account of the way her skin bloomed bright pink under his palm.

He loved it when she blushed.

Seth ran the pad of his thumb over her lips. She didn't pull away. Instead her eyes closed.

He wanted to tell her to keep them open. He needed her to know who she was kissing. There was always the risk that she'd be thinking about Manning while she was kissing him, but this wasn't the time to make demands on her.

This was his time to give.

Seth leaned in, pausing for just a moment about an inch from his goal. Her warm breath feathered softly across his mouth. Then he closed the distance between them and covered her lips with his.

Seth was no expert, but he'd kissed his share of girls. He thought he knew what to expect. He could read the signs, like when a spring storm came up out on the prairie. When he saw lightning in the distance, he knew he'd hear thunder in a few seconds.

Nothing in his past prepared him for this kiss.

His heart thudded so hard, he could hear it pounding in his ears. Surely she must hear it, too. But if she did, she gave no sign.

Instead, Angie raised her hands and draped her arms around his shoulders while the kiss went on and on.

It hit him suddenly that he and this woman were sharing a breath. Almost like they were exchanging souls if he wanted to go all new age touchy-feely about it, and yet, he had no idea what she was really thinking. Or feeling.

Maybe because he was swamped by his own emotions.

He was engulfed by a heady mix of tenderness and longing, of protectiveness tangled up with lust. Her lips were sweet as honey, but there was also a sting of pain in her kiss. It was as if he could feel her past hurts, her aloneness. The bone-deep sadness in her nearly suffocated him, but he wouldn't have broken off their kiss for worlds.

If it killed him, he wouldn't abandon Angie. Not ever. She'd had enough of that in her life already.

He wasn't sure how long the kiss lasted. Time sort of expanded and contracted around them. The only thing he was certain of was that she was the first to pull away. Not far though. In fact, she was still near enough to rest her forehead against his.

"That was . . ." she whispered, and he realized she was struggling for breath as much as he.

"Better?" He hoped so. "Amazingly awful" was a terrible black mark for a guy to have on his record.

"The best," she assured him.

He started to kiss her again, but she put a couple of fingers to his lips.

"I don't think we should do that again."

"Why the heck not?" After all, it was the best. Her words.

"Because I think it's time you went home."

"Why?"

"Because . . . I want you to stay," she admitted. "And you shouldn't."

Seth wanted to argue the point, but he could hear his uncle George in his head. Discretion is the better part of valor, the old man had told Seth often enough. He'd never really understood what it meant until now.

Seth could press on and Angie might let him stay. Anything could happen if he did, and while part of him cheered this line of thinking with great enthusiasm, a wiser part whispered the truth to him. If he pushed Angie now, he'd be violating her trust.

He didn't want her for just a night, he realized with a jolt.

He wanted her for a whole lifetime of nights. The revelation hit him with the force of a Mack truck.

Angie was the one. The only. He didn't know why for sure, only that it was so. Just as his aunt Shirley had told him, Angie "would do."

The bumps and wrinkles in her soul fitted perfectly with the ones in his. They were both better when they were together. They'd do for each other for the rest of their lives.

But Angie, like her Jane Austen heroine, thought she was stronger alone. Seth would have to disabuse her of that notion.

It wouldn't be easy.

"Okay," he said, and pressed a quick kiss to her forehead. "I'll go for now. But I'm coming back tomorrow."

"I'm counting on it."

A smile bloomed across her face. It lifted her cheeks and made her eyes dance. It was the smile he'd been wanting to see since the first time they met.

"That was exactly what I needed." Stretched out on the bed, Sabine raised her arms above her head, pointed her toes, and arched her back, catlike. "You always get all the kinks out."

"I'd like to get some kinks in. I've wanted us to try something kinky for months." Peter was already seated on the edge of the bed, pulling on his pants. That was the good thing about his deal with Sabine. She didn't expect him to hang around after their marathon in her big four-poster bed was over. It was a simple, effective arrangement that suited them both.

Most of the time.

"I could bring some toys next week," he suggested.

"We don't need them," Sabine said. "Really, Peter, all I want is a horizontal aerobics session and I'm good. You must be, too, or you wouldn't keep coming back every Thursday."

When they first realized they could fool around with each other without forming an emotional attachment, they'd agreed on Thursday as their standing night. That way they were each free to see other people on Friday and Saturday.

Not that either of them were into the idea of a real relationship with someone else. They didn't have the time. Billing a ridiculous number of hours each week didn't leave much for anything else.

To be honest, Peter didn't have the emotional energy to sink into another person. Why should he put himself out, knowing he might have to someday cut that tie? A small part of his heart he'd never admit existed still smarted over the way he'd had to push Ange out of his life.

Of course, it had been the right thing to do. He never doubted that. Being laser focused while he earned his law degree at Georgetown was the only way to get through the rigorous course of study. Being close to Angela Holloway had made him sloppy. He'd caught himself putting time with her ahead of studying more than once. To make it in the DC law game, he'd needed more than a *summa cum laude* asterisk on his degree. He had to network like crazy. During his time at Georgetown, he spent every waking moment he wasn't with his study group making connections that would serve him well once he graduated. He made it a point to suck up to his Ivy League classmates, who stood to inherit businesses or prestigious firms in the hope that they'd throw him cases later. Since Peter didn't come from money, he'd always had to try harder.

It would have been great to have a socially savvy girlfriend at his side who could help cement those ties, but Angie was hopeless when it came to working a room. She'd have been cowering in a corner.

Probably with her nose in a book.

Or worse, correcting my grammar in public. Who needs that?

In his more honest moments, Peter admitted to himself that he missed Ange. There was a sweetness, a vulnerability about her, that made him feel stronger. Angela had needed him.

Sabine did, too. But only for one thing.

"So before you go, tell me more about that UCFF case you think we can make in Oklahoma," Sabine said as he stood.

"Let's not go there." Peter pulled his Ralph Lauren polo shirt over his head. "The more I think about it, the less I like our chances."

"Why? It sounded like a slam dunk. A classic church and state deal."

She raised herself to her knees, pillows propped around her, her long blond hair tumbling around her shoulders. Peter looked away lest she seduce him back into the bed. He gave in to her wishes too easily when he was in a . . . suggestible state.

"We could make a big splash with it, you know," Sabine went on. "National news outlets love to cover this sort of thing every December. You can almost set your watch by it."

"I don't know." Peter sat down in a nearby chair and toed on his shiny black Ferragamos. He and Ange had lived together for most of a semester on less than the price of those shoes. And were ridiculously happy doing it. Peter shook his head at the memory. He wouldn't be satisfied with that simple life now.

But Ange sure was pretty first thing in the morning . . .

"I don't think we should pursue the case," he said. "It might look like we're picking on small-town America."

"Oh, who cares? Nobody gives a crap about flyover country." Sabine waved away his objection. "We can make a national name for ourselves with this. Give me the details again."

"It's just a Christmas pageant, Sabine."

"Bingo! They made our case with the name alone. If they had any brains at all, they'd call it a Winter Festival or better yet, something to do with the solstice. Can't go wrong going pagan. And they are using public property, right?"

"From what I gathered, they always have it on the courthouse steps. It's tradition."

"And the director." Sabine climbed out of bed, slipped into a silky robe, and cinched it closed with a tie belt. "You said something about the director being a public employee."

"A schoolteacher, yeah."

"Perfect. We might be able to get the NEA on board. Things like this just can't stand." Sabine's face was flushed. She always got excited when she scented blood in the water on the opposing counsel's side. "It's un-American."

"Is it?"

"They're trying to impose a *religion* on people, Peter. I mean, how intolerant can you get?"

Sabine had found her moral high ground. Peter wasn't likely to talk her down from it. He needed a legal point to skewer her with.

With which to skewer her, he heard Ange's voice in his head, as he reordered his thoughts.

"Don't we need a complainant?" he asked. "I don't think we can find anyone. It sounded like the whole town looks forward to this pageant each year."

Peter had overheard a number of conversations about plans for the Christmas pageant while he was in Coldwater Cove. From the college students at Bates to the night manager at the Heart of the Ozarks motel, everyone was chattering on about the pageant and what a fixture it was in the life of the place.

"Without a local alleging a violation of his rights, we don't have standing to bring a suit."

"Then we need to find one," she said, undeterred. "Maybe you should go back there for a bit."

"What reason could I give for returning to Coldwater Cove?"

"Why do you need a reason?"

"Because in that little town, a new face gets noticed. I had to explain what I was doing there to everyone I met."

"Well, that's not creepy at all." Sabine rolled her eyes. "How in the world do people live there?"

Quite happily, Peter almost said. The charm of the Town Square, the sparkling lake and green hills rising above it—there was a peacefulness about the place that washed away a little of the crusty cynicism that had built up around his soul.

But only a little.

"I'd go nuts there in a week," he admitted.

"Maybe a week is all you need. Look, why don't you go back to that little Podunk college and talk to them about endowing an English chair."

"We don't have the funds to do that."

"They don't know that, do they?" she said. "Talk to the teacher who's directing this sorry disruption of the American way. Maybe you can convince him—"

"Her."

"Her," Sabine repeated. She tapped her front teeth with her perfectly manicured fingertips as she studied him through narrowed eyes. "Why do I get the feeling you know this teacher from someplace else?"

"Because I do." He and Sabine had no secrets. She was going to wrangle it out of him anyway, so he might as well tell her. "She and I were at Baylor together."

"Don't you mean you were *together* at Baylor?" Sabine guessed shrewdly. "Don't forget. I know you, Peter. I can read you like a shoddily written deposition. Let the record show that you and this woman have slept together."

"I wish you wouldn't do that."

"Do what?" she asked, batting her eyes at him, all innocence.

"Make everything so . . . dirty."

"Because, darling, everything is." She crossed the room to him, letting her robe flutter open, and slid a hand down the front of his trousers. "How did you ever make it through law school without learning that?"

Peter roused to her despite his determination not to. He sighed. "What do you want me to do?"

"I want you to go back to Oklahoma and build a case. There's got to be a federal court somewhere near that Coldwater Cave place that we can file in."

In which we can file. He wasn't the fanciful sort, but he could swear he heard Ange's voice in his head for the second time that night.

"Cove. Not Cave." He could correct the town name at least. "Coldwater Cove."

"Whatever. Anyway, once we get ready to file, I'll tip a couple of journalists who'll eat this up with a spoon." She flounced away from him and settled before her vanity mirror. "The camera loves me. Let's aim for filing a couple of days before Christmas."

"The case isn't likely to be resolved in time to let the pageant go forward if we lose."

"We aren't going to lose. We *don't* lose," she snapped, a horrified expression on her lovely face. It was as though he'd suggested they contract Ebola just for fun. "But for once, the whole point of a lawsuit isn't winning. It's about stopping an egregious violation of religious freedom. All we need is a friendly judge who'll issue a stay that keeps the display from happening."

"It's not really a display. It uses real people, so I guess the Coldwater pageant is more like a play."

"I don't care if it's an off off-Broadway musical." She picked up a brush and attacked her hair with vigor. "We just have to stop it from happening."

"You kinda sound like the Grinch right now."

"Well, the Grinch is more politically correct than the Baby Jesus. If the people in Oklahoma were doing a play about

Who-ville, they wouldn't be inviting a lawsuit," Sabine said. "Honestly, how will people ever learn if we don't use the law to smack them around once in a while?"

Peter was glad she wasn't his enemy and it wasn't the first time he'd thought so. Sabine was a pit bull in the courtroom. When she thought she had a righteous cause, she fought even harder.

But Peter wasn't so certain they were on the side of the angels this time. Sure, he gave lip service to the popular interpretation of the First Amendment, that it was actually a guarantee of freedom *from* religion. But deep inside, he was still a son of Texas whose grandmother had dragged him to Sunday School every week during the summers he spent with her, whether he wanted to go or not.

It didn't turn him into the preacher his grandma had hoped he'd be. In fact, he was hard pressed to remember much about her little church except that his granddad would never join them.

But it hadn't hurt him to go. In fact, the Bible stories he'd been exposed to had come in handy years later in more than one literature class.

In the same spirit of pragmatic indifference to all things spiritual, if a bunch of hicks in Oklahoma wanted to dress up in bathrobes and reenact a bit of ancient history, it was no skin off his nose. He didn't see the harm.

And without demonstrable harm, how could they bring a suit against a town's Christmas pageant?

Sabine frowned at his reflection in her mirror. "I can see you're undecided about this. How about if I promise to drop the case after the holidays? That way we won't bankrupt Coldwater Crotch with legal fees."

"Cove. Coldwater Cove. At least get the name right, okay?"

"Okay, we're in agreement on filing, then." She applied a

fresh coat of lipstick. "In before Christmas, out by New Years. By then, media interest will have faded anyway."

"But we'll still have made our names known," he said.

Your name is your bond, Peter, his grandma had often said. *What will you give your name to?*

He knew his grandma wouldn't like him giving it to this. But he knew just as surely that he'd still do it.

Chapter 19

Shepherds and wise men and angels, oh my!

—Angela Holloway, who hopes she won't
run into any flying monkeys while
she tries to cast the Christmas pageant

"You certain sure you don't want me to be a wise feller, Miss Holloway?" Junior Bugtussle twisted the ball cap in his hands so tightly that the Finklemeyer's Feed & Seed logo stenciled across the front read Fink Fee & See. Angie had called most of her choices for the pageant cast and asked them to drop by her classroom after school was out for the day. She got the feeling Junior hadn't set foot in the high school since he'd *almost* graduated over ten years ago.

"No, I think you'll be perfect for the role of Head Shepherd," she explained. "If we use live animals, and I think we really should, we need someone who knows how to keep them under control."

Junior beamed under her praise. "Shirley Evans wouldn't never let us use real sheep and cows and such. Said they'd stink up the manger."

"Well, if our goal is realism, I don't suppose the original manger smelled like a hospital ward."

"No, I 'spect you're right about that." Junior scratched his head. "I could kinda hide a shovel in my robes, too. On account of, well, with real animals there's always a chance one of 'em will decide to . . . you know, answer nature's call."

"Ah! A wise precaution."

"See! I could, too, be a wise feller."

"Maybe next year, Junior." *Oh, my gosh, did I just say that? As if directing this thing once isn't enough for any sane person's lifetime!* "I really need you to wrangle the animals this time."

"Then you got it, Miss Holloway. Now about them animals, I got me a Guernsey cow what's about to drop a calf. She's a purty little cow and biddable as you could wish. You want 'em both in the pageant?"

"Why would we need both?"

"It'll make the cow more satisfied to have her calf next to her. If her bag gets heavy and she takes a notion that her baby might be hungry and it's not where she can get to it, well, I can't answer for the consequences."

Angie had a vision of a runaway Guernsey making a break for it and heading down Main Street as fast as her bovine legs could carry her. "All right. Maybe Seth could build a special stall for them inside the set of the stable."

"'Spect Seth Parker could build whatever you need. He's a right handy feller."

Angie smiled. Seth had been handy every night for the past week. He'd pick her up at her place and take her for supper at the Green Apple. Or she'd make a couple of peanut butter and jelly sandwiches and they'd sneak them into the Regal, where they'd watch another oldie-but-goodie movie together. One night, he even took her dancing at the Opera House when the local Big Band was playing. It wasn't clubbing by anyone's standard. There was no strobe lighting or hipster DJ setting the pace, but slow dancing with Seth Parker, all tangled up with his hard body and fresh masculine scent, was more than romantic. It made her feel safe in a way she hadn't in years.

"He is pretty handy at that," Angie said. Then because she was afraid Junior would catch her being sappy over Seth, she hurried on. "What other animals can you bring?"

"As I recollect, Mary rode her a donkey all the way to Bethlehem. Don't have one of them, but my neighbor up the road, he's got a zonkey."

"What's a zonkey?" Angie asked.

"Sort of a hybrid. Some fool put a donkey in with a zebra just to see what'd happen and 'bout eleven months later this sorry critter popped out." Junior shook his head. "Don't see too many of 'em."

"I bet not. What does it look like?"

"It's about the size of a burro, but the head's a little over-sized for the rest of him and if you get him in the right light, you can see some faint stripes. The durn thing ain't good for nothin' except eatin' and poopin'." Junior's ears went as red as the handkerchief poking out of his coveralls pocket. "Beggin' your pardon, Miss Holloway. I shoulda said makin' messes instead of poopin'. Dang, I did it again."

"That's okay, Junior. Could the girl who plays Mary ride this zonkey?"

"Guess so. It's gentle enough. I seen my neighbor's kids tryin' to ride it."

"Trying to?"

"Well, they ended up on their keesters most of the time," Junior admitted.

A striped burro dumping the Virgin Mary on her behind and going all rodeo through the crowd wouldn't put anyone in the Christmas spirit.

"But if we was to put a bridle on it, whoever you get to play Joseph won't have no trouble leading it along, I'll warrant," Junior suggested. "Who you figurin' to be Joseph, by the by?"

"Ian Van Hook," Angie said.

"That's good then. He's been taking kids what have been bullied out to the Hackbart Riding Center to give 'em a bit a confidence like. He's used to leading horses for them kids. The zonkey won't be much different."

"Isn't it stubborn?"

"It's a zonkey, not a mule. If Ian tucks a carrot in his pocket, it'll follow him anywhere. 'Course he might have to go along at a good clip to stay ahead of it."

"Okay, we'll give the zonkey a try." Angie envisioned all the paintings of the nativity she'd ever seen. There were always a few sheep. "Have you any lambs?"

Junior shook his head. "Wrong time of year. Lambs are born in the spring when the grass is fresh and there's plenty of it. But I can get my son Aaron to bring a couple of our smaller ewes. Maybe that'd do, and Aaron can be a shepherd along with me. Unless you got someone else in mind?"

Angie decided she could have as many shepherds as she needed to keep the folks who auditioned happy.

"The ewes won't wander off?" Angie imagined the courthouse lawn dotted with fuzzy sheep.

"Not if we bring ol' Bruno."

"Who's Bruno?"

"He's my sheepdog. If he knows you want the sheep to keep still, he's the one to make 'em do it. All he has to do is bare his teeth and they'll be like statues."

"You think Bruno will understand what I want him to do."

"Sure, he will. He's right smart. You want I should bring some goats too? Aaron's been bottle-raisin' a good-lookin' little ram. He figures on showing him at the county fair next year."

Angie did a quick mental count of the livestock—a zonkey, a cow and calf, a couple of sheep, and a large hairy dog. "No, I think what you've already offered will do."

"Yeah, I think so, too," Junior agreed. "Any more critters and nobody'll see the baby."

"And that's kind of important."

"Kinda? It's the whole dadgum point." Junior jammed his

cap back on his head. "If it wasn't for Baby Jesus, we wouldn't have Christmas now, would we?"

Angela nodded. It was easy to get caught up in the details of the pageant and forget the main thing. But there were so many details . . .

"Well, if that's all, I'd best get. Darlene takes on something fierce if I'm late for supper." Junior headed for the door, but stopped short. "It's getting a mite dark out. You want I should walk you out to your car, Miss Holloway?"

"No, I'm waiting for one more cast member to come. I'll be fine."

She was also waiting for Seth. They'd met for breakfast at the Green Apple that morning and he'd driven her to school. While she was meeting with a few of their chosen cast members in her classroom, Seth was trying to recruit Dr. Gonncu to be one of the magi even though he hadn't auditioned. Still, Angie thought he'd be perfect. The math professor had a dignity and stately bearing that would bring a regal touch to the pageant. Since she'd committed a faux pas at their first meeting by offering to shake his hand, she thought Seth might have more luck convincing him.

"He's not a Christian," Seth had said when she'd first suggested it.

"Nobody at the first Christmas was a Christian either," Angie had countered. "And Muslims regard Jesus as a prophet, so His birth would be important to them, too. Do your best to convince him."

She really hoped Dr. Gonncu would agree. Not that she was a fan of diversity for diversity's sake, but she wanted the pageant to represent every aspect of the community, including those who hadn't grown up in the area.

She'd been surprised when Asher Elkin, the stoop-shouldered, bespectacled owner of the small bookstore on the Square, had come to audition. The Jewish shopkeeper had told her out-right that he wanted to be one of the wise men.

"You see," he'd said, "my people are still waiting for the Messiah to come. Why shouldn't I play a soul who seeks him?"

It made sense to Angie and she was thrilled that Mr. Elkin had read well and, like Dr. Gonncu, would lend an air of grav-ity to the proceedings. She was sure Junior and his menagerie would deliver all the comic relief they'd ever need. Casting Mr. Elkin made even more sense when Seth told her a little about the bookstore owner after the audition was over.

"He loves Christmastime, and not just because it's good for business. I think it's the lights and decorations and family gath-ering and such," Seth had said. "In fact, he helped my parents keep the secret of Santa Clause going long after my friends stopped believing."

"How'd he do that?"

"Mr. Elkin has lived next door to my folks for years. My dad would often pop over on Saturdays to do things for him. He used to call my dad his *Shabbos goy,*" Seth had told her.

"What's that?"

"It's Yiddish for a non-Jew who does work on the Sabbath that an observant Jew can't. I thought my dad was a pretty good guy just doing those things out of the goodness of his heart until I learned he had a secret deal with Mr. Elkin."

"What kind of deal?"

"They worked out an arrangement so that when our fam-ily took off for the Christmas Eve service at church, Mr. Elkin was supposed to let himself in the back door." Seth had smiled that crooked smile of his at the memory. "My mom had told him where all our presents were stashed, and he played Santa for us by arranging everything under the tree so it would be there when we got home from church."

"That's a piece of evil genius." Angie hadn't ever believed

in Santa Claus. By the time she was moved to a home where her foster parents played along with the yearly ruse, there had been too many years in her past when she'd never had a Christmas. There'd been nothing in her stocking too often to believe in a jolly old elf. "Your parents are kind of sneaky."

"Yeah, but it was fun," Seth had said with a grin. "Even when I was eight and Tommy Thompson swore up and down that Santa Claus was really just our moms and dads, I was ready to knock him in the creek. I had the evidence of my own eyes. Neither of my folks ever left the Christmas Eve service early. They couldn't be Santa."

Maintaining such an elaborate fantasy for a kid struck Angie as questionable parenting, but the ruse was reinforced by the entire culture. And it had meant something to Seth when he was a boy. Now that he was grown, he appreciated the lengths the adults in his life had been willing to go to keep the magical side of the holiday alive as long as they could.

But what's more magical than the idea of God becoming a human being?

Angie was a little surprised at the number of times she'd had what she was beginning to call "God thoughts" lately. She was an indifferent churchgoer, making it to service maybe once a month. She chalked up these "God thoughts" to all the time she had to spend researching the Christmas story and its traditions.

When Seth had told her about his parents' scheme with Mr. Elkin, she thought they sounded like they'd be fun to know and she'd made the mistake of saying so. He immediately jumped on the idea of taking her over to his mom and dad's for dinner on Sunday.

She'd begged off. It seemed far too soon to meet the parents.

She loved being with Seth. He was terrific, actually. But

she'd fallen hard and fast with Peter. She was determined not to repeat that mistake. In fact, she always made sure they said good night at her door.

Seth's kisses were still hot enough to make her toes curl, but she sent him on his way before she unlocked her apartment. She wasn't sure she could trust herself to make him leave if she let him in. Angie ran her fingertips over her bottom lip.

A soft rap on the frame of her classroom door jerked her out of her "Seth thoughts," and made her look up. Emma Wilson was there, leaning on the doorjamb as if she wasn't sure whether she wanted to come in or go out.

"You wanted to see me, Miss Holloway?"

"Oh, good. Come on in, Emma." She was the last of the cast members Angie was planning to meet with that evening. Then Seth was taking her someplace special, but he wouldn't tell her where. It was a surprise, he'd said.

She couldn't wait.

But Emma apparently could. The girl lingered in the doorway, her eyes averted, her lower lip trembling. "I . . . I can't stay. I just came to tell you I can't be in the pageant, Miss Holloway."

"But I've already cast you as Mary."

At this news, Emma burst into tears.

Chapter 20

Beautiful mistakes happen.

—Angela Holloway

Angie flew across the room and, against her usual inclination to avoid physical contact, she put her arms around the weeping teenager. Emma clung to her, sobbing as if the world were ending.

"Come now," Angie said, patting her back. "It can't be as bad as all that."

"Oh, yes, it can. Worse, even." Emma snuffled loudly as she let Angie lead her over to a desk on the first row. Angie handed her a tissue and the waterworks subsided a bit.

"Did you and Tad break up?" Angie hoped so. Emma deserved better.

"No, but we will. He'll dump me for sure this time." Emma's eyes filled again. "I'm pregnant."

How many times had a young girl's life been changed forever with those two words?

It was usually the kiss of death for her education. So many girls dropped out of school because they were embarrassed by the changes in their body or felt tired all the time or suffered from morning sickness when they ought to be in Algebra class.

Or they opted to abort the baby and go on with their lives. Sort of. Angie had done a paper on it for one of her graduate classes. Teens who'd had an abortion were much more likely than their peers to abuse alcohol and drugs, probably to self-medicate their depression. Compared to adult women who'd had abortions, girls in Emma's situation who chose to abort were two to four times more likely to attempt suicide later.

"Tad doesn't know yet. He's gonna freak when I tell him. And then it'll be over for good." Emma blew her nose loudly.

"Maybe not." Even as she said it, she knew it was a kind lie. If the conversation Angie had overheard between them in the Green Apple was any indication, Tad Van Hook had already left Emma Wilson. She simply refused to pick up on the signals of benign indifference he'd lobbed halfheartedly in her direction. "Have you told your parents?"

Emma shook her head. "I can't."

"You should. They'd want to know."

"Not about this they won't." She studied her scuffed boots with absorption. "My folks have trouble enough of their own. They split up last month. Dad's in Muskogee with his new girlfriend. Mom is . . . well, she's sort of a mess right now, trying to hold it together for me and my little brother and sister."

Angie's heart ached for the whole family. "What do *you* want to do?"

"I want to go back in time and not get pregnant," Emma said softly. Then she met Angie's gaze directly. "I don't know what I want to do now. Tad will want me to get rid of it."

It. Angie was a stickler about the specific meaning of words and their misuse always annoyed her. "It" was so impersonal. The pronoun was used for a thing or maybe an animal if you didn't know the sex of the beast. Not for a person, no matter how small and incompletely formed.

"You're the one who gets to make that decision, not Tad," Angela told her. "You shouldn't let him pressure you one way or the other."

Emma swiped her eyes with the backs of her hands. "What would you do, Miss Holloway?"

Angela blinked in surprise that Emma would ask her such

a personal question. To be honest, she'd had a pregnancy scare of her own once. Her period had been a week late, but it turned out to be just stress from the all-nighters she'd pulled to prepare for finals. She was incredibly relieved when the test stick showed only one pink line. At the time she'd been finishing up her freshman year and had miles to go before she earned her degree.

A baby would have put everything she was working for on hold, but she knew she'd never abandon a child to the system. Somehow, with or without Peter's help, she'd have kept the baby.

She was grateful she hadn't had to broach that topic with him. The question was moot anyway. He'd broken it off with her the very next week, never knowing what a narrow escape he'd had with fatherhood.

"I don't think I can answer your question," Angie told her. "It's the sort of decision you can't make until you're faced with it. And I can't make it for you. No one can. I can only help you consider all your options."

Emma sighed. "If I decide to have this baby, I'll have to quit school."

"No, you won't." In the middle of the last century, girls who were found to be pregnant, but not the boys who helped them become that way, were summarily expelled from high school as a deterrent to others. Angie thought the policy was ridiculous when she first read about it.

As if a pregnant girl could get another one pregnant!

"Maybe not this year, but if I keep the baby, I'll have to quit school next year. I'd have to stay home to take care of it." Emma's brows drew together in a frown and she began fidgeting with her hands. "My mom has to work. Especially now that Dad's lit out. And I'd have to find a job, too, something at night so maybe Mom can watch the baby. If she will. You think she will?"

However the child had come into the world, Emma's baby would still be Mrs. Wilson's grandchild. A newborn was a bit of the divine, sent to remind the world there was always hope. At least, that's how Angela had always felt. How she thought everyone *should* feel.

Some of her foster parents hadn't.

But surely Mrs. Wilson would help her daughter care for the baby.

"That's one of the things you need to talk over with your mom." Angela gave her an assessing look. Emma's eyes were not only listless; there were dark circles under them no amount of concealer could hide. She probably hadn't slept in a while. The girl was clearly overwhelmed and needed the support of someone who loved her. Angie fervently hoped her mother would be that someone. "Look, you don't have to make all the decisions now."

"I do, if I want to have an abortion," Emma snapped.

"And if you do, you have to get your parents' permission. You shouldn't make all these decisions alone. How old are you Emma?"

"Fifteen, but I'll be sixteen next May."

Younger than the age of consent. "How old is Tad?" If he was eighteen, he could be in serious trouble.

"He'll be eighteen in a couple of weeks."

Just skated by a possible statutory rape charge.

"Tad can't be somebody's father. He's going to college on a basketball scholarship. It's all he talks about. If I'm gonna have an abortion, I need to do it quick. Right now, I can just take a pill, or maybe two, instead of having surgery." Her lips drew into a tight line. "We learned about it in health class."

There was more involved in a medical abortion than just taking a couple of pills. It would mean cramps from hell and bleeding for weeks, and if Emma waited until she was at ten weeks gestation, there was a chance she'd recognize the grape-sized shape of a baby in the tissue her body rejected. But Angela was trying to keep her opinions on Emma's options carefully neutral.

"You still don't need to rush to a decision. Whatever you decide, it's not something to be chosen lightly," Angie said, trying to project calm for Emma's sake. Inside, she was heartsick for her. "Every decision in life is a fork in the road. Every new choice puts you on a different path from the one you've been traveling. A door closes behind you, but new ones open."

It's just a pity so many life-changing choices hit us when we're too young, too trusting, and too stupid to realize how important they are.

"Well, my old choices weren't good. I certainly made the wrong one with Tad."

Angela took this as a positive sign. Emma was beginning to evaluate things realistically. Teenagers didn't do that very often. It gave her hope for the girl.

"It takes two to make a baby," Angie reminded her. "Don't lay all the blame on yourself."

"Everyone else will."

Oh, how I hate the "boys will be boys" mentality. "Not everyone. I don't."

"You're not from around here, Miss Holloway."

And if Angie lived in Coldwater Cove till she died, she still wouldn't be from around there. Small towns were like that.

Her cell phone rang and Seth's number flashed on the caller ID screen.

"Go ahead and take it if you want," Emma said, rising from her seat.

Angie shook her head and let the call go to voice mail. Emma's problem was urgent. Seth would wait.

"No, just a minute, Emma. I still want you to be Mary in the pageant," she told the girl.

"I couldn't."

"You gave the best audition, hands down. This baby doesn't

change that. And honestly, I think you know better than most how Mary must have been feeling at first."

Jesus's mother, too, had been young, and probably scared, despite her great faith. In biblical times, Mary might have faced much worse than unkind gossip from those around her. She might have been stoned to death if Joseph hadn't been a just man.

Too bad Tad was an irresponsible, self-involved kid.

"Yeah, but I didn't get an angel visitation. And it's kind of obvious I'm not a virgin," Emma said wryly.

"That may well be what Mary's neighbors thought about her, too. Maybe that's why she went to visit her cousin Elizabeth right away. She needed to see some family. Come on. I'll give you a ride home."

"All right." Emma stood and followed her out of the classroom, her boots shuffling along on the polished vinyl flooring. "You know you might get into trouble for casting me as Mary. Folks won't like it."

Emma was probably right. Angela hadn't even considered how the folks of Coldwater Cove might react to an unwed pregnant teenager as Mary. Since Angie had accepted the assignment, she'd fretted on and off about how her Christmas pageant would be received, and whether she was making too many changes in the town's tradition for its residents to absorb.

Suddenly, she didn't care what anyone else thought. Emma had given the best audition. She deserved to be Mary, no matter who didn't like it.

"You let me worry about what people think about that, Emma." She decided not to add, *You've got enough on your plate.*

Angie's phone went to voice mail again. Seth was starting to worry. It wasn't like her not to pick up. He started to punch in her number again, but figured if she *was* ignoring him on purpose, she'd just ignore him again. For the life of him, he couldn't think of anything he'd done wrong.

Lately.

A few days ago, he'd rushed her about meeting his folks. He knew it as soon as the words were out of his mouth. She'd seemed to shrink away from him. It was like watching a little turtle retreat back into its shell.

"What's eatin' you, Seth?" Lester asked as he straightened the silverware at the table Seth had asked the old veteran to set up in the sunroom of his ranch house. Because of Lester's experience waiting tables at the Green Apple, Seth had hired him to serve the catered meal that evening. Having once been a homeless alcoholic, but now clean and sober and reunited with his wife, Lester was always looking for ways to earn extra cash. Seth was happy to oblige.

"Nothing's eating me. I'm just wondering when Angie's getting home so I can go pick her up," Seth said, hoping tonight would go as planned. He had a lot riding on it.

If meeting his family was too hard, maybe Angie would be more comfortable with the part of Seth's world that didn't involve people. He'd decided to bring her to his home for the first time. It was situated on forty arable acres just outside of town. Seth had built himself a brick residence with an open floor plan and low horizontal lines, reminiscent of Frank Lloyd Wright's prairie homes. Snugged in the elevated oxbow of a meandering seasonal river, the house seemed to blend in with the bluffs and trees around it.

He'd been to Angie's place countless times. Even before they became a couple, he'd learned so much about her just from seeing what she surrounded herself with and how she lived in her apartment.

Angela kept her small space scrupulously clean. She craved order and loved books. One evening when he helped her bring in her groceries, Seth had caught her alphabetizing the cans in her pantry. She claimed it was on account of laziness. She didn't want to have to hunt through everything for a can of chicken soup. If it wasn't in the space where it was supposed to be, she knew she didn't have one.

Others might have said that quirk was a little OCD, but he thought it was adorable.

Seth wondered what his place would tell Angela about him.

During their dinner tonight, he planned to return the copy of *Sense and Sensibility* to her. He would also confess that he'd read it cover to cover, but he was more than a little confused by the ending. Willoughby didn't really get his in the end. After seducing one woman after another, that waste of skin was challenged to a duel yet lived to tell the tale. Then he got to marry an heiress.

And Seth wasn't completely sure Colonel Brandon, the character he most closely identified with, ended up with the right Dashwood sister.

Judging from Angie's scribbles in the margins, she wasn't so sure either.

Anyway, in the novel, the ladies were always suitably impressed by a man of property. Seth figured it wouldn't hurt his chances to let Angie see his answer to Delaford, Colonel Brandon's country estate.

His hand strayed to his pocket, where a small jewelry case rested.

Savory aromas from the meal they were going to share filled the sunroom. Seth had chosen to have Lester set up the table there instead of using the big dining room. The sunroom was more intimate, a smaller, yet more expansive space due to all the south-facing glass. It was still warm from the afternoon sun—an important consideration because Angie always seemed to be cold—but being a sunroom, you felt as if you were outside, which was important to Seth. He did most of his work outside. It felt right to him.

The shadow of the bluffs lengthened, throwing the landscape into shades of deep mauve and warm gray. Later, after they'd eaten, Seth would blow out the candles and they'd watch the stars wheel overhead through the big skylights.

Then, if the evening was going as well as he hoped, he'd take out the ring.

He checked his watch. Surely Angie was home by now. He pulled out his cell phone and called.

It went immediately to voice mail again.

What if, instead of ignoring him, she'd been in an accident? Maybe she was lying by the side of the road or in a hospital bed unable to speak because she was in a coma, or—

Stow it, Parker. You're being melodramatic. That's what you get when you spend too much time with an Austen novel.

Angie was probably in the shower.

Cheered by his imaginings of Angela all wet and soapy, he called out to Lester. "I'm gonna go pick her up. Keep everything warm."

Chapter 21

Screw one, screw all. It's the American way.
At least, it is if you're a lawyer.

—Seth Parker's opinion of
Peter Manning's profession

A sleek little roadster was parked in the small lot behind Angie's building. Seth didn't recognize it. There was no one in town who drove such an expensive car. Of course, his truck was pretty high dollar, what with all the bells and whistles and the heavy-duty towing package he'd had added on, but it was also a work horse of a vehicle. Not only would it haul whatever he needed, it served as his mobile office.

Seth couldn't imagine the roadster being good for any business purpose. At least no business in Coldwater Cove.

And who'd be stupid enough to drive it with the top down at the end of November?

He also didn't see Angie's car, but he figured she might have parked on the Square and gone up to her place using the long dark stairwell from the street. She didn't do it often, so he hadn't even been looking for her white Kia when he'd rounded the courthouse.

"You know that thing looks like a Storm Trooper's helmet going down the road," he'd told her when she first showed it to him. She'd stuck her tongue out at him. He figured she wasn't a *Star Wars* fan and didn't get the reference.

He was wrong.

"Maybe it does look like a space helmet," she'd finally admitted. "But it's more like *Doctor Who*'s TARDIS. My Kia's bigger on the inside than it is on the outside."

Angela was one of those rare females who understood both *Star Wars* and *Doctor Who*.

No wonder he loved her.

I love Angie Holloway.

He was still trying to wrap his head around the idea. Not that he wasn't absolutely convinced it was true. Just that he'd never thought it would happen to him so fast.

Or so completely.

He took the wrought-iron steps at the back of Angie's building two at a time. When he reached the top deck, his chest tightened. There were no lights on in her place. He rapped on the door anyway.

"She's not there," came a voice from the darkness.

In the dimness, Seth hadn't noticed the guy sitting on Angie's wicker settee. The man stood. Seth couldn't make out his features, but he recognized the voice.

"Manning."

"Good. You remember my name," the guy said. "I seem to have misplaced yours."

"It's Parker. Seth Parker."

"Good to see you, Parker. Hail the mighty spider killer and all that." Manning held out his hand to shake. Seth didn't take it.

For half a second, he thought about trying to be civil to Manning because he knew Angie would want him to. But this jerk had hurt her badly. He didn't deserve civil.

"Can't say it's good to see you again," Seth said. "That your roadster down there?

Peter smiled. The sly expression reminded Seth of a coyote after a kill. His teeth must have been bleached because they glowed in the dark a little. "I have one like it back in DC. I'm used to the power and speed, so I rented the same model in Tulsa for the drive down here."

"Hmph." Seth peered over the balcony railing at the car. "Kinda girly, isn't it?"

"It'd beat your truck in a race."

"Yeah, but my truck could squish your car like a grape. What are you doing here?"

"Come on, man. That should be obvious, even to a knuckle dragger like you," Manning said, all pretense of politeness gone. "I'm here to see Ange."

"Her name is Angela."

"Not to me."

Seth folded his arms over his chest. "She's nothing to you."

"Maybe not at present, but she used to be." Manning's grin was clearly designed to annoy. Seth itched to knock it off his face. "You can't deny I was there first."

"Watch your mouth."

"Or what?"

Seth bared his own teeth in an expression no one would mistake for a smile. "Or I'll break your jaw and it'll be wired shut for a month."

"Threatening a lawyer is probably not your smartest move."

Seth noticed Manning took a step back anyway. "It's not a threat. It's a promise. Stay away from Angela."

Manning cocked his head and narrowed his eyes, but he was careful to remain out of arm's reach. "She's a big girl, Parker. She can see anyone she pleases."

"She won't want to see you."

"She will. We parted on friendly terms last time," Manning said, and then added in a voice laced with innuendo, "very friendly."

Seth shook his head. "Not so much, I'm thinkin'. You took

her to dinner, sure. But then you slinked out of town without trying to see her again."

"Always leave 'em wanting more. That's my motto. But I'm back now."

"And I'm wondering why." Seth took another step toward him, but this time Manning didn't back away.

"That is none of your business."

"I'm making it my business." Seth glared at him and Manning glared back.

Just when Seth decided he wouldn't be able to keep from knocking the guy into next week, Manning's instinct for self-preservation must have kicked in. Peter dropped his gaze.

"You may want to hang out here waiting for Ange to show up, but I have better things to do," Manning said. "But don't worry, Parker, I'll see her soon."

Manning headed down the iron staircase, hopped into his roadster without opening the car door, and roared off into the night.

That's why he leaves the top down. So he can vault into the dang thing like some Olympic gymnast.

That move might impress the ladies in DC, but around Coldwater Cove, women were more likely to wonder if the car door was stuck.

Seth was glad to see the back side of the guy, but he was still worried about Angela's whereabouts. It wasn't like her to simply disappear. He was about to put in a call to the hospital to see if Angie had been admitted when a light came on in her kitchen.

Relief flooded Seth's chest. She must have come up the front way. He pounded the door harder than he meant to.

The sound of lowered voices and the scrabbling of soles on the hardwood came from inside. Seth heard an interior door slamming shut. Then the back door opened just an inch or two and Angie peered at him through the crack.

"Oh! Seth, I'm sorry. I forgot you were coming to get me."
She forgot? The ring in his pocket suddenly weighed a ton.

"I can't make it tonight," she said. "Something unexpected
has come up."

Who's in there with her? "What's going on?"

"I can't tell you. I'm sorry."

"Yeah, you said you were sorry already, but I'm not buying it."

He'd planned the perfect evening. He picked the right
wine to go with her favorite dish, lobster tails. Seafood did
nothing for Seth. He was more turf than surf, but he knew it
would please her out of all knowing. There'd be soft jazz on
the house-wide stereo system and once the stars began their
dance across the heavens, the sunroom would be as romantic as
Angie could wish.

Now everything was unraveling.

"Manning's back in town," Seth said, his tone gruffer than
he'd intended, but he couldn't seem to rein it in. "Are you
blowing me off to be with him?"

"What? No." Her brows arched in surprise. "Peter's in
town?"

"Caught him sniffing around on your deck a minute ago,"
Seth said, wishing he'd laid the guy out when he had the
chance. "As if you didn't know."

"I did not." She narrowed her dark eyes. "Of what are you
accusing me?"

Uh-oh. Perfectly proper syntax. She'd taught him what syntax
meant the other day. He already knew when her inner grammar gremlin popped out and she started talking like an Austen
heroine, she was seriously ticked off.

"Nothing. I'm not accusing you of anything. But what am
I supposed to think when I find the guy camped out on your
deck?"

"I had no idea Peter was in town, let alone here at my
place," she said emphatically, her shoulders tense.

"You sorry you missed him?"

"No." Then her shoulders relaxed and she sighed. "Look, Seth, I said I'm sorry I have to cancel on you and I mean it. I was really looking forward to tonight, but sometimes . . . things happen that you can't control."

Now that she was softening toward him, he felt more hopeful. "Aren't you going to let me in?"

"No."

"There's someone else in your apartment." It wasn't a question.

She didn't bother denying it. "Well, it's not Peter, that's for sure. Look, you have to trust me."

He hated to admit it, but she was right. If they didn't have trust in each other, they didn't have anything. "Okay. At least, tell me what's going on."

"I can't, Seth. It's . . . it's not my secret to tell."

"So it is a secret."

"For now. If I can, I'll explain later. I'm really truly sorry about tonight." She put a hand on his chest and he covered it with one of his own. "Whatever you had planned for us, I'm sure it would have been wonderful, but for now, just let it go, will you?"

"I might," he said as he leaned on the doorjamb, "if you give me a kiss."

Her eyes flashed to the left as if she were checking to see whoever was in the apartment with her. Then she stood on tiptoe and gave him a quick peck on the lips.

"You call that a kiss?" he said.

"It's all the kiss you're getting tonight." Then she pushed the door closed. Gently, but firmly.

"So, you and Mr. Parker, huh?" Emma rounded the corner from the living room and joined her in the kitchen.

"I thought I told you to stay in the bedroom."

"And miss all the action at your back door? No way, Ms. H."

"It's not nice to eavesdrop," Angie told her primly. She'd hoped the girl would stay put while she dealt with Seth. Not only did she want to keep her love life from the curious eyes of her student, but she didn't want Seth to know she was harboring something of a fugitive.

Emma's mother had kicked her out of the house.

"You're probably right," the teenager admitted. "Maybe it wasn't nice for me to listen, seeing as how you're taking me in and all, but it sure was fun. So, how long you two been together?"

"Not long."

"But long enough, I bet. Good on you, Ms. H.!" Emma twirled a lock of her hair around her finger. "Mr. Parker might be kinda old, but he's still pretty hot."

"Kind of old?"

"Well, yeah. He's gotta be, what? At least thirty, right?"

Angie shrugged. She hadn't ever asked his age, but she supposed he was in his early thirties. On the right side of thirty-five, at least. The Big Three-Oh was looming large on her horizon, too.

"You gonna marry him?"

"I don't know. He hasn't asked." Most of her friends from college were already married with children. Even Heather, her best friend in Coldwater Cove, was happily settled with her dot-com king of a husband, Michael Evans.

After Peter, Angie had figured she'd never marry. It was too risky to put all your emotional eggs in one guy's basket. But she was starting to rethink that.

"Why don't you ask him to marry you?" Emma suggested with grin. "Women can do that now."

Okay. Time to steer the subject away from me and Seth. "Is that what you're considering, Emma? Asking Tad to marry you?

Emma rolled her eyes. "I guess I'm thinking about it. I

mean, he'll graduate before the baby's born. He could get a job instead of going to college. Getting married would solve a lot of problems."

And cause a bunch of new ones. Angie kept quiet and willed her expression into one of careful neutrality. She could help Emma explore her options, but she couldn't advocate for a particular outcome. She was already breaking several rules by bringing Emma into her home.

"But if I do ask Tad to marry me," Emma went on, working things out as she spoke, "and if he says yes, I'll never know if it's because he loves me or because he feels trapped by the baby."

Oh, trust me, honey, he doesn't love you, Angie thought but would never say.

Emma plopped down onto the kitchen barstool. "I don't know what I'll do. Do I have to tell him?"

"Legally, probably not." Finally, a question she could answer. "But don't you think he should know? If he won't help you, perhaps his family will."

The Van Hooks were pretty well off. If Tad wouldn't take responsibility, his parents might step up for the sake of their unborn grandchild. Emma's family had punted her into the street.

Emma's forehead was creased by more worry lines than a kid her age should have.

"You want some ice cream?" Angie asked, hoping to cheer Emma up.

Her face brightened. "You got chocolate?"

"No, just vanilla, but there's some Hershey's syrup in the pantry."

"Now you're talking."

Angie dipped up two bowlfuls and split a banana between them. It wasn't exactly health food, but Emma was looking a little thin for a mom-to-be. After the ice cream, Angie would try to get a real meal down her. If she'd been thinking, she ought to have reversed those things, but just the mention of ice cream had clearly lifted Emma's spirits. That was more important than the food pyramid just now.

"Thanks, Ms. H.," she said as she dived into her bowl of icy sweetness. "And thanks for letting me stay here."

"No problem. The couch pulls out into a bed. And it's just temporary until everything gets sorted out."

Angie probably should have called the authorities. Emma was technically a minor. But she didn't want to get Emma's mother in trouble for kicking her daughter out of the house. Mrs. Wilson had problems of her own, but maybe she'd come around after she had time to think about her daughter's situation. Angie hoped Emma would be able to return home within a couple of days.

And besides, if Angela had called Child Protective Services, Emma would be placed in emergency foster care. It might be a good situation or foster care might make matters worse. Given her own experience with the system, Angie didn't want to chance it.

"Have you told anyone else about the baby?" Angela asked. "Friends, maybe?"

Emma shook her head. "Just you and my mom."

"Maybe you should keep it that way for a while, until you decide what to do," Angela said. "Except for your doctor."

"Why do I need to see a doctor?"

"Well, sometimes a home pregnancy test gives a false positive," Angie said, mentally kicking herself for not suggesting this first. If a doctor's test showed Emma wasn't pregnant, she would have upset herself and her mother over nothing.

Emma put down her spoon. "You think I might not be preggers?"

"It's a possibility."

"Okay. How do I get set up with a doctor? If I'm sick, Mom just takes me to urgent care to see whatever nurse practitioner is there."

She should have known Emma wouldn't have a regular family doctor. "I'll call my friend Heather. She works at Coldwater General. She'll know where you should go. If I ask her to keep it quiet, do I have your permission to share your situation with her?"

Emma sighed. "Why not? If I'm really pregnant, it's not like I'll be able to hide it for long."

Chapter 22

The Coldwater Cove Beautification Society announces its Annual Christmas Lights Contest. Displays will be judged on originality and holiday theme. How high the homeowner's utility bill goes as a result of the display is not a deciding factor.

—*The Coldwater Gazette.* The last bit was added specifically for George Evans, who nailed his electric bill, surrounded by twinkle lights, to one of his oak trees last year

"Glad you called to meet me for breakfast. I haven't heard from you since I dropped the pageant in your lap. I was afraid you were still mad at me." Heather Walker Evans slid into the booth across from Angie. It was a quarter to six, so the Green Apple Grill was mostly empty except for people like Heather who worked an early shift, and Angie who needed to be at the high school before her students. The usual breakfast rush didn't start until around seven and the retiree coffee crowd didn't turn up until after eight. "Does this mean you forgive me for forcing you into doing the pageant?"

"Yes." Against all expectation, organizing the pageant had been a net positive in Angie's life. She was happier, and more engaged with more people, but there was no denying the real cherry on top. Meeting Seth Parker. There was always a chance that she might have met him another way, but they hadn't hit it off immediately. She wouldn't call it instant dislike, but they certainly hadn't clicked like magnets at first. If they hadn't been forced to work together, they probably would've given each other a wide berth after that initial meeting. "I've definitely forgiven you."

"Good," Heather said, "because if you'd said no, I'd have to remind you that Seth Parker is by far the best guy I've set you up with since you came here."

"So it was a setup."

A grin stretched across Heather's face. "Of course."

Angie grinned back at her. "Thank you."

"That's what friends are for."

Ethel Ringwald hustled up to their booth and filled their coffee cups without asking if they wanted any.

"Where's Lester this morning?" Angie asked her.

"He's helpin' out in the kitchen for a change. Yesterday, when he was bussing tables, he dropped a whole stack of plates and broke every single one." A metallic clatter shot out from the rear of the Grill. "Never you mind that, girls. Lester stacks the pots wrong more often than not. Now he gets to wash them all again, but at least he'd have to act with malice aforethought to break one. Say! Laura put some cinnamon rolls in the oven this morning."

"So that's the bit of heaven I smell," Angie said. "I'll take one please."

"You'll take two," Ethel told her with mock sternness. "How are you going to keep warm out there if you don't fill up in here?"

Angie didn't argue with Ethel. No one did. Especially when Ethel told her customers they *deserved* a slice of pie because they'd cleaned their plates. Even if they objected, she brought them one anyway. The pie seldom went begging.

Forget about "suggestive selling." Ethel sold by decree.

Heather asked for the Hypocrite's Vegetarian Omelet. Lester's brainchild had become a Green Apple staple and had earned a permanent place on the laminated menus. Then Ethel headed back to the kitchen with their order, topping off coffee cups at a few other tables as she went.

"So how's the pageant going?" Heather asked.

"Fine. Well, almost fine. We're having a little trouble with the cast." Angie told her how well Emma Wilson, one of her freshman English students, had read the part of Mary. "But there's a problem."

"I'm not hearing one yet."

"Emma's pregnant."

Heather's lips formed a perfect "oh." "Is she still going to play Mary?"

"Yes, devil take the hindermost," Angie said defiantly.

"You'll get no argument from me." Heather held up her hands in surrender. "But there are those in town who won't take kindly to an unwed pregnant teenager as Mary."

"Then they need to read their Bibles a little closer." Granted the means of conception was different, but the Virgin must have faced the same threat of shame as Emma. "Besides, Emma just found out she's expecting. Chances are good the pageant will be long past before anyone else can tell."

"Ah, but 'telling' is something we excel at here in Coldwater. Emma told you. You told me. I'm guessing her family knows."

Angie nodded.

"And the FOB?"

FOB. Father of Baby. "Not yet."

"But when he does, this thing could snowball pretty quick. I'll support you in casting her as Mary, but you'd better expect some backlash."

Angie sighed. "That's the least of my worries. I want to help Emma if I can. So far, her family isn't up to the challenge, but I'm hoping that will change. In the meantime, I need whatever medical advice you can give me for her," Angie said, then added, "Bear in mind, she has no health insurance as far as I know."

"Let me see what I can do. There are a number of programs and organizations that offer help in this situation," Heather said.

"She knew you were going to talk to me?"

"Of course. Permission asked and given."

"Then give me her number and I'll make time to talk with her directly," Heather said. "There are privacy regs to consider if I'm doling out medical advice."

Angie took out her phone and shot her friend a text with Emma's contact info. She was only too happy to punt this part of her student's dilemma. Heather was a knowledgeable RN who'd make sure Emma found good medical care.

Of course, that left Angie with the formidable challenge of finding a place for Emma to live if her mom didn't change her mind and let her come home. If Angie let Emma stay with her, she'd be dealing with teenage drama made even more angsty by the fact that there really was something to dramatize this time.

Ethel returned with their order and the friends tucked into their breakfasts, making only a little small talk between bites. Angie knew Heather had to be at the hospital before her shift started at seven. Besides, Angie was expecting to meet another potential pageant cast member at the Grill around seven. It was Crystal Addleberry. She didn't want Heather to know Angie had asked her sister-in-law to participate in the pageant unless Crystal agreed.

Heather could be as dogged as Ethel when she thought she knew what was best for someone else. Angie didn't think Crystal could bear any more pressure than she was already under. She didn't need Heather pushing her to agree to be in the pageant.

"Now, tell me about you and Seth," Heather demanded with a sly smile. "You didn't like any of the other guys I set you up with, but this time I did good, right?"

Angie sighed. "You did."

"Okay, give. What's going on with you two?"

"The man makes my toes curl."

"Oooh! Toe curling is good. What else?"

"Well, we're together all the time." Last evening was the first one they'd spent apart since the night they went to the Regal to see *The African Queen*.

Heather chased the last of her hash browns around her plate with a biscuit. "So you like the same things? You two have a lot in common?"

Angie frowned. "I don't know that we do actually. He's not much of a reader, so we don't talk books, but we seem not to run out of things to say." Angie hadn't ever thought about whether they had common interests before. A niggling itch of doubt started in her chest. "Oh, no."

"What?"

"I was just thinking," Angie said. "Seth and I spend a lot of our time together working on the pageant and talking about it. What if once it's done, we have no reason to be with each other because we don't have anything in common after all?"

"But it's not all the pageant all the time with you two, is it?"

"No." She'd told Seth things she'd never told anyone. She'd shared her hurts and he'd made them better. But now that she thought about it, he hadn't told her much about what went on inside him. "I guess we're still getting to know each other, but even when I'm not with him, I can't stop thinking about him."

"That's a good sign." Heather eyed her critically, as if trying to diagnose her condition. "You know, there is something to the saying that opposites attract. Michael and I don't agree all the time. He's always telling me that if we don't have different points of view and different interests, then one of us is unnecessary in the marriage."

"That makes sense, I guess." At least Heather hadn't asked what Angie sensed behind her questioning gaze.

Do you love him?

If she did ask, Angie wasn't sure how to answer. Seth made her feel things she thought she never would. And even better, she trusted him, or at least thought she could. In all ways that mattered, he wasn't a bit like Peter.

And that was good.

Of course, she'd suffered from really bad judgment when she'd given her heart away the first time. What if she did it again, and it was the wrong thing to do?

When you give your heart away, it never comes back entirely whole. Do it enough times and there's nothing left.

Fortunately, Heather didn't ask the question.

"Michael and I have been married for about a year. In a lot of ways, we're still getting to know each other," she said. "But that's what makes it exciting. There's always more to learn about your spouse."

"What if you don't like what you learn?"

"I don't have to like it. But I do have to love Michael. I promised I would. It's part of the deal."

But sometimes deals get broken.

Heather checked her watch. She knew better than to go by the big clock hanging on the wall. Green Apple time was always about ten minutes behind the rest of the world.

On purpose.

"I gotta go," she said. "Keep me up to speed on the Seth front, and I'll keep you in the loop about Emma as much as I can."

"Sounds good," Angie said as Heather counted out enough cash to cover both their breakfasts along with a handsome tip, which she left beside her empty plate. Angie didn't object to her friend picking up the tab. As a thriving dot-com owner, Heather's husband had more money than God.

But it didn't stop his wife from rising to take the early shift at the hospital. Heather had a good bead on what was important in life. Being humble, useful, and helping others was at the top of her list. It was part of what drew Angie into her circle of friends and into the Warm Hearts Club.

Of course, sometimes Heather's helpfulness came in the form of some pretty dismal setups. But Angie forgave her for those early attempts at fixing her up with someone. Heather had knocked the ball out of the park when she'd arranged for Angie and Seth to be forced to work together.

Angie wasn't sure what would come of their relationship. All she knew was that every time she thought about Seth, her insides did a happy little cartwheel.

The bells over the Green Apple door jingled and someone whose insides hadn't done a cartwheel in a long time came in.

Crystal Addleberry.

Chapter 23

Perfect is the enemy of good. It doesn't
make sense, but it's often so.

—George Evans, retired lawyer who counseled
more divorcing couples than he cares to recall
because one of them knew exactly how their life
together was supposed to be and the other
couldn't bear how it was

Angie waved her over. "Hi, Crystal. Thanks for meeting me here."

"I can't stay long."

"Me neither." She planned to make it to the high school by a quarter to eight, early enough to beat her freshman English students into the building. One of her kids likely wouldn't make it by then. When she'd left her apartment that morning, Emma had been retching in the tiny bathroom. If the girl didn't have morning sickness, she was doing the world's best imitation of it.

So much for false positives.

"I'm surprised you didn't bring Riley with you." Remembering the time she and Seth had spent with the precocious child made Angie's heart glow warmly. There was something really appealing about a guy who could make a kid laugh when her family was crumbling around her. "She loves the Green Apple."

"Yes, but all she ever wants here is ice cream," Crystal complained. "You and I would never get a word in edgewise if she was around, so I dropped Riley off with my folks. Mom will feed her something nutritious and Dad will take her to school for me."

"I bet you'll miss them when they leave for their trip."

Crystal nodded. "But the cruise is all Mom talks about, so it's almost as if they're gone already."

Except that you can use them as an unpaid drop-in day care anytime you want.

"So, why am I here?" Crystal asked, looking around for someone to come clear away Heather's plate, flatware, and coffee cup. Since Ethel was shuffling around a table of four, Angie stacked up the dirty things and pulled them over to her side of the booth.

She motioned for Crystal to have a seat. "First, how are you doing?"

Crystal blinked at her. "I'm fine."

No, she wasn't. Her twinset had a pull on it. She was missing an earring and she'd managed to leave her house with mismatched shoes—one navy and one black pump. When Crystal sat and she rested her forearms on the table, Angie noticed that her usually flawless nails were chipped in a couple of places. Ordinarily, Crystal Addleberry looked as if she'd just stepped from a Lord & Taylor catalogue.

Now she wouldn't be terribly out of place at a thrift shop.

But Angela didn't know her well enough to press the issue. Instead she opened her bag and took out the picture of a star that Crystal's daughter Riley had drawn for her. She laid it on the table between them.

Crystal narrowed her eyes. "That looks like Riley's work. She never can get the sides of a star even."

Angie thought the lopsidedness was what made the star charming. "Riley gave it to me and I've had it hanging at the foot of my bed ever since."

"Then you, Ms. Holloway, know nothing about art."

Angie blinked in surprise. Seth wasn't kidding when he said his cousin was a perfectionist. Mothers usually saw their children's art through love lenses.

"I know you said you couldn't be involved in the pageant," Angie said, "but I wonder if you'd allow Riley to be in it."

"Riley? What can she possibly do?"

More than you can probably imagine. "I'd like her to be the star that guides the wise men to the Christ Child."

Crystal rolled her eyes. "My daughter would come closer to leading someone 'round the mulberry bush and talking them to death while she did it than leading them anywhere important."

"Actually, Riley isn't going to say a word. Here's what I have in mind." Angie drew another sketch from her bag. This one was drawn by Seth. The idea of Riley being the star had started out as a joke when Angie suggested they put Riley on a zip line and let her sail into Bethlehem dressed in a star suit. But Seth had taken the thought and run with it. He had a draftsman's hand when it came to building projects. The sketch made Angie's idea seem not only doable, but brilliant.

"Riley will be secured in the star mechanism up on the corner of First and Homestead." It was only a block off the Square on a slight rise, but with Seth's system of pulleys and rigging, Riley, dressed as a glittering star, would slowly pass over the heads of the townspeople who gathered to view the pageant. Finally, she'd come to rest on a small platform about five feet above the roof of the stable. "Seth will control the speed of her descent, so I promise you she'll be perfectly safe the whole time, swathed in glitter and fastened into a harness. He'll make sure she's not in any danger."

Crystal frowned at the sketch. "You know Riley ruined her last dance recital. I was mortified."

"She won't ruin this. I promise she'll make you proud," Angie said. "Look, I know the plays I direct at the high school will never win a Tony. But the kids who take part in them learn things about themselves. They come out of the experience with more confidence. Even if things don't always go as planned."

She hoped Crystal hadn't been there the night of the *Macbeth* production when her kilted ninth graders had accidently mooned the entire auditorium.

Crystal sighed. Then she met Angie's gaze. "Why are you doing this?"

"The pageant?" *Because I was hustled into it. Because my friend Heather was trying to set me up with your cousin Seth. Because I never learned to say no and mean it.*

"No, I didn't mean the pageant," Crystal said. "I mean why do you want Riley in it?"

Angie picked up the picture of the star again and held it up for Crystal to see. "Because when she gave me this picture, Riley told me she wants to be a star. Not every kid gets to have that kind of wish come true for Christmas. Seth and I can make it happen for her."

Crystal's eyes swam and she fingered her daughter's crude drawing. "She could use a wish come true."

"Couldn't we all," Angie said softly. "Look, I know it's none of my business, but if you're going through something right now, I—"

"You're right. It's not your business."

"Okay. All I'm saying is . . . if you want to talk, I'm willing to listen," Angie said, not sure why she offered. Even she had trouble believing the words coming out of her mouth. She'd never been one to stick her nose into other people's business. She always figured she had enough trouble keeping her own life on track. But Crystal seemed so very alone.

In a flash of insight, Angie realized the perfectionism for which Crystal was known was at the core of her problems. It poisoned her relationships. It soured on her own accomplishments. Nothing was ever good enough.

Crystal's frustration that things weren't going the perfect way she planned was why she was lashing out. In the woman's puffy eyes, Angie saw grief, bottled up and overflowing. If Angie could lift even a little of that burden, she was willing to give it a try.

"I'm not on the prayer chain," Angie assured her, "so whatever you say to me won't go any farther."

Crystal scoffed. "God save me from the prayer chain."

"They mean well."

"So did vivisectionists." Crystal put a hand to her forehead. "Sorry. You don't deserve that and neither do they. I grew up in that church. Marjorie and her crew really do care about people. It's just that when you know you need someone to pray for you, you realize you've really messed up."

Maybe that's the point. Knowing we've messed up. Yikes! Maybe I need to be on the prayer chain's list, too.

"And thank you for the offer," Crystal said, the rigid line of her shoulders softening. "I might take you up on it, Ms. Holloway—"

"Angie, please."

"Angie." Crystal's lips twitched in a micro-smile. "Okay. Riley can be in the pageant, but only if you tell me if she doesn't follow your directions to the letter. I don't want her to make a spectacle of herself."

Angie smiled wryly. "Well, she's going to be dressed as a star and flown over the Square, so being a spectacle is pretty much a done deal."

"I mean she has to listen to your instructions and follow them," Crystal said. "Perfectly."

Perfectly. That was a tall order for anyone, let alone a six year old.

"Maybe if you were at the rehearsals, too," Angie suggested.

Crystal pressed against the booth's backrest as if she were

trying to escape by melting into the green vinyl. "Oh no, I can't. My schedule is . . . well, I just can't."

Angie had the feeling that other than showing up for work, Crystal didn't want to be seen in public much. The fact that she and Noah were separated had been making the gossip rounds and Crystal didn't come out looking good in most of the accounts. She was too demanding, folks said. Too much of a nag. According to the wagging tongues, she'd driven her husband away.

Angie thought Crystal deserved a chance to learn to accept imperfection and that meant being around other people.

"I've found the best way to get anything done is to ask a busy person to do it," Angie said. "And you are one of the best organized, most meticulous people in town. Everyone says so."

That was the kindest spin she could put on it.

"Maybe I used to be, but now I—" Crystal stopped herself. "All right. If being a star means so much to my daughter, I'll let her do it and I'll try to be there, too."

"Great. Wonderful. Now, I have one more favor to ask," Angela said. "As long as you're going to be at the rehearsals anyway, would you be willing to play Mary's cousin Elisabeth?"

"Me? Why? I didn't audition."

"No, but I'm casting quite a few parts with people who didn't audition."

"You'll face some criticism for that," Crystal said.

"I'm beginning to think there's nothing I do that won't be criticized," Angie admitted. "I never said everyone who auditioned would get a part, but, back to Elisabeth. I think you'd be perfect."

"Trust me, I'm not perfect for anything right now," Crystal said softly.

"Maybe perfect isn't the right word," amended Angie, who prided herself on choosing the right word. Crystal was so touchy, so raw, she would have to tread with care. "Elisabeth wasn't perfect, and she didn't have an easy time of things. A woman's main reason for being in biblical times seemed to be to bear children. Elisabeth couldn't have any, so she was likely the focus of unkind comments. But she didn't give up. She eventually became pregnant, but at such an advanced age, her neighbors were still gossiping about her."

"Advanced age?" It was all Crystal seemed to hear about Elisabeth. "You think I'm perfect for the part because of my advanced age?"

"No, I didn't mean that." As the oldest of the Evans siblings, Crystal was probably closer to forty than thirty. "We'll have to do a pretty intense makeup job for you to look old enough to play Elisabeth."

"Then what *do* you mean?"

Angie drew a deep breath and fell back on the Christmas story. When in doubt, grammar and the written word were always her friends.

"When Elisabeth's unmarried pregnant cousin turns up on her doorstep, she welcomes her. She believes Mary's child is from God and encourages her. She rejoices with her when others might hide their faces. Elisabeth is strong. She's the sort of person you want with you in a crisis," Angela said. "I see that strength in you, Crystal."

Crystal worried her bottom lip, destroying the clean line of her lipstick. "I don't feel strong."

"But you've already shown me you are. I don't know what's going on in your life, but I know you've got more on your plate than most. And just like Elisabeth, you're willing to lay your issues aside to help someone else. You're making it possible for your daughter's dream to come true, for her to be a star."

"All right," Crystal said. "But if I do, you have to do something for me too."

"Sure. What?"

"You have to come to Thanksgiving dinner at my folks' house, you and Seth."

Angie already knew George and Shirley Evans and was comfortable around them. It would save her from having to meet Seth's parents. "Won't Seth's family expect him to be with them?"

"You can go there for supper. The Evans family is celebrating Thanksgiving at noon."

Two holiday meals in one day. Angie's stomach ached just thinking about it. "Your mother won't have a problem with us crashing the party?"

"Remember the Evans family motto. If a little is good, a lot's a whole bunch better. I'll have her call you with a formal invitation if it'll make you feel better." Then Crystal dropped her voice to a whisper. "Please. I need a few extra faces around the table."

Oh. That meant Crystal hadn't told her parents she and Noah were on the outs. Offering up Seth and Angie as a distracting buffer was actually kind of diabolically brilliant.

"I'll talk to Seth about it and see if I can get him on board."

"Good."

"We're having a first walk-through practice for the pageant at the park right after school today."

"Riley and I will be there." Crystal rose and headed toward the door. "If you have any trouble from Seth about Thanksgiving, remind him he owes me for that fishing boat incident and he'll come to heel," she called over her shoulder.

"Good to know." Angie made a mental note to corner Seth about it first thing when she saw him that evening. Then she took one last gulp of coffee, and even though Heather had left a prodigious tip for Ethel, Angie put a couple of dollars by her plate as well.

When she opened the door to go out, she was nearly bowled over by a guy trying to come in.

"Peter, what are you doing here?" Seth had told her he was in town, but it had totally slipped her mind.

What do you know? I really am over him.

"I'm here for breakfast," he said with an easy smile. "I hear it's the best place in town for Belgian waffles. Join me."

"I have to get to school." She pushed out the door and started walking across the Square. Peter dogged her footsteps.

"Then let's meet for supper. Harper's again?"

"No, I can't. I have plans." Seth had pretty much demanded a do-over after their special evening had been scuttled by Emma's predicament.

"Change them."

"You can't expect me to drop everything just because you breeze into town on a whim." *Oh, yeah. I'm so over this guy.*

"Trust me, Ange. You really want to hear what I have to say."

"Peter, I'm in a relationship now."

"It's that Parker guy, isn't it?"

Angie nodded.

"This isn't about you and me. I blew my chance with you long ago. I know that," Peter said, his handsome face looking so earnest she was tempted to believe he was truly sorry about how he'd ended things between them. "But that doesn't mean I don't care about your welfare. Your future. Give me a chance to explain what I have in mind."

Angie stopped walking and crossed her arms over her chest so she could look up at him. Her crap-detector was pinging off the charts, but Peter's clear-eyed gaze looked so sincere.

That must really go over in the courtroom.

"You've got one minute," she said, pointedly looking up at the clock tower on the courthouse. "Explain."

"I can't cover it all in a minute."

She started walking, but he caught her by the arm and stopped her. She pulled away and he held his hands up in the international gesture of surrender.

"Okay, look, Ange. My firm's been in preliminary talks with Bates College and, well, let's just say there are some exciting developments I want you to know about."

"About which I want you to know."

He laughed. "Some things never change. Thank God." Then he sobered. "Seriously, if not dinner, how about meeting me for drinks?"

She ran through her schedule in her head. Preliminary pageant practice slated for right after school. Seth had done mock-ups of the sets and the whole thing had been laid out at the park next to Lake Jewell. Angie had wanted to use the high school football field, but Coach Thompson wasn't having any of it. The Fighting Marmots were in contention for the state playoffs and there could never be enough football practice to suit him. The lake park would have to do for Angie's walk-through with as many principle actors as she could muster. The pageant practice shouldn't last more than an hour, and Seth wasn't coming to pick her up until seven.

"Okay," she told Peter. "I can meet you for a drink at six, but that's it."

And with that, she relegated Peter Manning to just another box to tick off on her very busy evening. The fact that her insides hadn't fluttered in the least when she literally bumped into him meant she was well and truly over him.

Besides, what harm could there be in a single glass of Chardonnay?

Chapter 24

Christmas pageants were invented to prove that
Murphy's Law isn't just a suggestion.

—Angela Holloway, who's losing sleep over
how many things can go horribly wrong

By the time Angie arrived at the park after school was out, the temperature had dropped to the midthirties and showed no sign of stopping its rapid descent. Heavy clouds threatened to loose shards of icy precipitation on the town.

"There's nothing colder than freezing rain," Angie muttered as she doubled her long scarf around her neck and wished she'd put her cable-knit beanie in her jacket pocket that morning.

All the prototypes for her sets were arranged along the park that sloped down to the Lake Jewell shoreline. Seth had built a humble-looking house set for Mary, and one for her cousin Elisabeth's home. There was a flat with a lick-and-a-promise of a pastoral scene roughed out on it. The shepherds abiding in the field would actually be abiding in front of the flat, which neatly hid the step ladder propped behind it. The angel would appear to them from the top of that not so dizzying height. Nearer to the lake, the manger scene was set, along with another house into which the Holy Family could migrate. Nobody would notice the move while the magi were processing their way to the center of the Town Square, following Riley, in the guise of a star suspended on a cable above them.

These weren't the final version of the sets. They hadn't been painted and the manger had no side or back walls yet, no stall stout enough to corral the cow and calf Junior Bugtussle would bring for the actual pageant, but the rough backdrops would do for a first run-through. Seth had obviously been busy, but Angie didn't see him there.

Instead, she found Junior's truck parked near the manger. He was trying to unload a bale of straw so big it barely fit into the bed of his pickup. Junior had tied ropes to the manger's main support on either side and then looped them around the bale.

"What are you doing, Junior?"

"I figure we need to get the cast used to trompin' through straw, so I thought as how I'd spread a little round for us to prac-tize on."

"No, I mean why have you tied the bale to the manger supports?"

"Oh, this here's an example of usin' my head and savin' my back, Miz Holloway. It'd take three men and a boy to move that big ol' bale by hand. This way, my truck'll do all the work. You see, when the truck goes forward, the ropes will pull on the bale and it'll slide right out, slick as snot."

There was something terribly not right about this plan, but Angie had majored in English not physics. She couldn't quite put her finger on the problem. Still, something made her call out "No! Wait!"

Junior didn't hear her. He was too busy jumping into his pickup and gunning the engine. The truck lurched forward, tearing up deep ruts in the dead grass.

The bale stayed firmly wedged in the bed. The ropes, however, pulled hard on the manger's main supports. It creaked, gave way, and then tumbled to earth like an out-of-balance Jenga tower.

Junior climbed down from the cab of his truck and lumbered around to survey the damage. Clearly befuddled, he took off his cap and scratched his head.

"Honest, Miz Holloway, I didn't see it going that-a-way," he said. "Want me to go home and get another bale?"

"No!" she said with more force than she'd intended. "We'll just have to use our imagination and pretend we have a manger this time."

Deek Atwood hurried up to her, clutching a long coil of electrical cables in his too-clean-to-be-normal hands. He'd been the town's resident computer and electronics geek before Michael Evans relocated part of his dot-com business to the area. Now Deek had plenty of other nerds to hang out with, and as a result, he'd come out of his shell.

And the apartment in his mother's attic.

"This is not going to work, Miss Holloway," he said emphatically. "There's no way to amplify the choir at each station. The mics we have are too directional to pick up a big group. The best you could hope for is one or two voices and—"

"And heaven help us if it's the wrong two voices," Angie finished his thought.

"It was a mistake to make the pageant choir open to all," Deek said. "Your ad in the *Gazette* invited both the tuneful and the tone-deaf. Everyone was encouraged to make a joyful noise."

When Angie wrote up the ad, she thought the alliteration gave it a little oomph. Now she wished she'd left the matter to the director, Mr. Mariano.

"I've heard the choir practicing," Deek said. "There may be some joy, but the emphasis is on noise."

Angie sighed. "We'll just have to hope the choir will carry without amplification, then."

"Oh, they'll be heard all right. I'm just not sure the folks who hear them will thank us," Deek said. "But that's not the worst of it."

"What else is wrong?"

"I've tried everything, but we don't have enough wearable mics for the main characters, and even if we did, I can't get the speakers to pick them up from one end of the park to the other. The speaker system nearest the action works with only a specific microphone."

"What can we do about that?"

"Anyone who moves from one set to another will have to change mics to the one calibrated for the next speaker. Your Mary and Joseph, for example, are going to have to change mics about three times by the time they reach the manger."

Angie shook her head. "That won't work."

"That's what I told you in the first place." Deek gave her a look that said he thought he was surrounded by incompetents and lesser beings who wouldn't know a router from a thumb drive if it bit them on the backside. "What's Plan B?"

Plan B? Even Plan A is nothing more than amorphous goo floating around in my head. We don't have a manger anymore. We don't have a script that doesn't involve sock puppets. We don't have a choir that can carry a tune.

What have I gotten myself into?

Even though ending sentences with a preposition was her number one pet peeve, Angie was too silently distraught to correct her own internal grammar.

"I'll have to let you know about Plan B, Deek." *As soon as I know.*

Other members of the cast were arriving. Emma had walked from the high school and her cheeks were flushed bright red from the cold. Aaron, Junior's son and official Second Shepherd, was walking with her. Aaron was a year behind Emma in school and it was obvious to anyone with eyes that he felt mighty important walking beside such a pretty girl.

Angie was glad for her. Clearly, her secret was still just that. Secret. She deserved a chance to enjoy the holidays without news of her pregnancy making the rounds.

If we can keep it quiet that long.

Ian Van Hook's sporty little mustang came to a stop on the street that flanked the park and the college freshman got out. Tall and lanky and utterly dependable, he'd make a good Joseph.

Angie had cast Jadis Chu, Michael Evans's personal assistant at MoreCommas.com, as the Angel of the Lord. The girl's unique piercings, like the silver chain that draped from her nose ring to her ear, and her spiky purple hair already gave her an otherworldly appearance in real life. Jadis arrived behind Ian, looking furtively around her at the others gathering. Angie couldn't wait to see what she could do with a little stage makeup to turn Jadis into a fiercely beautiful angelic being.

The petite Asian was a relative newcomer to Coldwater who kept to herself when she wasn't working. Angie had only met her because Jadis was friends with Heather, Michael's wife. Quiet, but intensely observant, Jadis was the ultimate outsider. Angie wanted to include her in the pageant because she knew what it felt like to be on the outside looking in. If being in the pageant could ease Jadis into more friendships, Angie would count that a win.

Dr. Gonncu and Mr. Elkin, two of Angie's magi, came striding across the park together, deep in conversation. Both men tended to speak with their hands and nodded in agreement frequently.

Angie smiled. A Muslim and a Jew at peace with each other. If the pageant accomplished nothing else, it looked as if these two very different men were finding common ground and becoming friends.

If only all the rest of us could, too. Then maybe there really would be peace on earth.

Angie's third magi caught up to the other two.

It was Noah Addleberry.

Seth hadn't wanted to cast him, especially after Angie had convinced Seth that Crystal should be Elisabeth and Riley the star.

"Folks will say the pageant is too full of the Addleberry family," he'd tried to tell her.

Angie had reminded him that for years, Ike and Lucinda Warboy, along with whichever of their progeny was age appropriate to be Baby Jesus at the time, had served as the Holy Family. "How is this different?"

"Ike and Lucinda weren't ready to lob grenades at each other."

"I don't think it's as bad as all that between your cousin and her husband."

"That's just it. You don't know how bad it is," Seth had told her. "No one knows for sure why they're splitting up. None of us do."

"But is the marriage over for sure?"

"Angie, don't stick your nose in their business."

"I'm not. But what if all they need is a way to see each other in a different light?"

"How is the pageant going to help with that?" Seth had asked.

"I don't know for sure," Angie had admitted. "That's the thing when you do theater of any kind. It may not be real, but it's often true. It shows us things about ourselves and others that we didn't realize before. And maybe that's what Noah and Crystal need. A chance to see each other not just as a co-parent or even as a spouse, but to see each other truly. Simply. As the person they fell in love with."

"That's asking a lot of a Christmas pageant." Then Seth had grinned. "Besides, don't you mean 'the person with whom they fell in love'?"

He corrected my grammar. Okay, Angie had decided at that moment, *I guess I do love him a little.*

"Don't try to distract me with proper syntax," she'd argued, but not very hard. "What if being in the pageant can help put a family back together? Isn't it worth a shot?"

In the end, Seth had given in and agreed with her cast choices.

But Angie began to fear he might have been right.

Crystal came storming across the park, Riley in tow.

"Why didn't you tell me Noah would be here?" Crystal demanded when she reached Angie. Riley squirmed, trying to free herself from her mother's grip.

"I wanna see Daddy."

Noah heard his daughter's voice and let the other two wise men walk on without him. He dropped to one knee and spread his arms wide. "Come on, Crystal. Let her go."

Whether Crystal released her or Riley wiggled free, Angie couldn't tell, but the little girl was suddenly flying across the park to her father's arms.

"What are you trying to do?" Crystal demanded.

"I'm trying to put together a Christmas pageant."

"Drop the innocent act. You arranged for Noah and me to both be in it on purpose."

"Yes, I did." Angie was suddenly tired of everyone second-guessing her. She decided to stop tiptoeing around Crystal. "It can't hurt for you and Noah to meet on neutral territory."

"How dare you interfere in my private life!"

"Remember where you are. It's not exactly private. If you think no one knows you and Noah are separated, you're only fooling yourself," Angie said. "I'm giving you a chance here."

"To do what? Beg him to come home?"

"No. To work it out. To fight if you have to," Angie said. "A marriage is worth fighting for."

Crystal slanted her a look. "Says the single schoolteacher."

Sometime between breakfast and now, Crystal must have gone home and changed her clothes. Her shoes matched and her makeup had been recently freshened.

"Okay, answer me this," Angie said. "Are you seeing someone else?"

"No, of course not."

"Is Noah?"

Crystal looked in his direction as if infidelity might be stamped on his features for all the world to see. She swallowed hard and then looked away. "Not as far as I know."

"Then you two need to work it out. You have a family, you and Noah. Do you know how lucky that makes you?" Tears trembled on Angie's eyelashes. She'd have given her eyeteeth for a stable family when she was a kid. "But even if you didn't have children, you need to reconcile for your own sake. The two of you loved each other once. You can learn to do it again."

Across the park, her husband was tossing their daughter into the air and catching her. Riley squealed with delight each time she went airborne. The corners of Crystal's mouth lifted in a small, sad smile.

"What if . . . he doesn't want me anymore?"

"He's here, isn't he?"

Crystal's gaze jerked back to her. "He knew I'd be here?"

"He turned down the part of wise man until I told him I was going to cast you and Riley in the pageant, too."

"Really?" The naked hope in her tone was almost embarrassing.

"Come on," Angie said. "Let's go make some Christmas magic."

Chapter 25

The problem with being perfect is that none of us are.

—Seth Parker, who wonders who died and
made him an unwilling marriage counselor

Seth settled into his truck cab, flipped on the interior light, and went over the day's work orders and receipts. He'd been spending too much time on the Christmas pageant and knocking off early to be with Angie. The high school building project was falling behind schedule.

He frowned down at the calendar on his tablet, but he still didn't see how he and his crew could catch up unless they started putting in longer days and weekends. Which meant overtime. Which cut into his bottom line big time.

Falling in love was a spendy proposition.

But Seth had made his name by coming in on time and under budget on his building projects. It was a point of honor with him. He was going to have to tip the life/work scales a little farther in work's favor for the next few weeks.

With all he had to accomplish, he was going to be as busy as a one-armed wallpaper hanger for a while. He hoped Angie would understand. After all, she'd probably be knee deep in pageant stuff until Christmas Eve.

They could talk about it later that night. After he popped the question. Then they'd have a long overdue conversation about his quickly filling schedule.

Hey, honey, yeah, glad you said yes. By the way, you probably won't see much of me till I get the high school addition done.

Maybe he should put off the proposal until New Year's Eve.

But he didn't want to do that. He'd waited too long to find Angie, too long to discover the other half of his heart. He didn't want to wait any longer.

His frustrated thoughts were interrupted by someone smacking the passenger side door. Noah Addleberry opened it and climbed into the cab without waiting for an invite. A biting wind followed him in.

"Man, it's colder than a well-digger's knee out there." Noah rubbed his hands together trying to warm them.

"What's up, Noah?" Seth hadn't expected to see him in the high school parking lot. Addleberry money was financing a large portion of the school project since the last bond issue had failed to pass, but this was the first time Noah had turned up on the job site. "Checking up on me?"

"What? No. You'll get the addition done, Seth. You always deliver. I'm not worried about that."

"What can I do for you, then?"

"Angie Holloway told me I could probably find you here," he said. "I need to talk to someone and you're close enough to understand where I'm coming from and far enough away to be objective. I hope."

"Okay. Shoot."

"It's about your cousin."

"You'll have to be more specific. I've got a lot of cousins," Seth drawled, trying to lighten the mood. When Noah didn't crack a smile, he added, "What's Crystal done now?"

Noah shook his head. "It's not her. It's never her. She hasn't done a thing. It's me. Or at least, she seems to think it is." The fingers of his left hand curled into a fist and he pounded his own thigh absently. Seth noticed that Noah was still wearing his wedding ring, but as far as he knew, the guy was bedding down on the family ranch not with his wife. "From the moment I get up in the morning till I go to sleep at night, there's just no pleasing her."

"Can you give me a 'for instance'?"

"Crystal obsesses about everything. If I miss the hamper and there's one sock left on the floor, she thinks the whole laundry room is filthy," Noah said with a shake of his head. "A few weeks ago, I was spreading mulch around the big oak tree in the backyard. She came flying out the back door, complaining that I was doing it wrong. According to the gospel of Crystal, I should have put down the edging before the mulch." He snorted. "I can't even dump out a bag of mulch to suit her."

Seth couldn't think of anything to say that wouldn't pour gasoline on the fire. Evidently, Noah didn't need him to speak, because he rambled on anyway.

"Then there's how she is with the kids. She's okay with Ethan. He's as perfect as she is, but the way she treats Riley just frosts me," he said through clenched teeth. "You know she's supposed to be a star in the pageant?"

"Yeah, *the* star."

"Well, we had the first rehearsal late this afternoon," Noah said as grimly as if he'd been witness to an execution. "I never should have let that schoolteacher of yours talk me into being in it."

Everyone seemed to know Angie was his. It made Seth want to grin from ear to ear, but he forced himself to stay sober for Noah's sake.

"What happened at the pageant practice?" he asked.

"Well, Riley takes her place just like Angie tells her to. Then she starts leading us wise men to the manger. At first, she keeps her eyes on the manger and her arms straight out because Angie told Riley they'll be like that in the star rig you're putting together for her to float down to the Square in." Noah gave him a sharp look. "She *will* be safe suspended in that get up, right?"

"Safe as if she was in her own bed," Seth promised.

"Anyway, Riley listens to the directions just fine at first, but she can't help being six. She starts skipping and dancing along the route she's supposed to walk. It's cuter than a basket of puppies, but Crystal almost comes unhinged. She charges across the park, scolding Riley for not keeping her arms straight and eyes ahead. She made Riley cry, Seth, and over such a stupid little thing."

Noah crossed his arms over his chest. "Crystal can't accept anything or anyone that isn't as flawless as she is. It kills me to see her tear into Riley like that. She's just a kid."

Seth felt for his little cousin, but he also pitied Crystal. She had a long history of chasing perfection and Seth had seen it crush her more than once.

"Is that why you left her?" he asked Noah.

"Partly. No matter what I do, she knows how I could have done it better. She wears me out," Noah admitted, then added, "Wouldn't you get tired of that, too?"

Seth was silent for a moment. "Is there someone else?"

Noah avoided his gaze. "No. Not yet, but I'd be lying if I said I'm not tempted. You know Sarah Bartlett?"

"The dance teacher?"

"Yeah." Noah glanced at him and then away. "Sarah has been . . . well, I've been getting a vibe off her when I pick Riley up from her ballet lessons for a while now. So I . . ."

"You what?" Seth growled. World-class nag or not, Crystal was still his cousin.

"No, nothing like that. I had coffee with her once at the truck stop out on the highway. That's all," Noah said defensively. "But to be honest, just talking to Sarah was better than sex with Crystal has been in months. Sarah made me feel . . . I don't know . . . like I was worth something."

"And Crystal doesn't."

"Not anymore."

Silence yawned between them and Seth felt duty-bound to fill it.

"It's not just you, you know. Crystal has been this way since we were kids. I remember her walking home from school in tears because she got a B on her report card," Seth said. "It didn't matter that she got A's in everything else. All she saw was the one B and it tore her up."

"Yeah, but—"

"I get that she's been hard on you, but she's always been harder on herself than anyone else," Seth said. "Did you know she wanted to play the violin when she was a kid?"

Noah frowned. "She's not at all into music."

"That's because when she was eight, she didn't play her piece perfectly at her first violin recital. She quit lessons the next day. I don't know why, but there's something in Crystal that *needs* to do things right," Seth said. "Don't tell me you didn't know she was that way before you married her?"

"Well, yeah. But back then it was great," Noah said. "She constantly tried to be exactly what I wanted her to be. She was . . . perfect."

Good-looking, well educated, and coming from one of the first families in the county, Noah was the type to expect perfection.

"Did you try to be perfect back?" Seth asked.

"Yeah." Then because Noah was basically an honest guy, he amended his statement. "No. I mean, I do my best. But hey, nobody's perfect."

"No. Nobody is. But Crystal thinks she has to try. And I'm betting she feels like you don't love her when you don't try to be perfect for her."

"I never thought of it like that," Noah admitted, "but she's just so exhausting. You get why I might be tempted by Sarah, right?"

"Just tempted?"

"Yeah, but that's bad enough, I guess," Noah said. "My marriage is sufficiently messed up without adding another person to the equation."

"It's good that you understand that. It means you and Crystal still have a chance."

"Do we? She—" He stopped himself from grinding on Crystal again. "If I'm being honest, I have to admit it's not all her fault. I give her plenty of mistakes to correct."

"And she needs to learn to let some things go. Let's agree that there's blame to be laid on both sides," Seth said. "Look, all this is way above my pay grade. The two of you need help, and I mean professional help to work this stuff out."

"You think Crystal will agree to counseling?"

"What woman ever said no to talking a problem to death?" Seth said with a raised brow. "But seriously, it won't be easy for Crystal to change. Perfectionism is a . . . well, it's the kind of weakness people pretend is a strength. She's gonna need your support to get through it."

"And . . . my love," Noah said.

"Yeah." Seth was feeling pretty smart about relationships at the moment. Men wanted to feel needed and trusted. Women wanted to feel loved and secure. When both parties worked at it, it was a winning combination.

He hoped he had Angie figured out as well as he did his cousin and her husband.

What with Junior dismantling the manger and Deek's technical problems, the pageant rehearsal had gone from bad to worse. Angie had been so sure putting Crystal and Noah in the cast would lead to reconciliation. Instead, they'd had a public blowup that left their daughter a sniffling mess and all the rest of the cast embarrassed bystanders.

"Do not get involved in other people's lives," she told her reflection in the mirror sternly. It would have been better if she'd never joined the Warm Hearts Club. Then Heather wouldn't have been able to coerce her into directing the silly pageant in the first place.

But then she wouldn't have met Seth.

Her chest glowed warmly at the thought of him as she dabbed a bit of perfume in the hollow between her breasts. He had something special planned for them, and since the evening had already been shoved once, he'd told her it had given him time to add a few things. Whatever it was, Angie was sure she'd like it.

Seth was going to ask her to marry him.

She felt it in her heart, in her head, in her bones. He'd ask and she'd say yes. They were going to become a family, and she'd never be alone in the world again.

It was kind of sudden. They hadn't known each other that long, but everything in her strained toward this man. Unlike Peter, who could convince anyone of anything whether it was true or not, Seth was a straightforward guy. What you saw was what you got.

Angie wished now that she hadn't agreed to meet Peter at Harper's. At the time, it seemed like the adult thing to do. She could have a drink with her ex and listen to what he had to say, and it wouldn't mean a thing.

It was all very casual. All incredibly mature.

Now she wondered if Seth would see it that way.

Especially since Angie was wearing her little black dress and strappy heels and had done her hair and makeup with unusual care. But she wasn't taking pains with her appearance for Peter, unless it was to remind him what he was missing. She'd dolled up for when Seth came by to pick her up later.

Effie wandered into the little bathroom and rubbed against Angie's legs.

"Well, this is a surprise," she said as she bent down to stroke the usually undemonstrative cat. The animal arched her back, as if to demand a more thorough petting. When Angie obliged, Effie turned on her suddenly and bit her hand. Then the cat shot like a bullet into the bedroom and dived between the pillows.

"What was that for?" Angie demanded. "You two-faced little . . . twink," she said, reaching for Crystal Addleberry's frustrated epithet for Riley.

Unblinking, Effie stared at her from her pillow fortress. Angie couldn't shake the feeling that the cat was trying to accuse her of something.

"I am not cheating on Seth," she told the feline. "It's just a drink with an old friend."

Effie hissed at her and then disappeared beneath the coverlet to form a suspicious-looking lump.

Angie checked the clock on her phone. To be on the safe side, she set an alarm so she'd have plenty of time to say goodbye to Peter at Harper's and get back home before Seth came to pick her up at seven.

Not that she was hiding the fact that she was having a drink with her ex. There was nothing to hide.

But on the other hand, what Seth didn't know wouldn't hurt him.

Chapter 26

To err is human. To blame it on somebody else requires a lawyer.

—Peter Manning, defending his profession
because no one else will

When Angie reached Harper's, she discovered Peter was already there, waiting at a table facing the door, obviously watching for her. His handsome face lit with a smile when he saw her.

He rose and pulled out a chair for her.

Very gentlemanly.

As she took it, his gaze sizzled over her slowly from head to toe.

Not so gentlemanly.

"Don't you look good enough to eat," he murmured into her ear as he pushed her chair in.

"Down, boy. I'm only here for a drink." She and Peter had always been quick with innuendo. It meant nothing now, but his frank admiration still made her feel good about how she looked.

She hoped Seth would be as appreciative when he saw how much trouble she'd taken with her appearance tonight.

Peter sat opposite her at the bistro table, signaled the server, and a bottle of chilled Chardonnay appeared.

"I only agreed to one drink," she reminded him as she eyed the bottle.

"One's a good start," he said amicably. "Let's just see where the night takes us."

"It takes me out of here in"—she consulted her phone— "about thirty minutes. I told you I have other plans this evening."

A shadow seemed to pass behind Peter's eyes, but his smile was still firmly in place.

"All right. Straight to business, then," Peter said, leaning one elbow on the table while he filled both their glasses. He raised his and she felt obliged to follow suit.

"To new beginnings," he said, and clinked the rim of his goblet with hers.

Angie repeated the toast, but she was sure the beginning she meant wasn't the same as Peter's. She and Seth were about to start something wonderful together. She was certain of it.

Then she was suddenly stabbed by a shard of guilt. Maybe she shouldn't have agreed to meet Peter like this. Thankful that Harper's lighting was on the dim side, she hoped no one noticed her there with him and felt obligated to tell Seth about their meeting.

Not that she was doing anything wrong. She was just having a drink with an old . . . friend. Yes, that's what Peter had become. Nothing more. In a city, they might have met anytime like this with no one the wiser, but this was Coldwater Cove. Nothing happened in a vacuum here.

And she was uncomfortably sure she didn't want Seth to hear about this little tête-à-tête from anyone but her.

Peter took a long sip of his wine and then set down the glass. "My firm is planning to start talks with Bates College about endowing a chair in the English department."

"That's great," she said, truly impressed. Peter's firm must really be successful if they could afford to fund a professorship, even at a small college like Bates. "The college intends to beef up its STEM classes, but it's foolish to ignore the liberal arts completely. There needs to be a balance between the two."

"I'm glad you feel that way," Peter said, "because as part of our negotiations, I'll tell the college we want you to have the position."

"Me?" If he'd said he wanted to give her a seat on a mission to colonize Mars, she couldn't have been more surprised.

"Why not you?" Peter said. "You've got a master's degree. You've been published. Now, don't look so surprised. I checked up on you. Your paper on the novels of Jane Austen is highly regarded in academic circles. You're more than qualified to teach at the college level."

"I never thought about it that way." She sipped the wine. It was full-bodied and buttery, and left her mouth with a crisp note of citrus. "I suppose I am qualified."

"Of course you are, Ange. More than qualified," he said. "Honestly, wouldn't you rather be teaching Shakespeare to English majors instead of high school punks?"

"My kids aren't punks. But I'd probably get less pushback from older students," she admitted. Elizabethan English was tough for some of her pupils. A few were barely reading at grade level anyway. "But if they don't get Shakespeare from me, a lot of my high school students won't ever be exposed to it."

"They might not ever be exposed to cholera either, but I doubt you'd hear them complain."

She leaned forward. "You don't understand. Shakespeare is good for them. It's like . . . taking vitamins for the mind. When you have to work to understand something, it stretches you. Then when the light goes on and the kids finally make sense of it, they feel so good about themselves. They've worked hard and they've accomplished something," Angie said with a contented sigh. "It's rewarding in a way that I don't think could be matched by teaching older students."

"Oh, I bet some older students could use some stretching, too."

She nodded slightly, conceding his point. A number of students at Bates were probably coasting through their classes. If she were their professor, they wouldn't be. When Angie had decided to be a teacher, she'd also decided to be a tough one. Those were the ones she remembered. The ones who'd challenged her, who taught her to question and reason things out. She wanted to pass on the gift of critical judgment and independent thought to her students, whatever their grade level.

"Say you'll think about it," Peter urged. "The salary bump alone is considerable."

He slid a piece of paper across the table to her. The figure he'd written on it was more than double her current pay.

"And let's face it," he added. "Which sounds better—high school teacher or tenured college professor?"

When Angie imagined the lively discussions she could have with students who took literature seriously, the offer was tempting. But she didn't like the idea of being beholden to Peter for her livelihood.

Seth would probably like it even less.

"I'll think about it," she promised. That was true as far as it went. She wouldn't agree to it, but she'd think about it. Especially on days when her ninth graders were giving her a tough time.

Oh, my gosh. I'm parsing my words like a lawyer.

"No, you know what?" she said, sitting up straight and putting down her wineglass. "That's not entirely honest. I won't take the position and no amount of thinking about it will change my mind."

"Why not?"

"If you attach strings to the endowment so the college can't hire whomever they want, you've hobbled the English department's academic freedom. That's not right," she said.

"And I can't accept something, not even a professorship, that's just handed to me."

"I don't understand your objection," Peter said. "People do things like this all the time."

"Not this people. If the college offered me a position under those circumstances and I accepted it, I'd have no integrity. How can I teach my students that things that are difficult to achieve are still worth having if my job was given to me as a favor?" she said. "Someday, I may teach at the college, but if I do, it'll be because I worked my way there. Because I *earned* my place, not because you bribed Bates to hire me."

"Ange, it's not like that."

"It's exactly like that."

"Wow. When you claim the moral high ground, you take no prisoners," he said. "What's gotten into you? You didn't used to be so black and white, so . . . rigid."

"I am *not* rigid," she said, aware that her affronted tone made her sound precisely that. "Look, I know not everything is black and white. There are gray areas. But there's far less gray out there than you think."

"God help us poor lawyers, then," Peter said with a chuckle. "Those gray areas are where we make our living."

"Look, Peter, I appreciate what you're trying to do for me and I hope your firm will gift the college with another English chair. They need it," she said, thinking about the one professor Bates already had. According to Crystal, Dr. Barclay loved to push the boundaries with experimental and radical means of expression. Someone who loved the classics would provide a nice balance. "But please don't insist on my filling the position."

"You're sure it wouldn't make you happy?"

She sighed. It might make her happy at first, and she could certainly use the extra pay, but in the long run, if she hadn't earned the job, she wouldn't be okay with it. Angie slowly shook her head.

"Then you're right to turn it down," he said.

She knew Peter well enough to recognize this as a strategic retreat. He hadn't abandoned his position yet.

"To be honest, Ange, I guess I was just looking for a way to make it up to you for . . . well, for how things ended between us."

Angie snorted. "And you thought giving me a leg up on my career would make everything all right? That's a little like saying . . . oh, I don't know . . . something like 'Hey, I nearly sliced off your finger and it's dangling by a tendon. Here, have a Band-Aid.'"

As soon as the words were out of her mouth, she wished she could stuff them back in. They were an admission of how deeply he'd hurt her. They laid her pain bare.

Peter didn't say anything for about half a minute. "I was an ass."

"Yes, you were."

"Probably still am."

She didn't say anything.

"Feel free to dispute the point." When she still didn't speak, he went on. "All right. I'm not the best one to judge whether or not I'm still an ass since . . . well, let's just say my moral compass hasn't been what it should be for a long while."

"Might be from hanging out in the gray area all the time."

"You're probably right. Seems you usually are," he said. "Let's change the subject before I downgrade myself from ass to total waste of skin."

That made her laugh. "What do you want to talk about?"

"Tell me about that Christmas pageant of yours."

"Do I have to?" she said with a sigh.

"Why? What's wrong?"

"Nothing really." Then because Angie believed in being truthful, she went on, "It's just not going quite as planned."

"Few things do," Peter said, raising his glass again and refilling hers. "I expected to be toasting Bates College's newest professor tonight and now look at me. Trying to escape being labeled a human toxic waste dump."

"I never said any such thing," Angie said. "Let it go."

"Only if you tell me about that pageant of yours," he said. "I can see it's preying on your mind. Tell me. Is that thing that resembles a broken-down manger at the lakeside park part of the problem?"

"Only part." Angie told him how Junior had demolished the manger with his truck, a bale of straw, and a couple of ropes. "But don't worry. Seth can fix it."

Angie expected him to say something snide about Seth, but he didn't. Maybe Peter was more mature than she thought. Instead, Peter started asking where the pageant would be held, at the park or on the Square.

"It's always been on the Square. Even though there's more room at the park, the Square location is about the only thing I'm not changing this year. I have to keep it on the Square." She told him about her casting choices for the pageant and how excited she was about the budding friendship between the Muslim math professor and the Jewish merchant she'd cast as magi.

"Wow, I didn't expect a place as 'white bread' as Coldwater Cove to have that much diversity," Peter said.

"Wait till you see our Asian Angel of the Lord. She's going to be terrifyingly gorgeous," Angie said. "And yes, I cast all of them partly because I want the pageant to show that the town embraces people of all races and faiths."

"Commendable."

Christian, she almost said, but towns couldn't be Christian. Only individual people could. Then she described what she thought would be the crowning glory of the pageant—Riley Addleberry's appearance as the star. She was so caught up in her vision of the child floating toward the courthouse that she didn't even feel her phone vibrating in the clutch she'd set next to her hip in the padded chair.

Peter seemed truly interested in all the pageant details, which surprised her to pieces. So she shared with him her hope that casting the Addleberry family would lead to a reconciliation between Riley's estranged parents before Christmas.

"Fixing a breakup?" Peter grimaced. "That's asking a lot of a Christmas play."

"That's what Seth said."

"He's smarter than he looks, then."

Maybe Peter's not so mature after all.

Then it hit her.

"Oh! Seth! Oh, no!" She grabbed her phone to check the time. She'd overstayed by a lot. The thirty minutes she'd allotted to Peter had turned into nearly sixty. "Thanks for the wine and . . . and for the Bates offer. I do appreciate it but—"

"No need to hurry off," he cut in.

"Oh, yes, there is. I'm late. Oh, gosh, I'm so late." She rose so quickly, she knocked the chair behind her backward. "I've got to go."

Angie practically flew out the door. Her heels were slowing her down, so she kicked them off and ran across the Square, clutching the strappy shoes to her chest. She was so intent on getting home quickly she didn't even feel the cold sidewalk under her bare feet. She unlocked the front door that opened down at street level and took the dark steps up to her apartment as fast as she could. When she hit her living room, she turned on the light.

That's when she heard the banging noise. Someone was pounding on her back door.

"Coming!"

The pounding grew more insistent.

"Oh, no. Oh, Seth," she mumbled as she skittered into the kitchen and threw open the back door.

Most evenings, he dressed down, rocking a plaid shirt and jeans. On his well-muscled body, they just worked. By anyone's measure, Seth Parker was hot, no matter what he wore. This evening, Seth had gone to the trouble of trying to look "date nice." His dark hair was still a little damp from his shower and he smelled wonderfully of leather and spice and clean male. His open collar shirt was topped by a well-tailored sports coat and his dark blue jeans were crisp and new.

"There you are," she said, trying not to let him see how short of breath she was.

"Yeah, here I *are*," he said with a trace of sarcasm. "Where were you? I've been here five minutes at least. I was about to call the cops and break in to see if you were okay."

"Well, that's overreacting a bit."

"Depends."

Oh, no. It's never a good sign when he speaks in one word sentences.

"On what?" she asked, keeping her expression carefully neutral. She'd been told she didn't have a poker face, but that didn't stop her from trying to appear innocent.

Dang it all, I am innocent!

"It depends on where you were, dressed like that," he said as he stepped over the threshold and into her little kitchen.

She swatted his chest with the back of her hand. "I'll have you know I dressed like this for you, you big dope."

She bent over to shove her feet back into the heels. When she straightened, Seth was just looking at her. He didn't say a word as he crossed his arms over his chest.

"Oh, all right, I was over at Harper's if you must know," she said with exasperation. "I met someone for a drink, but I'm here now and—"

"Who?"

"Whom?" she corrected.

"Really?" he said. "You want to play it like that?"

He was right. Seth had the moral high ground. She had technically been out with another guy, for however brief a time. Trying to fix his grammar wouldn't save her now. Her only play left was outrage.

"You know, if I want to meet a friend for a drink, I don't need to ask for your permission."

"A friend," he repeated. "Is that what you're calling Peter Manning now?"

"How do you know I was with him?" Even the Methodist prayer chain couldn't spread the word that fast.

"I saw his girly little roadster parked in front of Harper's when I came around the Square. Then when I find you're not home, well, I may be a few bricks short of a load when it comes to your literature stuff, but I can add two and two," he said, his jaw tense. "Why, Angie?"

It was so unfair for him to be angry. She hadn't done anything. Not really. "I don't owe you an explanation, Seth."

He didn't exactly flinch, but pain flicked across his face all the same.

"No. You don't owe me anything I guess," he said slowly. "My mistake."

Then he turned and left without another word.

Chapter 27

Treating a woman like a princess don't work
no more. You gotta treat her like a queen.

—Lester Scott, who's not the best one
to give advice on women

Seth slapped a putty knife full of spackle on the freshly hung drywall and spread it more or less evenly. His crew would be surprised when they came in tomorrow morning to find the classroom walls had been mudded and taped and were ready to sand before painting.

"There you are," Lester said, as he pushed back the plastic sheeting that covered the entrance and joined Seth in the unfinished classroom. He picked his way across the floor, careful not to trip on the wires that powered the flood lights Seth had rigged up to illuminate his work. "Been lookin' for you, boy."

"Why? I told you to go on home." Seth turned back to mudding the drywall. He had hired Lester to serve dinner at his house again that evening, but when he and Angie had their blowup, he couldn't bear to go back to his ranch house and face the old man without her. He hadn't confided in Lester that he'd hoped to propose that night, but the veteran had guessed and was full of suggestions Seth hadn't been able to put to use. After Seth had stormed out of Angie's place, he'd called Lester and told him to pack up the dinner, blow out the candles and take the leftovers home with him.

Seth didn't care if he ever saw another broiled lobster tail again.

"You deaf, boy?" Lester said. "I asked what you're doing."

"What's it look like? We're behind on this project. I'm trying to catch up." He smacked the wall with his putty knife harder than necessary.

"Easy, son. That wall didn't do nothin' to ya," Lester said. "So what happened with the girl this time? She blow you off again?"

"She didn't blow me off last time. Something came up with one of her students," Seth grumbled. Angie hadn't told him what, but at the time he'd figured it must be something pretty important or she wouldn't have sent him packing.

Now he wasn't so sure.

"Yeah, well, last time you came on home and you and me tucked into them lobster tails together, so's they wouldn't go to waste," Lester said. "Now you tell me you want me to take them home to the missus."

"Why didn't you?"

"My Glenda hates them things. Claims they stink up the house. Never argue with a woman when she says something stinks," Lester said sagely. "They got way better noses than us guys do."

"Yeah, maybe," Seth said. "But they don't have better judgment."

"Well, I might beg to differ with you there." Lester picked up a putty knife and began spackling over a few nail holes Seth had missed. "You're slippin' a little, son. These nails here are poking their heads out. It's not like you to miss stuff."

"I've been doing a lot of that lately." He'd missed a lot of things. Like how different he and Angie were. She was book smart. His intelligence ran toward reading blueprints and crunching numbers. He had a big extended family and it was fine with him. She was alone in the world and didn't seem to be in any hurry to let anyone into her aloneness.

"A woman can mess with a man's head sometimes. Makes him sloppy when he's thinking about her all the time," Lester conceded. "But usually, women make us better versions of ourselves. God knows my Glenda waited long enough for me to clean up my act."

"Yeah, well, my act is clean enough already." Seth was a straight arrow and made no apologies for it. "What you see is what you get. Maybe Angie just doesn't like what she sees."

"Maybe, but I doubt it," Lester said. "You're quite the catch. I hear what folks are saying, and ever'body who comes into the Grill says so."

Seth snorted. "Everybody except Angie Holloway. She can't seem to stay away from her ex."

"That feller from DC?"

"Yeah. Except he can't seem to stay in DC."

"She shut him out at the Green Apple this morning," Lester said. "He was all hot to take her to dinner tonight, but she told him no."

"She just didn't mean it," Seth said, refusing to be encouraged by Lester's story.

"Not that I'm one to carry tales, but the guy was pretty insistent. Said he had something important she'd want to know about, so if she wouldn't let him take her to dinner, would she just meet him for a drink."

"So that's what she did." Seth stopped working long enough to shoot a glare in Lester's direction. "What if I was out throwing back brews with an old girlfriend? Would that be okay, you think?"

"Well, I think it would depend on why you was there with your old girlfriend," Lester said. "My sense of what passed between the Teach and that DC feller, not that I was eavesdroppin' or anything—"

"No, of course not," Seth said with a roll of his eyes.

"Any-hoo, I got the feeling she agreed just to get away from him," Lester said. "I may not be much for readin' books, but I'm pretty good at readin' people. Angie wasn't fiddlin' with her hair or leaning toward him or doing any of the things women do when they're interested in a guy."

"No?"

"No," Lester said emphatically. "In fact, she was in an all-fired hurry to leave the Grill when he cornered her. Maybe she said yes to be polite. Women are like that."

"Angie isn't the sort to do something she doesn't want to do."

"Really? Wasn't it you who was tellin' me about how she felt roped into doing the pageant, but couldn't figure out how to get out of it without offending somebody?"

"Yeah," Seth admitted.

"Maybe her ex knows she's like that, not wantin' to be ornery to nobody, and he took advantage of her good nature."

"Well, she doesn't have any trouble saying no to me," Seth said.

"That's 'cause she thinks you're safe."

"Safe. Makes me sound like a toothless old spaniel. Maybe I should be dangerous for a change." Angie's book, *Sense and Sensibility,* popped into his head. No matter how steady, how reliable Colonel Brandon was, Marianne was all hot and bothered over Willoughby, who was sure to break her heart. "Women always go for the bad guys. Why is that?"

"I ain't sure they do. Leastwise, they don't stick with 'em if they got any smarts," Lester said. "My Glenda woulda never let me back into her life if I hadn't started cleaning up my act. Angie Holloway don't strike me as stupid. She won't be fooled by some slick-talkin' feller."

Maybe Lester was right. Maybe Angie was over Peter Man-

ning and Seth was upset over nothing. They spackled the wall
in companionable silence for a while.

"But why did Angie have to get so dressed up to meet that
guy?" Seth said with a frown. "She looked . . . well, that outfit
she was wearing ought to be illegal."

"She looked good, huh?"

"Oh, man." Good didn't begin to describe it. Just thinking
about the way that little dress hugged her curves got his motor
running.

"Yeah, I thought so. But she coulda been dressing like that
because she knew she was going to see you later and wouldn't
have time to change. Trust me. It takes a woman forever to get
fixed up to suit her." Lester gave him a weary look born of
long experience. "Besides, do you really think Angie is the
type to step out on you?"

"I don't know that she'd even think about it that way. It's
like she doesn't seem to think we're . . . well, that we're anything. Like it was nothing for her to see this other guy because
she and I are nothing special, if you get what I mean."

"Have you told her how you feel about her?"

In time spent together. In things done to please her. In
kisses that were quickly becoming not enough, but . . . "Not
in so many words."

"In how many words?"

"None, I guess." Seth really hadn't told Angie how he was
feeling. He just assumed she'd know.

"Guys are different. It's what we do that counts. With
women, well, they place a lot of store in what you say. But
mind, they want the whole package. You gotta back up your
words with actions," Lester hastened to add. "I told Glenda
how sorry I was for being a no-good drunken bum, but she
didn't let me back into the house until I reshingled her roof."

Working in silence, Seth thought about that for a while.

"Guess I've been coming at Angie backward, then. I've

been trying to *do* for her without ever saying what I *feel* for her. But that's . . . well, it's hard."

"Welcome to loving a woman," Lester said.

Lester got it without Seth having to say it. Why didn't Angie? He sighed and slapped more spackle on the wall.

"You know, there was a time when I'd a told Glenda I didn't even have feelings," Lester went on. "I did, o' course. I just didn't know how to recognize 'em or what to call 'em. Women got a leg up on us in that department."

"Maybe not Angie." She was pretty closed off about her feelings, but that probably came from being hurt in the past. And not just by Peter Manning. The long parade of foster families had something to do with it as well. She'd all but admitted that she had trouble forming connections with others.

"So, be honest now? You think she's really interested in that other feller?" Lester asked.

Seth stopped working for a bit. "No."

"Then what the heck are you doing here? Get back over to her place and apologize."

"Why should I apologize?"

"Because you're the man," Lester said as if it were self-explanatory and Seth was a dunce not to see it. "Might not be fair. Might even be true that you're not at fault, but nine times out of ten, if a man don't apologize, he may win the argument, but he loses in the end."

Something about that logic stuck in his craw. "If I go crawling back to her, she'll think I can't live without her."

"Yep," Lester agreed with disgusting cheerfulness. "But she won't believe it until you say the words."

Why were words so important? Seth had put a lot of thought and effort into this evening. He'd even arranged for a kid from the college with a classical guitar to come out to his house and play while they ate the catered meal Lester was supposed to have served. He'd gone overboard to show Angie how he felt about her, but she botched it all by stepping out with Peter Manning.

His insides still did a slow boil.

"I guess she's just going to have to keep wondering for a while," Seth said. "I'm not going to apologize."

"Okay," Lester said agreeably. "Only next time you put together a fancy do for two at your place so you can tell the girl how you feel, why don't you order prime rib? The missus likes that fine. She wouldn't mind me bringin' home them kind of leftovers at all."

Chapter 28

Men are why God created ice cream.

—Angela Holloway, who tries to have some
on hand for emergencies, but suspects not
even Chunky Monkey will fix her
man problem this time

After Seth left, Angie stripped off her little black dress, and pulled on her yoga pants and an oversized T-shirt. The outfit was her go-to "sluvvies" when comfort was wanted. It went hand in hand with Ben & Jerry's when comforting was wanted. She took her half-eaten pint from the freezer and settled cross-legged onto the couch for some empty calories therapy and a good cry.

It was so unfair. Seth acted as if she'd cheated on him, for pity's sake. It wasn't like she went on a full-blown date with Peter. All she did was meet him for a drink.

Honestly, she really hadn't even wanted to do that. Of course, there was a dark little part of her heart that believed looking good was the best revenge when it came to dealing with an ex. That bit of her wanted Peter to see she was completely over him, that she'd moved on. She wasn't the same girl he'd crushed all those years ago.

"Now I'm the girl Seth Parker crushed," she told Effie between sniffles. The cat kneaded her lap, circled twice, and then settled between her legs. Effie closed her eyes and started purring.

"Just great, cat. I'm a soppy mess and you're happy about it." Angie took another heaping spoonful of ice cream.

Cold stabbed the backs of her eyes.

"Better slow down," she warned herself, and dialed back the size of her next bite.

Then her kitchen door rattled and Emma Wilson let herself in. She'd given the girl a key, but Angie had hoped her student would be back with her mom by now.

Angie swiped her cheeks. It wouldn't do to let Emma see that she'd been crying. Of the two of them, she was supposed to be the adult. Emma had a lot more to cry about than she did.

But the heart couldn't weigh hurts like that. It was impossible to compare whose ache was worse.

"How's it going?" she called with false cheerfulness to the girl. "Have you had supper?"

"I'm not hungry." Emma came in and perched on one of the kitchen barstools, not quite in the living room and not really in the kitchen either. Sorta like where she was in life— betwixt and between.

"You need to eat something nutritious."

The girl eyed Angie's pint of ice cream. "Says you."

"All right. There's an unopened Cherry Garcia in the freezer. Grab a spoon."

"Now you're talking. Thanks." Emma hopped up and helped herself to the ice cream. Then she joined Angie in the living room, claiming the stuffed chair in the corner as her spot.

Emma gave Angie a searching look. "What's wrong, Ms. H.?"

"Nothing."

"Then you're wasting perfectly good ice cream," Emma said. "You and that old Mr. Parker have a fight?"

"He's not old." *The teen must think anyone over twenty-five is ancient.*

"But you did have a fight."

Angie conceded the point with a nod.

"Com' on, Ms. H. Dish the dirt. What'd your old man do?"

"He's not my old man."

"Sorry to hear that," Emma said, curving her spoon around the edge of the carton so ice cream wouldn't melt over the sides. "So you two broke up?"

Angie shrugged. If something so relatively minor could blast everything to pieces, were she and Seth ever really together in the first place? Of course, if he'd had drinks with an ex, it might not have seemed minor to her either.

"I am *not* discussing this with you," Angie said. "Did you go see your mom like we talked about?"

"Yeah." Emma's shoulders slumped.

"And?"

"Nothing's changed." Emma shook her head slowly. "She still won't let me come home. Says she has my sister and brother to think about and what kind of example would I be to them?"

"I'll talk to her tomorrow," Angie offered.

"No, please don't do that," Emma said. "It's not her fault. Mom's a wreck on account of Dad leaving her. She's got enough on her plate. The last thing she needs is some teacher hounding her."

Some teacher. I take the girl in, and she calls me "some teacher."

"I wouldn't hound her."

"You know what I mean. I don't mean to be ungrateful. I'm not. Really and truly," Emma said with emphasis. "I just don't want you to hassle my mom when it's not her fault I got myself knocked up."

"You didn't manage that on your own," Angie reminded

her. Tad should be made to shoulder some of the responsibility, but in so many ways, he was still a kid, too.

As a teacher, Angie had a duty to report child abuse, and failing to care for a minor child certainly fell under that mandate. Emma was only fifteen, too young to be emancipated. Angie was dancing dangerously close to the legal line by not turning in Mrs. Wilson (and the off-in-Muskogee-with-his-girlfriend Mr. Wilson), but she wanted to see if things would work out between Emma and her mom. She wouldn't wish getting caught in the grinding gears of the system on anyone.

"Does your mom know you're staying here temporarily?" Angie hoped the slight emphasis she gave the word *temporarily* would remind Emma that she needed to resolve her situation soon, but Angie hated to put additional pressure on the girl.

"Yeah, I told her you're letting me crash with you, but Mom's not registering much at the moment. What with worrying about her job and taking care of my little sister and brother and wondering how she'll make ends meet without my dad, well . . ." Emma's voice tapered off and she studied her cherry ice cream with absorption. "That's the thing about being a mom. I can see how it would wear you out after a while."

But if you're a mom, the kids are supposed to come first. Those are the rules.

However much she wanted to, Angie didn't say what she was thinking. Emma was trying to give her mom the benefit of the doubt, even if she wasn't stepping up when Emma needed her most. If Angie said anything against the girl's mom, the only one who'd be hurt by it was Emma.

The teen stirred her ice cream to "puddle" it a little. "I told Tad."

"Oh." Angie arched a brow at her. That was a brave step. "How did he take it?"

Emma shrugged. "About how I thought he would. He

freaked." Tears gathered, but once she blinked them back, her jaw took on a determined set. "He asked me if I was sure he was the father."

Angie nearly bit her tongue in two. A rant against men in general and Tad in particular was building inside her. It wouldn't help Emma for her to pile on, so she made herself stay silent.

"Anyway, I was so mad at him, I told him I'd have to check. Maybe it was one of, like, the other couple hundred guys I've been with. Then he got mad at me, the jerk. As if I would have slept with anybody else." The anger drained out of her tone to be replaced by deep sadness. "I loved him."

"Loved," Angie repeated. "Past tense."

"You pick up on stuff like that pretty quick. Guess that's why you're an English teacher." Emma took another spoonful of ice cream. "How can I love somebody who doubts me?"

Angie wondered the same thing about Seth.

Her phone vibrated in her pocket. *Forget speak of the devil. All I have to do is think of him . . .*

Part of her wanted to let it go to voice mail. The other part longed to hear his rumbly voice, no matter what he might say.

"I need to take this." Angie rose, disappeared into her small bedroom, and shut the door. Then she leaned against it and sank to the floor before she swiped the phone to answer.

"What do you want, Seth?" *Good start. Noncommittal. Tone not at all hostile. Totally vanilla.*

She heard him breathe deeply on the other end of the connection.

"You," he said softly.

Her insides tingled at that, but Angie bit her lip to keep from responding. Seth had all but accused her of cheating on him with Peter. He needed to apologize, and he hadn't. She couldn't let him gloss things over as if nothing had happened.

"I meant why are you calling?" she clarified. *Specificity. That's what's wanted. When in doubt, fall back on words that mean things.*

Silence reigned.

"Are you still there?" she asked in a small voice.

"Yeah," he said gruffly. "Look, I just hung up from talking to my cousin Crystal. She's a mess."

"I'm not surprised. Things didn't go well at the pageant rehearsal." This was a safe topic. Anything but the unspoken elephant in the room.

"So I heard," Seth said. "From both her and Noah. Neither of them are happy with the way things stand."

"I don't know how to make it better," she admitted, not sure she was talking about Seth's cousin and her husband anymore.

"Neither do I."

Maybe he wasn't talking about Crystal and Noah either.

"Maybe if Noah apologized . . ." she suggested.

"I'm not sure he's done anything he needs to apologize for."

Seth might have meant Noah. Or he might be talking about himself.

Dang! I wish I didn't know anything about subtext. It would be so much easier if words just meant what they mean.

"Noah left home," Angie said. "He might start by apologizing for that."

Kind of like the way Seth had stomped off before they'd had a chance to talk it all out.

Guess two can play this subtext game.

"Yeah, I think he regrets that," Seth said. "When a couple has problems, there's never a totally innocent party."

"I wouldn't say never," Angie said, a little testiness creeping into her tone. Then, because she valued truthfulness, she had to admit to herself that she wasn't as blameless as she tried to claim. If Seth had been out with an old girlfriend, she'd have been hurt by it. Still, she liked to think she'd have listened to his side of things before blowing it all out of proportion.

But feelings are funny things. Sometimes your mouth starts spewing the hurt in your heart before the words filter through your brain.

"You're probably right," she admitted. "Maybe . . . they both need to apologize."

"Yeah. The trick is getting one of them to go first."

"I'm not sure we can help Crystal and Noah with that," Angie said, wishing he'd just say it. Maybe she was the bad guy here, but it was suddenly of great consequence to her that Seth be the first to apologize. If he did, it would mean she was more important to him than his masculine pride.

And that would mean she was really important.

"Guess they have to decide what their relationship is worth," Seth said. "If they'd just . . . get to know each other's hearts, everything would become easy."

The notion sounded vaguely familiar. "How did you get so wise?"

A deep chuckle crackled over her phone. "From reading a Jane Austen novel."

"What?" The image of big, tough Seth poring over a romance novel made her laugh. "Oh, of course. 'If I could but know his heart, everything would become easy.' That's from *Sense and Sensibility,* isn't it? You've been reading that? Really?"

"Try not to sound so surprised. I'm not the knuckle-dragger you took me for," he said. "I'm housetrained and everything."

"I didn't mean that. I just meant it's not the sort of book I'd expect you to read."

"It's not," he said. "But you left your copy in my truck the day we met."

"So that's where it was." So much had happened since then, the book's whereabouts had fallen off her radar.

"I been workin' on it off and on since then."

Literature was safe. Angie could talk about that all day. "What do you think of it?"

"I think Marianne was a fool not to see what a louse Willoughby was from the very beginning."

"Even though you very nearly quoted Marianne?"

"She has her moments," Seth said, "but you got to admit, of the two sisters, Elinor's got more sense."

"Agreed. But you can't blame Marianne for being dazzled by Willoughby. He was . . . dashing and everything she'd ever imagined a man should be. It would have been considered a good match if Marianne had married Willoughby."

Seth snorted. "He's shiftless, irresponsible, and only looking out for himself. I wouldn't wish him on anybody. Reminds me of someone else we both know."

Peter. Angie saw the parallel right away. Peter had dazzled her at first, just as Willoughby had swept Marianne off her feet. And Seth embodied many of Colonel Brandon's sterling qualities—steadfastness, dependability, and deep, if unspoken, affection.

Maybe Seth knows something about subtext, too.

"Marianne came to her senses in the end," Angie said softly. "She realized Colonel Brandon was the much better man. In fact, I like to think she eventually apologized to him for not recognizing that right away."

"Maybe she did."

A pregnant silence hovered over them.

"Was there any other reason you called?" Angie asked. If he was going to apologize, now would be the perfect time.

"Yeah," Seth said, suddenly all business. "Crystal told me you promised to turn up for Thanksgiving at my aunt Shirley and uncle George's house. She says it's the only way she'll stay in the pageant. She also said I have to be there, too."

"Crystal seemed to think having us there will deflect attention from her problems with Noah," Angie said. "Though to hear her tell it, there will be a mob of people at the Evanses anyway."

"There will. There always is. Our pastor used to say the best time to show up at my aunt and uncle's house is mealtime. An extra mouth would hardly be noticed," Seth agreed. "Are you still okay about going?"

He hadn't apologized. But, then, neither had she.

"Yes, I'll be there." Angie had promised Crystal she would.

"Good," he said. "You want a ride?"

Kind of an awkward way to ask if I'll go with him, but when have we not been awkward? It's sort of our wheelhouse.

"There's only so much room to park in the drive and on the street by the Evanses' house," she said. "It would be silly for us to take two cars."

Not a ringing endorsement of our going together, but at least I didn't say no.

"Right. So I'll pick you up, then."

"Okay."

Silence grew again, a dark looming presence she wasn't sure how to escape. If one of them didn't say something of substance soon, she didn't see a future for them. But a hard part of her heart refused to let her be the first one to say it.

"Angie?"

"Yeah?" she whispered.

"I'm sorry."

Then the line went dead.

"Me too, Seth," she told the silence. "Me too."

Chapter 29

Getting along with women ain't no trouble. Just ask my
wife, Darlene. All it takes is for the man to do all the gettin'.

—Junior Bugtussle, whose wisdom
smacks of hard-won experience

The phone call was a start, but in no way did Seth feel as if the rift between him and Angie had been patched. His relationship with her wasn't the sturdy structure he thought he'd been building at all. It stood in shambles, more like the manger scene after Junior Bugtussle's truck had its way with it. Seth had some serious rehab work to do on both fronts.

After his quick apology, he had called her again early the next morning. Angie had agreed to meet for a quick breakfast that day and a couple of other times that week, but the Green Apple didn't really lend itself to private conversation. Especially since Seth now knew how very keen Lester's ears were, even when he didn't seem to listening.

They talked about the pageant, and about Angie's student Emma and her troubles, the poor kid. They even revisited his cousin Crystal's situation. It all came down to whether Crystal and Noah could forgive, make changes, and learn to trust each other again.

It seemed Seth and Angie could solve everyone else's problems but their own. They never quite got around to talking about the seed of distrust that had taken root in their relationship.

In some respects, it was a good thing that he and Angie were still a little bit on the outs with each other. For one thing, it meant his evenings were free. Which meant the high school addition was back on track because he could burn plenty of midnight oil on it. Now the project would be finished on schedule. And Angela was able to devote more time to writing a much-needed new script for the pageant.

They'd both agreed Coldwater Cove wasn't ready for Christmas with sock puppets, so Dr. Barclay's wildly weird version was scrapped.

But not spending much time with Angie meant that when Seth went to pick her up at around ten thirty on Thanksgiving morning, he felt as if he was just going through the motions. It was as awkward as their first date. Seth had originally hoped to take her to meet his folks later that day, but he doubted she'd be up for it now. Even though he'd apologized and she seemed to accept it, he was still walking on eggshells around her.

"Your student not coming with us?" he asked as he walked her from her back door down to his waiting truck below. He rested his fingertips on the small of her back as they descended the iron staircase. It was a little touch, just a slight brush of his fingertips, but he liked doing it. She didn't shrink away from him, which he took as a good sign.

Of course, it was just a matter of good manners. His hand at the ready meant he'd be able to catch her if she stumbled. But he was also touching her in a way not every other guy could. It felt chivalrous and sexy at the same time.

Just my hand on her lower back is all it takes to get me going. God help me if she lets me touch her anyplace else.

"No, Emma's not able to come. She's having morning sickness in spades today," Angie said. "When I suggested she eat turkey with us, she turned green as a gourd."

The fact that the kid was ill was no surprise. According to

Angie, the circle of people who knew the Christmas pageant's Mary was unexpectedly expecting had grown to five—him, Angie, Heather, Emma's mom, and the FOB, Tad Van Hook.

But since Seth and Angie had talked about Emma's pregnancy, be it ever so quietly, over breakfast at the Green Apple, he had no doubt Lester knew about it, too.

Which means if the news isn't fodder for the Methodist prayer chain by the first Sunday in Advent, I'll be mightily surprised.

"Emma is a total mess right now," Angie said as she hauled herself up into his truck. Seth wished she'd let him help her with that, but she always scrambled up before he could even put a hand to her elbow. "Remind me never to get pregnant."

"You don't want kids?" He loved Angie. Why else would he put up with her skittishness and unpredictability? And Seth wanted her to love him back, but "no kids" might be a deal breaker. Never mind that his parents expected him to present them with grandchildren someday, Seth had always seen himself as a dad sooner or later.

"No. It's not that. Kids are fine. Someday. Maybe. I'm just not a fan of pregnancy at the moment," she said. "A baby kind of takes over even before he or she's born. Talk about *Invasion of the Body Snatchers.*"

"I think that's the movie playing at the Regal next week," Seth said with a laugh. "Wanna go?"

"Not really." She softened the refusal with a grin. "It's been playing in my apartment for a while now."

Instead of taking Emma in, Angie could have taken her down to social services, but Seth had a pretty good idea why she hadn't. Given her past, the thought of surrendering anyone to the system would be as repugnant to Angie as a spider in a bouquet.

But it might be the best thing for all concerned. Emma could get some professional help, and involving a government agency might jar her family into action on her behalf. Right now, the girl seemed stuck in neutral, unable to decide what to do.

But Seth didn't think he should suggest the idea. He wasn't sure how Angie would react. He wasn't willing to risk another argument so soon after their blowup over Angie having drinks with Peter Manning.

Seth was no expert, but he was pretty sure that not being able to talk about certain things wasn't the sign of a healthy relationship.

That scumbag Manning was still in town, too. Seth had seen him hanging around the college and the courthouse, but at least he hadn't caught him on Angie's deck. Still, Manning's mere presence in Coldwater Cove irritated Seth. It was like a pebble in his boot that had become wedged under the insert. There wasn't anything he could do about it without tearing everything to pieces. The only bright spot was that as far as he knew, Angie hadn't seen the guy again.

But Seth didn't know everything.

After all, Angie had kept Emma's secret from him for nearly a week. If he hadn't caught her red-handed hanging out with Manning, he might never have known about their meeting. Angela Holloway had reservoirs of secrets he had yet to plumb.

That wasn't to say he didn't trust her. He thought he could. But because she kept things from him, it was obvious she didn't seem able to trust *him*. That stung. Seth had a lot of rebuilding to do if he and Angie were going to amount to anything.

One brick, one two-by-four, one nail at a time.

"Seth, I need to tell you something," Angie said as they pulled down the tree-lined street his aunt and uncle lived on.

Because her tone was so serious, he pulled to the curb and turned off the truck.

"Shoot."

She drew a deep breath. "I . . . I finished writing the script last night."

For that I turned my truck off? As personal revelations went, it didn't even crack the top one hundred. "Yeah?"

"I think the script is okay. Maybe good, even," she said hurriedly. "Would you give it a read before I hand it out to the cast?"

He shrugged. "Sure."

"Good." She nodded, apparently satisfied with his answer. "Because I . . . I wouldn't want to make *any* decision without talking to you about it first."

What is she saying? "About the pageant, you mean."

"Yeah, about that . . . and about other things, too."

May as well get down to brass tacks. "Does this have something to do with Peter Manning?"

"What? No. Why?" She narrowed her eyes at him. "Did you hear something?"

Should I have? "Like what?"

"Like why he wanted to meet with me that night."

"Oh, I've got a pretty good bead on why he wanted to see you." No mystery there. Manning still wanted her.

She shook her head. "It's not what you think. Peter isn't interested in me like that. At least, he shouldn't be because that's not going to happen."

"Good." He wished he was a man of more words. Good didn't begin to describe how it felt to hear that she was done with Manning.

"Anyway, when we met for drinks, he said his firm was going to endow an English chair at the college and the job was mine if I wanted it."

She might not be interested in picking up where she and Manning had left off, but that jerk wasn't the sort to make an offer like that unless there was something in it for him. "What did you tell him?"

"That I couldn't take it."

Relief settled in his chest. "You don't want to teach at Bates?"

"No, I don't want to owe Peter."

That's my girl. "Oh. Good." *Dang, do I even know any other words?*

"But, I just wanted you to know that . . . if I make any big decisions about . . . well, about anything *important,* I want to talk to you about it first."

Did she just lay a brick of her own? Maybe he didn't have to be the only one who was working on shoring up their foundation.

"That's good, Angie. I mean, I appreciate it," he said. This was better than an apology. This was a promise of good things to come. "Because if something important happens in your life, I want to be part of it."

"Count on it." She smiled then and it was *that* smile. The one that said she trusted him, that she needed him.

He did what any red-blooded guy would do. He leaned in to kiss her.

There was no hesitation, no second-guessing himself this time. This kiss was *meant.*

He knew it was so, because while his lips covered hers, the world sort of went away for a bit. Not that he wasn't still vaguely aware of the clicks of the engine as it cooled or the moan of the November wind outside his truck. Or that his extended family was expecting them to arrive momentarily. Or that he and Angie still had miles to go before they knew each other as deeply as he meant for them to.

It was just that those things were nothing at the moment. Even the right words, if he could find them, were nothing.

This kiss was everything.

He cupped her head. She was so delicate and small. It took every ounce of his strength to be gentle. His thumb caressed her cheek. It was all comforting and slow, like a tiny blaze that heats the whole room. That's how he'd been romancing this woman.

Time to turn up the heat.

He slanted his mouth on hers, and demanded a response. When her lips parted, he didn't need to be invited twice.

Sweet, warm, wet.

Seth was drowning in her and didn't care a bit. If Angie was the one who pulled him down, he was willing to go to the bottom with her. As long as she was there, he didn't care where he ended up. She might be a bundle of needs, and a bit scary in her neediness, but she was *his* little bundle of needs.

He'd love this woman till he was dust. Whatever she wanted from him, he was willing to give.

It was as if someone had suddenly turned up the volume on life. The rosy glow of her cheeks was brighter, her lashes curled on them more velvet-like. The nerve endings under his skin sent pulses of urgency through his whole body. The scent of her perfume wrapped itself around his brain and sang a song of wanting and tenderness and a thirst that could never be slaked.

Everything up to this moment had been a pale reflection of living.

This kiss was the real deal. He wanted Angela Holloway, all of her—her quirky humor, her deep silences, her hurts, her kind heart—he'd take it all.

So he poured his soul into the kiss. If this moment passed

without convincing her of what she meant to him, he feared his chance would never come again.

That's why when she pressed her fingertips against his chest, he hated to let her go. It took everything in him not to pull her tighter to him. His heart pounded unevenly, a wild and desperate and primitive drumbeat resounding in his ears.

Could she hear it? Was the same rhythm beating in hers?

When she opened her eyes, her pupils were so wide, the whole iris seemed black. He could almost fall into them.

"Seth," she said softly, her voice a little choked. "I . . . words mean everything to me, but I suddenly don't know what to say."

"Then don't say anything." Seth pulled her close and she melted into him, resting her head on his chest with a contented sigh. She grasped the lapel of his jacket and held on tight.

They spent a quiet few moments just listening to each other breathe. It didn't feel awkward. It didn't feel like a silence that needed to be filled.

It felt right.

"Your aunt and uncle are expecting us," she said after a bit.

Usually, Seth was glad he had a rollicking big family with lots of cousins and aunt and uncles. Now he'd give his left arm if he and Angie could be the only two people in the world.

"They'll wait a little longer," he said. The heat of the moment had passed, but a deep longing remained. The ache eased a bit as he simply held her.

Nothing earth-shattering had happened. No one had proclaimed undying love. He hadn't whipped out the ring he was still carrying in his pocket. They hadn't ripped each other's clothes off and gone crazy in his pickup, though part of him cheered that idea with enthusiasm.

But a line had been crossed anyway.

Something in him had touched something in her. And whatever they'd been to each other before, they were something else now.

Something new. Something strong.

And Seth hoped they'd never be the same again.

But he wasn't a betting man.

Chapter 30

*If you can count how many lights you're using in
your Christmas display, you're not using enough.*

—George Evans, who never regrets the extravagance
of his annual holiday decorations until the
electric bill arrives in January

From half a block away, they began to hear the music. Seth
parked his truck in front of the Evanses' house because the
drive was already full of cars belonging to other family members. When he turned off the engine, he recognized the tune as
a familiar, but juiced-up Christmas carol. The electronic whine
of synthesized holiday joy blasted from speakers behind every
bush and tree.

A gingerbread house made of painted plywood stood in
one corner of the yard, festooned with candy canes and dancing macaroons. Next to it, a life-sized nativity scene, complete
with bobble-head sheep, blocked the view of most of the west
side of the house. Several blow-up snow globes were strategi-
cally placed to fill any empty spaces on the wide lawn.

"Less is definitely not considered more here," Angie murmured.

Seth usually viewed his aunt and uncle's foibles through a
cloudy lens of affection. He tried to see their house through
Angie's eyes for a bit.

A bulky sleigh filled with wrapped packages and pulled by
six reindeer had been anchored to the roof of the two-story

home. There wouldn't have been room for eight animals due to their ponderous size. A pair of red-clad legs stuck out of the chimney. The black-booted feet moved back and forth, as if a slow-motion samba dancer were standing on his head.

"*Excess* rhymes with *success* around here," Seth admitted.

George Evans was puttering around beneath one of his oaks, a tangle of wires under one arm and a heavy-duty extension cord in the other.

"What's he doing?" Angie asked as they crossed the street toward the merry nightmare in the making.

"Every year, Uncle George puts together a Christmas display that would put Clark Griswold to shame," Seth explained. "His collection of decorations has grown over the years and I've never known him to retire any of them, so every December, he tops himself. The music is new."

Angie pulled her beanie down over her ears.

Probably to protect her hearing, Seth thought. "Maybe it'll grow on us."

"So will fungus, but it's not recommended," Angie said, raising her voice to be heard over the canned music. "Guess it's not just your aunt who believes if a little is good, a lot's a whole bunch better."

"Naw, it's genetic. Runs through both sides of the whole family," Seth admitted. "If you think this is a little excessive—"

"A little?"

"I'm just saying wait till you see it all lit up at night. Uncle George's strobes ought to come with a seizure warning for epileptics."

"There you are, Seth!" George shouted and waved a hand at him. "Come give me a hand with these cords. We'll hook up the rope lights wrapped around the oak trunks."

Seth helped his uncle untangle the cords and plugged lines from the base of each tree into the surge protector that led to the longest extension cord Seth had ever seen in a nonindustrial setting. The spoke-like arrangement of the cords spread across the lawn resembled a neon orange spider web.

"I gotta tell you, Seth, I think I finally solved my squirrel problem this time," George hollered with a wide grin.

"Really?" Seth shouted back. He wished for the hearing protection headset he usually wore on the job, but he'd left it in his truck. "How?"

"Simple. The durn things don't seem to like this music, nary one bit," George said. "I haven't seen hide nor hair of the furry little rats since I started playing it this morning at eight."

"You've been playing it that long?" Angie asked, her eyes wide.

"It'll only play from eight a.m. to ten p.m. Got the CD on a continuous loop. Good stuff, huh?" George beamed. "Come see the system I set up in the garage. It's state of the art."

At that precise moment, the music came to a sudden halt. Blessed silence reigned, and all Seth could hear was the whirr of the small motor on the Evanses' roof that kept Santa's legs wiggling in the chimney. Angie sighed audibly in relief.

"What the—" George bolted for the open door of his garage.

Seth and Angie followed.

"The cabinet where all the sound equipment's stored is still locked," George said, fishing for a key in his pocket.

"May not matter." Seth pointed to the hole where the main power cord went in. "Looks like this opening has been . . . well, enlarged."

Sure enough, there were telltale signs that a rodent of some sort had been gnawing through the rubber seal and surrounding wood. When George unlocked the cabinet, they discovered several cords had been chewed down to the bare wires.

"Well, there's why you haven't seen any squirrels in your yard for a bit," Seth said. "The whole bunch must have been in here working on the power cords."

"I had to special order all this," George said morosely, "It'll take a week to replace."

For which, the neighborhood should be joyful.

Seth clapped a hand on his uncle's shoulder. "Cheer up, Uncle George. You still have more lights up than anyone else in town."

His uncle smiled wryly. "I don't care about that. I only care about having more up than Mayhew."

In the matter of Christmas decorations, the rivalry between George Evans and his crotchety next-door neighbor, Mr. Mayhew, was approaching Hatfield vs. McCoy level. Each year, Mayhew tried to outdo Evans in overdoing lights, holiday scenes, and animated figures. The dueling displays looked as if a Christmas flea market had been gobbled up and then regurgitated out on the two properties, but this year, it did appear that Uncle George had Mayhew beat.

But it was only Thanksgiving. The Christmas season was just beginning. Between George Evans and Mr. Mayhew, there was no telling what new depths of poor taste would be plumbed on Oak Street.

"Come on in, kids," Shirley Evans called out the door that led from the garage to the kitchen. "It's too cold to stand out there. Almost everyone is already here. George, get on in and help me take the turkey out of the oven."

Angie followed Seth into the blessedly warm kitchen. But it didn't smell like typical Thanksgiving fare. There was an odd mix of spices wafting around her.

"Thanks for having us," Angie said to Shirley. She waved to Heather, who was busy setting the long table that had stretched beyond the dining room into the family room to accommodate the guests.

Angie's Angel of the Lord had been invited, too. Jadis Chu was helping her boss, Michael, carry chairs from other places in the house to fit around the long table. Angie was glad she'd been included. Jadis struck her as another orphan in the world. If the exotic-looking girl had family, Angie had yet to hear about it.

"How can I help, Mrs. Evans?" she asked her hostess.

"Shirley. We already settled that. And you can help by being our guest today. Next time, we'll put you to work," Shirley said. "Let's get you out of that coat. Here, Seth. Make yourself useful instead of ornamental. Take Angela's coat upstairs and lay it on my bed."

Seth obeyed as if the directive had come straight from heaven wrapped in a bolt of lightning. Angie would have liked to keep her jacket until she'd completely warmed up, but there was no arguing with Shirley Evans. Besides, the house seemed fairly toasty.

"It smells very . . . *interesting* in here." Angie's inner dictionary kicked in.

Interesting (adjective) 1. Holding one's attention 2. What one says when one can't say "good."

"Oh! That's because we're not having a traditional Thanksgiving meal," Shirley said, her eyes dancing. "In honor of our upcoming world cruise, we're going international!"

"But that is turkey in the oven," Seth said warily as he rejoined them in the kitchen.

"Yes, it is, but only because George wouldn't let me fix Peking duck. The man absolutely put his foot down. So we compromised," Shirley said. "What you're smelling is the Jamaican jerk sauce I just basted the turkey with. And all the side dishes are a taste from somewhere else around the world."

"But you made your cornbread dressing, right?" Seth said hopefully.

"Well, I made dressing, but it's not cornbread. It's made with Chinese sticky rice."

"I suppose you didn't make noodles either." Seth seemed

truly disheartened by the news. He'd told Angie the Evans family recipe for egg noodles was as closely held a secret as the launch codes for a nuclear arsenal. And it should be. As far' as Seth was concerned his aunt's noodles were good enough to serve a president.

"Well, no, not this year," Shirley admitted. "Instead, I bought some rice noodles to make Shrimp pad Thai appetizers."

"No pigs in a blanket? The kind you eat with toothpicks?"

"No, not this year. We'll use chopsticks instead. Like I told George, we're widening our horizons."

"But not our waistlines," George said with a sigh. "You know, not everything is improved by changing it out of all knowing."

"George, you can't cling to tradition all the time."

"Why not?"

"Well, for one thing, the usual Thanksgiving fare isn't all that good for you. Contrary to what my husband might think"—Shirley turned to Angie for support—"gravy is not a beverage and carrot cake is not a vegetable."

"Your international menu sounds"—Angie felt she should come to the former pageant director's defense, but all she could come up with was—"broadening."

"We're not likely to get broader eating that stuff," George grumbled.

"I'm smelling something quite spicy," Angie said. "What other dishes have you prepared?"

Shirley Evans shot her a grateful smile. "You must be smelling my Moroccan side dish—it's sautéed parsnips and dates in spiced yogurt."

"The Pilgrims never had any yogurt," George said.

"Or dates," Seth joined in.

"They might not have had turkey either," Shirley said, unperturbed. "But we will. What with the spice rub before it went in and the jerk sauce basting, it'll be blackened turkey. Oh, dear! That pot's about to boil over."

She raced away from them to the stove in time to save the cook top from a mess. It was likely too late to avoid a disaster on the dining table.

"I wonder how you'll all like my jicama and blood orange salad," Shirley said over her shoulder.

"Like Riley, we wonder how we'll like it our own selves," Seth whispered to Angie.

"Cousin Seth!"

"Speak of the devil." Seth knelt down and spread his arms wide. "Riley, come here, you little monkey."

Giggling madly, the child flung herself into Seth's arms and he hoisted her up onto his shoulders. Then he gave her a "pony ride" into the living room, being careful to duck in the doorway so she wouldn't bang her forehead on the head jamb.

Angie followed them as far as the living room, but Riley and her faithful steed kept going. They made a circuit of the foyer, the hallway, the family room that had been converted to an extension dining room to accommodate the long table, then through the kitchen and back past Angie. They didn't slow one bit as they started a second lap.

Crystal came to stand beside Angie as they watched the pair gallop around. Angie thought she looked more pulled together today. Her nails and hair looked salon fresh. Crystal had probably dropped ten pounds from stress, but her sleek linen slacks and cashmere sweater kept her from looking gaunt.

"Seth's good with kids," Crystal said.

Angie nodded. Seth was good with everybody.

"Noah used to be, too."

"Is he coming?"

Crystal shrugged. "I don't know. He's been told when the meal starts. I hope he'll drop off Ethan, at least."

"Noah is good with Ethan, isn't he?" Angie said, wanting to help Crystal find something good to say about her husband.

"He is, but then, Ethan's an easy child. He's never any trouble."

From the other room, the six-year-old terror of the Evans clan shrieked like a Banshee.

To Angie's surprise, Crystal smiled. "But in Riley's favor, there's never a dull moment when she's around."

"You never know what she'll say next," Angie said.

"True. And sometimes she says the wisest things. The other day she said she thought her dad was trying to find his way home, but maybe he couldn't pick out the right path and didn't want to get lost on the wrong one."

"That sounds like Riley," Angie said, glad to hear Crystal being positive for once. "She does have a way with words."

"It's my fault. I know it," Crystal said. Tears welled in her eyes, but she blinked them back. "I make him feel every path is wrong. I had everything—a great husband, a career, two sweet kids. It was good. Great even. But . . . I ruined it because it wasn't perfect."

"Nothing's perfect." Judging from the smell of something burning in the kitchen, their Thanksgiving feast certainly wasn't going to be.

"But if I change, I mean . . . I could change, couldn't I? If I tried . . ." Crystal went on, as if Angie wasn't even there. "I could stop looking for things to correct and be satisfied with the way things are."

"I don't think it's ever a question of only one person doing the changing."

"You're right." Crystal sighed. As a perfectionist, she also had control issues. And she was completely out of control at the moment. "Noah may not want to even try."

Angie searched for something comforting to say, but Crystal's phone rang at that moment.

"It's him," she said, her voice breathless and pathetically hopeful. She took a deep lungful and swiped the face of her phone to answer.

Before Crystal was able to even bring the phone to her ear, Angie heard Noah's voice shouting. "Come quick. It's Ethan. We're on our way to the hospital."

Then the connection was broken.

Chapter 31

Life is a string of moments, but those moments aren't a set of matched pearls. Some of them, the golden bright ones mostly, flee by, refusing to stay longer than a blink. Others are frozen in stillness, unwilling to budge and let some kinder, more hopeful moment take their place.

—Angie Holloway, on the passage of
time in a hospital waiting room

As soon as Crystal told her mother about Noah's frantic call, Shirley Evans took charge. She ordered Heather to the hospital stat. Being an RN and the only one in the family who could explain medical issues to the others, Heather flew out the door with Michael and Jadis hard on her heels.

Breathing hoarsely, Crystal was tearing through her purse looking for her car keys.

"No! You're in no condition to drive anywhere." Shirley ordered Angie and Seth to take Crystal to Coldwater General, and then volunteered to bring Riley up later.

"George can keep her entertained while I put all this food away. Then we'll join you at the hospital," Shirley said as she practically shooed them out the front door. Then at the last possible second, she grabbed Crystal into a tight hug and whispered in her ear, "I'll be praying every second, sweetheart. God's got this. Your little family is even dearer to Him than you are to me, and that's saying a lot."

Then, her eyes unnaturally bright with unshed tears, Shirley waved them on their way.

"Aunt Shirley may be a little nuts in the kitchen," Seth said as they climbed into his truck, "but she's exactly who you want beside you in a crisis."

Angie couldn't agree more. They all had their marching orders and knew what to do. But not even Shirley Evans could command them how to feel about it.

Crystal was unraveling by the moment. She talked nonstop all the way to the hospital, imagining every possible emergency, from broken bones to a ruptured appendix.

When Crystal gave him a chance to slip a word in edgewise, Seth offered a few comforting thoughts. Coldwater General was a good hospital, he reminded her. Doc Warner would make sure Ethan got the best care possible.

"And if it's something they can't handle here, Ethan can always be airlifted to Tulsa."

That was a mistake. It only made Crystal start imagining worst-case scenarios.

Angie kept quiet. She had no comfort to give. Bad things happened. Judging from the panic she'd heard in Noah's voice, this was bad. Angie knew full well that family was not forever. Her parents had been ripped away from her before she'd even had a chance to know them.

That hurt badly enough. She could only imagine Crystal's agony. She'd spent years loving her child, investing herself in him, only to have him injured or sick, possibly taken from her completely without warning . . .

How did people do it? How did they commit to each other? How did they give their hearts away knowing everything could be gone in a blink and they'd be left alone?

Crystal was out of the truck and running toward the entrance almost before Seth put his vehicle into park. Angie climbed out but didn't run after her.

Angie was too full of dread for that. She barely felt it when Seth took her hand. She put one foot before the other, and forced herself to push air in and out of her lungs, but she was numb inside as they walked toward the hospital's front doors. Crystal and Noah were about to be reminded that no matter what ties they'd forged, either with each other or with their son, none of them were unbreakable.

Life was precious. It was also fragile. Too fragile to bear. Angie hadn't been this deeply aware of her lonely, single "only-ness" in a long while. It pressed down on her like a heavy weight.

Noah wasn't the only one in the waiting room. It was ringed with other poor souls whose loved ones were receiving care elsewhere in the hospital. Some were trying to distract themselves with their phones or the dusty magazines, but they skewered the newcomers with a half-wild thousand-yard stare. It was a potent mix of hope that it might be a doctor with news and dread over what that news might be.

But Crystal didn't seem to notice the others. She only had eyes for her husband.

When Angie and Seth caught up to her, she was already in Noah's arms. The air around the couple crackled with suppressed panic. Heather and Michael were standing close by, their faces studies in worry and sympathy. Jadis had staked out the far corner and, eyes closed, appeared to be praying or meditating or sending "white light" or whatever it was admitted agnostics did in times of crisis. Judging from her intense frown, it didn't seem to be helping Jadis in the slightest and there was no telling how or if her intense concentration affected Ethan's well-being. Everyone in the room was afflicted with the paralysis of helplessness and afraid of what the next few breaths might bring.

Hospital waiting rooms are the anteroom of hell.

"Noah, what happened?" Crystal pulled back from their embrace far enough to look up at his face. "Were *you* hurt, too?"

Crystal's husband was a big, strapping guy. A respected member of the community. Looks, money, power—he had everything. Folks around Coldwater would say Noah Addleberry lived a charmed life.

Now the guy who had everything broke down and wept like a child. "Oh, God, it's my fault."

To Crystal's credit, she held him while his massive shoulders shook. "What do you mean?"

"It was my valium," he choked out. "Ethan must have gotten into the medicine cabinet and downed a bunch of tablets."

"When did you start taking valium?" Crystal asked as they sank onto the nearby couch together.

"Last week." Noah dragged a hand over his face. "I couldn't sleep without you—"

"So you're saying this is my fault?" Crystal interrupted, but then bit her lower lip to stop herself. "No, forget I said that. Please go on."

Noah drew a shuddering breath. "Anyway, I asked the doc to give me something to help me nod off." His voice broke and he half sobbed, "Oh, God, I'm so sorry."

Tears left dark mascara runnels on Crystal's cheeks. "Me too, Noah. Me too."

Noah held her tighter and they rocked back and forth. They were united again. Finally. But it was a broken sort of unity. It had taken the worst of things to bring them closer.

Angie studied the tips of her shoes. She wasn't aware that Heather had approached Noah until she heard her friend say, "How many tablets did Ethan take?"

"I don't know," Noah said in total misery. "I wasn't careful about how many I took—some nights more, some less—so I don't know. I brought the bottle, but Doc said it's not much help if we can't figure out how many pills should be in it. A lot. That's all I know. There should be a lot more."

"Where's Ethan now? Can I go to him?" Crystal asked.

"They're working on him in the ER, trying to get him to wake up." Noah stared at a distant point on the horizon only he seemed to see. "He fell asleep on the couch and just wouldn't wake up."

"I'll go see how he's doing," Heather said, and headed to the emergency room.

Noah swiped his eyes. "Aren't you going to rip into me?"

Crystal shook her head.

"But I deserve it this time," Noah said.

Crystal swallowed hard and moved, almost imperceptibly, a little bit away from him. But when she spoke, her words were gentle. "It was an accident, Noah. It's . . . it's not your fault."

"It will be if he . . ." Noah couldn't finish his thought, but they were all thinking it with him.

If he dies.

One moment Ethan was a nerdy little fifth grader glued to his iPad. The next he might be gone. He'd had so few moments. And for the short years of his young life, how often had Crystal and Noah made a mess of Ethan's moments. How much struggling for control, how much frustration, how much anger over things that didn't count for anything in the long haul, only to end up exhausted in a hospital waiting room together. All that flailing, all that fuss, over nothing of lasting importance.

And no matter what they did now, in a blink, their child could be gone.

Noah reached a tentative hand toward Crystal's, but at that instant, she began digging in her purse and emerged with a tissue. Angie didn't think Crystal had meant to avoid her husband's touch. It was just a chance miss.

And a missed chance. A moment to reconnect was lost.

How many missed chances could a couple survive?

Something like panic rose in Angie's throat. It was so hard to watch Noah and Crystal struggle toward each other, one step forward, two steps back. They'd never really come together at this rate.

Without a word, Michael Evans sat down on the couch on the other side of his sister and took her hand. Angie and Seth settled into the chairs across from them. No one said anything, but Angie noticed Seth bowing his head and closing his eyes. Though his lips occasionally moved, no sound came out.

At times like this, Angie wished she could pray and believe Someone was listening. She'd done it when she was a child, but she had no evidence that her words ever made it any farther than the ceiling above her head. Once she became an adult, she figured God was too busy to be bothered with the small doings of her life. Besides, she could take care of herself.

She had to.

But she wondered if it would be a cheat to try to pray now when things were terrible since she'd ignored God when times were relatively good?

Then, too, she'd have to care about someone to pray for them. And caring about someone was the sure path to devastation. She only had to look at the couple on the couch to see that. Crystal and Noah were both shattered, holding themselves together with the slenderest of things.

A bit of spit and baling twine disguised as hope.

Heather came back into the waiting room. Everyone rose to their feet in unison.

"Ethan has been moved to ICU," she said. "Doc Warner is doing everything he can."

"Like what?" Crystal asked. In anyone else, it would have sounded like a demand, but having been on the receiving end of Crystal Addleberry's truly demanding tone, they all recognized this as a simple plea for more information.

"Ethan's stomach has been pumped and he's been given flumazenil. That's a medication to reduce the effects of the valium," Heather explained.

"Is he awake?" Noah asked, his voice ragged. "Can we talk to him?"

Heather shook her head. "He's on a respirator."

Crystal gave a small gasp and Noah put his arm around her. She seemed to lean into him. "He can't breathe on his own?"

"Yes, he can. But Ethan was breathing so shallowly, his O2 sats were lower than the doctor wanted to see, so he ordered the respirator. Ethan's just getting some help with his breathing for now. This is a good thing," Heather said reassuringly. "Adequate oxygen flow protects his brain function and other organs."

"But when will he wake up?" Crystal asked, her tone small and vulnerable as a child's.

Heather didn't answer immediately.

"We should know more in an hour or so," she said, but the slice of silence before Heather answered had already spoken volumes. Ethan's life was balanced on the edge of a knife. It could go either way.

"So all we can do is wait?" Noah asked.

"No," Seth said. "All we can do is pray."

He held out his hands to Angie at his side and to Noah, who was across from him. As one by one the others joined hands, a circle began to form. Even Jadis left her corner and came to stand between Angie and Heather.

There was a time when Angie would have given anything to be part of a family for real. To be included in a loving circle, even a grieving loving circle. But now she felt as if she was being sucked against her will into a heartache waiting to happen.

It was selfish of her, but her life had been one goodbye after another. She didn't think she could bear another loss.

Even one that belonged to someone else.

Then, softly but confidently, Seth started talking to God. He didn't use any "thees" or "thous." He just spoke to God as if He was a friend he was used to checking in with on a regular basis. Sometimes there were long stretches of silence between sentences, as if Seth were listening for an answer.

In those silences, Angie heard only the ambient white noise of the hospital, a few beeps at regular intervals, the clack of shoes on vinyl floors and the low whirr and click of medical equipment. But then she began to hear the shuffle of feet on the waiting room's industrial grade carpet, and felt a hand on her shoulder.

Some of the other people in the waiting room had set aside their own pain and worry and had risen to join the circle praying for Ethan.

All Angie could do was wonder why they'd risk it for someone they didn't even know. Why offer up your hope if it was just as likely to be dashed to pieces as rewarded with a happy outcome?

When Seth finished praying, someone else picked up where he left off, asking for wisdom for the doctors and expressing thanks for Ethan's young life. The voice was strong and steady and . . . familiar.

That's George Evans, Angie realized, amazed that Ethan's grandfather could sound so at peace in crisis.

She felt a small hand reach for hers. Angie opened her eyes. Riley had wormed her way into the inner circle and was trying to separate Angie and Seth's hands so she could take her place between them. The usually chipper six-year-old looked up at her, her eyes enormous and solemn as a judge. Even though all the adults in her life were desperate with worry over her brother, Riley wasn't frantic. She seemed sober, but calm.

And far older than her years.

When her grandfather finished praying, Riley started in. Her voice small and reedy, she asked God to help her brother "get okay."

Simply. Trustingly.

If Ethan died, Riley was in for more hurt than she'd ever known. Not only would her brother be gone, Angie knew her parents were statistically more likely to divorce after the loss of a child. Plus, Riley's childish faith would be smashed to bits.

I'm a terrible person, Angie realized, heartsick over the moment of self-understanding. She wasn't proud of it, but she knew it was true. *I can't risk this. I can't be involved.*

Gently, she pulled her hand away from Riley's and put it in Jadis's. Then as the others continued praying, she slipped out of the circle, down the hallway, and out the hospital doors.

The wind bit her cheeks, but she turned up her collar and started walking home.

Alone. I may as well get used to it.

Chapter 32

*When folks start jawin' about whether some imaginary glass is
half empty or half full, I always wonder to myself, why don't
they just take a real one out of the cupboard and fill the
darn thing to the brim?*

—Junior Bugtussle, who thinks if you want
half a glass you should find a smaller glass

"Emma, I'm back," Angie called when she came through the
kitchen door, stamping her feet to get some feeling into them.
It was more than a mile from the hospital to her place. There
was ice in the wind's breath and Angie's toes burned with the
cold. "Emma?"

There was no answer, but the girl had left a note on the
counter.

*My mom called and wanted me to come for Thanksgiving dinner.
Maybe she'll let me stay. Either way, I'll call you. I've been thinking
about all the things I'm thankful for today and you're at the top of
the list, Ms. H. I don't know what I'd do without you.*

Emma

Angie sank onto one of the counter stools. Emma was only
fifteen, pregnant, and not sure where she'd be sleeping tonight.
Yet she'd been counting her blessings.

I really am a terrible person, she decided once again. All

she could think about was how Emma's moving out would affect her.

If Emma did move back home, Angie would be equal parts sad and relieved. She didn't want to admit it, but she'd enjoyed having another beating heart in the apartment. The cat didn't really count since Angie was never sure whether Effie would bestir herself to greet her when she came home.

But if Emma was once again her mother's responsibility, Angie wouldn't have to worry about her anymore. She wouldn't have to fret about what the girl decided concerning her pregnancy. Or if she should keep and raise the baby herself or give the child up for adoption.

Angie wouldn't have to care.

Or risk being hurt if things turned out badly.

Only that morning, Angie had pondered asking Emma if she could adopt her child. It had seemed a logical solution at the time. Emma could continue her education. She'd be able to see the child on occasion through the years. If Angie adopted the baby, he or she would never know the isolation and insecurity of a foster situation.

If Angie became an adoptive mother, she would finally have a family of her own.

That was what she'd meant when she'd told Seth she wouldn't be making any important decisions without talking to him first.

Now Angie was glad she hadn't mentioned an adoption to Emma. If she gave her love to Emma's child, she'd be destroyed if something happened to the baby. Ethan's sudden catastrophe proved that. She barely knew the boy, but Angie was still so shaken by his situation, she could hardly function.

I'm a miserable, selfish . . .

She wanted to add *heartless* to her list of sins, but the truth was Angie had a heart. It was just small. Whether it had atrophied from lack of use or shrunk because she'd kept it hidden to protect it, she wasn't sure. But she had precious little heart to offer anyone.

And Seth deserves so much more.

Angie took off her coat, made a cup of coffee, and sat on her couch, tucking her feet up under her. After a while, Effie came out to investigate. The cat snuggled up against her for a few minutes without purring. But when Angie didn't speak or deign to pet her, the feline moved to the far arm of the couch and glared in her direction. Finally, Effie hopped down and disappeared into the other room.

Evidently, it was highly unsatisfying to the cat to be ignored.

Shoe's on the other foot this time, huh, cat?

The light through the windows facing the Square grew dusky, but Angie didn't move from her spot on the couch. Every time thoughts of Ethan and the rest of the Evans clan invaded her mind, she chased them out with ruthlessness. She didn't dare hope. Didn't dare pray.

Heather was wrong. The whole premise behind the Warm Hearts Club was wrong. Being involved in other people's lives wouldn't make hers better. All it did was open her up to more hurt, more disappointment, more loss.

The only safety was in being alone.

A soft rap on her back door finally made her stir. Her feet had gone to sleep.

Kind of like my heart.

Her toes prickled as blood streamed back into them. In her heart, she felt nothing as she opened the door.

Seth stood on the other side.

"How is he?" she asked because she knew she should, not

because she thought she could bear to know the answer. She'd already tucked her heart behind a wall. Was this how it would be from now on? She'd go through the motions of appearing to care while tamping down her feelings like crazy to keep from being hurt by the caring?

"He's awake." Seth came in without being invited. "And breathing on his own."

"Thank God."

"Did you?"

"Did I what?"

"Thank God?"

"Seth, I—"

"When we finished praying, I looked up and you were gone." He cocked his head at her, his expression a mix of bewilderment and concern. "Why did you leave?"

Angie turned away from him. She couldn't bear to look at his face any longer. He was too dear. "I . . . I had to."

"Why?" he demanded.

How could she explain it? She wasn't even sure herself. She searched her feelings and came up with one true thing. It was something he might understand and not hate her for.

"I was afraid."

His tone softened. "What of?"

"Of Ethan dying." She raked a hand through her hair as she turned back to face him. She decided to lay everything out there. She owed Seth that. "Of God not caring."

"You think if Ethan had died it would have been because God didn't care?" Seth asked.

"Well, yes." What else was she supposed to think? If God was really all powerful, He could heal a little boy who'd accidentally taken some of his father's meds without breaking a sweat. If Ethan died, it would be because God couldn't be bothered to stop it from happening.

That kind of impersonal, unfeeling God was too terrifying to contemplate.

"Angie, that's not how it works."

"Really? That's how it works in my life." When he frowned in confusion, she went on. "Every time I got close to someone, they either died or left me or were taken away from me somehow. And God didn't lift a finger to stop it." She shook her head. "I just can't risk caring anymore."

"Even about me?"

Angie could scarcely breathe for all the caring inside her for this man. It was choking her. Seth had filled up the empty places in her soul until she was bursting with him. She wanted him with every molecule of her body. Her adoration of him bordered on idolatry. It was an old-fashioned sort of sin, but one she recognized in herself in a heartbeat. Every fiber of her being yearned toward Seth Parker.

Losing him would be her worst fear come to life.

It's too late, she realized. She couldn't save her heart from hurt by not caring for him. She already did. Seth was her next breath. He was her first thought each morning and the recurring theme running through her dreams each night.

"I can't care for you more than I already do," she said truthfully. Her chest constricted in pain. A single drop more love for him would make her heart stop. It wouldn't stand the strain.

His lips tightened into a hard line. "Then how are you going to live, not caring about anybody?"

"I don't know." Shoulders shaking, she burst into tears. "But if I don't get involved, if I don't let myself care—"

"Then you won't get hurt?" he filled in.

"Something like that," she managed to choke out between sobs.

He understands. She never thought anyone would.

Seth took her into his arms and held her close while she wept. She let him. She didn't have the strength to fight his love. A reservoir of past hurts bubbled up. All the times she'd come home to find her small suitcase packed, all the times she'd made friends at one school only to be yanked to another, every time she'd had to squeeze into yet another borrowed family, to call another stranger "Mom," to give a piece of herself to someone only to have it rejected or stomped on—all those blows to the heart rose to the surface and she wept them out.

And all the while, Seth held her. Finally, she was cried out. Drained.

"Here's the thing," he said softly. "Everything in life is a risk. If we decide not to take any risks, we aren't living anymore. We're just taking up space."

She didn't say anything. She wasn't sure her voice would work. And besides, just taking up space sounded safe.

"Angie, I love you." He put a couple of fingers under her chin and tipped it up so she had to meet his gaze.

He's not lying. I can see the love. What I can't see is the hurt that always follows. But I don't have to see it to know it's coming.

Seth dug into his pocket and came out with a small box. "I've been waiting for the right time to give this to you, and it turns out there is no right time. There's just now."

He handed it to her. It looked suspiciously like a ring box. Hands shaking, she took it. When she opened the box, she found an antique diamond ring—a large center stone, ringed with smaller baguettes set in gold filigree.

"It's beautiful."

"It was my grandmother's. She and my granddad were married for over sixty years. There's a lot of love, a lot of promises made good, already ingrained in that ring." He took one of her hands and sheltered it in both of his. "I'm adding mine today."

"Oh, Seth."

"Don't give me your answer. Not right now. I can see you need to think on this," he said. "But while you're thinking, I want you to remember this. No matter what you decide, Angela Holloway, I'll love you till I die."

Angie pulled her hand away from him and put a little distance between them. "That's just it, Seth. You'll die someday. I'll die. Whatever we do, it doesn't matter. We'll lose each other sooner or later." She gave him her back, unable to meet his gaze any longer. "I can't bear another loss. Especially not you."

Seth crossed over to her and put his hands on her shoulders, but he didn't force her to turn back to him. The warmth of his big rough hands penetrated even her thick sweater.

"God knows something about loss. After all, the reason we celebrate Christmas is because He let His Son leave heaven and come to earth," Seth said. "I gotta think that was a lonely choice. A choice full of loss."

"That's the least churchy explanation of the holiday I've ever heard," she said, turning in his arms to face him again.

Seth nodded, conceding the point. "Fancy words aren't my strong suit."

Angie smiled, despite herself. When they first met, she'd thought him a Neanderthal who only spoke in one-syllable words and incomplete sentences. Now she appreciated the depths of understanding behind those simple words of his.

"You said you were afraid God would let Ethan die. I was, too," he admitted. "But even if the boy had died, we wouldn't have been alone. God knows something about the pain of losing someone. I gotta believe if you let Him, He'll help you deal with your pain."

Even though she had no conscious memory of her real parents, she still felt their loss. Over the years, Angie had been an on-again, off-again churchgoer, depending on the devotion level of her current foster family at any given time. She knew the Bible stories. She remembered the words to some of the songs. But she wasn't sure God was really the sort to take an interest in her.

He hadn't demonstrated any so far. At least, not any she could see. But Seth obviously believed God could help her.

Make that "us."

Until she figured out how to care for Seth, or anyone else, without fearing the pain that was sure to follow, there wasn't much hope for an "us."

She leaned into Seth and stood on tiptoe to kiss his lips. He didn't need much encouragement to respond in a way that curled her toes. When he finally released her, she sagged against him.

"I have to warn you, I'm taking that kiss as a good sign," he said huskily.

"It is." Angie hoped it was. It hurt to hope, but she was beginning to believe not hoping would be even worse.

"Good," he said, "because I'm under orders to deliver you back to my aunt's house for supper, where you're supposed to help eat up some of her sad and sorry excuse for a Thanksgiving dinner."

Angie groaned at the thought of Shirley Evans's spicy mishmash of dishes. "I don't suppose I can plead for a rain check."

"Nope. When Shirley Evans sends a summons, attendance is mandatory," Seth said. "Besides, if we don't eat it, poor Uncle George will be stuck with those leftovers for a month."

"I guess the old squirrel fighter deserves our support," Angie said. "But I'm wondering if the highest and best use of that jerked turkey might not be to display it on the front lawn as a warning to other creatures."

Seth laughed. "Don't tell Uncle George. That's just the sort of desperate measure he'd be willing to try."

As Angie walked hand in hand with Seth down to his pickup, she wondered what desperate measures she'd be willing to try. Her dilemma couldn't be solved with traps. No gizmo would drive away the fear of loss.

Or give her a way to deal with it when it happened.

Chapter 33

*A lawsuit cannot be considered frivolous if simply
threatening one will make the other party knuckle under.*

—Peter Manning, on the many and
varied uses of the legal system

"What do you mean, you don't think we should proceed?"
Sabine's tone was carefully neutral. It was the same one she
used for deposing clients she suspected actually *were* guilty, but
she didn't want to know for sure.

"Just that. I still can't find a complainant," Peter said. Once
again, he'd had to place his call to his partner from the far edge
of the Heart of the Ozarks parking lot to find a measly single
bar of cell service. "Nobody in this whole town seems upset
about the Christmas pageant taking place."

Peter had even trolled the Samaritan House homeless shelter looking for a disgruntled drunk to use as his aggrieved
party. Not a soul would agree to take part in a suit against the
town's Christmas pageant, even when he offered a cash incen-
tive.

"I ain't gonna lie to you, man, I could use the money," one
of the frequent residents of the shelter had told him. "But the
folks hereabouts take pretty good care of the likes of us. Three
hots and a cot, if we agree to not bring a bottle in with us for
the night. Sandwiches to go and a warm blanket, even if we
don't."

"They force you to sobriety? How can they impose their values on you like that?"

"It ain't no big deal. They just hold out a carrot for us. There ain't no switch to beat us with," the man had explained. "Besides, reckon you'd want me to be sober if I agreed to sign on to your lawsuit thing."

"I'll only require you to be sober when you have to appear in court."

"But you ain't gonna be around here forever once that fancy-ass lawsuit of yours is done. Your money will go with you. So I asks you, what would I do after the ruckus dies down? I still gotta live here, you know. Ain't nobody gone give me a handout if I screw up the pageant for 'em."

"Not very Christian of them if they don't," Peter had grumbled.

"Well, maybe they would still help me out, at that. Folks 'round here are like that. But I wouldn't feel right takin' the help if I did 'em dirt like you want me to," the scruffy fellow had said. "Why don't you just ease on down the road, Counselor?"

So Peter had done just that. He'd frequented the Green Apple Grill by day and the Red Caboose Bar by night, half an ear cocked for malcontents. People complained about the weather and about politicians in general, mostly the ones in far off DC and a few in the state capital, but no one fussed about their own little corner of the world. For the most part, Coldwater Cove was pretty happy with itself.

And everyone seemed to be looking forward to the Christmas pageant with enthusiasm.

"I can't believe it," Sabine's voice crackled from his phone. To say that cell service was merely spotty was charitable in the extreme. "You mean *no one* will sign on to the suit?"

"No," Peter said. "I tried. Hand to God, Sabine, I tried."

There was silence for a few heartbeats, but then she came back with Plan B. "Then we'll file without a local. It makes for better TV if you have an upset resident by your side, but we'll have to make do. The principle is still sound, and the media will be on the lookout for this story. They always are. I know I said we'd wait till closer to Christmas to file, but you know what they say. It's better to be first than to be best."

"I don't know, Sabine," Peter said. "Maybe we should try to make the case elsewhere. This town is a dusty little backwater. What happens here doesn't hurt a soul. Why don't we save our powder for a fight worth fighting?"

"This fight *is* worth fighting," Sabine insisted. "Anywhere religion is being promoted by the government, it's worth calling them out. Besides, just filing the suit will accomplish our goals."

The only thing Peter thought it would accomplish was a string of disappointed faces in Coldwater once the townsfolk realized their precious pageant was going to be cancelled. From the old Vietnam vet who waited tables at the Green Apple to the statuesque dean at the college, everyone he'd met in the town would be upset.

Especially Angie.

He'd only seen her in passing, not even long enough to speak, since that night they'd had drinks at Harper's. Peter could still scarcely believe she'd turned down his offer to make her a professor at Bates College. The offer was totally bogus, but she didn't know that. She only knew it wouldn't be right to accept it.

Somewhere along the way, his timid little Ange had developed an acute sense of "oughtness," that elusive, almost instinctive feel for what was right or wrong, along with a spine of solid steel.

Sabine, who certainly had the spine, but not Ange's "oughtness," started talking again.

"This case is going to catapult us into the big leagues, Peter. You'll see. You can't buy this kind of publicity. We might even end up on a national morning news show or two."

Peter could almost see her preening. Cameras did indeed love his partner.

"There's no telling how many cases this will generate for us going forward," she said. "We'll be on every right-thinking organization's short list of litigators."

"I guess," he said noncommittally.

"I *know,*" she countered. "So I'll be in Tulsa tomorrow with a news crew ready to meet us on the superior court steps. I expect you to be there, too, Peter. Right?"

"There's just one problem with that."

"What?"

"Superior court convenes in the state capital."

"Hello? Like I said. Tulsa."

"Oklahoma City," Peter corrected.

"You're kidding me."

There wasn't enough bandwidth to do FaceTime on his phone, but he could practically see her rolling her eyes from halfway across the country.

"They actually think they have something that deserves to be called a city out there?" she demanded.

"Yes, they do, and it's where you have to be if you want to file in superior court in this state."

"Okay, I'll meet you in Oklahoma City, then," she said. "Right?"

He sighed. "Right."

"This is going to make us, Peter."

"Yeah."

"Don't get all excited on me," she said sarcastically. "I mean seriously. This thing has legs. It's going to drive a butt-load of business to our door. You'll finally be able to get that Ferrari."

"Yeah. That'll be good. See you tomorrow," he told her

more to get her to hang up than anything. When the connection was broken, Peter walked back into his slightly shabby, but scrupulously clean, motel room and plopped onto the sagging bed.

Angela Holloway would never own a Ferrari. She'd never have a vacation home on Aruba. She probably wouldn't ever make it to teaching at the college level.

But she had integrity. She knew how to pick her battles and which offers to turn down even if they seemed to advance her. Peter would bet she slept the sleep of the just each night.

He'd almost forgotten what that felt like. But he remembered well enough to miss it.

"Are you sure?" Phyllis Wanamaker asked. She was the owner of a shop called the Secondhand Junk-shun and her voice didn't usually sound so unsteady. "I mean, you saw the documents yourself?"

Marjorie Chubb allowed that the crackly sounding voice might be a technical issue. The captain of the Methodist prayer chain still wasn't very adept at setting up conference calls on all their cell phones.

Usually the prayer chain operated like a phone tree. One member would call two, the next two called four, and so on until all the prayer warriors had the information they needed to begin their assault on heaven. But for emergencies, Marjorie insisted they all learn how to participate in a conference call so the concerns could be shared at once throughout the whole group and praying could commence immediately.

And this was an emergency if Marjorie had ever seen one.

"I didn't actually see the documents, but I heard about the lawsuit straight from Wanda Cruikshank herself," Marjorie assured her prayer warriors. If the editor of the *Coldwater Gazette* said something was true, you could take it to the bank.

"How did she hear about it?" Glenda Scott wanted to know.

"Oh, you know how those media types are. They talk to each other," Marjorie explained. "It seems Wanda's got a cousin who writes for a little weekly in Oklahoma City, and as soon as the news hit his desk, he gave Wanda a call for a comment."

"What did she say?" asked Mrs. Chisholm, the oldest member of the group.

"How should I know that?"

"She didn't tell you?" Mrs. Chisholm said.

"No, I think she was too busy trying to find out what was what from her cousin to give him something printable from her," Marjorie said.

"Is it real?" Tilly Jean Iverson, the newest member of the prayer chain asked. "Can they do that, I mean?"

"Shut the pageant down? Yes, it appears they can," Marjorie said with a sigh. "A judge in Oklahoma City issued something called a temporary injunction."

"A junk-what?" Phyllis said. Evidently her ears pricked whenever "junk" was part of a word.

"An *injunction,*" Marjorie repeated. "It means the pageant can't go forward as planned."

The prayer warriors all began to talk at once.

"Till when?"

"Did you say Tilly? Oh, no. I think Tilly dropped off the call. Tilly Jean, you there?"

Several more voices chimed in asking after Tilly's whereabouts.

"Yep, I'm still here," Tilly Jean finally managed to get in. "Did Marjorie ever say how long the pageant has to stop for? Marjorie, are you still on the call?"

"Yes, I'm here."

"Well?"

"The pageant is hung up until the final decision is made, I guess," Marjorie said with a sigh. Conference calls weren't as efficient as she'd hoped. If everyone talked at once, no one could understand a thing.

"Who makes the final decision?" That sounded like Glenda Scott, a CNA at Coldwater General, but the connection was starting to break up a bit, so Marjorie couldn't be sure.

"The judge in the capital, I think."

"Well, why didn't he just decide then instead of *injuncting* us?" Phyllis said indignantly.

"I think the judge put off his decision because we wouldn't have liked it if he decided right then."

Marjorie wasn't sure who'd said this, but she thought it made sense. But maybe there was a spiritual reason for the delay, too. "If the judge had decided right then, we wouldn't have had the chance to pray over the problem."

This sentiment was met with a flurry of agreement.

"Wait a minute," someone said. "I think Tilly Jean got dropped off the conference call for real this time."

Several precious minutes were wasted while Marjorie punched at her phone trying to reconnect with Tilly Jean.

"This was so much easier back when all we had were party lines all over the county," Mrs. Chisholm grumbled. "No need for a phone tree to spread prayer concerns back then. We already knew what was what."

Marjorie was old enough to remember how folks in Coldwater Cove entertained themselves before cable TV came to town and sneaking a listen on their neighbors' calls had figured prominently. It probably wasn't what the phone company had in mind when they installed party lines, but it was blazingly efficient at distributing information.

"I'm back," Tilly Jean sang out. "What did I miss?"

"Not much," Marjorie said. "Okay, let's recap what we know. The state court has issued an injunction."

"And that means what?" Tilly Jean said. She'd evidently been off the call longer than anyone realized.

"That we can't go ahead with a pageant until there's a ruling."

"And when will the ruling be?" There was a little scritching noise as if Tilly Jean was taking notes. That wasn't unusual. A lot of the members kept a journal of their prayer requests so they could also record when the prayers were answered.

"We don't know," Marjorie said. "They have to convene a hearing. Then they'll set a date for a ruling."

"When is the hearing?" It was Tilly Jean again.

"Oh, foot! Wanda didn't tell me that," Marjorie said. "Well, God knows. All times are in His hands anyway. So we're agreed on what to pray, right?"

"That we get a good hearing?" Tilly Jean suggested.

"A good ruling," Marjorie corrected. "Agreed?"

"Agreed," came the unanimous reply.

The Methodist prayer chain's motto was the verse that said *If two of you shall agree on earth as touching anything that they shall ask, it shall be done for them of my Father which is in heaven.* Since there were a lot more than two on the prayer chain, they liked their odds.

"Oh!" Glenda Scott piped up. "I have a praise to report! Ethan Addleberry is being discharged this afternoon."

"Oh, good."

There were echoes of "Praise God" from all points on the conference call.

"So the boy's going home. Which home?" Marjorie asked. The split between Crystal and Noah had been quietly lifted up for some time now. "I only ask so we'll know how best to continue to pray for the family."

"To his home, home. The one with *both* of his parents," Glenda said. "Noah is moving back in."

This time the "Praise God's" were laced with copious "Hallelujah's."

"That's wonderful news, Glenda," Marjorie said. "If God can save a little boy, and save a marriage, I've got to believe He can save our Christmas pageant, too."

Chapter 34

*Sometimes things need to fall apart
before they fall into place.*

—Seth Parker, who believes there's always a
higher plan, but we may not be able
to make sense of the blueprints right away

"There's no saving it, Seth."

From the corner of his eye, he saw Angie refold the court documents and try to shove them back into the envelope. Even though the road he was driving wound along a three-season streambed, he reached over to cover her hands with one of his.

Her fingers were cold. She always seemed to be cold. He wished she'd let him warm her up, but she was still holding herself a little apart from him since his proposal. He wasn't good with words. Maybe action would convince her to say yes.

He just wasn't sure which action it would take.

"Come on, Angie. Don't be so negative."

"I'm not being negative. I'm being realistic. Face it. The Christmas pageant is dead and I'm the one who killed it."

"It's on life support, maybe, but not dead."

"The injunction sites us for using public property and we do. It mentions misappropriation of public funds because the director is paid by the county, naming me by name, so that's on me. If I weren't a teacher—"

"It would be a crying shame," he finished for her. "You're

a great teacher. And we'll find a way to make the pageant work, too."

"I don't see how. This is my fault."

"How do you figure?"

"I should have seen it coming. I mean, why else would Peter have been hanging around town so long? He was gathering evidence, building a case, and using me to do it. I'm such a stupe."

"No, you're not. It's not your fault he hung around. As I recall, you gave him the boot."

"You didn't think so at first."

"No, but that's because sometimes I'm a stupe," Seth admitted. "I shouldn't have doubted you."

"Maybe you should," Angie said. "I doubt myself. If I had the sense God gave a goose, I'd grab you with both hands and never let go."

"Now you're talking!"

"But, like I said, *if* I had sense . . ." Her voice faded away and she fell silent.

Angie was still wavering over her decision. She'd told Seth his grandmother's ring was safely tucked away in a drawer under her socks. He'd told her to take her time, but the waiting was killing him.

He'd given up the idea of a fancy dinner at his place. Instead of setting the table with his grandmother's china and silver, instead of hiring Lester to serve a catered meal, Seth had decided to just throw a couple of rib eyes on the grill. Then they'd watch the sun set behind the hills.

When they pulled off the highway and into the long winding drive that led to his home, Angie made suitably impressed noises. She loved the thick stand of pines that sheltered the house from the prevailing winds and the big live oak at the edge of his expansive yard.

"Oh, my gosh!" she said as she hopped out of the truck before he could make it around to open the door for her. He was going to have gear up with Angie if he wanted to be the gentleman his mom raised him to be. "Your house is gorgeous. I know you built it. Did you design it as well?"

"I put a couple of blueprints together to come up with the design." They walked up the flagstone walkway toward the cedar wraparound porch and front door. "It needed to fit the site and short of hiring an architect to create a plan from scratch, it was the best I could do."

She stopped in front of the door and smiled up at him. "Your best is pretty darn good. You know," she said as he stood aside to let her go first into his home, "in *Sense and Sensibility,* I always got the feeling that part of why Marianne softened toward Colonel Brandon was because if they married, she'd get to be mistress of his Delaford estate. Is that why you brought me here?"

"Well, since you brought it up, say the word and this could be your estate, my lady," Seth said. "So, how'm I doing?"

She pulled a face at him. "I'm not an Austen heroine. And if I say yes, it'll be because of you. Not your house."

"That's good. 'Cause I've been told I do kinda use antlers in all of my decorating." He opened the door and ushered her in. The house was undeniably masculine, filled with leather furniture and heavy dark wood.

"I like it," she said, looking around. "It suits you."

"And I'd like it better if it suited you, too." He pulled her into his arms for a sweet kiss. When they separated, her eyes were soft and shining. Then her expression turned impish.

"But would it suit Effie, I wonder," Angie said as she walked around the room, running her fingertips along some of the butter soft leather. "She's used to a much smaller domain."

"I suspect your cat would find a way to rule this roost, too."

Angie laughed. "Effie *is* used to being in charge. I'm glad you understand that we couldn't disrupt the natural order of things."

There were a number of things he'd like to disrupt out of all knowing, but Seth knew he had to let Angie come to him on her own terms.

He grilled the steaks. She made a salad and popped a bag of Uncle Ben's rice into the microwave. Seth didn't mind that she wasn't much of a cook. Angie had plenty of other things going for her.

Like she knew when to speak and when to let a comfortable silence settle over them. Plenty of people felt a compulsion to fill every hole in a conversation. To Seth, those quiet moments were fine. They were filled with a quiet knowing, a confirmation that all was well, and even if it wasn't, it would be so eventually.

It was something he took on faith. Just like he took that Angie would come around to a "yes" on that same faith. But in case she needed a nudge, he decided he ought to see if there was something he could do to tip the scales in his favor.

"So I read the script you emailed me," he said as they cleared the table after supper. "It was good."

"You sound surprised."

"No, I knew it'd be good. You've got a way with words, Angie," he said. "What I meant was it sounded like you weren't so upset with God when you wrote it."

"I'm not upset. I'm . . . cautious," she said, obviously still not ready to trust God completely with the uncertain future. "But you're right. Once I started writing, I started seeing the Christmas story with new eyes."

"Well, it'll make for a different pageant, that's for sure."

"No, it won't. There's not going to be a pageant," she said as she rinsed their plates in the sink, and then handed them to Seth to load into the dishwasher. "Peter saw to that."

Seth was quiet for a few minutes as he mulled over the problem. "So as I understand it, the main trouble cited in the lawsuit is using public property, right?"

"Yes. We can't have the pageant on the courthouse lawn. Or coming down a public street, for that matter. But that's not the only thing. It's me as well. I'm a public school teacher. I can't be the director."

"But I could."

She chuckled. "So, you're jonesing for a promotion from codirector to the Big Kahuna?"

"Why not?" He was self-employed. There shouldn't be any issue with the whole public employee deal. If Seth directed the pageant, they wouldn't be violating the injunction. Angie had already laid out the way the action should flow. She'd written the script. The cast knew what was expected of them. All Seth had to do was put the pieces together, and come up with a nonpublic piece of real estate for the pageant to come to life on. As a builder, that was sort of his wheelhouse.

But he didn't want to get her hopes up, so he decided to change the subject a little.

"How'd you come up with the idea for the way you wrote the script?"

She shrugged. "Since the pageant wasn't going to be confined to a single stage, Deek told me we'd have trouble with mics for our characters. So I needed to decide on a point of view character and let there be only one voice. If I told the Christmas story in just one person's voice, I figured that would make it easier, and it did."

"How'd you settle on Mary?"

"I'm a sucker for the underdog and I think she often gets shortchanged. She had the deepest relationship with God I can imagine," Angie said. "An incredible amount of trust. She must have been a remarkable person."

"So are you." Before she could argue that she wasn't, he

added, "Look, Angie, what if somehow, the pageant was able to go on?"

"Then there'd be a *Miracle on 34th Street* and all the angels would earn their wings," she said with a laugh.

And maybe, just maybe, if Seth could make the pageant happen for her, Angie could learn to trust him enough to get over her fear of loss. And trust God enough to heal her hurts, past, present, and future.

It was worth a shot.

Seth went to work on his new project the very next day. In his head, he dubbed it *Operation Wingspan* because whole companies of angels were going to be needed to make the thing come together.

He caught his first break when he went to talk to Zeke Warboy, the mayor of Coldwater Cove. Zeke was also the father of Ike Warboy, the former perennial Joseph. The poor man was still a little rattled by the legal attention his town had received. He'd never expected to be slapped with an injunction coming down from the state superior court no less.

"It's a pity. A real shame. Nobody loves the pageant more than me, even if my newest grandchild isn't going to be the Baby Jesus this year. And you let that little teacher—Ms. Holloway, is it?—anyway, let her know I don't hold it against her a bit that she was trying to change the cast this time. It's probably a mercy because young Cecil is, well, he's two goin' on terrible right now. He'd never lie quiet in a manger and look holy," he said. "But it doesn't matter anyway. We just can't go against the state on the pageant."

"How about if we move the pageant somewhere else?"

"That'd help." The mayor tapped his temple in thought. "You know, I just might have an idea. Let me make a call or two and I'll get back to you. But there's still the matter of Ms. Holloway being a public employee."

"Angie has bowed out of the pageant," Seth had told him. "She's no longer the director."

"Who is?"

"You're looking at him."

Zeke rolled his eyes. "Heaven help us."

"Amen. Make those phone calls anyway, okay, Zeke?"

Seth had left City Hall with a little more hope in his heart. Then he worked alongside his construction crew for the rest of the day. But while his body went through the motions, his mind was still looking for solutions to the pageant problem.

After the workday was over, his "worknight" was just beginning. Wherever they held the pageant, he figured it would need a number of raised platforms. These would serve as stages, elevating the actors above the gathered audience that would be looking on and following as the characters moved along on their journey to Coldwater Cove's version of Bethlehem. He'd been building the portable stages in the large barn on his property outside of town, figuring he could haul them in on a flatbed once they were assembled.

He wasn't expecting any company when a pair of headlights turned down his long drive. A car stopped just outside the pool of yellow light thrown by the lamp over the open door to the barn.

Tad Van Hook appeared in the doorway, shoulders slumped.

"Mr. Parker," he said, his gaze darting away after the shortest amount of eye contact on record.

"Yeah." Seth continued to pound nails while the kid shifted his weight from one foot to the other. "What d'you want?"

"A job, sir."

Seth's hammer paused in midswing. "Aren't you still in school?"

"Yes, sir, but I graduate this spring. I could work part time till then."

"I've seen you play basketball, Tad. You're pretty good." The Van Hook boy had been offered a free ride to a number of colleges based on his almost uncanny ability to put a ball through a hoop. "Aren't you worried a job will cut into your court time?"

"Yeah, I imagine it will, but I can't think about basketball now. I've got . . . other responsibilities."

Well, that's one way to put it. "You mean you want to work next summer till you're off to college, right?"

"No, sir. I'm looking for full-time work. Permanent. I'm ready to start anytime," the young man said earnestly. "I . . . I don't think I'm going to college, after all."

Seth eyed him thoughtfully. The last he'd heard from Angie about Emma's pregnancy was that Tad was totally weirded out by the idea of becoming a young father.

Maybe that's why God made it take nine months. To give us time to get used to the idea.

If Tad was ready to step up, take responsibility for his actions, and be an adult, Seth was prepared to help him be a man.

"Let's wait till the end of basketball season before you start working for me part time. But then only on weekends," he added. "And only if you can keep your grades up, too."

"Then once I graduate?"

"If you still want a full-time job, I'll make room for you on my crew," Seth said. It had taken him years to build up the skills and reputation to run a successful business in construction. The guys on his crew made a living wage, but none of them would ever get rich working at their trade. Tad, who'd grown up in one of the town's more affluent families, was in for a rude awakening if he intended to live on what he could make swinging a hammer. "You might want to keep your options open. Your decision could change between now and when you graduate. You let me know if it does."

"I don't think it will," the boy said. "At least not as far as I'm concerned."

Seth didn't want to ask. It wasn't his business, but Tad hadn't said anything about marrying Emma. Either way, if the young man was determined to take some responsibility for the child he'd fathered, it was a good thing.

"Thanks for the job, Mr. Parker. I won't let you down."

When Tad turned and walked away, he was standing far straighter than when he came in.

Growing up will do that to you. Even if you didn't intend to get there that fast.

Chapter 35

Somebody cue the bells. A bunch of
angels are about to earn their wings.

—Seth Parker, who never in a million years
expected to direct a Christmas pageant,
and certainly never one with this much riding on it

Seated at her kitchen counter, Angie was correcting the last batch of exams she'd give before Christmas. Papers were spread across the peninsula and more than a few of them were hopelessly pockmarked with red corrections. Her students all seemed to have a bad case of "holiday-itis." She hoped they'd do better after the Christmas break. They'd have to.

The results of the exam were so depressing, Angie welcomed the interruption of a knock on her back door. It was Emma.

"Come in quick. It's cold out there," she said as she shooed the girl in.

"I know. It's supposed to snow, Ms. H. Won't that be cool?"

No, it'll be cold. Very, very cold, Angie thought, but couldn't bring herself to dampen the girl's enthusiasm. It had been a while since she'd seen Emma this happy. "Can I get you some hot chocolate?"

"No. I can't stay. I just wanted to tell you that I've made some decisions."

"Good," Angie said cautiously. She'd been praying more of late, so it felt only natural to launch a silent arrow prayer skyward that one of Emma's decisions wasn't to end her pregnancy.

"Tad asked me to marry him."

Color me surprised! "He did?"

"Yeah. Guess he's got a job lined up with Mr. Parker's company and everything. Tad wants to take care of us." Emma put a protective hand on her belly.

Angie was waiting for the gush of excitement that was sure to follow, but it didn't come.

"What did you tell him?"

"That I didn't think it was a good idea. I mean, a couple of months ago I'd have jumped at the chance, but I've been doing a lot of thinking and I don't see it ending well for Tad and me," Emma said. "He might be okay with giving up his scholarship now, but he'd be bound to resent it later."

Angie nodded. "That's very possible."

"Anyway, we're not . . . we're just not as grown up as I thought we were. We can't raise a child. We're still kids ourselves."

"Have you decided to terminate the pregnancy?" There was such a hard knot in her throat, Angie was surprised the words came out.

Emma shook her head. "I can't do that. It wouldn't be right. Every time I thought about it, I was so sad. I can't. Even if it seems like it would be the easy way out right now, I don't think it would be easy in the long run."

"I'm glad you see that."

"But I also don't want to keep going to Coldwater High with my belly hanging out," the girl said.

"No, Emma, you need to finish school. I'll make sure you're not bullied and—"

"I'm going to finish," Emma interrupted. "Just not here. There's an alternative high school in the city where my grandparents live. It's for kids who have special challenges, so at least

I won't be the only pregnant student there. My grandma said I can stay with them till I graduate, so I'm transferring for the spring semester."

Angie wished Emma would stay in Coldwater Cove, but she understood the girl's urge to leave. "And once the baby is born?"

Emma sighed. "I'm really glad you cast me as Mary in the pageant, Ms. H., because I've been thinking about her a lot. She had a baby that she had to keep safe until it was time for Him to belong to the world. I have a baby I need to keep safe, too."

She rubbed her belly again, even though no bump showed yet. "But the best way I can keep him safe isn't to keep him myself. I have to give him to a family that will love him and bring him up like I wish I could. So I've already been in contact with a private adoption agency. My baby is going to a really sweet couple in South Carolina who can't have kids of their own. They're coming out so I can meet them once I get settled with my grandparents next month."

Tears trembled on Emma's lashes. "I wish I could do better. I mean, I thought about putting him in foster care until I graduate. Then I was thinking I could take care of him myself."

Angie sucked in a quick breath. That would mean consigning the child to the limbo of the system.

"But then I decided it wouldn't be right to let a baby get used to one set of folks and then have me yank him away from them," Emma said. "What do you think?"

"I think you're doing the right thing. You made a very loving choice," Angie said with relief. "What does your mother say?"

"She's on board. Tad's folks took a little convincing. You know, I really thought they'd be angry and claim that I was just a bit of white trash. I mean, like they'd think I was trying to sleep my way into the Van Hook family, but as it turns out, they've been . . . unexpectedly nice about it. They were all for me and Tad getting married. They were ready to be part of the baby's life."

Angie was too surprised for a response.

"But when I said no, Tad's folks helped with the private adoption thing. Turns out, they know the parents of the wife in that couple from South Carolina. And they promised to set up a college fund for the baby."

The Van Hooks could have taken Emma to court to force the child from her. Angie was grateful for their restraint. Everyone involved seemed to be putting the baby's welfare first.

Emma's chin trembled. "It's just so hard to think about giving the baby up."

"And it'll be even harder to do, but for what it's worth, you're making a good decision in a very tough situation," Angie said. "I'm proud of you, Emma."

The girl unexpectedly threw her arms around Angie. "Thanks, Ms. H. That means a lot."

Angie patted her student's back. "And I'm sorry you won't get a chance to be Mary in the pageant. You'd have been wonderful."

Emma pulled away, dried her eyes, and smiled. "Well, as it turns out, I *do* get to be Mary. Come with me." She took Angie's hand. "You'll need your coat. It's cold out there."

"Where are we going?"

"To the dress rehearsal. The pageant is going forward."

"How is that possible?"

"Oh, we had a little help from some angels," Emma said with a wink. "And your Mr. Parker."

Emma and Angie walked the two blocks from the Square down to the park that stretched along the lakefront and sloped upward to greet the stately two-story homes that lined Maple Street. The mock sets were gone and in their place, substantial-looking stages with incredibly detailed backdrops dotted the wide expanse of winter-brown grass.

"No, this can't be right. We can't use the park for the same reason we can't have the pageant on the Square," Angie said before she realized that Emma had already left her to join the rest of the cast assembled in the middle of the park.

"The park isn't public property," came a dearly familiar voice from behind her.

She turned to find Seth, with his thumbs tucked in his pockets and a big grin across his ruggedly handsome face.

"It turns out the park belongs to the Founder's Club—you know, the one made up of the Sweaseys, Addleberrys, Van Hooks, and Bradens—all the first families in the county," Seth explained. "They've tried to donate the park to the town over the years, but the council always says no. If they accepted it, the city would have to maintain the park. This way, the Founders Club is on the hook for mowing and upkeep and insurance."

"But what if the Founders decided to develop the park and build something here?"

"I guess they could, but they'd all have to agree to it, and when have you known those families to agree about any-thing?" Seth said with a laugh. "Plus, the town council would have to okay a zoning change."

"What's it zoned for now?"

"A landfill. Can you imagine what would happen if the Founders Club tried to actually dump garbage in the middle of town? By the lake, no less. Every soul in Coldwater Cove would boycott their businesses and ride them out of town on a rail. No, I think we can count on the park being here till the Second Coming. So once we got the okay to hold the pageant at the park, we had our perfectly legal, nonpublic owned loca-tion."

"So the Founders Club families did agree on something."

"Hey! It's Christmas. Peace and goodwill and all that," Seth said. "And as to the other specific objection in the lawsuit, you are no longer the director, so the town's off the hook on that count, too."

"And what a group of private citizens agree to do on privately held land doesn't fall under the injunction!"

Seth put two fingers between his teeth and whistled loudly enough to be heard in the next county. "Places everybody. Take it from the top."

"Mary treasured up all these things and pondered them in her heart."

Angie's gaze jerked to the nearest oak, where a speaker was wedged into the lowest crotch of the tree. Mrs. Chisholm's voice had come from it. Seth must have had the old librarian record the narration Angie had written. Her voice came again.

"That's what my friend Luke wrote in his gospel. What he couldn't capture with his words was the longing I felt as we waited for the Messiah to come. The whole world groaned under the weight of Rome."

The wheelchair bound retired librarian might be the poster girl for curmudgeons everywhere, but after years of countless read alouds, Mrs. Chisholm's voice was still full and expressive. She was perfect as an elderly Mary, giving her remembered account of the Christ Child's birth. Seth had done well casting her.

"We were taught that all things would be set to rights when the Messiah came. He would reign, the rabbis promised us, in the spirit of David and his kingdom would cover the earth with righteousness."

Hand in hand, Angie and Seth wandered toward the stage located farthest from the lake, where Emma, dressed as Mary, was sweeping a humble, first-century-type house. Then the girl stopped sweeping and bowed her head.

"So we prayed. We hoped. We waited."

Mrs. Chisholm's voice was coming from another speaker located near this stage. Angie realized that with only one narrator to amplify, Deek had been able to set up a sound system that played throughout the park simultaneously.

"And God answered our prayers . . . in a way I never could have expected."

A group of people had gathered around Mary's stage and at the end of Mrs. Chisholm's words, they began to softly hum "O Come, O Come, Emmanuel."

Then Angie's ears pricked to the soft chug of a generator powering a fog machine. Thick mist poured onto the stage.

"Anyone who has ever wished to see an angel has never met one. They are fierce and terrible . . . and beautiful beyond belief."

Suddenly a strobe light pulsed, making Angie blink in surprise, and then Jadis Chu, in full angelic regalia, appeared in the mist. Her wings were diaphanous fronds, accented with glitter swirls and shards of reflective metal. Her makeup was reminiscent of a Kabuki actor, stark white with shades of purple and vermillion accenting her strong features.

Emma fell to her knees. Jadis was so intensely striking, Angie almost felt as if she should, too. Mrs. Chisholm's voice came again.

"Even more than Gabriel's appearance, the angel's words frightened me. I was favored, the angel said. All generations would call me blessed. For God intended to use me, the lowest of his handmaids, to bring His Son into the world."

The humming throng around Angie turned out to be the pageant choir. From behind the stage, Mr. Mariano blew into a pitch pipe, and began directing the spread-out members of the choir in a haunting rendition of "See, Amid the Winter's Snow."

The group began to follow Emma as she left the first stage,

and, singing as they went, walked across the park to the next platform, where Crystal, as Mary's cousin Elisabeth, was waiting to greet her.

Mrs. Chisholm's narration continued. The choir provided more a capella traveling music when Mary was joined by Joseph. Ian lifted Emma onto the back of a strange-looking little creature that could only be the zonkey Junior Bugtussle had promised to bring. Then, they continued their journey toward the stable situated near the lake.

Mrs. Chisholm's recorded narration went on as Emma and Ian reached the stable, complete with a cow, calf, and an extra stall for the surprisingly sweet zonkey.

"Jesus was with God when the earth and the stars were called into existence from nothing. It is his voice in the thunder, his power in the rolling sea. He made the world and everything in it. Yet in all his creation there was found no room for him."

Joseph and Mary disappeared behind the wooden structure for a moment and when Emma reappeared, she was carrying a lifelike doll, carefully swaddled, in her arms. She laid the doll in the manger and sat on a three-legged stool beside it, all her attention turned to the baby.

Seth must have rigged some lights under the straw because streams of illumination emanated from the manger bed.

"He ought to have been born in a palace, swaddled in silk, and warmed by a fire. But God's ways are not ours. Instead he came into this world in a stable. Straw was his bed. The ox and ass lent their warmth and sweetened the air with their breath. I remember he cried softly that night. So I reached down . . ."

Emma did as Mrs. Chisholm said.

". . . and held God . . . in my trembling hands."

The choir began singing "Away in a Manger." The carol was soft and sweet, but Angie almost wished for silence. Even though she'd written the script, the enormity of God becoming a helpless babe was so overwhelming, she couldn't take in much more at the moment.

"I knew from the beginning that Jesus was no ordinary child. He belonged to the ages, to all peoples and races. He was chosen as our ransom, the Lamb of God, slain from the foundation of the world. Still, I hoped he would be just mine for a season."

A tear slid down Emma's face and Angie knew she was thinking of her own child, the one who would never be hers.

Not even for a season.

Then the focus of the play shifted to a different stage in another part of the park, up the hill from the stable. Jadis made another appearance as the angel on a platform raised above a spot on the dry grass where Junior Bugtussle and his son Aaron were keeping a flock of two wooly sheep with the help of their dog, Bruno. They looked suitably afraid of the angel despite Mrs. Chisholm's reminder that the angel had told them not to fear.

The choir launched into "Angels We Have Heard on High." Bruno tipped his nose to the sky and joined in on the "Glorias," but other than that, it really did seem as if the host of heaven could not keep silent. The morning stars, who sang at creation, cried aloud that the salvation of God had come to earth.

Then when the song had ended and Jadis had disappeared back into the fog-machine's mist, the shepherds bolted toward the manger in a rush, babbling about signs and wonders. Junior and his son seemed determined to see the Child, the Holy One, with their own eyes.

Once they reached the manger, Junior and Aaron bowed low to Emma and baby with so much reverence, Angie wouldn't have guessed it was only a doll if she hadn't known.

When the gathered choir began singing "The First Noel," she found herself singing along with them.

When the song ended, Mrs. Chisholm's voice began again.

"Except for those months when I carried him beneath my heart, Jesus was never only mine. Others sought the true king as well. In a distant land, they studied the heavens. They pored over scraps of prophecy. And then a star led them as they traveled from far away."

Angie turned to see Riley ensconced in the star harness. Her smile was almost brighter than the spotlight that lit her up and as she began her slow descent on the zipline toward the manger scene, snow began to fall. It shimmered in the light like diamond dust drifting to earth. The air was crisp and fresh, and Angie wished Riley's moment of being a star could last forever.

Dressed in the outlandishly gorgeous costumes of the magi, Riley's father, Noah, Dr. Gonncu, and Mr. Elkin followed her to the stable. Apparently, Seth had decided moving the Holy Family to another location, while scriptural, wasn't necessarily good theater.

"Over sand dune and wadi, past ziggurat and temple, their caravan came." Angie could hear Mrs. Chisholm's voice coming from several speakers all around her. "Their horses and camels were swift to obey their desert-born masters and faithfully bore those seekers to worship at my son's feet. Unlike the shepherds who came with full hearts, but empty hands, these visitors brought worthy gifts—gold, as befitted a king; frankincense, to honor Jesus as their high priest; and—"

Noah opened a cast of fragrant spice at Emma's feet. The scent washed over Angie, sweet as honey, sharp as a blade.

"A fist closed around my heart when they revealed their last gift. It was myrrh. The spice used to anoint the dead."

The choir started singing again, but Angie didn't hear

much of them. When she'd wrote the words Mrs. Chisholm was reading, it really hadn't sunk in to her that God did know something about loss. But Seth was right. He'd lost His Son. Jesus had come to die.

"He was my son. My heart. My beloved. He is that fragrant essence that lifts the heart of man in the cool of the evening. If I close my eyes, I can still smell the sweet perfume of grace."

Seth put his arm around Angie as the choir began singing again. Angie leaned into him. Seth had taken the scattered pieces of the pageant and pulled them together into wonderful wholeness.

She figured he could do the same with her, if she'd just let him love her. And God, too. She knew now she'd never be able to push God into a far corner of her heart again.

"And so Jesus came. Against all expectation. Against all reason. He left heaven, forsaking that realm of perpetual light to take on our darkness. He gave up the power of God and clothed himself with our dust and weakness. He was willing to do whatever was necessary to redeem his poor, lost creation."

"He couldn't bear to see us banished from Eden again. He wants us to be with him, not only in this world, but in the one to come. And once death closes my eyes, I believe I will open them again to see only light."

Mrs. Chisholm had never sounded so sure, so confident, and so much less like the fuss-budget Angie knew her to be. Could she have felt as changed by the pageant as Angie did?

"Jesus was born. Not only for Israel. Not simply for eager shepherds or wise seekers. He came for us all. And that means everyone."

The choir launched into a spirited rendition of "For Unto Us a Child Is Born."

When they were finished, Seth turned to her. "Well, what do you think?"

"Yes."

"Yes, you like it?"

"Yes. Yes, I like it. Yes, to you. Yes, to everything." She threw her arms around him. "Yes, to taking a chance even if I lose because I can't bear the thought of not being with you for the rest of my life."

He lifted her and twirled her in a circle. Stars wheeled overhead. Snow was still falling. It stuck to Angie's eyelashes, to Seth's hair, to the ground and the trees. It covered them with a sparkle of magic. Of love. Of faith. Seth finally set her feet back on the ground but didn't let go of her. "Okay, then. Let's go."

"Where?" Angie asked, though it really didn't matter. She'd go anywhere with this man.

"To your sock drawer, of course. I want to see my ring on your finger before you change your mind!"

"There is zero chance of that." She put a hand behind his head and pulled him down for a long kiss. "Not now. Not ever."

Recipes from Coldwater Cove

Holiday Cheer!

Shirley Evans may believe in experimenting on her family with esoteric dishes, but there's a lot to be said for the tried and true. So I'm sharing some of my family's recipes that have been handed down for a couple of generations. Like all classics, they've stood the test of time— Grandma Jewell's Pink Lemonade Salad, Aunt Mary's Pumpkin Bread, and Mom's Ridiculously Delicious Buckeyes.

My Dear Husband tried to claim that even though my grandmother called this first recipe a salad, it is not a salad since there's no lettuce involved. To which I replied, if potato salad can be a salad, and three-bean salad can be a salad, and chicken salad can be a salad— well, you see where I was going, and he could, too, because he threw up his hands and declared the pink lemonade dish a salad.

Don't you love it when a man sees reason?

Anyway, this salad is light and cool and a perfect palate cleanser.

Grandma Jewell's Pink Lemonade Salad

(Yes, I named Lake Jewell after her!)

Ingredients

Ritz cracker crumbs
12-ounce can partially thawed pink lemonade
1 can Eagle Brand sweetened condensed milk
16-ounce carton of Cool Whip

Directions

Crush half a sleeve of crackers with a rolling pin. Spread across the bottom of a 9-by-13 pan. Save some to sprinkle on top.

Whip remaining ingredients in a bowl. Spoon onto the cracker crumbs. Sprinkle the reserved crumbs on top and refrigerate till served.

Aunt Mary's Pumpkin Bread

My sweet aunt suffers from macular degeneration, so the pumpkin bread recipe I received from her is written in super-large print. She doesn't let her vision issues get her down in the kitchen. She's a wonderful cook, and this holiday treat is perfect for a cold winter day! Add a cup of coffee (not one of George Evans's!) and you've really got something.

Ingredients

4 eggs
1 cup oil (Canola is my choice)
⅔ cup water
2 cups pumpkin (Yes, I use canned pumpkin, but if you're the clever
    sort, I'm sure you could use the real thing if you puree it down
    to a pie-filling consistency.)
3 cups sugar
1 teaspoon salt
1 teaspoon cinnamon
1 teaspoon nutmeg
2 teaspoons baking soda
3⅓ cups flour
Nuts (Aunt Mary doesn't specify what kind or how much, so I file
    this under baker's choice! Add them or not at your pleasure.)

Directions

Beat together all the wet ingredients, then add the dry one at a time, finishing with the flour. Pour into buttered, floured loaf pans (makes two loaves) and bake at 350 degrees Fahrenheit for one hour.

Mom's Ridiculously Delicious Buckeyes

I have no idea why these last Christmas treats are called buckeyes, but they really are ridiculously delicious. My mom always says it's because they're made with love.

Ingredients

1 cup butter
2 cups peanut butter
3 cups powdered sugar
1 teaspoon burnt sugar flavoring
1 12-ounce package of semisweet chocolate chips
½ bar paraffin

Directions

Soften butter and peanut butter to room temperature. Mix and add powdered sugar and flavoring. Roll into small balls and chill for two hours. Melt chocolate chips and paraffin. Using toothpicks, dip balls into mixture, place on sheet of waxed paper, and chill.

Hope you enjoy trying some of my family's special treats. Along with the holiday suggestions, please accept my wish for you and yours to have a blessed Christmas, and lots of love in the coming years.
Holiday Hugs,
Lexi

A COLDWATER
WARM HEARTS
CHRISTMAS

Lexi Eddings

ABOUT THIS GUIDE

The suggested questions are included
to enhance your group's reading of this book.

Discussion Questions

1. At the beginning of *A Coldwater Warm Hearts Christmas,* Angie overhears a conversation between two of her students that sounds eerily familiar. She wishes she could intervene and tell Emma to stand up for herself. Do you think she should have spoken up? Or was she right to mind her own business?

2. Angie uses grammar as both a shield and weapon. Do you have any idiosyncrasies that help you cope with the world?

3. When Seth first meets Angie, he doesn't think she's his type. When is the turning point? What makes him start to take an interest in her?

4. Shirley and George Evans win the Limeberger's Funeral Home Bucket List Contest. Even with all his grumbling about the expense, do you think George will enjoy his world cruise? Why or why not? What's on your bucket list?

5. Angie says, "In literature or in life, it's hard to get very far if you keep rereading the same chapter." What do you think she means by that? What is she stuck on? Has there been a time in your life when you felt yourself repeating past mistakes or refusing to move on?

6. Angie leans on her Austen heroines and Shakespeare characters to help her know what to do. Are there any literary characters who have informed the way you approach certain situations? Early on, Angie refers to Tad Van Hook as a Willoughby, after a faithless fellow in *Sense and Sensibility.*

Does your family have a shorthand that lets you communicate volumes just by mentioning a fictional character's name?

7. Crystal gets embarrassed by what Riley says and does. Has that ever happened to you? Or are you tickled by the funny things kids say? Care to share your favorite?

8. Seth says perfectionism is the kind of weakness people pretend is a strength. What does he mean by that? How does perfectionism damage a person's self-esteem? What can it do to relationships?

9. When fifteen-year-old Emma Wilson turns up pregnant, Angie wants to help her. She feels she has to walk a fine line between offering alternatives and persuading Emma to take one path over another. What do you think of the outcome? Do you wish Emma had done something else?

10. Peter Manning and his partner Sabine weren't able to completely disrupt the town Christmas pageant with their lawsuit. What do you think about public holiday displays? Is there a place for faith in public discourse? How should we balance the free expression of religion with the rights of those who feel offended by it? Is there a way to find "peace on earth" over this issue?

Read all the Coldwater Warm Hearts books!

THE COLDWATER WARM HEARTS CLUB

The lake is crystal blue, the hills roll for miles, and breaking news travels via the Methodist prayer chain. But don't let the postcard fool you. Coldwater Cove, Oklahoma, leavens its small-town charm with plenty of Ozark snark.

For Lacy Evans, returning to flyover country is the definition of failure. She had everything she wanted—an award-winning design firm, a chic city condo, a handsome, aristocratic almost-fiancé. Then her boyfriend ran off with her receptionist and her clients' money. Now she's out of business and crashing on her parents' couch. When she slides into a booth at the Green Apple Grill, she's feeling lower than a worm's belly.

But Lacy's old classmate Jacob Tyler is happy to see her. Coldwater's football hero came back from Afghanistan short part of a leg and some peace of mind, but he's counting his blessings, and Lacy could be one of them. Then there's her ex, Daniel, wearing a sheriff's badge and a wedding ring, but looking like young summer love. And a host of unlikely serendipities: The selfless do-gooders who sneak around taming curmudgeons and constructing second chances. The Fighting Marmots. The sprawling, take-no-prisoners Bugtussle clan.

Lacy thought she knew her hometown, and herself. She just wanted to get on her feet and keep running. But the longer she stays, the more she finds to change her mind . . .

"A unique take on what it means to go home again."

—Kristan Higgins, *New York Times* bestselling author

A COLDWATER WARM HEARTS WEDDING

Everyone longs for a place to be loved and accepted, warts and all. And Coldwater Cove has its share of warts! But while this cozy corner of the world is home to just about anyone who wants to put down roots, the way has been barred to Michael Evans.

Mike's dad saw to that some ten years ago when he ordered him to leave town and never come back. But when Michael learns his mother is battling breast cancer, not even the animosity between him and his father can keep him away. Of course he didn't figure on getting roped into being best man at his sister's upcoming wedding, but as long as Michael's back in town, he figures he's got a second chance with the girl who got away—Heather Walker.

Long-legged Heather has had a love/hate relationship with the town bad boy ever since he christened her "Stilts" in middle school. She was voted most likely to succeed. Michael seemed destined for the state pen. Even so, she hopes there's more to him than leathers and a Harley, for his family's sake if nothing else. But while her fascination with him grows, a decade-old secret involving a member of *her* family threatens to tear them apart. . . .

"Readers of sweet romance will fall in love with Coldwater Cove. Lexi Eddings's talent shines in this edgy, fresh story."

—Kristan Higgins, *New York Times* bestselling author